Kissing the Countess

WITHDRAWN

*Also by Susan King
in Large Print:*

Waking the Princess

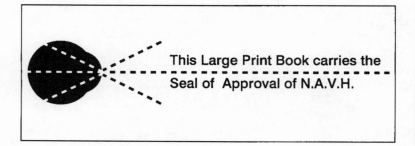

Kissing
the
Countess

Susan King

WHEELER
PUBLISHING

Published in 2004 by arrangement with NAL Signet, a member of Penguin Group (USA) Inc.

Wheeler Large Print Softcover.

The text of this Large Print edition is unabridged.
Other aspects of the book may vary from the original edition.

Set in 16 pt. Plantin by Ramona Watson.

Printed in the United States on permanent paper.

Library of Congress Cataloging-in-Publication Data

King, Susan, 1951–
　　Kissing the countess / Susan King.
　　　　p. cm.
　　ISBN 1-58724-629-5 (lg. print : sc : alk. paper)
　　1. Highlands (Scotland) — Fiction.　2. Nobility — Fiction.　3. Large type books.　I. Title.
PS3561.I4833K57 2004
　　813′.54—dc22　　　　　　　　　　　　　2004041776

*For Audrey LaFehr,
my wonderful editor*

As the Founder/CEO of NAVH, the only national health agency solely devoted to those who, although not totally blind, have an eye disease which could lead to serious visual impairment, I am pleased to recognize Thorndike Press★ as one of the leading publishers in the large print field.

Founded in 1954 in San Francisco to prepare large print textbooks for partially seeing children, NAVH became the pioneer and standard setting agency in the preparation of large type.

Today, those publishers who meet our standards carry the prestigious "Seal of Approval" indicating high quality large print. We are delighted that Thorndike Press is one of the publishers whose titles meet these standards. We are also pleased to recognize the significant contribution Thorndike Press is making in this important and growing field.

Lorraine H. Marchi, L.H.D.
Founder/CEO
NAVH

★ Thorndike Press encompasses the following imprints: Thorndike, Wheeler, Walker and Large Print Press.

Acknowledgments

Thanks are due to Jennifer Wingard for sharing her considerable expertise in geological matters, and for finding me a lovely fairy crystal of my very own for good luck.

I owe very special thanks to Dougie and Jenny MacLean for warm Scottish hospitality, and again to Dougie for his inspiring music, and for a funny story about mountain climbing.

She loves me, she loves me not —
This Highland pride is all I've got

Standing here on Cadderley
Between the burn and the turning sea
I gaze across at these golden hills
I'm looking all the way to eternity

No trace of where we have come
No trace of songs we can hold
for our young

Lose our language to greed and gain
All washed away by a southern rain. . . .

— Dougie MacLean, "Eternity"

Prologue

Scotland, the Northwest Highlands Summer, 1849

Along the road that curved beneath the fairy mountain, a hundred Highlanders came in slow procession. Some walked, carrying bundles on their backs and children in their arms, while others rode in creaking, overloaded carts. Sunlight filled the glen, dazzling over mountain snow beds and heathered slopes, gleaming on the loch. No head was bowed, no shoulder was stooped, as each man, woman, and child looked around to capture in heart and memory the beauty of Glen Shee, the Glen of the Fairies.

Catriona MacConn watched them from where she stood on a steep slope. She crossed her arms tightly, as if binding her heart could ease the ache she felt. Sighing, she glanced at her brother. Finlay MacConn stared down at the trail of people and carts and fisted a hand at his side. Tall and sturdy like his younger sister, though his hair was dark while hers glowed the color of bronze, he wore a jacket and kilt, his stockinged legs powerful from years of climbing the hills.

Shading her eyes, holding back tears, Catriona looked down at the man who watched from the roadside, seated on a sleek dark horse. The Earl of Kildonan watched as his factor and men rode along the straggling line of travelers, hastening the people onward with shouted commands.

Galloping across the glen on a bay horse, another man rode to join the earl, pulling up beside him to gesture as if angry. Catriona did not recognize the dark-haired man, but his agile build, the neat cut of his brown suit, the confident way he handled his horse, and his bold advance to the earl told her that he was a gentleman, perhaps a kinsman. The earl also gestured as they carried on what appeared to be a hot dispute.

"Who is that with the Earl of Kildonan?" Catriona asked. "The one with his black hair blowing about. He's got a wild look to him, as if he's displeased about something."

"I think he is the earl's heir," Finlay replied. "Called after his father, so George Mackenzie would be his name. You may not remember him, for you were young then, but he lived at Kildonan Castle when he was a lad. That was before the countess took her children and left her husband altogether."

"Oh! I remember a black-haired, shy lad who liked to walk in the hills alone. I would not know him now, though." Catriona felt mercifully distracted from the dismal sight of the procession.

"He's been away ten years or so, living in the Lowlands with his mother," Finlay said. "Mrs. Baird told Father that he's come back to make sure of his inheritance, with his father selling land and clearing the crofts. There is no love lost between those two, or so says Mrs. Baird, who works at the castle now."

"So the son is like the father. Perhaps they are arguing about who gets the larger share of the profits from the sheep that will run on the earl's lands." She sniffed. "A sad day when Highland lairds do not care for the dignity of the people, or for the good of the land itself."

"It did not used to be so, in the days of the chiefs, when this glen was a stronghold for Mackenzie warriors and their kin. The lairds of Kildonan watched over their tenants as carefully as they did over their own families. Or used to."

"Nothing is as it used to be, nor will it be again," Catriona said. Standing in silence, she watched the cavalcade wend past the foot of the slope where she and Finlay stood.

Some of the women wailed, and some threw their plaids over their heads in grief. Catriona felt more tears prick her eyes. She placed her hand at her throat, where her pulse bounced, and swallowed, wanting to cry out in communion with them. Many of the people leaving now were friends and kinfolk to the MacConns.

"If the Glen of the Fairies is emptied of its humans, then the *daoine sìth,* the people of peace — the fairies themselves — will go into mourning," she said. "The magic of this place and its legends, and the beauty of these mountains, will diminish. The fairies will fade from grief, or so says Morag MacLeod."

"The fairies must be used to the clearings by now, Catriona," Finlay said wryly. "Thousands have been forced out of their Highland and Island homes, where their kin lived for generations. This has been happening for decades."

"Then we must pray that this is the last of the clearings."

"It may be, at least in our glen. The Earl of Kildonan is making more sheep runs, hiring only a handful of Englishmen and Lowlanders to shepherd them. More economical than a hundred Highlanders on the same land, he claims. The rest of the land, I hear, will be rented out for a hunting reserve." His frown was bitter and deep.

"What will happen to the stories and the songs of this glen?" She sighed. "I wish I could capture all that wisdom and magic somehow, keep it for future generations. Our culture is leaving, too, carried away by the people to other lands. I dream of saving the glen — the land, the people, the heritage."

She shrugged. "But that is just a dream. Who am I but the minister's daughter — and he is losing most of his parish today."

Finlay put his arm around his sister. "Sometimes a dream is enough. If we nurture it and let it grow, it will become a stronghold." He gazed at the mountains on the other side of the glen, where golden sunlight poured over snowy peaks. "I wish I could save it, too. But I would save the people and bring back every one of them. Had our brother Donald lived to see this day, he would have done anything he could to stop this."

Sighing as she thought of bright, brave Donald — who had died on the upper slope of this very mountain — Catriona watched the sad procession. "If Father were a crofter instead of the reverend of Glenachan, we would be leaving, too. And neither you nor Donald nor Father could stop that."

A gust of wind billowed her skirt and the plaid shawl she wore over her shoulders. Loosened from its single braid, her hair streamed out, a bright banner of Celtic red-gold. She pushed it back and stood beside Finlay in silence, feeling strangely, sadly, like an honor guard.

The wailing rose again from below them, and Catriona saw an old woman on another hill raise her hands to the sky. The plaintive sound echoed against the hills, resounding, growing as other women joined the lament.

The resonance magnified and deepened, as if the mountains themselves cried out to see the people depart.

The sad beauty of the melody stirred through Catriona's heart. She loved these old songs, and she could not bear to think that grief and emptiness would replace all that magic and joy.

"The hills themselves are crying," Finlay said. "Look there, at the runnels filled with water, rushing down the hillsides like streams of tears."

Catriona nodded and took her brother's hand. The singing continued on the road below, and she lifted her head and began to sing, too, softly at first, then with clear power. The song was a *tuireadh,* a lament Highland women sang at funeral processions, and its melody twisted the heart.

> *Where shall we go to make our plea*
> *When we are hungry in the hills?*
> *Where shall we go to warm ourselves*
> *When we are chilled with cold?*
> *Hiri uam, hiri uam . . .*

The sound rolled outward, lifting into the mountains, and Catriona closed her eyes and felt the music fill her soul.

"Father, listen to me, I beg you," George Evan Mackenzie, Viscount of Glendevon, implored. "This is not the way a Highland chieftain tends to his people."

"Do not spout nonsense at me about Highland custom," the earl replied. He was a large man, gruff and gray, his suit and hair both the dull color of pewter. "Mr. Grant, see that those stragglers hurry up, or we will be all day about this," he instructed the factor. "They have to reach the coast by nightfall, to camp out by the docks and board the cattle ships on the morning tides."

"Cattle ships!" Evan rounded his stallion, the bay reacting to his owner's agitation by snorting and sidestepping.

"Aye. We've arranged for some of them to have passage to Canada. The rest will go to Glasgow to find jobs there."

"With what skills? These people have lived here for generations. Most of them have never been to a city, let alone another country. They know nothing but these hills and the way of life that has endured here for centuries."

"That is the problem, that stagnant, simple society of theirs. They are a complacent and lazy people, walking about the hills tending to their small flocks and herds, their small crops, their small crafts. They have no ambition, no skills other than weaving and herding and storytelling. They would never learn anything new if they stayed here. They will flourish and do well outside the glen. We

15

are doing a service for them by sending them away from here."

"Service! Perhaps the poor who crowd the cities, their children's limbs misshapen and their bellies empty, would like to know that it is for their own good," Evan snapped. "These are Highlanders, healthy and proud, happy in this glen. Land and kin are everything to them. If you send them out of these hills and take them away from their kin, you remove their very soul."

"Then their Highland soul is doing them no good at all and should be removed, like a canker. When I agreed with your mother that you should come north for a bit after your last term at university, I did not expect you to come spouting the same babble your mother sings. Tiresome, that save-the-people righteousness," he barked. "I *am* saving the people — by sending them on their way, to a better life than this backward, savage existence."

"A cold rationalization of arrogance and greed," Evan said. "I hoped you had changed in these last years. I hoped that when Mother left you and took Jeanie and me with her, you would come to realize what is most important. These Highlanders know what to value — family and land. Love and the gifts of this world are all we have in the end. But you do not see that. You destroy what you could save." He waved an arm toward the people.

"Keep babbling like a charity matron, and I'll take that land and inheritance from you and give it to your sister. She, at least, respects me," the earl growled.

"I used to respect you, Father," Evan said. "As for the inheritance, there will be little left but a hundred thousand sheep and stubbled hillsides if you empty this glen of its most valuable resource, the people and the Gaelic culture, and sell off the land for profit."

His heart pounded as he looked around at the beautiful power of the hills and the sky and at the line of people whose faces showed the same strength and pride. His childhood memories of Glen Shee were precious to him. He loved it here, and he felt a fierce need to protect this place and its people. In the few days since his arrival to the land he had always felt was his home, despite the differences of his parents, he had felt the depth of his attachment to Glen Shee and Kildonan.

And he was powerless to stop what his father had decided to do. The clearings had been practiced widely in the Scottish Highlands for compelling economic reasons. Evan did not give a damn about financial gain or economic improvements if it meant destroying the dignity of this place. He cared about the people and the land. In a way, he had been torn away from here years ago by his mother's decision to leave his father and the Highlands. To some extent, he knew what these people were feeling now, and he hated watching the pain on their faces.

"I am paying off debts so you will have a decent inheritance," his father said. "I will make a fortune for you and your sister from the sheep that run on these hills. You will be happy about it eventually."

"I can find no happiness in this," Evan said.

"There are damn good reasons for this. Evictions seem cruel, but these folk will benefit, and so will we. Highlanders live like savages. When a Highland family holds a croft, hundreds of acres support a small kailyard and barely a hundred sheep. Now this glen will produce, really produce. Sheep by the thousands, enough wool to clothe the Continent, and all of it managed efficiently by a few men and their families."

"Then let these people herd those sheep for you."

"I would, but they'd rather wander the hills or sit by the hearth telling stories. I need men to count sheep and mark them, move them from field to field to keep them fat, gather them in the spring and shear them, then prepare the wool and take it to market."

"They could do it," Evan said. "You show them no respect, Father, yet you want respect for yourself."

"Fifteen Lowland men will do the work of two hundred lazy Highlanders. Good God, what is that caterwauling?" The earl turned abruptly. "It makes my skin crawl."

"A song of mourning," Evan snapped. "They are losing their homes and the life they knew." He understood a little Gaelic, having learned some from his Highland nurse as a boy, but he did not need to comprehend the words. He knew grief when he heard it.

"I'll be glad to leave this place myself," Kildonan said. "I'll hand over the running of the estate to my factor, Mr. Grant, once the flocks and the shepherds are in place. I plan to come back every few months for hunting and fishing, but I cannot live here all year. Never could. These mountains haunt me. I cannot sleep here." He looked around.

"Then you do have a conscience," Evan said.

"I do not need my own pup snapping at me. Go back to Edinburgh and build bridges or whatever the devil you've decided to do. Engineering is no occupation for a peer of the realm, but suit yourself. You should have chosen the ministry, with all the pontificating you've been doing since you came back here."

"I should have read for the law. Then perhaps I could have found a way to stop this."

"Go on. Leave — before I decide to send you away forever," the earl thundered. "I

19

hoped you would see the worth in this. But you have all the stubborn ideals of youth. There's no convincing you. Ride out if you do not like what you see here."

Evan rounded his horse before his father finished speaking. His fury and his grief were as big and terrible as the mountains that surrounded the glen. Riding past the column of Highlanders, he heard the wailing song of the women echo in his soul.

He could not look at them as he passed. He wanted to apologize, to rectify their tragedy, but he was powerless. He felt ashamed to be the heir of the man who had brought such catastrophe to the people he traditionally should protect.

Evan had returned to Kildonan Castle and Glen Shee hoping to reclaim some of the happiness of his childhood, hoping to reason with his father now that he himself was a man. But George Mackenzie, Earl of Kildonan, was not interested in the opinions of a university engineering student. He was interested only in proving himself right and making himself rich — at a cost that Evan could not bear to think about.

As he cantered away, he heard another female voice raised in song. The clear, sweet sound sent chills up his spine. He looked up the hill that soared beside the road.

A young woman stood in the heather high on the slope. She was tall and slender, bright and beautiful, wrapped in a tartan shawl, her red-gold hair rippling outward. Beside her stood a young man, and for a moment Evan wondered if they were a vision — they seemed so much a part of the ancient beauty of the glen, like a pair of Celtic gods come to watch over the desolation the day had wrought.

The girl sang the lament with such poignant sadness that Evan stopped to listen out of honor and respect. The afternoon sun turned the mountain snows pink and gold and spilled fire into the glen. The singer glowed with her own fire, with a proud, brave spirit, and others turned to look, stopped to listen. Even the old earl paused to stare upward.

Her clear, haunting voice shivered through Evan's heart and imprinted itself there. When the last note faded like the clean strike of a bell, he sighed with it. That voice was desolate but not defeated.

Then he rode away, carrying his grief with him, taking the happiness he had known here and the feeling that he had lost his own future in this beautiful glen. After today, he could never return to Kildonan and Glen Shee with his head held high.

But he felt a little balm of healing from the Highland girl's song, and he took that with him, too.

Chapter One

Scotland, the Northwest Highlands
November, 1859

Clinging to a wall of rock with his fingers pressed into narrow crevices and his hobnailed boots propped on a ledge inches deep, Evan Mackenzie, Viscount of Glendevon and lately Earl of Kildonan, took a deep breath. He rested his brow on his upraised arm and contemplated his dilemma.

He was alone on a nearly vertical rise of rough black gneiss in a cold, buffeting wind and heavy mist. Sleet pattered the rock around him, rendering it slippery as the devil, and he could scarcely see past his own reach. And his only companion had disappeared over half an hour ago.

The mist was thick and cold, and he couldn't see worth a damn. One wrong step along his precarious path, and he might stumble and even plummet. The deep corries and natural chimneys along the black mountainside would claim him long before he reached solid ground, over two thousand feet below.

This was only what he deserved for

breaking his vow and coming back here, he thought wryly. He had kept his distance from Kildonan and Glen Shee for years, but the mountains had lured him, the silent call of their memory stronger than the practical demands of his inherited property. His father had died in a shooting accident while hunting several months earlier, and Evan had finally found it necessary — unavoidable in fact — to return north.

Glancing down, he looked into the dense white cloud that swathed the mountain just below his booted feet. Strangely, he felt as if he floated on an amorphous cloud miles above the earth. That thought was a bit too close to the angels for comfort, he told himself grimly.

"Fitz!" he shouted. "Arthur Fitzgibbon! Where are you! Damn, where the devil are you?" he finished in a mutter. His words came back to him in an eerie, muffled echo.

Silence, but for the whine of the wind. So far he had heard nothing unusual — no crunch of rock as a man stumbled, no shout, no cry of distress. Evan was sure that Professor Fitzgibbon had descended not long ago, for he was not keen on climbing through mist and rain, although the two men had planned to conquer at least one peak today if the weather held out.

Younger and stronger, Evan had clambered far ahead by the time Fitzgibbon had called that he wished to turn back, and Evan had answered that he wanted to go a little higher, but would soon follow. Fog and spitting rain had obscured the view, so Evan had not realized that Arthur was no longer scrambling behind him.

No doubt Fitz was on his way back to Kildonan Castle to warm his feet before the fire and enjoy a dram while he waited for Evan to trek back. Fitzgibbon was a good fellow, but not the most practical of souls. His mind was probably lost in geological observations as he hiked the few miles back to the castle. He would assume that Evan would take care of himself, and his biggest regret would be missing the upper sections of the mountain.

Evan could report on that well enough. The rock wall was a mix of black gneiss and white crystal, striped like a wild zebra and treacherous as the devil with a coating of verglas, a thin transparent layer of ice. He pulled a small ice pick out of the canvas knapsack he wore on his shoulders. Hacking intently into the verglas, he improved his next fingerhold and moved upward.

Imagining the comforts of a hearth fire and a glass of whisky only made Evan more aware of the chill that invaded his feet and hands and the hunger that twisted in his belly. He could not blame Arthur for giving up adventure in favor of a hot toddy and a blazing fire.

However, Evan did not usually choose comfort over risk. He liked the sting of danger now and then. Suddenly the afternoon's challenge had a little more sting in it than he had planned.

Looking around, he felt a keen sense of isolation. He clung to the shoulder of the ancient stone mountain like Jack upon the sleeping giant. There was no quick or safe way down, or up, from this point.

He had returned to Kildonan and Glen Shee to settle some matters on his estate and to try himself against the mountains that he remembered so well from boyhood. Having scrambled in the Alps and climbed in various parts of Scotland, he had not found anything to compare to climbing the Torridon mountains of northwest Scotland. Much lower in height than the towering Alpine peaks, lacking their pristine fantasy beauty, still the ancient, powerful majesty of the Highland slopes both astonished and humbled him. The raw, primeval strength of these hills seemed to have erupted from the heart of the earth itself.

Blowing on his cold, bare fingers, for he preferred to climb without gloves, he stared into the vat of milky fog around him. Groping, he found another hold and pulled himself up with the strength of his hands. He had the security of a rope tied around his waist, its upper end knotted to an iron claw hooked over a rock far above. Easier to go up, he knew, than down just now. At least he could see a little ahead, while the visibility below was obliterated. Once he found a safe perch, he would rest there and wait for the mist to clear. Then he would make his way down.

Grim, determined, he ascended by increments. This section was the most difficult part of the climb, with or without mists and slippery surfaces. Until now, the climb had been simple, a steep hike with a few risky hand- and footholds along the way. The day had begun with mist and drizzle, but nothing to worry about. Had he known that sleety rain, deep fog, and cold temperatures were sweeping toward the northwest Highlands from the Isles, he would never have attempted to scale the rock wall that led toward the split upper peaks of the rocky mountain.

He tugged on the rope tied around his waist, feeling the hidden grip of the serrated iron claw a few yards above him. Pulling on the taut Manila rope, he inched upward, choosing his holds cautiously. More than once he plunged his fingers into snow, trying to find a grip.

Fear began to eat at his will and wrench in his gut. He ignored it, focusing only on the next hold, the next upward surge. The sleet came so fast now, pattering on the rock all around him, that every hold was a slippery threat. The blessing was that the heavy sleet tore through the mist so that he could see the mountaintop that towered above him. Far to the left, he also glimpsed the rugged beauty of snow-covered slopes on a level with his perch. He had climbed far higher than he had realized.

The wind shoved at him, but he inched upward. Another gust rolled him sideways, knocking him against stone. He lost his hold and slid downward, but the rope caught him, and he found niches for his hands and feet. Moving upward, he slipped again, but rope and claw kept him from falling.

Finally reaching the wedged claw, he yanked it out and tossed it higher, where it snagged on a shelf. After testing the rope, he began to move upward, then felt the claw slip. He grabbed. The ice was honeycombed here, rotten with rain.

His support collapsed, the claw sprang free, and he slid violently downward. The rock had just enough incline that he was able to stay with that angle, grabbing rock and tufts of grass and growth and ice. Somehow he stayed with the incline, while his body made an undulating path in the resident snow like the tracks of a sled.

Bumping, bouncing, he descended helplessly, unable to catch hold of anything long enough to stop his downward hurtle. Soon, he knew, he would careen wildly out into the misty air and plummet straight down.

When the moment came and he sailed, panic was followed by unexpected bliss. Weightless, he surrendered to the fall.

Moments later, he slammed hard against a ledge.

"You've a long walk down to Glen Shee, Catriona. You may not reach home before the storm hits," Morag MacLeod said, gathering her plaid shawl over her rounded shoulders, to protect her thick gray hair from the cold drizzle. Turning her back to the mountain slopes, she peered at the misted glen far below. "You can stay the night in our little house and wait out the weather. My husband always likes your company, too."

"Thank you, Morag, but a little rain will do me no harm." Catriona shrugged and drew her own plaid higher over her head. "And my father and brother will be waiting supper for me. I'd best hurry."

"Let that old witch, your aunt, take care of them for once. And your father's cook will be there, unless she has gone home early with the bad weather. You do too much in that big house. The reverend's sister has made you into little more than a servant, Catriona Mhór, and that is not right. Plain Girl — *tcha!*" Morag shook her head. "That title does not suit you — the one who takes care of the others in her family all her life and neglects her own happiness for their comfort. You are not even plain." She peered close at Catriona, her cheeks bunched like wrinkled apples, brown eyes gleaming.

"Plain enough," Catriona said, shifting the heavy basket she carried. She and Morag MacLeod had been out on their weekly walk through the hills, gathering finished knitting from some of the Highland women who lived in the hill crofts — the stockings, mittens, and blankets they collected would be donated to the Highland regiments. "Who would marry me? Tall as a man, I am, with hair as red as fire. I try to be content running my father's household, though it is a lonely life," she admitted. "But I do not care to wait for some man to take me for a wife. I do not mind helping my father and my brother. Aunt Judith was not always there — she has only come to stay since her widowing."

"She is there now, and plans to stay now, I think. Your contentment is of little concern to her. And she will be quick to criticize your lateness today, I'm sure," Morag grumbled. "Well, you'd best hurry because of the weather. More than rain is in those clouds, I think. The way my old bones are complaining, we may even have snow tonight." Walking beside Catriona, the older woman clutched her faded plaid. "Now, sing the new song I taught you today. Do you remember it?"

29

Catriona lifted her head to sing as they walked, feeling the cold mist and drizzling rain on her cheeks. The haunting melody was easy to remember, but she struggled to recall the verses, which told a story of a lost lover returning from a sea voyage.

"*Oh-ho-ri-ri-o,*" Morag joined her in the refrain. "*Oh-ho-ri.*" The old woman clapped out the rhythm, her strong, rough voice harmonizing with Catriona's higher tones. "Good," Morag approved. "Are you going to write this song down, too, in that way you learned at the Edinburgh school, with those odd symbols?"

"Musical notation? Of course. I have written down all the songs I have collected over the years — over a hundred and thirty songs now. I hope that will please old Flora MacLeod. . . . Did you tell Mother Flora that I would like to meet with her to learn some of her songs?"

"*Ach,* I told her — the old crazy woman," Morag muttered.

Catriona laughed in surprise. "She's your grandmother!"

"Grandmother by law — my husband's grandmother. She says she's over a hundred now, though I don't believe it — she says whatever she likes. I think she's a lunatic, with her talk of meeting the fairies when she was young and learning their songs from them."

"Whether or not it's true, she is a wonder, Morag. She has more songs in her head than you or I could ever learn. My own mother learned to sing from old Mother Flora when I was small, so I would like to learn from her myself. I've gathered as many Gaelic tunes as I could from every Highlander who would sing for me. Many of the finest came from you, of course," Catriona added, glancing at her friend.

"I've taught you all that I know." Morag shrugged. "Mother Flora does have some rare old tunes that will be lost when she is gone. You do good work, Catriona MacConn, in saving the old Gaelic songs."

"My mother began collecting the local songs, but died before she could complete her work. I do it in her honor and in honor of the culture that is fast disappearing from this glen."

Morag nodded. "We'll go see Flora soon. We've tried for years to convince her to come live with us, but she refuses. So we bring her what she needs and visit her often. And still she sends us away threatening to cast spells on us. Me in particular." She snorted.

"Perhaps she will refuse to sing for me, then."

"She said she remembers your mother, but she would not promise anything for you. Your voice would please the fairies themselves, and it should please even Mother

Flora. The old she goat," Morag muttered.

"We'll never get up there today." Catriona peered at the thick mist that ringed the mountaintops. "Those clouds are getting darker, and the rain is turning to sleet."

Morag glanced up. "A strange feeling tells me you should stay with me and my John tonight. Come with me. Our house is only a few miles from this spot, and you will not have to cross the fairy bridge — it will not be easy if the stones are slick."

"I'll be fine, dear. I like hillwalking, and I do not mind the rain. And the bridge — you know we always leap across that like goats, you and I." Laughing again, Catriona gave her friend a hug. She tugged the old woman's shawl higher in a motherly way, although Morag was over seventy.

"Let me have the basket, at least," Morag said. "The knitted things we've gathered from the Highland wives will get wet if you carry them down to the glen." She took the bulky basket Catriona held. "We'll meet Wednesday by the bridge and go to see Mother Flora. And by then . . . will your brother have good news for me?" She lifted her brows meaningfully.

"About your kinfolk who left the glen?" Catriona shook her head. "I do not know, Morag. He tried to find them — even went to Glasgow to inquire — but he has had no success yet. Did you tell Mother Flora that my brother is trying to locate her kin?"

"Not yet. Ten years is a long time, and they went far away, some of them. Well, I will hope, and wait. Perhaps Finlay will have good news for our family, too. I know he recently brought some MacGillechallums back to their abandoned homestead on the slopes of Beinn Alligin," she whispered conspiratorially, as if the hillsides could eavesdrop. "Angus MacGillechallum was out there watching the sheep, as he agreed to do. And no one the wiser except those of us who would never tell."

"So long as the new earl keeps away from Glen Shee, Finlay can bring in whomever he likes to do the work of the estate. I'm so glad he was appointed Kildonan's factor," Catriona answered. "He will do well for the land and its people."

"And the new earl never the wiser," Morag said. "As if he cares. He will grow fat and rich from the sale of Kildonan wool, though he takes no interest in the process."

"And that is fine. Then we can do what we like."

"True. Now run, Catriona Mhór. Let those long legs carry you home!" Morag waved, then turned to hurry along a narrow track that led over a hill.

As Catriona continued on her way, the drover's track wended downward between ancient pines clinging to steep hillsides. The wide path was rough and overgrown, for no cattle came this way any longer, though she saw numerous sheep and a few wild goats stubbornly grazing, undisturbed by the weather. She jumped lightly over fallen trees and moved quickly downward.

Overhead, the clouds gathered heavy and dark as they swept in to crowd the surrounding mountains, and the rain grew colder, carrying stinging sleet.

Perhaps she should have accepted Morag's invitation after all, she thought. The way was slippery enough that she decided to avoid the old stone bridge and take the longer, safer route on the drover's track. But in this weather, not much would be safe if ice began to accumulate from the falling sleet. Glenachan House, her father's manse, was several miles from this point, no matter which way she went.

Drawing her plaid over her hair, she hurried onward.

Opening his eyes, Evan moved a little, realizing that he had come to a safe landing on an outcrop of rock. The mossy ledge was coated with sleet. Breathless and fog blind, head aching severely, he peered around.

The gneiss wall soared far above him, and he could see the trail of his fast descent in the snowy ramp along its incline. He had slid downward a long way, but his actual fall had not been far. He had hit his head, but otherwise thought he was unharmed. His knapsack was still strapped to his back, and the rope was still tied to his waist, though he had lost his ax.

All he had to do now was gain his feet and walk. From here, he thought he could find the drover's track that crossed the hills nearby, which would lead him easily to the glen. Shifting, groaning a little, he tested himself, then rose gingerly to hands and knees. After untying the rope and claw and shoving them into his knapsack, he edged along the ledge until he reached a broad swath of hillside that angled into the rockier heights of the mountain.

The heathered ground was littered with stones and boulders, and the fog was so thick that he could not see a path. Aching in every muscle, he stood slowly, his balance uncertain, and moved forward.

Strangely, he heard a voice singing through the sleet and fog, its echo sweet and mellifluous. He had heard that magical voice before, and it sank into his heart now as it had done then. Suddenly he remembered a lovely girl with red-gold hair standing on a hillside in sunlight as she sang a haunting tune.

Vision or reality, she became his compass through the fog, his goal and his sanctuary. He had to find her. Slipping on iced grass, then struggling to his feet, he moved toward her voice.

Dizziness and the steep incline of the hill overtook his senses, so that he did not know if he walked or stood still. Then he realized that he was tipping, and he sank slowly to his knees. A moment later, his head hit turf and heather.

Shivering in the cold dampness, Catriona continued the new song that Morag had taught her. She clenched her mittened hands to warm them, for the temperature was dropping fast. Sleety rain had deposited a thin coat of ice on the rocks and grass, and she walked cautiously. If she fell up here, alone on the mountain path, she might not be found for days.

She glanced up at the rocky precipice that rose beside the path, much of its massive bulk hidden by fog. The slope she climbed was high, yet a mere foothill to the ancient mountain. Above, crags and walls soared toward snow-covered peaks not visible through the mists. Legends wove through those crags and caves like bright threads in a tapestry, told in the stories and songs that Catriona had heard all her life.

Shivering again, she drew her woolen plaid higher over her head to cover her hair, tucking her copper-sheened braid over her shoulder. Morag's prediction of snow might prove right after all, she thought, for the wind had a bitter edge.

The old track followed the angle of the hill, skimming down toward the glen and her father's rectory at Glenachan. The ice made the ground so treacherous that she had to go carefully.

The song about the lost lover distracted her as she tried to master its poignant melody and multiple verses. Once she was home, and warm and dry, she looked forward to making a good copy of the notes she had taken about the new song. She had written the words in Gaelic and English and transcribed the melody, as she had done with all the songs she had learned over the years. The pages of her notes for this song and some others were folded securely in her pocket.

Daylight was failing rapidly, but she knew the way well. She was glad for the warmth of the long plaid shawl that covered her from her head to nearly her ankles, and glad for the thick layers of her green jacket and skirt, flannel petticoats, and woolen stockings. Her brother, Finlay, had insisted on studding her boot soles with small nails for a better grip as she walked.

She hoped that Finlay had decided to stay at home, after all, today, and not ride to Inverness as he had planned. For nearly two years, her brother had dedicated much of his time to finding exiled Highlanders and relocating them to their old crofts in Glen Shee. He had found jobs on the land for as many as he could. The people were more than willing to work as shepherds for the vast numbers of sheep that roamed the slopes and fields of the glen and its mountains. The sheep belonged to the current Earl of Kildonan, who had not returned to the glen in the months since his father's death. Finlay all but ran the estate himself and made decisions with increasing boldness. Sometimes she wondered if Finlay's deep, quiet grief over the loss of their brother Donald years before drove him to take chances now. Donald had loved the glen and its people, and like Finlay, he would have risked anything to help them, had he lived.

She worried that one day Lord Kildonan would return and demand to know why his sheep were being herded and clipped by the same Highlanders his father had run off the land. If and when that day came, she hoped Kildonan would be such a wealthy man from the profits of those same wool clippings that he would not care if Highlanders, Englishmen, or fairies ran his Highland estate. His father had not cared about the details of the estate in the last year or two of his life — hopefully the son was the same in that regard, for it had proved convenient for Finlay's efforts to help the Highlanders of Glen Shee.

But she knew Finlay risked arrest or exile from the glen if the new earl ever discovered, and disliked, what her brother was doing. Until then, she could only hope that Finlay took no undue chances and placed only as many families on the land as the estate's needs could support.

Lost in her thoughts, glancing around at the thickening white mist as she walked, she did not see what lay prone in her path. Tripping suddenly, she looked down and gasped.

At her feet, a man lay facedown and motionless, his arms flung forward, so that she had stumbled over his tweed-coated arm, the rest of him half-hidden behind a crop of large stones.

Sinking to one knee, Catriona reached out, then hesitated, afraid the man was dead. When his fingers moved slightly, she breathed out in relief and touched his shoulder.

"Ach Dhia," she murmured to herself. "Dear God. Sir! Sir," she said, shaking him a little, but he did not rouse.

Chapter Two

He was dark haired and hatless, his body tall and long limbed. His face, only partly visible, had a firm and handsome profile, and he seemed about thirty years old or so. Catriona noted that he was well dressed, his jacket and trousers of good, heavy tweed, his gloves of supple brown leather. His well-cobbled boots had thick, hobnailed soles — a climber or hillwalker, then. A knitted scarf was draped around his neck, and a canvas knapsack rested on his back, its single strap crossing his torso.

He must be one of the holiday climbers who sometimes visited the area hoping to challenge themselves on the mountain slopes. Undoubtedly he had companions who would look for him.

She glanced around, but saw no one through the drizzling sleet; nor did she hear anyone calling out as if searching. The only sounds were sleet pelting stone and the cold moan of the wind.

Resting a hand on his back, she felt his breath rise and fall. Gingerly she swept back his dark hair, silky cool, damp with sleet. Blood darkened one side of his forehead.

Seeing the small gash and dark bruise there, she gasped in sympathy.

Tucking his scarf higher to help warm him, she wondered what best to do. They were isolated on this high slope, and the man was not able to walk on his own. He was tall and hard muscled, and though she was tall and strong herself, she did not think she could support him along the icy slopes to the glen.

The nearest house was Glenachan, but it would take her too long to get home in these conditions. She could not leave him here to suffer or possibly to die from injuries or exposure to the freezing cold. As it was, she did not know how long he had been lying there unconscious.

She touched his cheek and slid her fingers under his scarf and collar to feel the pulse in his neck. His skin felt cold, and he was pale under the dusky shadow of his beard. She had to help him, and in such bitter weather, both of them would need shelter.

She rested her hand on his soft, dark hair for a moment, thinking. Years ago, her eldest brother, Donald, had fallen while climbing this same mountain — Beinn Sitheach, the Mountain of the Fairies. The weather had turned that day, too, to ice and cold.

With no one to help him, Donald had died alone of injuries that need not have killed him. By the time her father and Finlay searched and found him, he was gone — and her father had been injured from a fall on that awful, heartrending day.

Having endured that, she would not let tragedy befall this stranger, no matter who he was, no matter what it cost her to help him. If she stayed with him, he might be saved — but he could die if she left him here while she fetched help. Somehow she would find a way to bring him to shelter and safety.

Remembering that a little ruined shieling hut was located farther down the slope, she knew she must take him there. After easing the knapsack off his back, she set it aside. Then she stood, leaned down, and grasped the man under the arms.

She knew she could manage his greater size by dragging him and did so, advancing with care, glancing over her shoulder through mist and rain.

As she pulled, his head lolled on her hip, and his weight — while not overmuch for his height — threatened to pull her to her knees, but she went onward, determined.

The wind beat at her, buffeted her plaid, stung her cheeks. Freezing snowflakes dusted her face and the man's sagging form. She slipped once, falling hard to one knee, but she kept his limp head from hitting the ground.

Resting her brow against his dark hair for a moment, she struggled to her feet. Then, breathing hard, she summoned sheer determination and pulled him the rest of the way.

The little stone hut was set a hundred feet or so off the path in a turf clearing, in the lee of the upthrusting hill. Pulling and huffing, Catriona dragged the traveler along, his heels digging snakelike tracks in the new snow.

Built of stone and thatch, the place had been deserted a long while, she knew, by shepherds who once used it for a summer hut when they brought the cattle to the uplands. Still, its ruined condition would be preferable to complete exposure.

Catriona tugged the unconscious stranger through the doorway. Immediately she saw that a portion of the roof had collapsed, for a corner was piled with musty old thatch and broken rafters. Chill winds and sleet burst through the roof and the modestly sized interior was dank and dim.

Feeling the strain of her task, Catriona maneuvered the man across the room toward the cold hearth and laid him on the earthen floor. She removed her plaid and wrapped it around him, using his finely woven scarf to cushion his head. He opened his eyes slightly, heavy lashes black against his pale cheeks, and mumbled something. She glimpsed the rather startling hazel green of his eyes before his eyelids closed.

Then she went back outside, shivering without her plaid, to grab a handful of snow,

43

which she wrapped in her handkerchief. Once inside the hut, she sank to her knees beside the stranger and applied the makeshift compress to his forehead, where a cut seeped blood, staining his face, shirt, and tweed jacket.

Cleaning his skin gently, she saw him flutter his eyelids a little, though he did not fully awaken. She rubbed his bare hands with her mittened fingers, still shivering herself.

She glanced around. The hearth was crude, but a stack of old peat would provide fuel for a fire, if it was not wet. She went to the hearth to stack a few crumbling peat bricks there, and finding an old flint on a shelf, she worked at it until it struck a spark. Several attempts finally produced a smoking peat, which she coaxed into a flame. Catriona sat back and watched the flame grow, casting a feeble light over the man who lay near her.

She studied his face for a few moments. Handsome and strong in appearance, he looked healthy enough despite the bruise and small cut on his brow. She did not recognize him, though there was an elusive familiarity to his face.

Holding her hands out to the increasing heat of the flames, she looked around. In the gathering dusk, the gloom in the shieling hut was deep and dismal but for the small glow of the hearth. The temperature, even a few feet beyond the hearthstones, was freezing.

She heard icy rain pelting the outer walls and saw a mix of sleet and snow spilling through the hole in the roof.

Frowning, she realized that she could go nowhere now. She could not leave the man unconscious, and she could not make her way down to the glen in the icy darkness. She gazed at the man's unknown, rather striking face, and wondered how the two of them would survive this bitter, dangerous night.

Before she could worry about that, she had to tend to the stranger. The bruised cut on his head was obvious enough, but she did not know if he had any other wounds or injuries.

Drawing off her mittens, she bent forward and gingerly patted his broad shoulders and arms, then touched his chest, where he wore a brown woolen vest and white linen shirt beneath his buttoned jacket. His suit was of good tweed in brown and cream, earthy colors that flattered his smooth, lightly tanned complexion. Fine creases around his closed eyes hinted that he was an avid outdoorsman. The taut, strong body underneath his clothing revealed athletic strength.

His shoulders were broad and square, his torso hard and lean wherever she touched him. Though she was hesitant at first, she had to know the extent of his injuries, and grew bolder, exploring his chest and flat abdomen, then his lean hips and long, muscled legs. Slipping her hands beneath him, she probed his back and skimmed her palms down his legs, then wiggled his feet in their hobnailed boots. Relieved to find no obvious broken bones or other injuries, she discovered, to her blushing surprise, that it was rather pleasant to touch his long, lean, perfect form.

He was a beautiful man, handsome and virile, and her imagination strayed, conjuring a vision of lying in his arms, sheltered against that hard, powerful body. Shocked at her wayward, insistent thoughts, she sat back and watched his face for signs of pain or discomfort.

His hair was deep brown, while his brows, thick lashes, and clean-shaven beard were black. She touched the square strength of his jaw, his beard rasping on her skin, and then she traced a fingertip over his beautifully chiseled mouth, his lips soft and cool, his breath faint and even.

His eyelids fluttered again, a flash of mossy green and brown, the dark, calm colors of the forest. She drew her hand away and he closed his eyes again. His breath eased out, long and slow, and she realized that he slept.

After pulling the plaid up to his chin, she turned to look around in the bright flickering light of the hearth. In a dark corner, she saw a sagging bench and a few utensils on a shelf — a small iron kettle, a bowl, tongs, a fire poker.

She rose to her feet and fetched the kettle, remembering that she had some dry oats tucked in a packet in her skirt pocket, a habit she had formed long ago when taking long walks in the hills. Wondering if the stranger carried any other food, she turned toward his knapsack.

If they had to spend a long, dark, cold night in this hut, they would need not only heat, but sustenance.

Firelight and warmth and gentle hands upon him. He knew that kind touch now and had come to treasure her grace and comfort while he lay there, unable to move. He did not know how long that had been, or where he was, or who she was. But he was deeply glad to be alive and grateful for her care of him.

Her hands lifted away, having brushed his forehead again. Turning her back, she began to sing in lilting, breathy Gaelic. Although he did not understand all the words, the sound was calming.

Opening his eyes, Evan watched the young woman dip a wooden spoon into the contents of an iron kettle set on stones over a hearth fire. Gleaming waves of hair formed a loose, coppery halo, sweeping gracefully over her cheek to twist in a long braid. She did not look at him, continuing to hum as she stirred. Firelight flowed over her like red gold.

She looked younger than himself, perhaps early twenties. Tall and long limbed beneath a moss-green gown, her body curved like an hourglass, slender through the waist and full at hip and breast. Despite weariness, his body contracted lustily to see that womanly shape, but he glanced away, unwilling to stare with evident desire at his nameless and lovely savior.

He glanced around. They were inside a small, crude stone house in sad repair. The walls leaked the outside cold, and part of the roof had collapsed into a corner. Had he not known better, he would have thought himself caught in the Middle Ages, or in some legend of enchantment, with a beautiful girl stirring a magic cauldron, her soft chant rising with the smoke of the fire.

Dimly he recalled that he had fallen while climbing. The accident existed only in torn bits of memory. He tested himself further — Evan Mackenzie, lately of the Lowlands, born in the Highlands. Viscount of Glendevon, recently Earl of Kildonan following the death of his father seven months ago.

Good, he thought. His brain was intact, at least.

Ending her song, the girl came toward him. He looked into a pretty oval face with pleasing features, surrounded by a glorious halo of bright hair sheened like a mix of copper and bronze. Her eyes were large and gray-blue, and her translucent skin had a fine scattering of golden freckles. She had an appealing freshness, a simplicity that was beautiful, an honest face, a gentle manner and voice. He wished she would sing again, for he felt something healing in the sound.

Other than that sweet, quiet singing, she had said little that he recalled. She had not attempted to babble on cheerfully at him, for which he was grateful.

She said nothing now, though she glanced at him with keen blue eyes. Her smile was shy, and she turned to stir the kettle again. The calmness about her seemed to affect him, too, for he drew a slow breath and felt steady and soothed as he glanced around and took stock of his situation.

Shifting slightly, he put a hand to his head and felt the thickness of a bandage over a tender spot. He ached everywhere, head to foot, but he was comfortable in his warm nest, which consisted of a plaid blanket wrapped around him.

The girl turned and smiled again, a wooden spoon in her mittened hand. Her face brightened in an impish way. She had the strong-boned good looks common in the Highlands, but her hair was extraordinary, and when she smiled, Evan saw that she was astonishingly lovely.

She spoke quietly in Gaelic, and he looked at her without reply. "You are awake," she said then in English. "Good."

Still he stared at her, fogged by weariness. He vaguely remembered a terrifying fall from the mountainside, resulting in a hard slam against rock. He knew he had crawled toward a safer place and recalled sleet and ice and unforgiving winds.

But he did not recall how he came to be here alone with a Highland lass. Staring at her, he blinked, then nodded.

She tilted her head. *"Parlez-vous français?"* she asked. *"Capisco l' italiano, abbastanza bene. . . . Sprechen-Sie Deutsch?"*

Now here was a complete surprise. His Highland angel was multilingual. He blinked again, bemused. "That is more than my poor brainpan can handle just now, lass," he murmured. "English will do. I believe I fell . . . quite a distance." He rubbed his bandaged head.

"Ah," she said. "You are an English holiday climber?" She spoke the lilting, precise English typical of a Gael who had acquired the second language in school.

"A climber, aye, but a Scotsman."

"Aye? You sound English."

"Eton College," he explained. She nodded her understanding, then blew on the spoon to cool its steaming contents before leaning forward to offer him a taste.

He swallowed, closing his eyes at the satisfying taste of a hot brose. He detected a healthy dash of whisky mixed with a thick broth of water and oats. It slid down his throat like fire.

She turned away again, and he glanced around. The dim little room was a dank ruin. He smelled stone, earth, the sweet must of peat, the clean, cold snap of wind and snow.

Icicles hung from an ugly tear in the roof, and a gaping hole in the thatch revealed a magical night sky, filled with swirling snow-flakes.

Snow drifted inside, blanketing the rubble of the fallen roof. The little hearth fire gave off some heat, but the hut, ruined and open to the elements, was as cold as an icebox.

The girl felt the chill, for she shivered. Mittens and indoor clothing were not enough protection against the elements. Her green skirt was plump with petticoats, and her high-collared jacket conformed nicely to her full bosom, but her clothing would not provide enough warmth in this keen and killing cold.

He, on the other hand, felt snug inside the plaid. Looking down, he realized that he was wrapped in her shawl, for the tartan, consisting of colors crisscrossed on a creamy background, was the sort traditionally worn by Highland women. Watching her shiver and sniffle so that he could be comfortable, he felt a pang of guilt.

"Miss —" he began.

"Catriona," she said. "Catriona MacConn."

"Pleased to meet you, Miss MacConn. It is . . . Miss?"

"I am not married," she said, stirring again.

Spinster or not, she was an angel to him, and she was shivering. And if she was not some man's wife, that made their strange situation marginally less awkward. There would be no husband furious with him for spending time alone with the man's wife, though there might well be a father or brothers. But it could not be helped. He would do his best to be gentlemanly.

But she was feeling the cold just as he was — and he had the only blanket in sight. He opened the plaid in invitation. "Miss MacConn, meaning no disrespect — would you care to come sit beside me and get warm?"

"I am fine." As she spoke, she chafed her arms with her mittened hands. Her breath frosted in the air.

"Lass, don't be a fool. Come get warm before you perish of the chill." Evan beckoned to her a bit sternly. He did not have much patience with mincing feminine modesty where none was needed — he certainly did not intend to play wolf to her lamb — nor did he enjoy watching self-made martyrs who suffered nobly so that others could benefit.

He did not know this girl, but he would

have guessed her to be forthright and practical, and not a victim of convention.

"Miss MacConn," he said. "It is absurd for me to sit here comfortable, while you are shaking with cold."

She stared at him, clearly tempted, and stepped forward.

Chapter Three

She looked from the blanket to him, hesitating. "I am not that sort of girl, I assure you." Her teeth chattered.

"Nor am I that sort of man." He sat up, leaning his shoulders against the cold, damp wall, where the wind cut through gaps between the stones. "But I will not watch you suffer while I lounge about recuperating. I believe you saved my life, Miss MacConn. I am in your debt, and I cannot dismiss that lightly."

"You owe me nothing, sir. I could not leave you there."

"I owe you a great deal. If you prefer, we'll share the blanket by turns. I'll tend the fire and stir your concoction in the kettle, while you wrap up and get warm." He eased himself to his feet, placing a hand on the wall for support when his head spun and every aching muscle protested.

"Sir, you must not —" She rushed forward, slipping her arm around his waist and tucking her shoulder under his arm. He leaned on her, noticing that she was a strong girl and could easily support him. But he refused to sit when she pushed him downward.

Relenting, she helped him toward a wooden bench beside the fire. The thing was warped and rocked a little, steadying when he leaned back against the wall.

She knelt by the hearth to stir the bubbling contents in the kettle. "You should rest," she said. "You seem to have no broken bones, but your head injury concerns me. And you suffered some exposure to the cold — I do not know for how long."

"I'm fine," he said, although he still felt aches and weakness. But his physical nature was strong and hardy, and he did not easily admit complaints. "Whatever is bruised will mend." He tipped his head, puzzled. "How did I come to be here in this place, with you?"

She sat back on her heels and looked at him. "I found you near the drover's road that runs over the hill — Beinn Sìtheach, we call it — Beinn Shee, the Fairy Mountain. It is the tallest peak beside the great mountain called Beinn Alligin."

He nodded. "I was climbing the one called Beinn Shee. I did not make it to the top, though." He shifted, stifled a wince.

"No one ever has," she said quietly. "Do you recall falling?"

"Aye. A friend and I started out early in the day in the mist, but we thought it would clear. As we worked our way up, the storm blew in from the northwest, bringing rain and then sleet. My friend turned back, I think. I lost him in the fog. I hope to God he did not fall, too."

She frowned. "I saw a man crossing the glen floor as I came over the old track. The fog had cleared enough to see into the glen, and I did think it odd to see a gentleman walking alone in poor weather. He had a pack on his back, and wore a jacket, knickers, and a hat, like a sporting gentleman. But no gun."

"That would be Fitzgibbon." Evan felt relieved to know that Arthur had made it safely down from the mountain. "I could not descend safely, so I went up, looking for shelter." He told her the rest, as much as he remembered. "It was something of a nightmare," he finished, and he touched his brow. "I hit a rocky ledge rather hard and then tried to crawl to safety, but fell again. It's a blur to me now."

"I found you collapsed beside the path, nearly chilled to death, with your head bruised and bleeding. I knew this shieling hut was not far down the track, so I brought you here."

"I'm eternally grateful, Miss MacConn. But how did you manage it?" He sat forward. "I must have walked, though I do not recall that."

"I dragged you here."

"What? I am amazed as well as grateful. That was a Herculean task. I am not a small man."

"Nor am I a small woman. I could hardly leave you there to fetch help." She rose to her feet. "Sir, it is so cold in here. You must cover up and keep warm."

He felt the cold intensely, but had not forgotten that she felt it, too. She paced, rubbing her arms, and the tip of her nose was a delicate pink.

"Miss MacConn, I insist that you take a turn under the blanket and get warm. Please," he said, pointing toward the plaid. He left the bench, hiding the effort it cost him to move, and lowered to the floor beside the glowing hearth. Then he took the spoon from her and dipped it into the kettle.

"Be careful. It's hot," she said.

In response, he pointed toward the plaid. She crawled into the cocoon he had abandoned and drew the blanket to her chin. Her boots stuck out.

"Tuck your feet in," he ordered. She smiled at his tone, and he smiled, too, feeling a little surprised at himself. Generally he had greater reserve with strangers, but he felt at ease in her company. He sipped from the spoon. "This is good. Like a brose, but not sweet."

"I used oats, melted snow, and whisky," she said. "I hope you don't mind, sir, but I found your flask of whisky in the knapsack and mixed it with snow and the packet of oats that I had with me. I always carry dry oats with me when I walk out in the hills."

"Lucky for us that you did. Whatever I have is yours, Miss MacConn." She had saved his life, and that had begun to dawn on him more completely. He would have offered her more than the contents of his knapsack — he would have given her his fortune, his estate, his very person had she needed anything. He might have died if she had not come along, and if she had not had such compassion, courage, and determination.

Suddenly he felt a strong surge of affection for her, as if he had known her a long time. An odd reaction, since he tended to be reserved upon meeting someone. But no one had ever saved his life before. Gratitude formed a bond with her that felt tangible and strong.

"There are some more oats in my pack, though not much," she said. "We do not have much to eat other than that."

He set down the spoon. Despite growing hunger, he did not want to consume more than his share, but when he offered her the spoon, she shook her head.

"I'm not hungry just now. I fear we will have to stay here until daylight." She looked anxiously at the door, which swayed on worn hinges, buffeted by the wind. Snow blew in through chinks in the walls and through the gap in the roof, sifting down to the floor.

"I'm sure we'll be fine. The storm will blow through soon, and then we can leave.

The glen isn't far from here, is it?"

She shifted to sit up, leaning against the wall and pulling the plaid around her. "The track goes over the hills rather than directly down, so it's more than three miles to the glen floor and another mile or so to my father's house from that point. The track is steep and overgrown and treacherous in bad weather. And you should not exert yourself with such a walk just yet, with that head injury. You probably have other bruises and aches as well, though thankfully no broken bones." She blushed in the firelight as he glanced at her. "I had to examine you," she explained.

Seeing the embarrassed flush on her cheeks, Evan smiled. "Well, I'm glad you did," he said, to put her at ease. "I can make the descent if the weather clears, but it does seem as if we will have to spend the night here, Miss MacConn." He looked at her soberly. "I hope you do not feel too awkward about that."

She shrugged, a brittle show of bravery. "What choice do we have? We'll manage. We have a fire, some food, and . . . one blanket." She frowned. "Perhaps your friend will come for you."

"Fitz? Perhaps, but not guaranteed. A good fellow, but he tends to assume all is well and goes about his business. Besides, the storm will prevent anyone from searching for us.

Your family will be concerned, I'm sure."

"My father and brother will worry when I do not come home. My . . . eldest brother died under such circumstances, many years ago," she murmured. "He was climbing on Beinn Shee when he fell, but he was not found in time."

"My God," he said softly, genuinely touched. "How terrible for your family." He set down the spoon and leaned toward her, still seated by the fire.

"My father . . . took it very hard. Donald was the oldest of my parents' six children. My father was also injured on the day of the search, and he . . . well, he has never been the same. Turned sad and fierce that day and found his solace in strict religion." She shrugged. "But we have all managed, in our way. As I said, they will be concerned if I do not return from these hills — and will surely come look for me when the weather allows."

"Well, I think we will easily get down to the glen in the morning, before they even have a chance to come out. And no one need be the wiser about our adventure here, if you wish," he offered impulsively. "We can arrive separately."

She tilted her head, then gave a pensive nod.

The wind howled, and sleety gusts rattled the walls. Catriona MacConn looked around anxiously. "This shieling hut has been here a long time. It was used long ago, when the shepherds and their families brought the cattle to graze on sweet grass in the high hills. No one has been here for decades, I think."

Evan moved to sit with his back against the wall, bringing him closer to the girl. "We could stuff the larger holes and block the gap in the roof to cut the winds," he suggested, glancing around. "I might be able to wedge something between the rafters."

She rubbed her arms. "I knew there was rain coming, but wintry squalls are impossible to predict and are common in autumn. We could have even colder temperatures and more snow before morning. If so, we could be stranded for days."

"All will be well," he assured her. She returned his gaze quickly and frankly. Catriona MacConn came of strong, practical Highland stock, and he felt sure that she would remain calm and reliable if their adventure became a true ordeal of life and death.

"I hope so, Mr. — I have not yet learned your name."

"Mackenzie. Evan Mackenzie. Pleased to meet you, Miss MacConn." He smiled, holding out his hand, touching her fingers lightly. Though they had touched before, that brief intentional contact sent a subtle shock through his body, and he felt an inward astonishment. What was it about Catriona

61

MacConn, he thought, that set his senses reeling and distracted him so thoroughly?

He did not offer his titles along with his name, keeping them to himself as usual. His peer status made him uncomfortable, for it set him apart in his work as an engineer of bridgeworks. Uncertain of his inheritance due to the rift with his father, he had devoted himself to earning a livelihood and establishing a reliable reputation. Long ago he had made it a habit to introduce himself as Mr. Mackenzie, and outside of rare formal occasions, he seldom needed anything more than that. In the recent months as Lord Kildonan, he had used it sparingly.

As for his reliable reputation — well, that had suffered greatly two years earlier, and he himself had shattered with it to some extent. He did not want his name and title shattered, too, here in Glen Shee, because of his father's deeds here.

"Mr. Mackenzie." She smiled politely, and he was enchanted once again by her fleeting fey quality and the pretty, elusive dimples that graced her cheeks. "There are many Mackenzies hereabouts. Are you related to some of them?"

"I might be," he said carefully. "I consider myself a Lowlander, although my father's people were from this region, and my mother was born in Inverness." He did not add that he had spent some of his childhood in Glen

Shee. Those memories were precious and private, and he did not want to discuss his late father or his current situation. Instinctively he knew that Catriona MacConn would not be pleased about his identity if she knew all of it. He did not want to spoil the necessary camaraderie that would help them endure the night.

"Well, you're Highland by blood at least, if not by upbringing," she said. "Mackenzies have been the lairds of Kildonan Castle and the estate of Kildonan in Glen Shee for generations. They have held the title of earl for less — perhaps twenty years."

"Aye," he said. "I'd heard something of it."

"Perhaps you know the current Lord Kildonan, or knew his father, the late earl."

"I . . . have heard of them." He moved away and began to stir the brose again. Knowing he should tell her, he resolved to do so later, once they were safely down the mountain.

"The old earl was an awful man, to be honest, Mr. Mackenzie, though I beg your pardon if he was your kinsman. I am sorry the man died — he was shot when he set down his own gun while deer stalking, and that is no way for a man to go — but to be truthful there were many who were not unhappy when he left us."

"Indeed," Evan answered flatly, though he felt a fresh pang at losing his father while so many things between them were still un-resolved.

"I have not met the new earl, but I suspect he is no better than his father. He has not bothered to come north yet, and his father died months ago."

He glanced at her, tempted to say that he had been diving off a damn sea rock as an assistant on a lighthouse project during those months. The news of his father's death had not reached him quickly, and the man had been buried by the time Evan had found out about it.

Obeying his instincts, and hearing Catriona's contempt for the earls of Kildonan, Evan kept his identity to himself. Aware of his father's misdeeds, he did not expect the people of Glen Shee to warmly welcome the new Earl of Kildonan.

"Did you know the previous earl, Miss MacConn?" he asked.

She shook her head, her shoulders and back leaned against the wall. Evan noticed that she shivered. He was not very comfort-able himself, even beside the little fire. Bit-terly cold air seeped into the room through a multitude of cracks and crevices.

"I did not know him personally," she an-swered. "He caused much trouble and sad-ness in this glen when he evicted the people to make room for sheep so that he could se-cure his fortune. They say it is a vast fortune indeed, and I hear the new earl plans to sell much of the land, and not bother himself with running the estate." She lifted her chin, a slight motion that Evan thought revealed pride and a hint of some inner hurt.

She loved this land deeply, he realized. So did he, although he was aware that his actions as earl did not prove that.

He frowned. Catriona, and the rest of the residents of Glen Shee, did not know that the new earl had no choice but to sell some land and rent out the castle and hunting reserves in order to generate needed funds. Evan's father had left considerable debts — sheep were lucrative, but the earl had been extravagant — and the new earl had obligations on his own.

Following the bridge collapse that had killed three of his crewmen and friends, he had been helping to support their three widows and eleven fatherless children. Having arranged for a modest yearly income for each family, he was also determined to see the children properly educated. His private income as an engineer covered some of those expenses, but after meeting his father's debts, he found himself forced to sell part of Kildonan to make up the difference.

Although the Parliamentary commission that oversaw the construction of bridges in Scotland had cleared Evan of any responsibility in the tragedy, he had not cleared himself. He did not know if he could forgive himself. The memories of that day would haunt him for the rest of his life.

Although he could donate money and take a personal interest in the welfare of each family — and particularly each child — he could never make up for the loss of three excellent men. And he wondered still, to this day, if he could have saved them.

"I see," he replied slowly. "If the earl plans to alter the estate, I suppose he has his reasons. Have you always lived in this glen, Miss MacConn?" He felt an urge to change the topic.

"I have. And I saw the people leave this glen, years ago. I can never forget that sight," she murmured.

Evan had also seen that long trail of people leaving the glen. "Your family stayed?"

"My father is the parish minister. It is a Free Church rather than an Established Church. Hardly any people are left to minister to here."

He knew the Free Church had adopted a strict dogma, having split from the more moderate Established Church of Scotland several years ago. "I see. Miss MacConn, what makes you sure that the new Kildonan will be anything like his father?"

"Because my brother is his factor, Mr. Mackenzie. And Finlay has told me how the new earl neglects his property, leaving it to his factor to run, not caring a whit about the land or the people. But the profit from the wool, aye, that's very important, isn't it?" Her blue-gray eyes fairly sparked.

"Factor?" *Oh God,* he thought, and he shoved long fingers through his hair. *Finlay MacConn.* He knew the name, but as yet had not met the fellow. Evan's sister, Lady Jean Gray, came to Kildonan regularly and had met with young MacConn, who had been the old factor's assistant and had replaced the man upon Grant's death, just before Evan's father had passed away.

And here he sat, alone in a compromising position with his factor's sister, the daughter of the reverend of the Glen Shee parish. With each passing moment, he felt that it was wiser for him to keep his identity to himself until the risk of their situation had passed. If Catriona knew who he was, she might not want to stay with him at all. He would not be the cause of her shivering in a corner to keep her distance, as she did now, or perhaps running outside altogether.

Much better, he told himself, to stay on neutral and equal ground with her for now. Later, when they were warm and well fed and convention was restored, they might even find cause to laugh about this.

"Neglect?" Evan asked. "He . . . neglects this place?" He had never seen it quite that way. He had been out in the remote

Hebridean Isles working on engineering projects when his father had died and had no time or leisure to come up here. His sister and brother-in-law enjoyed taking holidays at Kildonan, and so he left it to them to see to the running of the estate. Jean and Harry had reported that the new young factor was competent and trustworthy. Evan had assumed all was well.

"All but abandoned it to his sister to run, my brother says," Catriona went on. "Did he return after his father's death to meet his tenants? Does he intend to right the wrongs the old earl did here? He could bring back the people who were forced to leave Glen Shee. He could ask Highlanders to watch his thousands of sheep for him. Has he done any of that?" She folded her arms. "Not at all, Mr. Mackenzie. It's very sad, that."

He frowned. "Aye. It certainly is. I can see where you might get that impression —"

"Impression! He is continuing his father's legacy. He enjoys the profits from the sheep, and he charges money to allow tourists and holiday climbers to come here."

Evan looked away. The rentals and tourists had been his father's idea, and the profit from that was healthy. He and Jean had even talked of building an inn or hotel. He shook his head, half to himself. There was much he needed to learn about Glen Shee, apparently.

Catriona sat straighter and looked at him.

"Oh, dear. Mr. Mackenzie. Oh dear, are you —"

So she had figured it out that quickly. Well, he would face the consequences. "Am I who, Miss MacConn?"

"Are you one of those who paid to take a climbing holiday on Lord Kildonan's lands?"

"No, Miss MacConn," he said with a sense of relief. "I can assure you that I have not paid for that privilege."

Chapter Four

Catriona stood back and looked around the hut with a sense of satisfaction. She and Mr. Mackenzie had crammed chinks in the drystone walls with thatch taken from the debris of the roof. The wind still howled, blowing damp and freezing cold, and sleet still mixed with snow to filter through the remaining holes in the roof, but she did feel less draft.

"Oh, Mr. Mackenzie, please be careful," she said, turning.

Evan had broken apart the wooden bench to wedge the planks between the roof beams. He reached overhead to secure the makeshift patch and block more of the cold air.

"I'm — perfectly — fine," he answered, pounding the plank into place with his fist. Catriona had seen him wince in pain more than once as he worked. Tall enough to assist him, she stepped forward to prop up one end of the bench while he fitted it between the rafters. Mackenzie glanced at her briefly. "I always liked tall lassies. Now I know why." He grinned.

Holding the piece, she knew she blushed at his teasing compliment. She stole a glance at

70

him as he worked, admiring the animal power of his shoulders, the long grace of his back and legs. She watched the muscles shift and bunch beneath his shirt, for he had removed his jacket to work in shirtsleeves and vest. Remembering the smooth firmness of those hard muscles under her hands earlier, recalling her own curiosity about what it might be like to lie in his arms, she felt her cheeks heat fiercely.

She had rarely had thoughts like that before, and what was more disconcerting, they persistently returned, bobbing up no matter how often she pushed them down.

"There," he said, stepping back and lowering his arms. He glanced at her. "It seems a little warmer in here."

"Less drafty, at least. Mr. Mackenzie, please rest. I fear you will overdo, and I do not know how serious your head injury might be. We must have the doctor look at you back in the glen."

He looked surprised. "There's a doctor of medicine here?"

"Almost. Mr. Grant is the laird of Kilmallie at the other end of the glen, but he studied medicine at university, although he did not complete his degree — his father, who was the earl's factor, died and the son was called back here. But he is a competent doctor for our needs. You should consult Mr. Grant about your head bump later. Are you

71

staying at the Torridon Inn in Glen Shee? Mrs. MacAuley runs the only accommodation in the glen. But perhaps you are staying with friends here."

He avoided answering, certain she knew everyone in the glen. "I might consult Mr. Grant. I'll see how I feel tomorrow. There, that should hold." He stood back.

"I do feel a difference."

"Politely said, Miss MacConn, but it is still bitter cold in here." He glanced around. "Where shall we sleep? I apologize for being so direct, but it is getting late. We need to make a bed."

"Beds," she corrected. "There's only the one plaid and our jackets, but it's only for tonight. You take the blanket, Mr. Mackenzie, and I'll borrow your coat, if I may."

"You take the blanket."

"You need a comfortable place to rest, Mr. Mackenzie. I'm concerned about your injuries. I insist." She folded her arms like a stern nursemaid.

"Perhaps we should share." He knelt on the floor to spread out the plaid. "After you, Miss MacConn."

She stared at him. "Surely you don't expect us to sleep in the same bed."

"Why not? We'd stay warm that way." He looked at her. "The only way we'll get through this beastly night is to share warmth, Miss MacConn."

"Share warmth! You — I trusted you!" Still, as she looked at him, she felt no alarm — only a dark, secret excitement.

"I promise, you can trust me." He inclined his head.

"I am not — I will not —" She stopped awkwardly.

He sighed. "I have no designs on your virtue, Miss MacConn. Our situation is serious. Either we protect ourselves from the bitter cold, or we suffer for the sake of propriety and risk our health. Which shall it be?"

"When you climbed in the Alps, I am sure you did not have to share warmth with your companions."

"It was easier to keep warm ten thousand feet up in the Alps than in this frosty hovel scarcely one thousand feet up, I assure you. We had tents, hot water bottles, extra clothing, blanket beds, campfires, and plenty of hot food. A tent gets very warm with two or three occupants, even in frigid temperatures. You and I have no tent and no way to keep warm. That roof is partly patched, but tonight this place will be cold as the very devil."

"Then you had better find a way to keep yourself warm."

"I am trying," he drawled. He looked hard at her. "I like a challenge, Miss MacConn, but one night in this little freezing box could be more risky than a night on the Matterhorn."

She sent him a sour glance. "We will manage."

"Survival needs resourcefulness as well as courage and determination, Miss MacConn. What we must do to stay alive here is obvious. How we reconcile that with society is the problem."

"Stay . . . alive?" She stared at him.

"If the temperature continues to drop, and if we fall asleep unprotected, we could freeze to death. I thought you knew."

"I — I did not think it was that dangerous."

"Likely we will be fine. But there is an element of uncertainty. Though," he said, patting the plaid, "I suppose being proper counts more with some women than common sense."

"I am not so proper as you think. Oh! That did not come out right," she said hastily. "I mean, of course I have common sense."

Evan smothered a smile. "I would think you no less the lady if we were to rest beside each other, keeping each other warm."

She regarded him warily. Evan Mackenzie was right. They would need to share physical proximity and warmth. His confidence and integrity reassured her, and he seemed a gentleman who would not take advantage of their unique situation. But she should not put herself in a compromising position.

"We will take turns," she decided. "I will stay by the fire and tend it while you take the blanket. Then we will change places."

He sighed. "For a quiet lass, you have a formidable nature." He turned and went to the blanket, lowering himself to the floor.

Sitting down beside the fire, she took the poker to stir the crumbling peat bricks, which were smoking more than she liked to see. The brose was thickening, too, as it simmered in the kettle. She would need more snow and ice to thin it so that it would not cook down to an inedible paste. She should melt some ice for drinking water, too, or later collect some from the fast burn outside the shieling hut.

Mackenzie stretched out in the blanket and soon fell asleep, for she heard the steady rhythm of his breathing. Catriona knew that he was bruised and aching and would need sleep, but she resolved to rouse him later to be certain that his head injury had not gotten the best of him.

Shivering, amazed at such a sharp chill and icy storm for early November, she tended the fire. When Mackenzie began to snore lightly, she stood and soon slipped through the door. Using the wooden bowl she had found in the hut, she packed it full of snow, then brought it back inside to add it to the thick, simmering brose in the kettle. She sipped some of the hot brew to ease the ache in her stomach.

Then she lay down in the darkness beside the fire. The earthen floor felt like a freezing slab beneath her, and she curled, tucking her skirt and petticoats around her legs. The weak little fire did not radiate much warmth.

But Evan Mackenzie lay an arm's length away, and suddenly she very much wanted to slip inside the blanket with him just to feel toasty again. Instead, she lay there shivering.

Waking in the night, Evan saw that the fire had diminished to a few bright, glowing threads of heat in the stacked fuel. As he sat up, he noticed that the air had turned astonishingly cold. The girl curled by the low fire, apparently asleep.

Easing himself out of the blanket, wincing at stiff muscles, he went outside to attend to necessities and was shocked to find a sheeting of ice nearly everywhere he looked. Sleet still pelted the ground and the little house. Back inside, he shut the door and made his way in the darkness back to the fireside.

Time for him to take a turn on the floor and let her have the warmer plaid. He crouched down beside the girl and saw that she trembled with cold even in sleep, her arms crossed tightly, her long legs tucked under her skirts.

He touched her shoulder. "Miss MacConn."

She started. "Aye," she whispered, her voice hoarse, as if she were coming down with a cold in the head. If nothing else, that forlorn little voice decided him.

"Miss MacConn, are you familiar with the old custom of bundling?"

She peered up at him. "Aye, it is still practiced here."

"Then I'm sure you've had opportunity to bundle with your own young man."

She sat up. "Young man? No one has ever courted me."

He blinked. "I find that hard to believe."

She shrugged. "I am the plain girl."

"The what? You're not plain at all."

She laughed, a soft, delightful sound, unexpected. In the firelight, he saw a dimple flash in her cheek. "No, Mr. Mackenzie. It is another custom in some parts of the Highlands. I am the youngest of my siblings, and so I am called the Plain Girl. The one who stays at home as her parents age and runs their household. She never marries."

"Ah," he said. "You agreed to that?"

"Not really. It was always assumed that would be my place in the family. My mother passed away years ago, my older sisters married and moved away from the glen, and one of my brothers has left Scotland to seek his fortune. I remained at Glenachan to care for my father and my brother Finlay." She looked at him, and he saw a little spark of defiance. He wondered how completely she had accepted that fate. "So I have never been courted, and I have never bundled with a suitor. Besides, there are not many young men left to court anyone in the glen now."

He nodded. "Because of the clearings?"

"Aye, because of the greedy Earl of Kildonan."

He let out a long breath. Once again it was hardly the time to admit his identity. "I see. So Plain Girls never wed?"

She fed a few chunks of peat to the fire. He saw it smoke and not quite catch. "Sometimes they will, after their parents are gone. Usually by then it's too late. They are old spinsters, set in their ways and past the age of childbearing."

"I think you will have suitors no matter how long they have to wait for you."

She glanced at him. "Thank you, but there's no doubt I'm quite plain. I'm . . . well, I am called Catriona Mhór."

He had retained some Gaelic from boyhood, and the word was simple enough. "Big Catriona?"

She nodded. "I'm taller than my father and my sisters and brothers but for one, Finlay. Strong as an ox, my father says of me, and my aunt says I am built for working."

Evan did not like the aunt or the father much, he decided. He watched the faint glow of the hearth turn her hair the color of new flame. "You are tall, but surely not big. My sister is nearly as tall as you are, and no one calls her big. Nor are you plain. You should be called . . . Catriona Bhàn," he murmured, drawing out the whispery "v" sound of the Gaelic word. "Fair Catriona. I know a little Gaelic."

"Oh!" She looked away. "That's . . . very kind." She sounded as if she had never had a compliment before.

"And I would be honored to bundle with you. After all, Miss MacConn, you are freezing, and so am I. Shall we — ?" He pointed to the blanket.

She regarded him warily, then looked with longing at the abandoned blanket. "Very well, Mr. Mackenzie."

He went toward the blanket, and she followed. They sat side by side, and within moments, she deftly refolded the blanket around them and lay back, as he did. The material wrapped over him and under her, with its end tucked between them.

"Interesting." He folded his arms over the cloth.

"Keep your arms inside," she said in the darkness.

"Oh." He slid his arms under the material. "I promise to behave myself, Miss MacConn. But you had better, also."

"I will." He heard the humor in her voice.

"Are you comfortable?"

"Quite." He heard the chatter of her teeth. "Well, almost." He saw a puff of frosted air as she spoke.

Lying in silence, he felt himself arouse and tighten. He had not slept beside a woman for a long while, and his body reacted to her nearness. As warmth collected in the space between them, he felt a distinct throbbing of flesh, a surge in the blood that signaled gathering desire. Although the feeling grew more insistent with the passing of each silent moment, he certainly did not intend to act upon the sudden compelling urge to take her into his arms.

She lay still, and soon he realized that she slept. Sensing the trust implicit in that letting go, he smiled to himself, and tried to follow suit. But his thoughts kept returning to her, to her lush shape and quiet, sultry voice, to her gentle touch and her irresistible nearness.

He tried to assuage himself with the knowledge that after a few hours in the cold little hut and their chaste little nest, they would awaken to morning sunshine and melting ice and snow. Then they would make their way to the glen, and home.

Catriona MacConn had a home and a hearth and a family who waited for her. Evan lacked that in Glen Shee. True, Kildonan Castle was his now, and it had been the home he loved most in his life. But after a decade away, his return felt awkward. He felt unwelcome, unwanted here. Although he had dreamed of belonging in Glen Shee and Kildonan again, the truth was that he did not.

He sighed, yearning for the comfort of a home, a place where love, and family, and smiles waited just for him. But that dream felt as elusive, in that moment, as simple physical warmth.

Rising carefully from the bundled blanket in the middle of the night, Catriona tiptoed to the door and cracked it open slightly. She peered out at a world gone white. Snow flew sideways with the force of the wind, and sleet pelted the walls of the house. Chilled by the icy wind in her face, she rubbed her mittened hands over her arms.

Poor weather or none, she had certain needs, and she and Mr. Mackenzie would need more drinking water as well. Besides, she had awoken feeling thirsty. Fetching the wooden bowl quietly, she then stepped outside, into a bitter blast of wind. She hurried to the far end of the building, seeking the shelter of an abandoned byre that sagged behind the shieling hut. After quickly tending to her needs, shivering all the while, she straightened her clothing, then headed for the burn at the base of a little hill nearby.

Sleet fell fast and needle sharp, and the

wind shoved at her. Bowing her head, she half slid down the incline, ice-crusted grass slippery beneath her feet. She fell to her knees, dipped the bowl into the stream, wetting her mittens inadvertently. Clambering back up the hill toward the shieling hut, she stumbled, then righted herself, then slid again.

Her feet went out from under her, and she slid over the frosted grass and splashed into the burn, its banks edged with icy-coated grasses. The shocking sensations of wet and cold penetrated her layered clothing, and she gasped, floundering.

Sunk inches deep in a trench of fast-flowing, icy water, she fell to her hands and knees in the water. Crying out, she scrambled to her feet, grabbing her saturated skirts, and half ran, half fell up the incline to hurtle toward the house.

Bursting inside, she saw Evan Mackenzie sit up in the darkness, then get to his feet. Catriona ran to the hearth and fell to her knees beside its heat. Tearing off her wet mittens with her teeth, she fumbled at the lacings of her leather brogans with trembling fingers.

Mackenzie came toward her. "What happened?"

"I fell in the burn," she said frantically. "I tried to get a bowl full of drinking water for us — ach," she exclaimed in dismay, as she finally drew off her loosened shoe and saw how wet the leather was and how saturated her woolen stocking.

Her fingers were shaking, red with cold, and the chill was seeping into her limbs like knives. Her skirt and petticoats were wet through to her chemise and knickers. Thin slivers of ice had formed on the hem of her skirt, some of it melting near the fire.

"Here, let me get the other shoe off," Mackenzie said as he knelt beside her. He took hold of her foot and shoved the wet hem of her skirt out of the way. Undoing the lacing quickly, he pulled the shoe off, turning the pair upside down by the fire.

"Your stockings," he commanded. "Take them off."

She did not protest, but reached under her wet skirt as modestly as she could to unfasten the ribbon garters that held the stockings on her upper thighs. She rolled each knitted length down her legs and stripped them off. Mackenzie snatched them and spread them beside the hearth. Catriona folded her bare legs and feet under her skirt, seeking warmth. But she only shivered more, for her skirts and petticoats were freezing wet.

"*Ach Dhia*," she said, teeth chattering. "I am s-so cold."

Mackenzie turned and whipped the blanket off the floor.

"No — we cannot risk getting our only blanket wet."

"Then take my jacket," he growled, tugging it off and draping it over her shoulders. He took her hands in his and rubbed them between his palms. His touch felt divinely warm, and she gasped at the sheer relief of the sensation. "I'll rub some warmth into your feet," he said, bending.

"I — I can wait until the stockings are dry."

"Don't be a fool. That could take all night. We've got to warm you quickly, or you'll be ill."

"I'm s-s-strong." Her teeth chattered. "I never take ill."

"You will take ill tomorrow unless we do something now. You'll have frostbitten toes, if nothing else." He slid his hand under the dripping hem of her skirts, and his fingers found her foot with a delicious shock of warmth. Reluctantly she shifted to allow him to take her bare foot in his hands.

As his firm caresses brought warmth and blood flow back into her toes, she moaned a little. "It stings a bit," she admitted.

He rubbed more gently, and his fingers slid over her ankles and up under the wet hems of her cotton knickers, warming her lower legs. The feeling was intimate, dangerous, and delicious. She gasped as the heat of his touch spread through her limbs.

Teeth still chattering, she sat quietly, knowing she should never let a man touch her so boldly. But she needed warmth, and she had given him permission to help her.

She wanted this, she realized, and felt as if some hidden wellspring within her had been tapped. Warmth and desire began to flow through her in a way she had never known.

Suddenly she wanted to feel his hands all over her body. She had wondered what his embrace would feel like, and she had always wondered what a man's loving caresses and soulful kisses would feel like — she had known only inept fumblings in a dark loft with a young man who had been a friend of her brother. Those brief and immature fondlings had hinted at deep and magnificent secrets in her body, as yet untapped and unknown.

Watching the glossy dark crown of Evan Mackenzie's hair, she felt an urge to caress that silkiness and to touch him as well, and to let him touch her anywhere. *Anywhere,* she thought, heart beating faster. She closed her eyes and sighed, imagining his arms around her, his rough cheek brushing hers, his lips on hers, so gentle, so loving, so safe.

Shocked by her wayward thoughts, she stiffened under his massaging fingers and pulled away. "Thank you," she said, teeth still chattering. "That's enough, I'm sure." But it was not.

He glanced up. "You'll have to take off

those skirts. The hems are soaked."

"They'll dry if I sit by the fire."

"Those wee embers will not dry anything." He took her by the shoulders to look at her earnestly. "Listen to me. If you stay in those garments all night, you'll take a severe chill."

"I'll be fine," she insisted. But his hands on her shoulders were strong, and she saw a new fierceness in his features.

"Get those wet things off, or I will do it for you."

Chapter Five

"No — I —" Catriona pulled away from him as if alarmed.

"I am not threatening you, if that is what you think," Evan said, still holding her by the shoulders. "Modesty is admirable, but right now it could jeopardize your health, even your life."

"My life?" She stared up at him, shuddering with cold. Her cheeks were too pale, her lips a faint blue. Her teeth literally rattled together. He wanted, suddenly and wildly, to take her into his arms and kiss warmth into her. Sweet as that would be, it would not solve the immediate dilemma.

"Aye, your breath could slow, your body temperature could drop. Your body would be unable to warm itself. If you fall asleep like that, you might never wake up. It feels almost warm, that sort of deep chill, and can lull you into being almost comfortable. You fall asleep, and if that happens, to be frank, you could die." Grasping her shoulders, he tried to convey his passionate concern.

"You sound as if you know what that's like."

"I do. Now get those things off." He knew far too well.

"Were you . . . exposed to cold conditions

while c-c-climbing in the Alps?" she asked, shivering.

He shook his head and bent to take her feet again to cup and warm them. "We kept warm and dry in the Alps, as I told you. No, it was underwater that I learned the dangers of real cold." He glanced at her. "I'm a master undersea diver. We risk severe chills every time we go down."

"D-diving! How inter-interesting," she said, shivering almost violently. "I've seen p-pictures in books. Did y-you have trouble there with the cold, Mr. Mac-mac-kenzie?"

He frowned and reached up to tug his jacket more securely around her shoulders, rubbing her arms. Hesitating, he decided to share a little of the truth. "Aye, but not under the sea. A bridge collapsed on a river in Fife. I was there."

She gasped. "Did you fall into the water?"

He shook his head and rubbed her hands gently. Despite the pleasant distraction of her soft skin and slender, lovely fingers, his thoughts were elsewhere. "I dove into the water with another fellow. We did what we could to help and rescued those who had fallen, but three men died that day. It was not the fall or the debris that killed them, but the cold water. They were in it too long before we got to them."

"Oh, how awful," she murmured. "D-did you know them?"

He nodded. They had been friends and members of his work crew. The bridge had been his own design, his own project. He looked away. "I worked with them. I . . . I could not save them. One of them died in my arms."

In the two years since the incident, he had said little about that day to anyone. Certainly not to anyone he had met only a few hours earlier. He felt somewhat amazed at himself now for doing so.

"Oh, Evan," the girl whispered. He felt soothed, hearing his name so soft upon her lips. "How did you come to be there when the bridge collapsed?"

"I am a bridge engineer. It was my project. My pride and joy," he said bitterly. "It fell while still under construction. We could not save . . . everyone." He spoke unemotionally and sat back, hunkered on his heels. His hands draped, empty, over his knees. He could not look at her.

Catriona touched his arm. "I am so sorry," she whispered. "Was it long ago?"

"Just over two years ago," he answered.

"Tragedies take away parts of our souls, I think," she said.

He glanced at her quickly. He had never thought of it in those terms, but he knew she was right.

And he knew that she understood. From what she had told him, she had lost a brother to a tragic incident, and her father had been deeply changed. She had seen the people leave the glen, too, at his own father's orders. Catriona knew about the deep hurt of the soul, as he did.

Her words were like a soft light upon his heart. Suddenly he understood something more about himself, why he had wandered, wooden and subdued, through life afterward, abandoning bridge projects for dock works, lighthouses, canals. Burying himself in geometrically beautiful designs and mathematical formulas, he had shut himself off from the love and friendship that others tried to offer him.

"It can take a long time to recover from such a blow. Some n-never d-do," she added. She was still shivering too much, her body struggling to raise its own temperature.

He narrowed his eyes, struck by the depth of her sympathy and understanding. In the space of minutes, she understood him as no one else had in two years. She had summed up his hurt and his sense of being lost, and offered him a balm.

His friends and relatives wanted him to get on with his life by now. His mother wanted him to find a pleasant society girl and marry, wanted him to build a fine new bridge to replace the other one both literally and in his mind. Somehow she was convinced that both actions would cure his heartache, his guilt, his self-recrimination.

Catriona MacConn did not know him at all, yet she knew how he felt. Part of him was indeed still missing. He needed ample time to heal, a chance to find that lost bit again, if he ever could. The tragedy had destroyed part of him, heart and soul. He had recovered as much as he could by keeping himself tightly guarded and speaking very little about the experience.

But he could not shake the feelings off, and now suddenly he knew why. A part of his soul had torn away, spiraled out, left him on that day. He could not get it back.

He frowned thoughtfully, then nodded. "Thank you, Miss MacConn." She could not know why he thanked her. "So you see, I do know what severe cold can do." He rose to his feet. "And I will not let you suffer that tonight. Can you stand?" He held out his hand to her.

Nodding, she let him assist her to her feet, her hand curved in the hollow of his.

"Now take off your petticoats and your skirt," he said. Seeing her hesitate, he shrugged out of his jacket and draped it around her shoulders. "Put that on, and we'll get you under the blanket. Go on," he urged, and turned away to allow her privacy.

Shivers ravaged her. She had never felt so frozen, as if her body had turned to marble.

She had to get out of her cold, wet clothes *now*.

When Mackenzie turned away, she removed his jacket, then pulled at the loops that buttoned her own, for that had to come off before the dress. Her fingers trembled violently. Her body shook, muscles tensing, jaw clenched, teeth knocking. She wondered if she would ever feel warm again. Her fingers were so awkward that she could not undo the buttons, and she made a sound of frustration.

"Are you finished?" he inquired, back turned.

"I'm — having difficulty," she admitted.

He turned and came toward her. Without asking permission — he was the sort of man who preferred action to discussion, she realized — he opened the button loops at the waist of her jacket and moved up, his fingers quick and sure.

Silently he drew her jacket open, then worked the long row of tiny buttons that ran up the bodice of her dress from waist to high neck. Catriona's heart slammed; her breath quickened.

As his fingers brushed over the valley between her breasts, she silently moved his hands away. She opened the rest of the bodice buttons. Beneath the dress, she wore a chemise but no stays. The upper body of her chemise was dry, but the lower hems, and her petticoats and knickers, were as wet as her outer skirt.

Mackenzie glanced toward the cleavage of her breasts, then turned away quickly. Catriona wriggled free of her bodice and sleeves and pushed the dress over her hips until it pooled at her feet. She snatched up his tweed jacket and slipped her arms inside the satiny inner lining of the sleeves. Though too large for her, it felt good.

"The rest of it," he said, glancing over his shoulder.

"I cannot —"

"Miss MacConn, take off whatever is wet. Please," he added, his voice gruff. "For your own health. Those things must dry."

She knew he was concerned about the cold, but suddenly she wished that he could be passionately concerned about her, only her. Sighing, she wriggled out of her soggy petticoats and dropped them, standing then in damp chemise and knickers.

Then her mind conjured something wild, something exciting. She imagined taking off the rest of what she wore, imagined his gaze upon her, and felt her body rouse and tingle. Somehow she knew how his lips would taste, knew that his embrace would be powerful and tender, knew he would pour his passionate, quiet fire into her like the heat she craved.

He had said she was not plain and had

called her Fair Catriona. No one had ever complimented her like that. His interest, however slight, had a magical, irresistible allure.

Suddenly she wanted this night, already dangerous, to turn wild and intimate. She was alone with a kind and beautiful man, and these hours together could become a wild miracle, a bright, hot glow that would change her plain existence forever. She wanted something secret and unforgettable with him.

Her heart slammed with her daring thoughts, and her fingers trembled. Drawing a deep breath, wondering if she had gone lunatic from the cold, she undid the tape of her knickers and shrugged the garment off. The creamy cotton puddled at her feet, wet and clammy cold, and she was glad to be out of it. She shivered, but it was with the boldness of her action.

She kept her chemise on, for the shorter hem was only damp, and she could not bring herself to remove every stitch. Pulling Evan's jacket close, she was glad that its length hid her torso and the upper part of her legs. She drew a breath, for the scratchy wool smelled of spice, fresh air, and, somehow, of him.

Mackenzie turned, and his gaze took her in slowly, head to foot and back again, his hazel-green eyes intent. Facing him, she knew her breasts were scarcely hidden by the thin cotton shift under his jacket. She felt her nipples tighten as his glance skimmed her, and she felt her face heat in a blush.

One thing to imagine him loving her, she thought, suddenly mortified, quite another to stand before him nearly unclothed, as if offering herself to him. What was she inviting?

But she knew what she wanted and felt compelled to plunge ahead into the unknown. She scarcely understood the powerful urge she felt. Her heart pounded as she met his gaze.

Then she made herself look away and stooped to gather her dropped garments. The chemise and jacket did not adequately cover her long thighs and left her knees bare. "I — I need to dry my things," she mumbled.

Evan snatched her plaid from the floor with a savage motion, and tossed it over her. She clutched the wool around her and covered her limbs as she spread her wet things out to dry.

Mackenzie took up his silver flask, opening it to hand it to her. "There is a little left in here," he said brusquely. "Drink it. Then lie down."

She nodded, feeling self-conscious and embarrassed. Sitting, she tucked her legs beneath the plaid and took a sip from the flask. The burning liquid poured down her throat, and she coughed, then felt the wonderful fire of it spread. Her body tingled, her heart thudded. She could hardly look at him now.

Yet her dreams and impulses still drove her. She was lonely, had been for a long time, watching other girls marry and have children while she had tried to accept her dull future of caring for her father and brother. Not only was she curious about physical love, but she realized that she was deeply attracted to Evan Mackenzie. And she was certain that there would never again be another night like this in her life.

He had tapped her loneliness with his kindness, his concern, his patience. Touching him, tending to him, she felt her natural curiosity and imagination stir. He had roused thoughts and glimmers of passion in her with his passing touch, with heartbreakingly beautiful smiles that sparkled deep in his eyes, so that she knew he was thinking of her, looking at her.

But that was all in her imagination, she told herself, conjured by that newborn wildness in her. He was grateful for her help, and that was all. He was a handsome, educated gentleman, and she was an ordinary Highland girl, and when the weather cleared tomorrow, she might never see him again.

But once — just once, those wilder urges insisted. Ignoring that, she held out the flask to him. "Thank you."

He shook his head. "Again. You'll need more to warm you."

In silence, she took another sip, then another when he motioned for her to do so. The swallowed fire expanded, wrapping her in comfort. She gave him the silver flask. "No more," she said. "I have not eaten much. It will make me ill."

He took the flask and drank from it, his lips covering where hers had been. She watched the slide of his powerful throat.

"Mr. Grant says a person with a head injury should not take much whisky," she ventured.

"Mr. Grant has never been stranded in a shieling hut on a cold night, alone with a bonny lass," he said in a dry tone. "Now lie down and go to sleep."

She stretched out inside the plaid, the wool faintly prickly against her bare legs, and pulled it up to her chin.

Evan Mackenzie sat beside the fire, propping up his knee to lean his arm there. He took up the poker and jabbed at the blackened peat bricks. The fire smoked. For all the poking and shifting he did, the crumbling peat would not glow any brighter.

"We need to add more fuel," he said. "But the rest of the peat in the corner is damp."

"My skirt," she said quickly.

"We're not that desperate yet," he drawled. "You have lovely legs, Miss MacConn, but you will need that skirt when we leave here." He cocked a brow at her.

She shook her head. "In the pocket of my

skirt there are some papers. We can burn those."

He reached for her skirt, groped, found the folded pages. "Are these letters?"

"Notes," she said. "I've written down some Gaelic songs."

"Aye?" He glanced at the pages. "Oh, I see. Musical notations." He looked at her as if puzzled.

"That is why I was out hillwalking today. I am collecting the old Gaelic songs from some of the Highlanders in this glen," she explained. "I've been learning them for years and writing down all the songs I learn."

"Fascinating," he said, his slight frown thoughtful. "So you can transcribe musical notation and speak not only Gaelic and English, but French, Italian, and German, as well."

"And a little Greek," she said.

"Not the typical Highland mountain lass, are you?"

"I'm a minister's daughter," she said. "What did you expect, that I spend my time walking the hills in bare feet and ragged skirts, babbling in Old Irish and following a flock of sheep? Education is an important concern in the Highlands, as elsewhere in Scotland. I had tutors, and I spent two years studying in Edinburgh. I'm as well educated as you are. Well, but for engineering principles."

"I cannot write in musical scale," he said.

"Nor can I manage Italian. So we are even."

She smiled a little. "Burn those pages, Mr. Mackenzie. They will give us some light and heat, at least for a while."

"I cannot burn these. There are several songs here, with the melody carefully transcribed, and the verses translated in Gaelic and English. This took a great deal of work."

"There are only ten songs there, and I can redo them. I remember most of them, and Morag MacLeod, my friend, will help me with the rest. Burn the pages, Mr. Mackenzie. We have no choice."

Relenting, he tossed the pages on the fire one by one. Light and heat bloomed. Catriona watched the papers crumble and spark, and closed her eyes, trying not to regret the lost songs, glad for the heat. She could re-create those pages, though it would take some time.

She watched Evan settle on his side by the hearth. "Mr. Mackenzie, you will be cold without your jacket," she said.

"You need it," he said. "Your wee songs are keeping me warm." He smiled, and she laughed. Then he leaned his head on his bent arm. "Good night, Miss MacConn."

"Good night," she murmured, feeling a sudden disappointment to lie alone in the dark and the cold. She drew her knees up, trembling with the chill despite the jacket and plaid. Earlier, straight, strong whisky had created a hot core in her belly, but as that sensation faded, she felt again the knife edge of the freezing winds that sliced through every crevice in the hut.

Lowering the plaid, she peered at Mackenzie. The papers had burned down quickly, and the brighter light was diminishing. In the glow of the crackling peats, she saw that he was still awake. And she felt instantly guilty, for he lay without blanket or jacket, while she had both.

"Mr. Mackenzie," she said. "Are you very cold there?" She knew he was — that question hardly needed forming.

"Well, I am beginning to wonder what else we can burn," he drawled. "There might be some dry roof beams."

"I am still cold, too." Trembling, she drew a breath. "Would you mind . . . if we bundled again?"

"Not at all." Hearing the note of relief in his voice, she was glad she had offered. As he rose and came toward her, she felt a lightning stab of anticipation and could have counted every thudding beat of her heart.

Crouching, he touched her cheek. "You do feel cold."

"I cannot . . . seem to get warm. Oh," she exclaimed, as her body convulsed in new shivers. Her feet and toes felt like ice, but there was an undeniable tremor of physical excitement, too. "The chill in here seems worse since the fire died down."

"It does," he agreed. He sat, removed his boots, and then opened the blanket to settle in beside her. They lay face-to-face, and he folded an arm under his head, then slipped his outside arm over her. Spreading his hand open, he rubbed her back in circles. She felt his stockinged feet touch hers, lending her bare feet a little protection.

Closing her eyes, she rested her cheek on his shoulder, exhausted from continually fighting the cold. She shuddered as her body tried to create heat, and she pressed closer to him.

"Come here," he said, wrapping both arms more securely around her. "The air is miserably cold, and this plaid is thin for two to share. Miss MacConn, the best source of heat we have is each other."

She nodded silently, still shivering while he rubbed her back vigorously for a few moments. Circling an arm around his waist, she stroked his shoulders and back to bring him some greater warmth as well. Her fingers grazed over the satin backing of his vest, and she felt, under the layered cloth of shirt and vest, the remarkable width of his shoulders and the smooth, hard contour of the muscles along his spine.

When his massaging palm skimmed over her lower back and down to the upper curve of her behind, she drew a quick breath. A feeling stirred in the core of her body, a melting, tingling sensation. She sighed out, wanting more, but he drew his hand slowly upward again to shape and press her shoulder.

Heat gathered between them, and she felt his hand on her head, sweeping over her hair, then down her back. Somehow it did not matter that she was in a stranger's arms, nearly unclothed. She felt as if she had always known him. His physical heat and his caring wrapped around her like another blanket.

As her body began to throb under his gentle caress, she knew that desire had begun to heat her from within — and she wondered if he felt that, too. His touch felt like fire suddenly, burned through the cloth. She began to breathe with him, and every part of her being craved more of his touch.

"Are you still cold?" His voice, low and close, made her shiver, made her close her eyes.

"Aye, a little." Her heart thundered, and as she lay in his arms, she felt passion flutter and stir. She shuddered, but not from the chill any longer. "And you?"

"A little." His breath brushed her cheek, and as she moved her head, his lips touched the corner of her mouth. Her heart pounded, and a rush of desire poured through secret places. She tilted her head in the darkness, and her nose nudged against his.

Sighing, she tipped her head back and let her mouth meet his. So easy, that first touch, so cool and tender. This did not feel wrong, she thought — it felt innocent. Dear God, it felt like she had found heaven. She pulled in a soft breath, opening her lips for more.

His arms tightened around her, and his mouth moved over hers, and suddenly he was kissing her harder, deeper, with such strength and passion that she felt it strike down through her feet. She thought she might melt from the pure bliss of it, feeling as helpless as butter over flame.

Chapter Six

She had never been kissed like that, never. She had not known that it could feel like a fall from a great height or like a pouring of liquid sunshine, hot and splendid. Nor had she realized how desire could spread heat from within.

He claimed that she had saved his life, but she knew without doubt that he was saving hers. His caring, tender touch and his deep kisses were rescuing her from the oblivion of loneliness to which she had long been consigned.

Just once, she would follow will and desire and discover what love felt like. Just once, and then he would be gone from her life. For now, she wanted to let him fill her with more of his fire. In seeking bodily warmth, she had unleashed a feverish power and deep need within her.

I need you, she wanted to say. As he kissed her again, she shuddered with pleasure. *And I've needed this so much.*

Whatever the price would be, she would gladly pay it. Will and desire drove her onward, compelled her.

Evan drew back a little, touched her hair

with his hand, a sweet caress. "Warmer now?" he whispered.

"Some," she breathed, nudging toward him for another kiss.

"Your toes still feel cold," he whispered, as his feet caressed hers. She slid her fingers over his jaw, through the thick gloss of his hair. "So do your hands. Here."

He opened the buttons of his vest and his shirt, baring his chest. Slipping his hands under the jacket and around her waist, he pulled her close, nearly skin to skin, with only her thin chemise between them. Her belly fluttered, her breasts tingled. A bliss of searing warmth radiated from him.

Angling her face to his, she waited, and a moment later he kissed her again, tender and exquisite, so that she opened her mouth to his and sighed. To feel so safe, so comforted, so loved, even if only for a brief time in her life, was the most wonderful feeling she had ever known.

His hand at her waist smoothed over her lower back and her hip, then slid along her outer thigh. Moving upward again, his fingers grazed along her rib cage, shaping her there, his thumb grazing the side of her breast. She closed her eyes, allowing him to explore her curves and hollows, touch her however he pleased, for his caresses stoked a deep fire within her.

As his fingers moved again, she sucked in

her breath, for he contoured his palm over her breast, and his fingertips roused her tightening nipple. She gasped then, for he lowered his head and his mouth traced over her collarbones and lower still, until his breath heated her breasts through the cloth of her chemise.

Arching toward him, she felt his hand nudge aside the cloth of her chemise. Quick and sure, his hand settled over her bare breast, his touch delicate at first, then firmer, until she moaned out, fearing she might dissolve from the sheer pleasure of it.

She slid her own fingers over his bared chest, kneading warm skin dusted with springy hair, her palm following the planes of hard muscle. Pressing herself against his hips, she felt him harden against her, and she moved a little, trying to ease the growing, demanding ache deep inside of her. He shifted his head and took her mouth again, his kiss deep and strong, his fingers kneading her breasts, her nipples, so that a sort of lightning struck through her.

Desire came fully alive within her then, beating its wings against the cage of her body, struggling to burst free. Writhing, crying out softly, she silently asked for more.

He moved his hand downward, over the bunched chemise, until he found her thigh and tucked under the damp hem of the cloth. She waited breathlessly, her belly fluttering. As his fingers eased over the apex of her thighs, then gently slipped into the hidden cleft, she gasped again.

At first his touch astonished her, and then her body flooded with luscious, white-hot fire. With soft cries, she rode his touch, rocked with it, felt as if she turned molten. Suddenly she felt herself climbing, then reaching a blissful peak that she had not even known was there, like a burst of light in darkness.

Mind and reason no longer held sway as a magnificent inferno built in her and the craving grew with it, until she could not bear it. Pleading with her body, with her hands and her mouth, she wanted to feel him deep inside of her, knowing somehow that only that would ease the hunger he had roused in her.

Sliding over his bared chest and flat stomach, tugging at his clothing, at draw-strings and hooks in the darkness, she touched him boldly, her heart pounding. She had not known what to expect, but he felt wonderful to her, like velvet over warm steel, powerful and beautiful. Feeling an urgent desire, she arched against him, whimpered, pleaded for what her body understood better than she did herself.

Slipping her fingers along the length of him, she felt him surge in her hand, sensed his gasp as his lips touched hers. And his fingers touched her, too, tracing exquisitely over her breasts, sliding downward over her belly, raising a deep flutter of excitement there. Then he began again to caress that secret part of her, and under the astonishing tenderness of his fingertips, she felt once more that glorious sensation spiral through her.

Yet it was not enough, for the craving grew insistent, more powerful than anything she had ever known. Responding to instinct, she opened her legs, writhed against him. He groaned low and moved, his grip fervent on her waist. Now she suddenly, overwhelmingly, knew what she wanted, and she could not wait, could not.

Arching toward him, shifting, she felt him slip into her, felt him harden and push, gently at first, until she felt a small burst of pain and gasped. By the time she drew a new breath, the subtle shock of his entry eased into a wave of relief. Moaning with the deep, indescribable pleasure of it, she heard him groan low, and she pushed down over him, taking him into her fully. She felt him throb inside of her, part of her now, and she cried out as he thrust, hard and deep, to satisfy the deepest need, body and soul, that she had ever known.

Rocking with his rhythm, she felt the drumbeat of her own heart as her body merged with his. Wrapping her arms around him, she felt him shudder in her arms, breathe out, grow still.

Then he swore something under his breath and pulled away quickly, separating his body from hers. Holding her tightly for a moment, he breathed hard and fast. Catriona felt the damp sheen of sweat on his back through shirt and vest and felt her own body dampened, as well. She felt exhilarated, relaxed, fearless. She felt deliciously warm and safe.

But he shook his head. "No," he whispered, half to himself. "Dear lass — God, I am sorry. That should never have happened." He rolled away from her, sat up, pushing the plaid away. Chill air invaded their nest, sweeping away the warmth, the passion.

She felt her heart sink in that moment. "Please — Evan, wait," she said, reaching for him. "I did not mind —"

"I minded," he snapped. "Now go to sleep. You're warm now. We're both warm — blast it, that's how all this started, and it went too far. I took it too far. Damn," he whispered, shaking his head. "How could I — Catriona, I thought I could be near you without that. But what happened was certainly not what you needed."

But it was, oh God, it was. She knew it as surely as she knew her own name. She would never have a moment like that again. She drew breath to tell him so, but he turned away abruptly and rose to his feet.

In the darkness, she watched him cross the hut and open the door to step outside into the bitter cold. The chill entered the room, flooding the emptiness where he had lain beside her.

Closing her eyes against sudden tears, she curled tightly in the lingering warmth inside the blanket. The thrill he had given her faded, replaced by a loneliness more intense than ever.

In his arms, she had felt beautiful, enchanting. In the wake of his rejection, she felt plainer than ever, big and clumsy and undesirable. She had always thought that love would not be hers, but Evan Mackenzie had given her a little hope. He was strong and beautiful and kind, and she deeply, keenly desired him. But he did not really want her. Tomorrow they would both return to their lives and forget each other.

Finally the door opened and he came back inside, returning to kneel beside her. Catriona pretended to be asleep, her back turned to him. After a while he lay down beside her again, and she did not stir. His breathing deepened and finally slowed, and she felt herself drifting to sleep.

She still felt cold, for the shared warmth under the plaid was nothing compared to the fervent heat they had created between them earlier.

Evan woke with Catriona tucked in his arm, her head on his shoulder. His breath frosted in the air as he exhaled, and he felt icy drafts leaking through the walls and roof. The hour must be near dawn, he thought, for gray light filled the little house.

Although he did not hear rain, he knew that the slopes leading down to the glen would still be dangerously slippery. He and Catriona should stay in the shieling hut a little longer.

With a strange clarity of thought, he knew that he wanted to stay here with her as long as he could. He wished they had the freedom to blissfully explore each other, as they had begun last night, when her passionate response had stirred him fiercely.

What the devil had he been thinking, to love her like that? The memory felt like a hot dream now, but it had been far too real. The girl was charming and gentle and had slipped past his usual defenses. And then he had lost his customary control.

Holding her close, he felt desire resurge. But disgracing her was no payment for saving his life.

Tightening his arm around her, he sighed with regret mingled with longing. She sagged against him, warm and trusting in sleep. They had both needed heat last night, and the succor of another soul in this lonely place. But what would follow next, once they left this hut?

He owed her an apology, and more, though

111

he was not yet sure what to do, what to say to her. He had acted neither rationally nor gentlemanly. The damage was done. Her innocence had been intimately breached, and he was at fault for that — despite the fact that she had been curious and willing.

He scarcely knew her, yet he desired her and felt bound to her. Long after he left the shieling, his heart would belong, a little, to her. No woman had ever had quite so intense an effect on him or so much natural power to drive him to madness. She had soothed him, suited him, understood him as no one ever had before, though he could not explain why.

Dipping his head, he kissed her brow. The magic still coursed between his body and hers — he could feel it like a magnet's pull. But the weather would soon clear, and the world waited for them, and all this would end.

He was exhausted, and she was asleep, and nothing needed solving quite yet. Holding her, he felt himself sliding back into dreams alongside her.

"Catriona!"

She stirred, hearing her name, thinking Evan had spoken, although the sound was oddly distant. She opened her eyes to bright morning sunlight seeping into the shadowed interior. She had slept far later than she had thought she might.

He lay beside her, his arm circling her. The warmth felt wonderful. "Evan," she whispered. "Did you call me?"

"What?" He blinked at her sleepily.

"Catriona!" The voice shouted again. "Where are you?"

Then she knew. "My father," she blurted, sitting up. "He's outside —"

"Catriona! Are you in there?"

She scrambled out of the plaid, but Evan pushed her down, pulling the wool over her. "Stay there," he murmured, getting to his feet. She reached toward him. "Stay down!" he said. "You're not dressed."

"Oh, no," she groaned, remembering that she was not. She clutched the plaid.

"Catriona!"

Then the door burst open, and pale light poured inside, silhouetting a giant of a man wearing a black suit and a bowler hat crushing a leonine mane of hair. He cast a formidable shadow as he stood gripping a long walking stick.

"Catriona," he thundered, peering into the dim interior. "Are you in here, girl?"

"Here, Papa." Heart slamming, she half sat and drew the plaid blanket to her chin. She glanced anxiously at Evan Mackenzie, who stood tall and calm beside her pallet.

"Thank the Lord! She's here!" Reverend Thomas MacConn shouted over his shoulder, waved, then crossed the threshold. He moved stiffly, using the walking stick like a cane. Four men came in after him, their large forms further blocking the light as they swept in fresh, chilly air. Catriona shivered.

"Girl, are you safe?" her father asked, striding forward. "The Lord be praised. We feared that something awful had happened again on these slopes —" He stopped, staring at Evan. "Sir," he growled. "And are you who I think you are?"

"Aye, no doubt." Evan inclined his head. "Greetings, Reverend MacConn."

"Papa, I'm fine," Catriona said hastily. "We were caught by the storm — oh, Finlay!" She greeted her older brother with relief as he came toward them. "And Mr. Grant," she greeted the third man, Kenneth Grant, the laird of an estate at the far end of the glen, who acted as the doctor in the glen. The fourth man she had never seen before. Good Lord, did her father have to bring the entire village in his search party? Soon the whole glen would know of her disgrace.

Under four gazes that registered various degrees of surprise and suspicion, she felt keen embarrassment. She sat on the floor in her chemise, her hair flowing loose. The plaid was obviously the only makeshift bed in the room, and it had clearly been shared. And the man beside her was dressed in shirtsleeves, unbuttoned vest, and trousers. Even worse, his shirt hem was untucked, his black hair mussed, and he had no boots on.

Surely the truth seemed as crystal clear as the cold morning air that poured into the shabby ruined interior. Kenneth Grant kicked the door shut behind him as if to punctuate a tone of disapproval, even anger.

As her father, brother, and the two others stared at Catriona and Evan, a few seconds felt like a slow agony.

Her father grew red in the face as he turned to Evan Mackenzie. "You, sir!" he said in English. "How is it you are here with my daughter, in a — shameful state!" It was not a question. Her father was not a man to ask, but to inform.

Evan regarded him calmly. "Reverend MacConn, I assure you there is an explanation."

"We were stranded in the storm, in the freezing cold," Catriona said. "Mr. Mackenzie was injured in a fall —"

"Injured?" Kenneth Grant asked. "I act as the physician in the glen, sir. Miss MacConn — are you unwell or hurt?"

"I'm fine," she said. "But Mr. Mackenzie —"

"It's nothing," Evan said.

"Mr. Mackenzie?" her father asked. "Is that what he told you his name was?"

She looked from him to Evan. "I do not understand."

"That is not just Mr. Mackenzie," her father said, glowering. Catriona looked at Evan in surprise. He glanced away.

"Father, they need the food and the plaidies we've brought with us." Finlay hefted a knapsack over his shoulder. "They have had a bad time of it, no doubt. First we should get them home and let Mr. Grant treat them. Later we can learn the details of their wee adventure."

Evan shoved a hand through his rumpled hair and glanced at Finlay. "Thank you, sir."

"I want the details now," her father growled.

"The important thing is that they're safe," Finlay said.

Grant nodded. "True. And if the gentleman is hurt —"

"They look hearty to me," Reverend MacConn said. He folded his arms and glared at Evan.

"Good grief, Kildonan, what happened to you?" The fourth man stepped forward. "Deuced good to see you, sir. Bad night, eh?"

"Bad enough, Fitz," Evan said quietly. "Good to see you. Miss MacConn, this is Mr. Arthur Fitzgibbon."

"I feared the worst when that storm blew in yesterday and you did not return," Fitzgibbon went on. "So I rode back through the glen and met these gentlemen, who were out searching for Miss MacConn. We had to wait until the weather cleared to come up here,

116

though. Bad night all around, with that ice, and no picnic coming up here this morning, either. What luck to find you both together, Kildonan."

Catriona felt her heart falter as realization suddenly dawned on her. She stared up at Evan. "Kildonan?" she whispered.

"Aye," he said, his gaze on hers steady and grim. "I am Lord Kildonan."

Chapter Seven

Catriona said nothing as the group carefully walked the long drover's track, which was still treacherous with ice. She avoided glancing at Evan Mackenzie — Lord Kildonan, she reminded herself bitterly — and concentrated on watching her father's progress. His old back injury made long, steep walks difficult for him now, but Thomas MacConn refused to accept her hand on his arm on the rougher parts of the terrain. His rejection of her help — and his silent but clear disapproval of her situation — hurt more than she wanted to admit.

Still silent upon reaching her home, she was swept away by her aunt, Judith Rennie, and their family friend Mrs. MacAuley, who ran the glen's only inn. Swept along on a tide of anxious cries, surrounded by the swishing black skirts of the two widows, Catriona let the women guide her upstairs to her bedroom, where a hot bath, fresh clothing, and a hot meal awaited her.

She felt Evan watching her as she walked away, but she did not glance back, although she heard him ask Arthur Fitzgibbon to ride back to Kildonan Castle to fetch Evan's sister, who Evan said should have arrived at the castle that day to meet him. So there was even more Catriona did not know — he had been at his castle for a few days, apparently, and she had not heard about it.

Leaving Evan standing in the hallway, Catriona felt drained of physical and emotional energy suddenly, as if his quiet strength had shored her up for the past twenty-four hours. Now it had been withdrawn. For her, Evan Mackenzie no longer existed as she had known him. And now that she was back in the tense and critical atmosphere of her father's manse, she felt herself pull inward protectively through silence and dull compliance.

All she wanted was to rest and to be left alone. She needed time to think about what she had done and what must come next. She felt hurt and weakened. Her father and her aunt were furious and shocked by the fact that she had spent a night alone with a man, but the greatest blow was Evan's deception, which felt like a betrayal. He was not the kind, loving stranger she had thought; nor was he a man she could dream of endlessly, later, when she felt lonely.

Instead, he was the son of the hated Earl of Kildonan and reputed to be no better himself, and she had allowed him — in fact had encouraged him wantonly — to use her.

They had shared risk, and warmth, and intimate passion, but he had not shared the truth with her. She did not know if she could forget, let alone forgive, that.

Nor could she bring herself to look back at Kildonan himself, though he stood in her hallway, watching her, his silence as grim as her own.

"Considering the exposure to severe cold and a fall into icy water, I'd like to be sure there's no lung ailment, Miss MacConn. Excuse me while I check the health of your heart and lungs." Mr. Grant leaned forward and thumped gently on her upper chest. Seating himself beside her on the horsehair sofa in the drawing room, he tapped his fingertips up and down her back in a pattern, angling his head close to listen.

Sitting straight backed and breathing slowly, Catriona was glad that Mrs. MacAuley had tied her stays loosely after she had bathed and changed into a fresh gown of gray-and-blue-striped silk. She waited in silence while Kenneth Grant completed his examination.

Her aunt waited in silence, too, standing by the closed doors of the drawing room while she chaperoned the doctor's examination. Hands folded primly, handsome face pulled in a harsh frown, Catriona's aunt Judith made her disapproval of the entire situation clear. The widow of a Perthshire laird, Judith

Rennie was a strong-minded woman with an iron will. She had quickly surmised that Catriona's experience with the Earl of Kildonan was not a dangerous adventure but a shocking escapade.

Although the misinterpretation offended her, Catriona was not surprised by her aunt's conclusion. Nor did she have the energy to correct Aunt Judith. Guilt, if nothing else, silenced her. She had been very foolish, indeed, just as her aunt thought. Sighing, she glanced at Kenneth Grant as he leaned back.

"All seems well. One moment." He picked up his stethoscope and placed it against her chest, listening through the layers of her clothing. "Aye, clear." He removed the stethoscope and laid it aside. "You're in excellent health, as always. Just tired, I think."

"Aye, tired," she agreed in English, the language normally used in her father's household but for the kitchen and the nursery when she had been a child. Her father conducted his church services in Gaelic for the benefit of his Highland parish, but at home he demanded English in dining room and drawing room.

Kenneth Grant glanced up. "Your niece had taken no harm from her ordeal, Mrs. Rennie, but she will need rest for a few days. I'd advise against long walks over the hills until you have your strength back, Miss MacConn. No going about with Morag

MacLeod," he cautioned.

"Catriona and Morag MacLeod have work to do — they collect the knitting assignments, as you well know," Judith Rennie said. "A worthy charitable act that must be done regularly."

"A few days will make no difference," Grant answered.

"She is in good health, and I understand Lord Kildonan is in good health, too. Not so much the emergency, was it, Catriona?" Judith looked smug.

"The situation seems to have been serious, Mrs. Rennie," Grant said solemnly. "Lord Kildonan has a knot on his head and is bruised from his fall down the mountainside. He is a lucky man and fortunate to have such a strong physique. He needs only some rest to be hale and hearty again. And he insists that Miss MacConn saved his life. You must be proud of your niece for her Good Samaritan deed, Mrs. Rennie."

"She is a minister's daughter, and exemplary behavior at all times is expected of her, though with Catriona exemplary is not a word that always applies," Judith replied with a sniff.

"We endured some terrible conditions, yet we are both well and unharmed," Catriona pointed out. "I should think that would be cause for giving thanks, Aunt, especially in this household."

"Of course we are thankful and glad no other tragedy occurred — I do not think your father could have borne it if it had," her aunt replied. "We are also quite distressed by the matter."

Catriona sighed. Grant glanced at her, his expression grim and humorless. She had never felt quite comfortable with Grant, who was overly serious and scowled much for a man of his age — scarcely a decade older than she was herself.

"If you're finished, Mr. Grant, the reverend would like to see Catriona in his study. My dear, come along." She opened the door and tipped her head. "The earl is already meeting with your father. They are waiting for us."

Catriona's heart pounded at the thought of seeing Evan, speaking to him. "Go ahead. I'll . . . be along in a moment."

Sniffing again, Judith Rennie left the drawing room, leaving the door partly open.

Grant took her hand. "Let me check your pulse once more, my dear Miss MacConn. You have suffered an extraordinary ordeal."

And her aunt was the better part of it just now, she wanted to say, but sat beside him in silence. Then, as he nodded and set her hand down, she smiled.

"Thank you, Mr. Grant, for coming out to Glenachan, and for your help in searching for me and for . . . Lord Kildonan."

"I was glad to be of some help," he said,

123

his brown eyes narrowing. He was a tall man with a square face and a thick shock of dark brown hair. As laird of Kilmallie, twelve miles away at the easternmost end of Glen Shee, he did not come often to Glenachan. Kenneth now ran his inherited estate, which he had expanded with sheep runs that had begun to make his fortune. Yet he still found time to act as the glen's only doctor, the nearest full physician being thirty miles away in Kyle of Lochalsh. "I'm always delighted to help you in particular, my dear Miss Catriona."

He sometimes referred to her by her first name, for they had known each other for years — since she had been a girl, in fact, though he had been only an occasional visitor to the manse then. He smiled, quick and flat, as if it pained him to do so. Grant lacked a sense of humor, she knew, and his somber, earnest nature was sometimes trying.

"Not everyone is delighted with me just now," she said.

He frowned. "Reverend MacConn is understandably upset, of course. He was very much afraid that you had met with an accident. I dosed him for nervous ailment last night, he was that worried. And he did ask me to speak with you, miss, to determine if you were . . . well, harmed in any less obvious way."

"Lord Kildonan behaved like a gentleman,

if that is what you imply," she said. That was true enough. She had not behaved like a lady, but she was not going to give details to anyone.

Grant stared hard at her. "Your father fears that you were . . . compromised. The blanket was obviously shared."

"We had to share it for warmth," she answered. "It was terribly cold. My father and my aunt may not understand that we were in danger of our lives in the shelter of that hut, but you, as a doctor, must assure them that we had reason to share the blanket. That does not mean I was compromised."

"So you did share it. Well, I'm sure this will all blow over, like last night's storm."

She nodded silently. If the details became known, the storm would become a tempest. "I must go to my father," she said. "Is that all, Mr. Grant?" She stood, and he did as well.

"One more moment of your time, Miss MacConn," he said. He smiled that curious, thin smile that held no humor or lightness, and went to the door, closing it securely.

"Shutting the door is not necessary — nor proper," she said, stretching out her hand to open it again. "I am in enough of a kettle with my aunt just now." She meant it for a jest, but he did not laugh. The doctor, always serious, never seemed to quite understand jokes, she reminded herself.

"Nor was what you did proper, my dear," he said. "If only I had known."

"Known what?" She moved past him, but he took her shoulder. She turned, puzzled at first, then alarmed, for he seemed angry in that hard, grim way he had. "What is it? Did my father or aunt ask you to . . . speak to me about anything further?"

"I wish I had known that proper Miss Catriona, the Plain Girl of Glenachan, was willing to spend the night in a man's arms," he said in a low voice. "I would have pressed my own interests earlier." He took her by both shoulders. "Now I wonder if it is too late."

She tried to shrug him away. "What do you mean, too late?"

"I was there, my dear. I saw you sitting in the pallet you shared with him. You looked so beautiful, with your hair loose, your cheeks rosy, your lips — seeing that, it cut me to the heart," he said, and then he brushed his hand over her cheek. "I want what you gave the earl so freely. I deserve that more than he does." He took her by the shoulders again.

"Take your hands off me," she said, fierce and low. Her heart beat hard, her head whirled. Had she missed some sign in him of affection for her? Some sign of a hidden, almost cruel temperament? He had always been serious and grim, though impeccably polite.

126

"I've known you for years, and I would have pressed my suit with your father, but you were the Plain Girl — the one who agreed never to marry. And now this! Much better if you had run off and wed someone. That would have been less of a shock than this — giving yourself to the Earl of Kildonan, of all men!"

"He was a gentleman when we were alone, as I told you," she said. That was true for the most part. "And I am no man's mistress, if that is what you think. Let me go."

"Everyone in the glen knows that the old earl kept a Highland mistress — more than one. It appears that his son means to do the same."

"Not with me," she said, pushing against him. "I am done with him — and what happened last night should not interest you or anyone else. Leave me be."

But he caught her in his arms, pulling her to him. "Listen to me. Keep still and listen," he hissed, while Catriona struggled. "I know about your brother."

She grew still. "My — brother?" she whispered.

"Finlay MacConn has been bringing back some of the people who were evicted from this glen years ago. He is setting them up again in their former homes."

"How . . . ridiculous," she said, her voice muffled. How did Kenneth Grant know?

Finlay was always very careful, and so far had installed families only in remote areas of the glen.

"I've seen them," Grant said. "I was hunting on my land where it borders Kildonan, and my dogs ran off in pursuit of a stag. I chased them a far distance, and I saw smoke curling up from what should have been an abandoned croft. Then I saw that ancient Mr. MacGillechallum, who was thrown out of his home with his old wife. Both of them sitting outside in the sunshine by their little house — and the house had a new roof and a new door. What do you think of that?"

"I do not know what you're talking about," she said.

"Oh, you do," he said, holding her hard at the waist. "I think you have been helping him. You and Finlay are well-known for walking the hills for hours, full days, at a time. That old wifey was singing a tune that day, one I've heard you sing, dear girl. A strange old Gaelic tune, and where would you have learned it but from that old woman?" He tilted his head and hummed a little of the melody.

The beautiful old song seemed eerie and thin, rendered in his flat voice. She stared at him. "Let me go," she said coldly, "and leave this house. When my father and brother learn that you have put your hands on me in so vile a manner — and you a doctor — there will be plenty said, and done, about it."

He pulled her close enough to whisper in her ear. "What do you think the new earl will say about all this? His factor taking estate decisions into his own hands — Kildonan will have him arrested for it. The sheriff at Inverness and the magistrate of the Torridon district always supported the old earl. And now Finlay MacConn . . . and his beautiful sister . . . have gone against the law. Those people have no right to live on this land. They are not tenants approved by the landowner. They are not capable of doing hard work or paying the rent."

She stood motionless in his grip, feeling an ugly swirl of fear. "What do you want of me? Why are you bringing this up now?"

"I want you to kiss me, dear Miss Catriona," he murmured angrily. "I want to know for myself what you shared with the Earl of Kildonan."

His lips traced along her cheek, and she shuddered. When his mouth touched hers, she felt a wave of revulsion and anger. She buckled against him, but he yanked tightly, a big, strong, determined man, with no bit of lightness or humor in him. All was grim in his view of the world, and Finlay's offense — and hers with Kildonan — had triggered something cruel in him.

Kenneth kissed her then, his thin mouth

hard and cold. She twisted her head away.

"Now listen to me," he growled. "I will report your brother's activities to the earl and the sheriff, and I will see those old folk, and everyone else Finlay has brought back, thrown out of their homes again. They have no right to be there."

"What do you care?" she said, writhing in his grip.

"More than you know. Kilmallie lands border Kildonan policies. The earl plans to sell those acres. I intend to acquire them, but those old folk will not stay on the land if I have anything to say about it. The earl has prospective buyers coming to look at the property. Wealthy men who will either convert the rest of the land into sheep runs or develop it into a vast hunting paradise."

"No," she breathed. "I thought it was just a rumor. He cannot really do that."

"He can. Any folk Finlay installs will be sent away again by Kildonan or the new owners — or me, if I can get that land. But I think you and I can make a little bargain, my dear."

"What do you mean?"

"I will keep your brother's activities to myself," he said, "and you and I will keep one more secret." He yanked her close, her hips against his own. Even through layers of petticoats she could feel the ridge of his erection. He ground himself against her and dipped his head to kiss her.

"You will give me whatever you gave Kildonan," he said. "If you are his mistress, you must be mine, as well. And I will pretend to know nothing about your brother's plan."

She froze in his arms, staring at him.

"I have the right, now that you have declared yourself available." He slipped a hand behind her head and kissed her again, but she pulled away in disgust. "That is the price of my silence, Miss Catriona. Your earl will never know, and your brother will be safe. I will acquire the land I want . . . and Kildonan will be a rich man and off to the Lowlands again. He will not care what happens to his bonny Highland mistress."

She only stared at him. Grant kissed her cheek.

"Until later, my dear." Then he let her go and opened the door, stepping out into the hallway.

Catriona stood there for a long minute, limbs shaking. She felt so faint, suddenly, that she rounded to sit on a chair, bending to lower her head, afraid she might pass out.

Chapter Eight

"Lord Kildonan, sit down," Thomas MacConn said solemnly. "Finlay, leave the door ajar for your aunt. She and Catriona will be along soon."

Evan sat in a leather chair opposite the reverend's desk while Finlay stood near the window. The small, crowded room was dominated by a mammoth desk and leather chairs arranged on a worn carpet. Crammed bookcases and a large stone fireplace lined the walls, and dark drapes partially blocked the light.

"Father, I'm sure Lord Kildonan is exhausted and would like a chance to rest before he is interrogated," Finlay said.

Thomas MacConn sent his son a grim look. "We need to resolve the matter without delay."

"Of course. I understand the family's concern," Evan said.

The reverend seated himself behind his desk and folded his hands over his stomach, below the silver watch chain that crossed his black vest. He was a large, imposing man, and Evan could well imagine his commanding presence and gruff voice intimidating his parish, particularly one with the strict views of the Free Church. "Very good, sir," Thomas MacConn said. "And I'm sure you can also understand that my sister, Mrs. Rennie, is upset, too. I asked her to attend our meeting and to bring Catriona in, as well."

Evan nodded, keeping his expression neutral, although his heart jumped at the thought of facing Catriona again in front of her family. The meeting did not promise to be pleasant, and he had no intention of revealing the truth of what had happened in the shieling hut. Whatever he owed Catriona — and he did not doubt he owed her — should be resolved in private between them.

"Lord Kildonan," Finlay said, "while you were consulting with Mr. Grant, Mr. Fitzgibbon rode to Kildonan Castle to inform your family of your safe return."

"Thank you. My sister and brother-in-law will appreciate knowing that all is well."

"Now, Lord Kildonan," the reverend said, "Mr. Fitzgibbon told us you went climbing on Beinn Shee yesterday and lost each other in the mist. The weather turned poor. All that is very unfortunate, of course. What I want to know now is how you and my daughter came to be alone in the shieling for a day and a night."

"Certainly. After I lost Mr. Fitzgibbon, I had a fall while climbing," Evan said. "Miss

133

MacConn came along the drover's road and saw me and assisted me to the shieling hut. The storm grew worse and stranded us there. The slopes were iced over, and there was no question of attempting to get down to the glen."

"A dreadful experience, I'm sure," Finlay said. "That hut is in bad repair and would not offer much shelter. I have been intending to hire a carpenter and a thatcher to fix it up. With your permission I will arrange that."

"My permission?" Evan lifted a brow, puzzled.

"The hut is on your land, sir, since the estate of Kildonan includes the whole of Glen Shee in its eighty-two-thousand acres. Indeed, much of Beinn Shee is yours, as well." Finlay straightened and bowed his head a little. "Sir, in the commotion, I had no chance to introduce myself fully. I am the factor for Glen Shee and Kildonan. I took over for the previous factor, the elder Mr. Grant, after he died. You and I have not had a chance to meet yet. Most of my dealings have been with Lady Jean and Sir Harry."

Evan nodded, already aware that Finlay was his factor. "Aye, Mr. MacConn. My sister has mentioned what an admirable job you've done on the estate."

"Thank you, sir." Finlay leaned against the wall and crossed his arms. He was a tall young man in his late twenties, large framed and slightly padded in the torso, with dark brown hair, blue eyes, and pale skin that flushed easily. There was honesty in his attractive features, and Evan saw a resemblance to Catriona. Jean and Harry had often praised the new factor.

"As soon as possible, Mr. MacConn, we'll meet so that you can apprise me about matters at Kildonan," Evan said.

"Of course. Sir, I apologize for interrupting your story. Do go on — the weather turned on you quickly. That happens in this part of the Highlands. It must have been devilish cold in that shieling."

"It was, but we managed," Evan said.

"We all saw that a hearth was in use and a kettle over the fire," the reverend said. "Perhaps you were not as uncomfortable as it might seem."

"The roof was open to the elements. We did have a small fire, but the peat was damp and quickly burned out. A few oats and some whisky was all the food we had between us."

"My daughter," Reverend MacConn said, "only partakes of strong drink for medicinal purposes."

"Under the circumstances, this was medicinal. We were freezing. Miss MacConn suffered greatly from the cold and damp and was showing all the early symptoms of the freezing death, but without complaint. Sir, you should be proud of your daughter. Her behavior, in my estimation, is without reproach." Evan knew he was the one at fault. He looked hard at the father, who harrumphed.

A tapping sounded on the door, and Mrs. Judith Rennie entered. Evan had met the reverend's sister upon his arrival, and clearly recalled her cold reception. Dressed in unrelieved black except for a white lace collar, she wore a perpetually severe expression on her thin face. He drew up a chair for her, and she sat with scarcely a nod, her back arrow straight, her hands, mittened in black lace, folded in her lap. They looked capable of clawing or clutching.

"Judith, my dear, Lord Kildonan has explained that he and Catriona were stranded by the weather," the reverend said. "They had no other way to stay warm in that dreadful hut."

"Oh?" Mrs. Rennie fixed Evan with a stare, her eyes an eerie pale gray, her iron-colored hair tucked under black netting. He nearly shivered under that chilly glare. "I suppose you decided it was your gentlemanly duty to keep the lass warm. She was without her proper clothing when you were found together."

"Her outer things were wet. Should I have let her freeze while I saw to my own comfort?" He returned her stare calmly. "Would that have been more appropriate behavior

136

than sharing a jacket and a plaid?"

"He has a point," Finlay said.

His aunt huffed. "No one should have been up on that mountainside overnight in such weather. There is no excuse for it. You could have come down, both of you."

Evan glanced away quickly, impatiently, controlling his temper. Finlay snorted and sent Evan a sympathetic glance.

"Finlay, see what's keeping your sister," Thomas MacConn said. "She was to come as soon as she finished with Mr. Grant."

"She will be here soon enough. She will not want to miss this either," Finlay said.

Bemused by Finlay's quiet rebelliousness and squelching a streak of resistance himself in the current company, Evan glanced toward the door. Anticipating Catriona's arrival, he felt like an anxious schoolboy.

"Lord Kildonan, it is true that Catriona was caught in a state of undress," Reverend MacConn said. "Can you explain that?"

"She fell in an icy burn, and her clothing was wet. She was chilled to the bone, which was dangerous in such cold temperatures. She was shivering violently, her teeth banging together, and she was blue around the lips. I suggested that she remove her wet things, have a little whisky, and . . . bundle with me in the blanket to keep warm."

"Ah, bundle," Finlay said. "That makes sense to me."

"Not to me," Mrs. Rennie said. "They were alone. He told her to do these things — and she complied. What else do you suppose he told her to do? Thomas, I feared the new Lord Kildonan would be no better than the old, and now it is proven. Luring a young lass like that — oh!" She sniffed into her lacy handkerchief.

Evan's temper soared, fast and hot, but he quelled it by placing his fingertips together in a controlled arch. "I assure you the young lady was not harmed. And you have no reason to judge me by my father's behavior."

"You were alone for a day and a night," Thomas MacConn said. "You could easily have taken advantage of the girl when she was so vulnerable."

How on earth was he to answer that? "I admire your daughter, sir, and treated her with respect." Well, he had, in a way. Frowning, he gazed at them defiantly over his steepled fingers.

"The lass will not admit to anything either," Mrs. Rennie said, "out of some misplaced loyalty, I suppose."

Evan regarded them in cold silence, keenly aware of his growing loyalty to Catriona and his anger toward her hard-hearted aunt and her stern father, who showed surprisingly little backbone. The brother, though, seemed worth his weight in gold.

He would not explain last night any further. Catriona was clearly in deep disgrace, and he had caused her ruination. The awareness sat on his shoulders like a heavy stone.

"Thomas, the implication is clear," Mrs. Rennie said.

Thomas MacConn frowned. "Aye. The lass is ruined and in a state of sin." He glared at Evan. "And you, sir, are to blame!"

Standing, Evan leaned forward and smacked his palms on MacConn's desk. "All that we did," he said, low and fierce, "was help each other survive."

"A convenient way of wording it," Mrs. Rennie sniffed.

Evan sucked in his breath. True, the girl had been innocent, and he had gone too far. His passion and flaring need for her had taken him by surprise, overwhelming his will and common sense. Offended by the lack of compassion in a righteous household, he knew he had little defense.

"I have the utmost respect for Miss MacConn. And it was hardly a romantic rendezvous," he snapped.

"However indelicate it may be, we must know what happened last night," the reverend's sister said. "Did you —"

"Judith, that hardly matters now," Thomas said with surprising reasonableness. "The fact is that they were alone and unchaperoned overnight, and that is the awkwardness of it."

Judith Rennie gave her brother a stare so

139

fierce that Evan thought the big man might buckle under its force. Then she turned her pale gaze on Evan.

He was not about to give way to tyranny. "I will not discuss particulars. You are determined to make your conclusion, madam. What difference the details?"

Mrs. Rennie gasped, while Finlay huffed a laugh. "My guess is that they behaved themselves. Catriona is strong willed but level-headed, and my sense is that Lord Kildonan is a gentleman and can be trusted."

"Everyone knows about this, or will soon enough," Mrs. Rennie insisted. "Word will go all the way to Inverness and Fort William and beyond. You know that Mrs. MacAuley loves to gossip. She will write to her kin in the cities, and your father's name will be attached to this horrible scandal."

"It would be more horrible if the girl had frozen to death — pardon me, Father, but you know it is true," Finlay said. "In her wet clothing, buttoned to the neck, while Kildonan sipped whisky and borrowed her plaid to warm himself. If it were me, I would have done the same as he did — helped the lass, whatever it took and however it appeared to others later." He nodded to Evan.

"It is a disturbing situation," the reverend said, and he lifted his hands as if he did not know what else to say or what to do. "I thought I had lost the lass — but this — this is almost worse." He shot Evan a furious glare.

"Regardless, Catriona cannot live under the minister's roof after this," Mrs. Rennie said. "We are simply too upset and distressed, for so many reasons. And it's unthinkable for her to stay in the reverend's house while in a state of sin."

"How can you suggest that?" Finlay asked angrily.

"I shall simply have to stay here myself and take over the running of this household," Mrs. Rennie sighed. "We have kin in Glasgow who might take her in."

"Glasgow!" Finlay burst out.

Evan sat forward. "You have my sincere apology. Hold any grudge against me that you like. Do not punish the girl."

"An apology is not enough," Mrs. Rennie replied. "Catriona is not some dairy lass to be taken at the whim of the earl. This is not the Middle Ages."

"Madam, that is an insult," Evan said. "She saved my life."

"It may be best that she leave here for a little while," Thomas MacConn said. He glanced almost guiltily at his sister.

"My brother could lose his living over this scandal," Mrs. Rennie said. "You do not know what you have done, sir. Or perhaps you do," she added.

A dark ferocity rose up in him — anger or

will, guilt and remorse, or all of those. Evan stood, breath heaving, and turned to the reverend. "You would condemn her and send her away from her home and this glen, for saving a man's life?"

"I —" Thomas MacConn looked down. "She was a brave lass, but I am not convinced that you both needed to stay the night."

"It pains us," Mrs. Rennie said, though Evan had not addressed her. "But her father is God's representative. He must uphold only what is virtuous."

"Compassion is virtuous, madam," Evan snapped back. "Gratitude for her safe return is virtuous."

Blasting out an angry, exasperated sigh, he spun away, fisting his hands, his thoughts roiling. Catriona would be sent away — and like the Highlanders who had been cleared off this land, he realized, her bright, warm spirit would wither if she left the glen that she loved.

Her brave rescue of him and her generous act of loving him, would reap heartbreak for her, and it was all his doing. He already carried the burden of another catastrophe, which he believed he had caused, at least in some part. Last night had taken no lives, but he had ruined something beautiful all the same — a bright, innocent Highland girl.

But this disaster he could right. She had

saved his life, and he owed her a rescue in return. He knew what he must do.

Turning, he regarded her family. "I will marry the girl."

"You what? Oh! Catriona!" Mrs. Rennie's voice was hushed.

Heart pounding, Evan glanced up.

Framed in the doorway, Catriona stood very still, her face pale, her eyes wide with a look that bordered on shock. She stared at him — only at him.

"I said," he murmured, watching her, "that I will marry Miss MacConn, if she will have me."

At first Catriona was not sure what Evan had said, as if he spoke in some strange language. Staring at him, she felt caught in his thrall as he moved toward her. His gaze was penetrating, the hazel green of his eyes intensified by the sunlight that filtered between the curtains. She could not look away.

He approached her. "Miss MacConn, will you marry me?" His tone was soft and low, his gaze wholly on her, as if they two were the only ones in the room.

Stunned, she stepped back. What had he admitted to her family about last night? Her father watched her with a sad and disappointed expression, while her aunt glowered, thin fingers twitching. Finlay regarded all of them with the bemused air he often adopted. He, at least, would not condemn her.

Clearly they surmised the worst. She felt a sinking sense of dread and humiliation. An earl would never offer to marry a minister's daughter after a brief acquaintance, except in a case of utter scandal.

She and Evan both knew that there was reason enough for scandal and reason enough for marriage. They had shared a night of adventure and compassionate desire, but now they were caught like fish on a righteous hook.

She certainly did not want to marry him. But she had overheard what was said before they all saw her standing there, and she did not want to leave Glenachan and Glen Shee. And with Grant's murmured threats still echoing in her head, she simply did not know what to do.

"Miss MacConn." Lord Kildonan — she could not erase his title from her mind — came closer and took her hand before she could run. The intimate touch of his warm skin over hers, for neither wore gloves, conjured a precious reminder of last night.

She had wanted to keep those memories safe and private to nourish her for the rest of her lonely life at Glenachan. Now they had been taken from her, open to discussion and judgement.

But he was not the dear Mr. Mackenzie who had held her in his arms so tenderly. He was the son of the hated Earl of Kildonan and even more a stranger to her now. She could not trust him any longer. She had been a fool, drawn in by his charm.

Grant had said that Evan truly intended to sell off much of the land, leaving Kildonan Castle and the glen in the hands of others. Marrying him would mean leaving the glen with her husband — she could not do that, nor could she support his decision to sell.

"No," she said suddenly, pulling her hand out of his. "No!"

"Hear me out," he said fervently, quietly.

"No," she hissed. "I cannot marry you!" She whirled away, but he caught her arm and held her in place. That hard grip reminded her of struggling with Kenneth Grant only minutes before, and she twisted more desperately.

"Catriona, stop," Evan said. His hand was firm, but not violent, and strangely calming. She drew a breath, stilled.

"Catriona, whatever is the matter?" Judith Rennie rose from her seat. "Behave yourself."

"Lass, this is the best thing," her father said, his voice a powerful rumble where he sat at his great desk. "I am glad to have you safe, of course — my lass, I feared for your life on that mountain. You know that. But I cannot condone the rest of it, and I will not have my youngest daughter behaving in such a wild manner. Lord Kildonan has offered to marry you. I want you to accept."

"It is the only way to make up for this shameful situation," Judith Rennie said.

"No." She probably sounded like a child, and she certainly felt like a fool, controlled and forced into a loveless marriage. She wrenched her arm again, and this time Evan released his hold.

Spinning, she gathered her skirts and ran down the hallway. At the stairs, she streamed upward, skirts floating, feet flying.

Footsteps thudded behind her, and she looked back to see Evan striding down the hallway, his face creased — not in anger so much as utter determination.

"Catriona!" he called, his deep voice reverberating throughout the house as his steps pounded toward the stairs.

Chapter Nine

The sound of more pounding feet told her that the others followed Evan. Reaching the top of the steps, Catriona hurried down the corridor to her bedroom, opening the door and spinning to close it quickly. As she did, she glimpsed Evan, Aunt Judith, and her father coming up the stairs.

She slammed the door and leaned against it, breath heaving. Behaving like a spoiled girl was completely unlike her — generally she was always outwardly calm and kept her feelings to herself — yet she had done this almost compulsively, reacting out of temper and heart-pounding fear. Now she closed her eyes and waited.

She could hide in the solitude of her room and reason out what she should do next before facing them again with her decision. Clearly she had to refuse Evan — she felt betrayed and hurt by the truth he had withheld from her. Though her heart yearned for Mr. Mackenzie, she could not marry the Earl of Kildonan. As for Kenneth Grant's blackmail — she simply did not know what to do about that and felt powerless and angered.

Once she came out of her room, she knew

she could reason in private with her father, but she did not expect mercy from her aunt. Judith's heart had turned into a hard kernel years ago when life had embittered her somehow. She had a habit of squelching happiness in herself and others before it could blossom. Ever since the death of her mother, Catriona had lived in her aunt's harsh shadow. Judith had felt duty bound to play stern surrogate mother to her brother's six children.

Catriona's five brothers and sisters were older, and as they moved away one by one, she had lost their sheltering influence like protective layers peeling away. She and Finlay were left as the subjects of Aunt Judith's determination to mother them through control and correction. She had cowed her own brother, Thomas, years before, and he still did all her will. Finlay was an easygoing sort and had simply ignored his aunt's demands.

But Catriona had tried to please her, earning herself constant small criticisms and the label of Plain Girl. She was to have no life outside her father's home and no family of her own. Judith's plan for her ensured Thomas's and Judith's comfort and stole away Catriona's own cherished dreams.

Loving her father, she had tried to accept it, hoping to act as the buffering influence in the household, protecting him from Judith's sharp-edged nature.

And now Judith, who always wanted the upper hand at the manse, would convince the reverend to either send his daughter away — or force her to marry the Earl of Kildonan.

Catriona would rather leave her beloved glen than become what she most resented — the aristocratic authority in Glen Shee. The marriage would separate her from the people and heritage of Glen Shee as much as if she had been sent into exile.

A knock on the door startled her, rattled through the wood and shook her shoulders as she leaned there.

"Open the door," Evan said, pounding.

She put her mouth to the crack of the door. "Go away!"

"I need to speak with you," he said quietly and sternly.

"Well, I do not need to speak with you. Go away!"

"Open this door!" He smacked his hand against it.

"A young lady does not open her door to a gentleman," she said. "A gentleman does not ask to be admitted to an unmarried girl's room. Nor does he beat on her door."

Hearing silence, she thought he had gone. She rested her brow against the wood and fought tears.

"If the young lady spends the night in the gentleman's arms," he whispered, his voice floating through the crack in the door so that only she could hear him, "and if the gentleman asks her to marry him, then the rules have changed."

"Only if the young lady accepts. You do not want to marry me. And you do not have to!" The last she shouted loud enough for the benefit of her father and aunt.

Silence again. Then she heard a creaking as if he leaned a shoulder against the wood. "Catriona, open this damned door."

"No."

"There are several people with me in the hallway who would love to hear our entire conversation. I will conduct my business with you one way or another. Open the door or share this with everyone."

Muttering that they should all go away and leave her be, she turned the handle and yanked the door open so fast that Evan nearly fell through the gap. He caught the doorjamb and glared at her, and she returned his glare boldly.

Behind him, she saw her father; her aunt; Finlay; Peggy, the little housemaid, who stood with an armful of linens, her mouth agape; and Mrs. MacAuley, standing with Glenachan's chubby cook, Jessie, peering up from the lower landing.

"You can talk to me from where you stand — and all of *you* can go downstairs," she told the others.

"Now I have no doubt that you must

marry the earl," Judith said. "Obviously you two are on very familiar terms. You will be a countess — why refuse that? Either marry the man or leave Glenachan House. Tell her, Thomas!" She elbowed her brother.

"Papa?" Catriona looked past Evan toward her father. "Will you send me away if I do not marry him?" She phrased that plaintively in Gaelic.

Thomas MacConn sighed heavily. "Catriona, it is not proper for you to stay here now. The sin of this outweighs . . . all the rest of it. Though I know you saved the man's life — he has compromised you. Let him make that up to you. To all of us." He looked away, and suddenly he looked old to her, grayed and sagging, weak where he had always seemed strong.

"Think of your father's position in the kirk," Judith said, "and what he has worked for all these years. He could lose the living of this manse, and we would all have to leave."

Evan sighed, his hand on the doorframe. Catriona glanced at him. While the others had spoken, she had felt his presence beside her, strong and protective, like a rock in a storm.

"Mrs. Rennie," he said, glancing over his shoulder, "I am attempting to resolve the matter. Please go downstairs and give us privacy — all of you." He drummed his fingers expectantly on the wood.

Judith Rennie huffed and whispered to the minister, who shook his head, took her elbow, and guided her toward the stairs. One by one, the others filed down the steps after them.

Evan turned back to her, his tall form filling the doorway, his long arm in the same tweed jacket he had worn yesterday, his bulk blocking her from escaping past him. His hand on the doorframe prevented her from shutting the door.

"Now," he said, "hear me out."

She looked up at him and nodded, her heart pounding so hard she thought he would see its bounce under her bodice. Part of her was angry with him — yet part of her wanted desperately to accept his offer, on the remote chance that last night had meant as much to him as it had meant to her.

He kept his hand raised just beside her head. "I . . . admit that I have made a dreadful mistake."

Her heart sank a little. "By asking me to marry you? I agree." She lifted her chin.

"I mean I made a mistake last night when I . . . took advantage of our situation. And I apologize." He spoke so softly that any eavesdroppers in the stairwell could not have heard. His intimate tone and his closeness took her breath away, stirred her heart unwillingly. "Let me make it up to you."

"We were both distressed," she whispered

fiercely. "You do not need to make up anything." She felt a blush in her cheeks. Last night she had desperately wanted to be loved, and she had pushed for it to happen — yet Evan was the one offering apologies and recompense. "I would rather this be forgotten. I would rather no one ever knew."

"My dear lass," he drawled, "it is too late for that." He reached out to trace his fingertips along her jaw, tilted up her chin with a knuckle. "And now we must deal with the consequences of our . . . adventure."

"Only because you told them too much," she snapped, angling away from the thrill of his touch. "I thought what happened was for us alone," she finished in a whisper.

He leaned even closer. "Their imaginations did the work. Your aunt has a naughty turn of mind. As for what happened last night, that remains our secret." His gaze searched hers. He stood so close, with only the span of the doorframe separating them, that she could feel the warmth of his breath, could see his thick eyelashes, and noticed the honey-gold and moss-green colors in his irises. "I promise."

"Perhaps it is better if we forget this . . . *Lord Kildonan*."

"Ah, so that is the troublesome point."

"You could have told me," she said between her teeth.

"I intended to tell you, but when you

ranted on about my father and earls in general, it seemed awkward. And I did not expect visitors to our little mountain chalet first thing in the morning. I thought we had time yet."

"Time for what? More deception? Or more . . . adventure?"

"Time for honesty. There is no doubt that I wronged you. And I should have told you immediately who I was."

"If I had known who you were, there would have been no opportunity to wrong me," she snapped.

"Obviously you are not in a forgiving mood. But the only solution now is for you to marry me."

The deep, mellow register of his voice was so compelling to her, by its nature, that he could have said anything, recited a rhyme or read an advertisement, and she would have felt a fillip of pleasure. But what he murmured was the stuff of her most precious dreams — a handsome man offering her a romantic escape from a dull life of drudgery and loneliness.

Yet the dream was offered without love, the most essential element of the fantasy. She looked away, shook her head. "You would not marry me otherwise, Lord Kildonan, so you do not need to marry me now. They have forced you into this."

"No one forced me," he said sharply. "I

suggested it. I owe you a rescue."

"That is no reason for marriage."

He leaned near. "What if there is a child?" he murmured.

She drew a breath. That thought had occurred to her, too, when she had let go of reason to experience rare passion last night. "Then that would be my consequence and my concern."

"I disagree," he growled.

Shaking her head, she stepped back and pushed the door shut, stopping short of mashing his fingers. "Please go," she said.

In answer, he pushed on the door so firmly that she could no longer hold it closed. As it gave way, he crossed the threshold. She stepped back into the room with the force of his entry.

Evan strode inside, kicked the door shut, and took her by the shoulders. "Listen to me, you stubborn lass. I compromised you, but I will honor my obligation. We both know a child is a possibility. Marriage seems to me to be the only reasonable solution."

"Bearing an out-of-wedlock child is not the catastrophe in the Highlands that it is in the Lowlands and elsewhere," she said. "Such offspring are often welcome in Highland homes."

"Perhaps so, but not in this Highland home, I would guess," he said in an intense tone. Leaning forward, he lowered his voice so that no one, even standing outside the door, could hear him. "You'll find no forgiveness for that here. If they send you south, you could end up doing factory work while your child grows up on the streets. I've seen such children," he went on. "Have you?"

She glanced away. "I have."

"Aye. Bowed legs, swollen bellies, wandering the streets half-naked while their parents slave for a pauper's wage. Highland children are straight and strong and beautiful, walking the hills with their families. The child of an earl would have all the advantages without the suffering. Now which should ours be, do you think?"

The images he evoked tugged at her heart, but she shook her head. "The question is pointless. There will be no child."

"How do you know? Did you use methods against it? I did not," Evan said. "I could not think — you were so . . ." He paused, glanced away. "The situation got away from me. And you will not know if you are with child for several weeks."

"Women know their . . . phases, sir. If you are so adamant about this, we need only wait a little while," Catriona said, cheeks blazing. "Then you will know there is no need for marriage."

"And if you are wrong?"

She glanced away, knew she must relent.

"If so . . . then we would have to marry, if you are still willing."

"I am willing now. Waiting is out of the question, since I had not planned to stay in the glen for long. And I will not have a child of mine born after a six-month marriage, I assure you."

Something turned, needful and poignant, deep inside. Every instinct told her he was a good man, a man of integrity and kindness, and that they could make a marriage, even from this accursed start. Yet she privately knew that she had cajoled him into loving her and that he felt obligated. Nor could she easily forgive him for concealing his identity.

She had wanted only to be loved last night, just once. But she had fallen too deep, too far. Now she did not know what to do. Tears stung her eyes, and she shook her head in silence.

"Listen to me. That heartless raven of a woman," he ground out, "will send you away. Let me take you out of here."

"So you can pack me off somewhere far away from you once you decide I am not truly fit to be a countess? No." If she ever married, she wanted love, devotion, partnership.

"Catriona — what is it that bothers you so about this?"

She stood in silence, unable and unwilling to tell him all her doubts and fears — and she could not tell him what Grant had threatened and what he had told her about Evan's intentions in Glen Shee. She turned her head and did not answer.

"Do not make this so blasted difficult."

"We have no basis for a real marriage," she finally said.

"We had the makings of one last night," he murmured. "Shall I remind you?" He reached out and pulled her to him, dipping his head to kiss her with such tender richness that her head spun and her knees gave way. He held her up with his easy strength, and she wrapped her arms around his neck and let him kiss her again.

Dazed, she felt herself responding to the powerful desire that had overtaken her last night. When he pulled away, she stood with her eyes closed, her breath quickening.

"Well?" he asked. "Do you remember now? We have the makings of a marriage — you cannot deny it."

She looked at him then. He towered over her, the only man she knew who was taller — and stronger willed — than she was. Her heart surged, and passion tugged at her, intimately, hopefully. He possessed some sort of magic in his hands, his lips, his voice, that sank easily into her and untied the knots, weakened her resolve.

"I know," she whispered. She felt her knees trembling, felt her body, her soul, hurtle forward, when she tried to resist. "I will . . . marry you." She looked up. "And your debt will be paid."

His hands tightened on her arms. "Catriona, my girl," he murmured, "somehow I wonder if I can ever make it up to you."

She gazed at him in silence, suddenly wanting to be kissed again, as if that could erase the strife and doubt.

He let go of her and turned away. "Come downstairs — we'll inform your family." He opened the door.

Catriona saw her aunt standing in the hallway outside her room as if she had been eavesdropping through the oaken door.

"So," Judith said. "I see you have made your decision. A good thing — you two were alone far too long. Lord Kildonan, I came up to tell you that your sister, Lady Jean, and her husband, Lord . . . Lord Henry . . ."

"Sir Harry Gray, madam," Evan supplied tersely.

"Aye. Lady Jean and Sir Harry have arrived and are anxious to see you." She frowned. "I do not have the stamina to inform them of this awful scandal, so I will leave that to you. Come along, Catriona." She whirled away and headed for the stairs, then spoke over her shoulder. "Your father wants this deed done tonight."

Glancing frantically at Evan, Catriona pushed past him. "Tonight?" she said as her aunt trounced down the stairs.

"The reverend insists," Mrs. Rennie answered, pausing on the landing to look up. "We have begun the arrangements."

Catriona gasped and stepped forward, but Evan grabbed her arm and pulled her back. "Let it go. What difference tonight, next week, next month? The sooner we are married, the sooner you are free of this so-called disgrace. And the sooner you are out of this house," he murmured.

She whirled to direct her anger toward him. "This is my home! I do not want to leave it like this, so fast."

"They will force you to leave or marry. And I owe you a rescue. Frankly, I think you need one."

"You're wrong," she snapped.

But she knew, in her heart, that he was right. Her life had begun to change in the first moment she saw him, and it would never be the same.

Chapter Ten

"Your father, the previous earl, attended my parish church." Holding a dainty teacup in his tough, squarish hand, Thomas MacConn looked at Evan. "But you and Lady Jean were raised in the Lowlands, as I recall." He frowned. "Do you attend kirk, sir?"

"Of course. Regularly." Evan glanced at his sister, who sat beside Catriona. Lady Jean Gray, dark haired and beautiful in the first blush of early pregnancy, watched him, her expressive brown eyes wide. She glanced at her husband, a large, handsome fellow normally brimming with good spirits, who pressed his lips together grimly. Beside them, oblivious to the rest, Arthur Fitzgibbon took a bite out of a biscuit, crunching audibly.

Evan was glad that Jean and Harry had come to Glenachan after learning of the mountain rescue. Arriving at the manse, they had managed to hide their astonishment when Evan had taken them aside to explain about his impending marriage, to be performed that night.

Jean had kissed his cheek gently, while Harry had declared genially that Evan should stay off mountains if climbing got him into that much trouble. Jean had gone off in search of Catriona to welcome her to the family, a gesture Evan greatly appreciated.

"Our mother made sure we attended church every Sunday," Jean said with her usual calm, "no matter where we were at the time, whether in Edinburgh or at her estate in northern England."

"Did you attend services in the Established Church of Scotland or the Free Kirk?" Mrs. Rennie asked.

"Actually neither." Evan set his teacup down. He would have done anything to escape the last tense, awkward half hour, but for Catriona, who sat on the horsehair sofa beside him in relative silence. He would not desert her.

Mrs. Rennie huffed. "I knew it! You're a Mary worshiper!"

"Aunt Judith!" Catriona burst out.

"If he's a Catholic, he won't be able to marry you tonight, lass," her father said. "Not without obtaining a dispensation."

"We attend Anglican services," Evan said sharply, resenting the whole business. "When in Scotland, we attend a Scottish Episcopalian church, or an Established Church. Does that meet your standards?" He had endured enough of his soon-to-be in-laws, and his admiration for Catriona had increased tenfold. He was more than willing to marry her to get her away from this.

"Good," Thomas grunted. "The Anglicans and the Free Church recognize one another's wedding ceremonies. We'll go ahead with it tonight, as agreed."

Catriona drew a breath. "Papa, I do not want —"

"We must do this quickly," Judith Rennie said. "I apologize, Lady Jean, Sir Harry," she said, turning toward Evan's sister and brother-in-law. "This is not the best welcome for your first visit to the manse. So very awkward."

"Not at all, Mrs. Rennie," Jean answered. "I am so relieved that my brother is safe after his disappearance yesterday, and I'm grateful to your daughter for her bravery and generosity. Their dangerous adventure was quite romantic, I think."

"And I'm sure, under the circumstances, marriage is a good solution. It seems to suit everyone here." Harry smiled.

Bless them, Evan thought. Harry was a kind, if blustery soul, and Jean had a sunny nature that was irresistible to most people around her. He was glad to see Catriona brighten and relax a bit.

"Papa, I need some time to prepare for my wedding," Catriona said. "A few weeks —" She glanced at Evan, and he knew that she thought if there was no child, she could be free of the marriage. But the disgrace would always be with her.

"The wedding is not as important as the marriage," Judith said. "You cannot spend another night in a state of sin."

Aye, Evan thought. He was glad to rescue Catriona MacConn.

"Kildonan, sir! What an odd day this has been," Arthur Fitzgibbon said as he approached Evan, who was walking on the grounds of the manse.

"Aye, Fitz," Evan said grimly as Arthur fell into step beside him. "Quite a day, I agree."

He said no more as they strolled the path that cut over an expanse of neatly trimmed lawn that sloped downward toward a small loch in the distance. Modest flower gardens spread to either side of the grass, and the graveled path and a few stone steps accommodated the natural incline of the land. The gardens held few flowers this late in autumn, though chrysanthemums, holly bushes, and low evergreens lent good color to the beds.

Behind them, the manse was a stately two-story building of gray stone, its mullioned windows shuttered with heavy draperies. Off to the left, Evan saw the parish church at the edge of the grounds behind some trees, its fieldstone walls and steeple picturesque. Ahead, the smooth surface of the lochan mirrored the dusky twilight. Attracted by the glimpse of mountains on the opposite shore of the loch, Evan walked toward the near

164

shore. Arthur accompanied him, footsteps crushing pebbles.

"Shall I offer congratulations?" Arthur asked.

Evan noted the doubtful tone. "Thank you. I hope you plan to stay for the wedding."

"Of course. Wouldn't miss it," Arthur replied. "Miss MacConn is a charming girl, and one cannot blame her family for wanting this marriage, given the, er, circumstances. But I must say I think it's a mistake for you to do this."

"Oh?" Evan glanced at his friend, not entirely surprised to hear Arthur's opinion. Fitzgibbon was older than Evan by a decade, of medium height and with a strong build, his brown hair graying, his mustache and sideburns thick. He had so far not married and was a pleasant fellow, if preoccupied with his own interests. As an author and a professor of natural philosophy at Edinburgh University, he made studies of glacial formations and mountainous land masses in particular. Evan had taken classes under Professor Fitzgibbon, and they had formed a friendship based on geology and the pastime of mountain climbing.

When Arthur had taken up mountain climbing in Europe, he had convinced Evan and other friends to go on a climbing holiday in the Swiss Alps. Evan had gone reluctantly, but he had discovered that the exhilaration of being so far above the world had helped erase some of his dark grief over the devastating bridge collapse. Since then, he had climbed the mountains of Wales and the Grampians of Scotland, and he had looked forward to returning to Glen Shee, which was bordered by some of Scotland's highest mountain slopes.

"Fitz," he said, "I've learned to trust you while scaling sheer rock and picking my way across the ice fields of the Wetterhorn, but I am not sure I can trust your opinions regarding marriage. It is not your preferred state. But I have always wanted a wife and a family. It's time I did something about it."

"Marriage of convenience, then," Arthur said. "Won't have to think about it. Just get it over with. It's the only way I could be persuaded to marry — but the timing is deuced awkward. Climbing club and all."

"Ah," Evan said, nodding. "The Scottish Alpine Climbing Club — it slipped my mind in the excitement." Recently, he had agreed to host the same climbing group that he had traveled with in the Swiss Alps well over a year ago. The energetic force behind the club was his cousin, Miss Jemima Murray. She and several others were to stay at Kildonan Castle while conducting a hillwalking tour of the Highlands. Evan and Arthur had planned to undertake some local mountaineering with them.

But he had not planned on being a newlywed. Frowning, he shoved his hands into his trouser pockets. What a time to bring home a bride. Kildonan Castle would be as full as a resort hotel.

"Have our guests arrived yet?" he asked.

"Not yet," Arthur said. "They were delayed by the same poor weather that hung you up, but they expect to hire two coaches and make the trip to Kildonan in a day or two. Good that they missed the trouble over your disappearance and all the rest of it."

"All the rest of it," Evan repeated wryly, amused at Arthur's capacity for glossing over details that did not directly relate to Arthur or to climbing or geology.

"I look forward to good climbing days in the weeks ahead and the chance to investigate some of my glacial theories. You'll be free to join us, I hope."

"Of course," Evan replied. "I do not yet know if my . . . bride will join our party. It would not be right of me to desert the girl quite so soon after we are married."

"Bring her along. Highland girls are avid hillwalkers," Arthur observed. "Though this marriage business is difficult."

"Unavoidable, Fitz," Evan said. "It's a bit of a scandal, but will soon be forgotten."

"Nothing wrong with trying to get out of it, if you ask me. Give it some thought. Apologize to the girl and her family and offer them funds. Take care of the problem."

"She's the minister's daughter, and I'm the earl of this region," Evan pointed out. "I will not follow in my father's footsteps. Every Highlander in this glen would soon despise me. Likely most of them do already," he muttered.

"Miserable business," Arthur commented. "But . . . were you such a rascal with the lassie that there's no way out of the wedding?" Arthur peered at Evan. "Not my concern, but people will talk."

"Let them. I am determined to do this. No matter what happened when we were alone, she is in full disgrace."

"If her family tosses her out on her ear, find her a wee cottage somewhere and pay her upkeep until she finds a husband. That would give you . . . certain rights, anyway. Could be good."

"I owe her more than that. She saved my life. If not for her, I could have died on that mountainside."

"Well, I did come back for you," Arthur muttered.

"Aye, I know. Thank you for organizing the search party."

"So it does not matter who you wed, just that you wed?" Arthur asked. "The earl must have an heir and all that."

Evan shrugged. "I admit there are provisions in my father's will, certain rights to the properties, that require that I marry and produce an heir."

"Aha," Arthur said. "Hence your hurry."

"I can marry anytime in the first year to gain those rights, so it is not particularly an issue. And yet I find myself rather insistent about going through with this." He half laughed, stopped to look up at the darkening twilight sky. "Odd indeed."

"You're doing the chivalric thing, I suppose. The girl has a fine figure and a bonny face, though she's a wee bit dull for a countess. She'll do, though."

"Aye, she'll do." Evan paused to look out over the loch in the gathering darkness.

"Huh, look at the time." Arthur popped his watch open, then shut. "You'd best get ready."

"There's little for me to do now. Lady Jean brought me a fresh suit of clothes, without knowing that I needed to dress for my own wedding." He indicated his plain black suit, black silk vest, and neckcloth of dark silk. "So I'm ready. But go ahead. I'll be along soon — I've got some thinking to do."

"I'm sure of that," Arthur said, and he turned to depart.

Evan looked out over the dark, glassy surface of the water, which reflected gray dusk overhead, and the long cluster of hills and snow-topped mountains on the opposite side of the loch. There would be rain later tonight, he thought. Not a good omen for a wedding — but nothing yet had brought good omens for this wedding.

He frowned and glanced down, watching the water lap cold and clear to touch the leather toes of his black boots. Tonight he would make a wedding promise to a girl he scarcely knew.

Yet in some way he did not understand, he felt as if this was right. He owed his life to her, and he took the debt seriously. And he wanted to be sure that any child was given a name and a family — and a father.

Father. Was that it? he wondered. Was it the possibility that he might become a father? If he ever did, he would not abandon the child as his own had done, to fine houses and good educations and little or no good paternal influence. He wanted to be sure his own child, son or daughter, knew him — and felt safe, cherished, and loved.

Perhaps that was what spurred him toward this enormous step, he thought. He felt strangely calm and determined about his choice. Something deep had awoken in him when he had lain with Catriona MacConn in his arms — something deeper than need and lust.

As Earl of Kildonan, he would need a countess. But Evan Mackenzie wanted a wife and a companion. He wanted a family and love. And Catriona had a sort of simple, compelling magic for him that he could not explain.

He did not think it was possible to love the

girl after a day and a night with her, but it was long enough to recognize her finer qualities. She would make a fine countess and a fine wife.

He only had to convince her of that after the marriage, and convince her to stay with him. It would take more than an exchange of vows to keep this countess, he knew.

What did one take when leaving one's home forever?

Catriona stood in the middle of her small room, the simple space unadorned but for a framed engraving of the Torridon Mountains, a gift from her mother; a white coverlet stitched by her grandmother; and a few shelves of books that Catriona treasured.

Sighing, she turned. Aunt Judith had told her that her things would be sent on to Kildonan Castle, so that she need only pack what she would require for a few days. She had filled a leather portmanteau with clothing — a few blouses and skirts, two day gowns, and underthings to go with them. She needed a second case for her bulky petticoats, for shoes wrapped in paper, and for her books and the notes for her song collection.

Her garments were not numerous, though they were of good quality — her mother had taught her early that fine fabrics and well-made garments reflected good breeding. But she lacked a countess's wardrobe, she thought with a frown.

She did not know what being a countess would mean for her — whether she would find herself in lofty social circles, or simply carry on her life more or less as before, with the exception of . . . a husband.

A husband and a family — were those truly for her? The dream seemed hardly capable of coming true, for it had an unexpected edge, the irony of who she was marrying and how little she really knew about him.

"You can come back anytime you like." Finlay's voice filled in the silence.

She whirled, holding one of her nightgowns. The door was ajar, and her brother leaned there, regarding her calmly.

"No need to pack in haste," Finlay said.

"I'm just bringing a few things. I'll get the rest later." She put the nightgown into the portmanteau and chose other garments from those folded on the coverlet, placing them in the bag as well. She glanced up at him.

"You can supervise the packing of your things later, and we'll bring them up to the castle. Or you could leave them here, Catriona." He watched her solemnly. "Until you have settled into your new life and are sure you will stay."

"I'm no longer welcome here," she said stiffly, and she turned away, fighting tears.

"You'll always be welcome wherever I am," he said quietly.

She nodded, then sobbed and covered her face for a moment. Finlay crossed the room to put an arm around her.

"I do not think I can do this, Finlay," she sniffled.

"He's not such an ogre, your earl." He patted her shoulder. "You two did look rather good friends when we found you in the bothy," he murmured in a light tone. "What could Father do but demand a marriage?"

She nodded glumly. "But . . . I am not ready to be any sort of countess — especially not of Kildonan! I've been the Plain Girl all my life, Finlay. Marriage was never planned for me."

"You deserve some happiness, if you ask me. Though this does throw our own wee scheme awry. You certainly cannot help me out in the way that we planned." Finlay frowned. "What we are doing poses too many risks for you now, Catriona, as the countess."

She looked up at him, remembering Kenneth Grant's threats. "Finlay," she said, "perhaps you should stop doing this —"

"I won't," he said. "I've got one family ready to bring out of the Glasgow tenements. And I'm still trying to locate some of the MacLeod clan. I won't stop now, even if it means I'll do it alone, without your help."

"We were told that the new earl cared less

than his own father about matters on the estate. But now that he will be in residence at Kildonan Castle, he could ask some difficult questions. I do not want you to take such a risk."

"Perhaps this will be a blessing in disguise."

"How so?"

"Just make sure the earl does not inquire too deeply while I continue my work. Once I get these families into cottages in the remote hills, no one will be the wiser for a long time. The shepherding and gathering and clipping will be done for the year, and the earl will be a wealthier man . . . and he will not much care how he got that way."

"This one is not like his father," she said. "If he puts his attention on the estate, he will shortly discover what you have been doing."

"Then you will have to charm him out of suspecting."

"He and I scarcely know each other, Finlay."

"He will listen to you. How could he resist?" Finlay smiled. "Just gain me a little time to finish what I've begun."

She sighed. "I'll try." She turned away to gather more things to put into her portmanteau.

But in order to stop Kenneth Grant from making good on his threat to expose Finlay and send the Highlanders back into exile, she would have to become his mistress — at the same time that she became Evan's wife.

She closed her eyes, sensing a cold lump of fear in the pit of her stomach.

Chapter Eleven

Clenching her toes nervously in flat slippers of black silk, Catriona could feel the silver coin that Lady Jean had given her for luck tucked under her left instep.

Luck. She almost laughed at the thought.

Even now she stood beside the Earl of Kildonan, being married before her father in the parish church of Glenachan. A handful of witnesses sat in the front pews of the little church — her aunt and brother, Evan's sister and her husband, and Evan's friend. The darkness inside the whitewashed interior was relieved only by the glow of some candles. A chill in the air and the sound of fine rain on the windows reminded her of the night that had brought about this sober little wedding.

She wore her best day dress of cobalt-blue silk, the bodice and skirt trimmed with simple bands of black ribbon. Wide sleeves spilled over creamy half sleeves done in *broderie anglaise*. A pretty gown, she knew, though more suited to teatime than one's own wedding.

Lady Jean had kindly suggested arranging late yellow chrysanthemums from the garden inside the church, but Aunt Judith had insisted that Catriona be married without flowers or veil in accordance with her sinful state. Instead, she carried a small Gaelic Bible that had belonged to her mother and wore a little black bonnet trimmed with white lace and black ribbons. With her rich waves of red-gold hair subdued beneath the bonnet, she knew she looked a somber, rather ordinary bride.

The dimly lit church, her father's grim voice, the cool atmosphere, and the steady patter of rain all suited a Plain Girl and her plain little wedding. Yet despite the sober ceremony and her reluctance to marry the Earl of Kildonan, Catriona felt a strange, fluttery excitement dance inside of her. She had never thought she would marry, and for a moment, she closed her eyes and savored that fact alone, let the solemn, sacred words her father intoned wash over her.

She allowed herself to believe, in that instant, that her most precious dreams were coming true — love and happiness, children and a home of her own, a husband's lifelong comfort and affection. Then she sighed. This was not a love match, but one born of necessity and obligation.

In the soft candlelight, though, her groom did not look like a man submitting to a forced marriage. He looked like a prince from a fairy tale, strikingly handsome in his black frock coat and trousers, with black silk vest, white shirt, and neckcloth of blue silk. With his dark hair waving over his brow and his hazel eyes brilliant in the candle glow, he was beautiful. There was no other word for it, she thought, and she caught her breath a little as she looked up at him, hardly able to believe that this handsome, virile man was willing to marry her at all.

He met her glance and smiled, and though it was quickly gone, it warmed her to her toes and gave her a moment's reassurance. Throughout this ordeal, she had noticed how gracious Evan Mackenzie had been about the union.

Reverend MacConn murmured the vow in Gaelic and asked the groom to repeat it. Looking at Catriona, Evan lifted a brow to signal that he did not understand.

"Say 'I will,' " she whispered. "That is . . . if you want."

Evan frowned slightly. Heart pounding, Catriona watched him and wondered if her groom was about to change his mind.

"I will," he said quietly. A moment later Catriona repeated her own vows in Gaelic, then English as Evan had done, and Evan took her gloved hands in his own.

A wave of dizziness spun through her, as if she felt the ripple of magic that bound her life to his through the promise of the vows. Closing her eyes, she could not shake a sense of unreality, as if she had stepped into a dream where time moved both fast and slow and the thud of heart and blood overtook all other sounds.

When Reverend MacConn pronounced them man and wife, Evan glanced at Catriona.

"It is done," she whispered in translation. "Now we —"

"Kiss," he murmured, leaning close. "That much I know."

He touched his lips to hers so tenderly that her heart stirred, and her body stirred, too, though her father stood glowering over them.

Married. Catriona felt stunned.

Sheer panic set in like a cold wind.

Heart beating hard, Evan waited — giving no sign of his sudden wave of doubt — while Catriona used an old-fashioned feather pen to sign the registry book in the rectory office. What had he done? Dear God, he was actually married.

A breath, two breaths later, he realized that he still felt strongly — despite that moment of trepidation as the shock set in — that what he had done was proper, wise, and the only thing to do to resolve the situation.

He glanced over her shoulder as she wrote her name. *Catriona Elspeth MacConn*. He had not known that Elspeth was her second name. He knew very little about his bride, although he already knew some of her most intimate secrets.

Musing that his mother was also named Elspeth, he wondered what she would think of her new daughter-in-law. The dowager countess was on holiday in Spain with friends, unaware of what had happened in her son's life.

As soon as possible, he would write to inform his mother of his marriage, although he feared it would bring her back to Scotland like a whirlwind. She wanted nothing more for him than to see him married. He was sure that his mother would welcome Catriona warmly, just as Jean had done in their mother's place, and he smiled to himself.

Taking the pen, he signed his own name. *George Evan Mackenzie.* He hesitated, then added *Earl of Kildonan, Viscount Glendevon.* He sensed Catriona stiffen beside him as she watched him write out his titles.

The witnesses to their wedding in the church stood watching them, the silence awkward inside the rectory office. Jean, who was willing to pretend that the wedding had been a joyous occasion, stepped forward and embraced the bride, giving her another tearful, happy smile.

"Welcome to our family, Catriona," Jean said. "Evan, congratulations." She turned to kiss his cheek. "I hope you are both very happy."

"Aye, er, congratulations," Harry said, shaking Evan's hand and then Catriona's. Arthur followed suit, as did Catriona's brother. Reverend MacConn gave his daughter a dry peck on the cheek, and her aunt gave her a stiff embrace.

Evan took Catriona's elbow to guide her toward the door. Holding her slender arm in his hand gave him a sudden, surprisingly tender feeling of protection. He had wanted, after all, to get her away from the family who did not value her as they should.

The deed was done. His obligation to her was fulfilled. Love had nothing to do with this match, born of guilt and gratitude. Yet a little hope stirred in him nonetheless, for he had always wanted a family. Perhaps this would lead to happiness for him — and for his bride, too.

He glanced down at Catriona in the darkness as they crossed the lawn heading back to the manse for a late supper before leaving for Kildonan Castle. The others followed quietly behind them.

He was aware that they had no bagpiper to herald them, no tossing of shoes, no singing or carousing going on around them. The bride had no ring, no veil, no flowers, no dancing or music, either. Her family's strict religion forbade some of the joyful elements of a wedding, but he knew that even Free Kirk weddings were not usually this dreary.

She deserved a fine wedding and a happy celebration, he thought. And if anyone deserved to be Countess of Kildonan, it was she. No one loved Glen Shee more passionately than Catriona MacConn, and no countess could serve its interests better. Evan knew he had made a good choice in that — if only he could convince her to remain his countess.

He envied her the love and the bond she had for her native Highlands. As a boy, he had loved these lands deeply, too, but he had been torn away from them and transplanted. Now, thanks to his father, the people of the glen would not trust him.

Soon he would have to tell Catriona about his decision to sell much of the land, rent out the castle, and leave this place entirely, freeing himself of most of his duties as a Highland earl. He also had yet to tell her about the guests who were about to arrive at Kildonan Castle. Some of them were coming particularly to discuss a potential purchase.

Married but twenty minutes, and already he had secrets.

Seated opposite her husband on the leather bench seat inside the closed gig, Catriona saw that Evan knitted his brow in pensive silence and fisted his hand against his mouth as he gazed out the window beside him.

She could well imagine his regret over this hasty marriage. She still felt stunned by the quick wedding and the stiff farewell with her father and aunt. Sighing, she looked out her own window at the steep, dark silhouettes of the mountains that ringed the long glen.

She and Evan rode alone, for Lady Jean and Sir Harry, who had brought the one-horse gig to Glenachan House, had borrowed Reverend MacConn's pony carriage for their return a little earlier. Lady Jean had wanted time to alert the household staff that the earl would be bringing home his bride.

The bride was not eager to arrive, she thought. Pressing herself into the corner, she gazed at the evening sky and wished the driver would slow the vehicle to a crawl or turn it around altogether. She had not been ready in heart or mind to leave her home and family, and she feared that her marriage would not redeem her in the regard of her father and aunt for a long while.

She blinked back tears and stole another glance at Evan Mackenzie. He sat with one ankle crossed over his knee, his profile still pensive as he watched the passing landscape.

He looked no happier than she felt. A tear slid down her cheek, and she wiped it angrily with her glove. Evan glanced toward her.

"Madam?" he asked softly.

"I suppose we will be there soon," she said, hoping idle conversation would help her overcome the urge to cry. "It's but twelve miles from Glenachan to Kildonan Castle."

"Aye. You'll see the castle on your side

first, if it's not too dark." He leaned over to share her view through the window. "It's a beautiful sight when the moon is out, as it is tonight. Ah, look there."

Catriona tilted her head and saw the castle in a wash of moonlight. She had seen Kildonan Castle often from a distance, but had never been inside — and she had never imagined it would be her home one day.

Perched on the shore of a small lochan and backed by the dark hump of low mountains, the castle had a fairy-tale beauty. Its pale stone walls, various turrets, and conical roof caps seemed enchanted in the moonlit setting.

"Oh," she gasped impulsively. "It's beautiful."

"Aye, grand," he murmured. "A bit too grand for my taste, and expensive to upkeep, but it will do."

Soon the coachman turned the carriage onto the long drive that looped in front of the castle. Acres of smooth lawns and tiered gardens surrounded the building, an older central tower flanked by two rectangular wings fronted with palatial windows, the whole a blend of tidy symmetry and intriguing whimsy in a wild, rugged Highland setting.

"The original castle was the central pele tower, built by an earlier laird of Kildonan in the sixteenth century," Evan said. "The wings were added in the eighteenth century by my great-grandfather. The exterior walls are of native sandstone, but they have been harled, that is, coated with rough, textured plaster for a uniform appearance, which also helps seal against the weather. It will need another coating soon, I think — a time-consuming project, if the plasterers can be brought up here."

"We are in a remote area," she agreed, glad of a neutral topic to discuss. "But I'm sure some local Highlanders could do it. You need not hire painters and plasterers from Inverness or Glasgow to come all the way up to Kildonan."

"A good idea. I'll ask your brother to find some local men to do the work. I'm sure the crofters can easily learn the technique of harling the castle walls."

She swallowed quickly, nodding.

The carriage rolled up the long drive, gravel crunching under the wheels. Catriona nervously smoothed her blue skirt and short black cape, then straightened her black silk bonnet. For a few moments, entranced by the sight of the castle, she had forgotten that she must face the household staff as the new Countess of Kildonan.

Evan cleared his throat. "I should have mentioned this earlier, but it slipped my mind in all the commotion this evening. We are expecting guests at Kildonan in a day or two."

"Guests?" she repeated. "So soon?"

"Two cousins and some friends planned to tour the Highlands this month, and so Jean and I invited them to spend a little time at Kildonan. They are interested in doing some hillwalking and climbing in the area."

"Oh," she said, a little dumbfounded. She wondered if these were the guests who were coming to look at Kildonan Castle and the earl's lands with a view to purchasing them. "How nice," she said with no enthusiasm.

"I know it's not easy for you to deal with guests so soon, but I doubt we'll see much of them. They are coming to have a look at Glen Shee and the castle."

Ah, she thought. So she was right. She turned her face away in the darkness and felt a plummeting sense in her stomach.

"They are all experienced climbing enthusiasts and intend to do a good bit of hiking and so forth. I traveled with some of them myself, and we climbed in the Alps. With luck, madam," he said, "you will not need to socialize with them beyond breakfast and the occasional dinner. They'll have a busy schedule."

"Will you be climbing with them this time?" she asked.

"I had planned on it. Of course you are welcome to join us. I'm sure the guests would love it. And you might enjoy it, too."

"I . . . Perhaps," she said uncertainly. The

idea of facing the household staff tonight was hard enough. Facing Evan's cousins and friends after this scandalous marriage, and meeting prospective buyers interested in taking over Glen Shee — and playing hostess to them — was too much to bear thinking about.

"If you plead headache now and then, you can manage to avoid some of the hostessing duties," Evan said, as if he understood some of her reluctance. "Lady Jean will be here for a few more days, and I will be available to act as host."

Her pride stiffened her. "I rarely have the headache," she said. "I intend to do whatever is expected of me."

"*All* that is expected of you?" he murmured, watching her.

Realizing the deeper implication of his words, she felt a blush heat her cheeks. What she wanted and desired — to be in Evan Mackenzie's arms again, to share love and loving with him — conflicted strongly with so much else — his identity as Earl of Kildonan and her urge to protect her brother and the people of this glen. How could she desire this stranger, who stood poised to ruin her life and change the glen she loved?

Her body and her heart had developed a distressing breach of interest. She frowned and turned away to look out the window.

As the gig's horse slowed to a stop,

Catriona glanced toward the castle entrance and saw the front door open. Several people filed out to gather on the wide terraced steps in the moonlight.

The vehicle lurched as the coachman climbed down. Evan stood, ducking to exit, then turning to assist Catriona. She felt her stomach roll anxiously as Evan handed her down to the ground.

"Welcome home," he said quietly.

Home. She closed her eyes in anguish, and for a moment solid earth seemed to sway beneath her feet. She felt Evan's hand under her arm, lending her surprising strength.

Their faces were unfamiliar, their names vague. Evan nodded pleasantly and strolled alongside Catriona as the housekeeper, Mrs. Baird, introduced the new countess to the staff. He paid close attention, for he had arrived at Kildonan only days ago and scarcely knew most of the servants himself.

Mrs. Baird and her husband, Robert Baird, the butler, had been at Kildonan since Evan's boyhood. The others were not so familiar to him, and hearing their names again, he despaired of keeping them straight. The cook and stableman were married, and most of the housemaids and grooms were either their children or their kinfolk. In addition, they resembled one another to a remarkable degree.

Beside him, Catriona greeted each person

as he or she was introduced, taking their hands and repeating their names. They all smiled and brightened as she did so. Evan saw that her calm nature and kind, lovely smile quickly earned her their loyalty.

Although he had walked this gauntlet of introductions when he had first arrived, he followed Catriona's lead, repeating their names and taking each hand as he did so — and found their faces and names immediately fixed in his memory.

He had already learned something from his countess, he thought, and smiled to himself.

"Here are Maggie and Deirdre, the upstairs housemaids," Mrs. Baird was saying. Two pretty brown-haired girls smiled and curtsied awkwardly. Catriona murmured a polite greeting, and Evan nodded. "Bethie is the downstairs lassie, and Seona is the kitchen maid." They nodded and dipped in turn, one a plump redhead and the other dark and slim, again as young as the upstairs maids. "Davey and Allan see to the chores inside and outside the castle, and wee Robbie works in the stables." Three lanky youths, scrubbed clean, nodded solemnly, hats in hand.

"And this is Mr. MacGillechallum," Mrs. Baird went on. She had an imperious, unapproachable air, as did her husband, the butler, Evan noticed. But the MacGillechallums, as a whole, were a smiling, bonny lot. "Mr. Gillie — as we call him — runs the stables.

And Mrs. MacGillechallum, his wife, does our cooking."

"Gillie will do, aye," MacGillechallum said, his voice deep, his hands rough and large as he doffed his hat. Evan nodded and shook his hand, as did Catriona.

"I go by Mrs. Gillie, or Cook," said his wife, a short, robust woman who resembled the young housemaids. "The lads and lassies are our sons, daughters, and nieces. And we know *you* well . . . Lady Kildonan." She smiled at Catriona, who tilted her head. Mrs. Gillie then whispered to Catriona in Gaelic.

Catriona pressed the cook's hands and murmured a reply.

Evan's knowledge of Gaelic was not extensive, but he had learned the basics from his nurse years ago. He knew that Mrs. Gillie thanked Catriona for some sort of help, while she replied that she and her brother Finlay had been glad to do it.

Puzzled, Evan leaned toward her as she turned away. "I see you know Mr. and Mrs. Gillie," he said.

He could have sworn she turned fiery pink. "Oh, we helped Mr. Gillie's old parents, who, ah, live in the high hills."

Hearing his name called, Evan turned to see Jean and Harry coming out of the house to add to the welcome. Evan kissed Jean, then waited while Jean embraced Catriona warmly.

"Come in," his sister said. "We've been very busy in the last hour, and I hope all is ready."

Evan took Catriona's elbow to guide her toward the entrance. Then he paused, reminding himself that he was entering his home with his bride. Quickly he swept her into his arms, and she gasped in surprise, looping her arms around his neck.

For a tall girl, she was not heavy, and he easily carried her over the threshold into the foyer, where he set her on her feet to excited applause from those watching on the front steps.

He leaned close and brushed his lips lightly over hers. The feeling of her mouth under his was tender and delightful, and he closed his eyes, wishing for more, knowing in every fiber of his being that he had made the right choice in marrying her tonight, though others doubted it — including the bride.

"Welcome to Kildonan, Catriona." He took her gloved hands and looked down at her. "I hope we can make the best of it."

She glanced up at him. "Perhaps," she whispered.

A stunning moonlit view of the mountains through the large windows of her bedroom caught Catriona's attention as soon as she entered. While Mrs. Baird closed the door and set a hurricane lamp with a flaring candle on a table, Catriona turned slowly.

The sheer size of the room took her breath — lofty plastered ceilings, tall windows, and high, pale walls created a sense of spaciousness that even the large four-poster bed could not diminish. Drapes, coverlet, half canopy, and a chaise longue in serene creamy damasks and pale floral chintz harmonized with an expansive Belgian carpet in a green leaf pattern. Small oil paintings, polished mahogany furniture, and a glassed bookcase graced the room as well.

Compared to the simple decor and modest proportions at Glenachan House, this bedroom seemed like a queen's chamber. She murmured in admiration as Mrs. Baird pointed out the private dressing room, water closet, and large, tiled bathroom. Deirdre, one of the housemaids, was already in the bathroom filling a porcelain tub with steaming water from brass spigots for her evening bath. The girl looked up with a shy smile as she stacked thick linen towels.

"A cistern on the roof supplies hot and cold water for this floor and for the kitchen," Mrs. Baird explained. She held herself stiffly and seemed so formal and expressionless that Catriona wondered if years of serving the previous earl had made her humorless. "Sometimes we have a bathwater shortage if there are several guests. Then water will be brought up for your requirements."

"Thank you," Catriona replied. She stopped short of revealing that she had always taken baths in the closed pantry of Glenachan House late at night — a cistern and a private bath were astonishing luxuries to her.

Mrs. Baird opened another door. "This leads to the small sitting room that you share with Lord Kildonan. His room is through that opposite door there."

Peeking inside, Catriona saw a cozy room with a small fireplace, a window, and armchairs and a small sofa in leather arranged on a worn Oriental carpet. The opposite door was partly open, and she saw a smaller room, dark and cozy, with deep green walls and mahogany furnishings. Then she heard Evan's voice as he spoke quietly to someone, perhaps a servant. A moment later, he appeared at the connecting door, about to close it.

His gaze touched hers, piercing and intent, and then he clicked the door shut.

"Deirdre will be your lady's maid for now, until you choose one you prefer," Mrs. Baird said. "The previous countess was not in residence at Kildonan, and Lady Jean brings her own girl."

Catriona nodded, unsure what use she might have for a lady's maid or indeed how she might choose one. "I'm sure Deirdre will do a fine job," she said, smiling through the door at the girl, who was arranging lotions on a tray with fresh flowers.

After Mrs. Baird left, Deirdre helped Catriona out of the blue silk gown. The young maid had an unobtrusive manner and a gentle touch, and Catriona felt herself begin to relax as Deirdre unwound and brushed out her hair. While Deirdre unpacked her two portmanteaus, Catriona closed herself in the bathroom and sank into hot, fragrant water. Sighing, she closed her eyes.

Only a day ago, she would have sold her soul for such heat and comfort. And in a way, she had. Remembering Evan's touch on her naked body, the heat and pleasure of his skin against hers, her mind further conjured the feel of his lips and hands. She wondered if Evan expected to share her bed tonight, or if he instead shared her reluctance toward their hasty marriage.

Moaning low, she sank slowly into the hot, rose-scented water until she was nearly submerged, her hair floating out in rich streams of dark bronze. Her body craved the exquisite power of his touch, but her heart was a jumble of uncertainties.

Chapter Twelve

Standing before the connecting door late that night, Evan paused. This was his wedding night — he certainly knew his rights, but he was not sure what his bride wanted of him. Tightening the belt of his maroon silk dressing gown, he knocked, heard her soft answer, and entered the room.

Catriona glanced up from the book in her hands, her eyes wide and a little wary. Enthroned in the big bed, sunk deep in lacy pillows under an ivory coverlet, she looked lush and beautiful. Her long, graceful form was swathed in a prim white nightgown with a high buttoned neck and weavings of pale blue ribbons.

She looked vulnerable, too, he thought, though there was a touch of wildness in the gleaming reddish hair flowing over her shoulders. The sight of her stole his breath, and his body clenched in response. He moved toward her.

"Good evening, madam," he murmured.

"Lord Kildonan." She picked up her book and flipped pages nonchalantly. But he saw that her fingers trembled.

He wondered where to begin, what to say.

Shoving his hands in the pockets of his silk brocade robe, he glanced around. New fabrics had been installed recently, but the furnishings were those his mother had used years ago. The leafy carpet had been here then, too. He remembered tracing its design with small fingers, long ago, in happier times.

"I trust you are — No, please, go ahead," he said, when she began to speak and stopped.

"I only meant to say that it's a lovely room and quite comfortable." She folded her hands in a prim manner. "Was this your mother's room?" she asked.

"Aye. My parents used this suite years ago, before . . . she left him. She was no more fond of him than you were," he said wryly. Catriona blinked and did not comment, but he saw comprehension in her eyes. "My sister had the rooms redone after he died." His newly redecorated room was smaller and cozier than Catriona's, in dark greens and dark wood — he liked its warm cavelike feel. "I had not seen the changes until the other day."

"And you did not expect to give this room to a wife," she said crisply.

"Well, not so soon," he admitted. God, he was discussing the room as if he were the housekeeper rather than her groom. He did not know what note to strike with her.

Last night she had come willingly into his

arms when the compassion of strangers had blossomed into poignant, stirring intimacy. He wanted that natural magic back again for both of them, but did not know how to re-capture it.

He walked toward the bed. "What are you reading?"

She peeked at the spine as if she did not know herself. "I found it on the book-shelf. . . . Sir Hugh MacBride, *The Enchanted Briar*." She flipped a few pages. "Oh! This is inscribed by the author — 'To Master Evan. Yours affectionately, Sir Hugh. Dundrennan House, Christmas, 1840.' "

"I turned twelve just before Christmas that year, and he gave me the book as a gift. I'd forgotten it was here. My sister had borrowed it at one time," he added. "She came here far more often than I ever did."

"I see. So you'll turn thirty-one in De-cember?"

"Aye. And . . . might I ask? I don't even know your age, though I suspect you're not nearly as old as your bridegroom."

"Twenty-six in September. Quite the spin-ster."

"Not any longer," he said, watching her. Nearing the bed, aware of her intent gaze, he knew they both used the conversation to edge closer, to explore each other. He had never felt so tentative, and he did not like it. He was a man of action and quick decision.

In the shieling hut he had known just what to do. Following heart and instinct that night, he had allowed need and passion to lead him along a path of fire.

Now he danced along a pretty path of social convention, though he burned to pull her into his arms and make love to her again, fully and fervently. Legitimately. He must let her know that he was willing to honor the marriage, though the dance was intricate, its design delicate. With one wrong step, hearts and hopes could shatter.

She looked down at the book. "It's very interesting that you knew Sir Hugh personally. I have always loved his poetry."

He did not want to talk about poems. He wanted to take the blasted book from her and fling it across the room and pull her into his arms. But he could not, and he knew it.

Instead, he sat on the foot of the bed, his weight sinking the mattress a bit. "Catriona," he said, leaning on his hand.

She raised her knees to draw her feet away from him. "Did you know Sir Hugh well?" She turned more pages.

He sighed. "I know his son and heir. And I was fortunate to be invited to his home during several school holidays. I attended Eton and then Edinburgh University with Aedan, who is now laird of Dundrennan, and Aedan's cousin Dougal Stewart. We are good friends still. Perhaps you might meet them someday."

"Perhaps. How interesting to have known such a great man."

"To be honest, I saw little of him. I spent my time fishing and hillwalking with his sons and nephew and yearning rather pitifully after his bonny daughter and nieces. Romantic poetry was only a means to an end with the lassies . . . although I think I made a fool of myself." He grinned sheepishly.

She laughed, and he loved its musical sound, like notes up and down a scale. "Then I'd better put this away." She gave him a mischievous look and slipped out of bed to cross the room and replace the book on the bookshelf near the chaise longue.

Golden lamplight haloed her form and shone through the translucent fabric of her nightgown. He could see her full, round breasts, her beautifully shaped legs, the sultry curves of her hips and slender waist. His body surged at the sight, but he only crossed his arms and lifted a brow slightly.

He had known her only briefly, true — but he knew more than most grooms knew about their brides on the wedding night. He already knew her lush curves, the way she tasted, the sound of her breathing as she slept in his arms, and he could not forget that easily. She worked some magic over him, all unknowing, and he was caught fast — and could not explain any of it.

"My dear," he said, and stood, coming toward her. Lord, he thought, he did not even know how to address her. "I thought we should . . . discuss our arrangement."

She turned, folded her arms over her bosom. "Arrangement?"

"Aye. Our meeting and our marriage came as a shock to both of us. I know you are not the most content of brides."

"We scarcely know each other," she pointed out.

He inclined his head. "Marriages have been made from less."

"Aye — but it still puzzles me that you went through with this." She narrowed her eyes thoughtfully. "Does the earl need a countess so much? A convenient Highland girl and her family to take care of Kildonan in his absence, perhaps, and smooth his way with the local people?"

He frowned, felt his temper stir. "Do not be insulting. You know I did what I thought was right. And I think we could give this a fair chance. It is a beastly business to undo a marriage." His parents had lived separately for twenty years to avoid the ordeal of divorce in the courts. "And we cannot simply annul our union."

"We cannot," she agreed. "I thought you wanted to wait a few weeks to see if —" She stopped. "If a child comes of it."

"Whether or not it does," he said, "we know we can get along well with each other."

"We had to get along in that shieling hut, or perish. And I thought you were — Mr. Mackenzie. A man I could trust."

"You could trust the earl, if you tried." He huffed a laugh. "And besides, what was I to tell you? 'I am the gentleman you loathe most in the world. Come sleep beside me'?"

"I would have appreciated the choice," she snapped.

"If I had told you, madam, we would both have frozen."

"Why do you want this?" she asked bluntly.

He paused, frowning. He did not know how to explain that he felt compelled to be with her, that he felt desire, respect, and a kinship of lonely souls with her.

A small war was waging inside him between fierce craving — physical desire and some deeper, indefinable need for love — and his logical self, which cautioned him to go slowly, dance the dance, and see what came of this.

He did not know how to explain that he had closed off his heart for two years — yet he felt healed in her company, felt understood and whole inside. No woman had ever affected him like that before.

But he could not voice any of that and open himself up so much, even to her. Pride and natural reserve made him shrug. "I am accustomed to risk, and I am willing to take this chance," he said simply. "But I see that you are not."

"I will not merely accept this because it is convenient," she said crisply. "Good marriages are made of far more than . . . attraction and necessity." She blushed.

"You mean love? That's a rare thing, my lass. I've seen it happen for others, and read of it, but I doubt it's portioned out to everyone who makes a match. Still, many marriages do quite well without the ideal of some great, eternal love . . . or so I hear."

She watched him, brows tucked. A little light seemed to go out of her eyes, and he cursed himself for speaking his mind.

"So you do not expect . . . love from this, yet you wish to continue?"

He hesitated. "I think we have chosen well, though fate took the upper hand. I think I have found the right countess for Kildonan," he said, "and you got your much-needed rescue. You would be in poor straits without this marriage, I'm afraid."

He knew that was cold, but he could only reveal so much of his feelings at one blow. He felt compelled to be with this girl above all others, but he did not know why. He was not one to question himself endlessly. He followed instinct and courage. His instincts said this would be good for both of them. And he would be damned if he would spend his wedding night discussing love, when he had always believed it could not come to him.

"I know our first meeting was unusual, but —"

He laughed outright, could not help it. She pursed her mouth, and he nodded. "Go on."

"And so our acquaintance is based on desperation and fear and . . . the need to survive."

"It was rather pleasant helping each other survive."

She scowled at him. "What if we are not compatible without duress or danger? We got along then because we had to. But otherwise, and ordinarily, we have little in common."

"We have this glen in common," he said, wafting his hand toward the window, where the moon was a clean slice of light over the dark, primeval mountains. "We have our educations and our Highland heritage. We have our shieling hut . . . and our wedding."

"Our wedding." She looked away. "Our somber wee wedding."

"Not a very celebratory affair, true. But I thought the bride was lovely," he added quietly. His glance slid down the length of her body for a moment, where the candlelight shining through her gown had continually drawn his gaze.

She seemed to realize suddenly that he could see through her nightgown, for she snatched a paisley shawl from the chaise longue and swept it around her shoulders. Its folds did not obscure his view of her excellent legs.

She crossed her arms. "If only we could start over. . . . But the marriage is done now."

"I have no desire to fall off a mountain again," he drawled.

"I meant only that most relationships that lead to marriage begin with introductions, friendship, then . . . courting, and finally an agreement that marriage suits both. We began in a backward manner."

He stared at her, stunned by his next thought. Whether a dance, a pathway, a mountain to climb, or a marriage — one had to go step by step. "We could . . . start again, you know. Without the mountain or the ice storm. Just . . . start again."

"We could." She looked up at him, her eyes vivid. Then she thrust out her hand. "I am Catriona MacConn, sir. The minister's daughter." She smiled.

She had elusive dimples when she smiled, which he had not seen often. God, she was beautiful, he thought. Smiles and laughter transformed her pleasant face into something extraordinary.

"And you are *not* Mr. Mackenzie," she said.

His lips twitched, and he laughed a little, something he did too rarely these days. "Lord Kildonan." He took her hand, her fingers slim and cool in the cage of his, and he bowed deeply. The chaise longue stood between them like a barricade.

Her dimples deepened, her blue eyes sparkled. In her translucent gown, her wild, fiery hair loosened, her breasts lifting beneath the fabric, she was more than enchanting — she was passion itself.

Looking at her, he felt something like a blow, like a heavy rolling punch to heart and gut, and he wondered suddenly if he had begun to fall, desperately and astonishingly, in love.

He had climbed mountains, sunk deep into the ocean, had risked his life countless times. He had not quailed at stepping open-eyed into an impulsive marriage to save this girl's dignity. But nothing ever made him quake as much as the thought that he had actually fallen in love.

Could that be the source of what compelled him to her?

Heart thundering, he did not let go of her hand, but walked around the barricade of the chair, so that she turned to face him. He drew her slowly toward him. Something burned in him to be said, and it had nothing to do with courteous little games to ease the awkwardness between them.

"We can start again if you wish," he said in a low voice. "This is your wedding night, when you should have all your will. But I do not think we can wipe clean the slate and make a little innocent friendship between us to see where it leads."

"If we had been introduced as the earl and the minister's daughter — perhaps we could —"

"Could we?" He pulled her still closer, and she did not resist. "What would you have felt if you had met me for the first time in the vestibule of your father's church or in some matron's drawing room at teatime? Tell me." He slid his hands to either side of her face, cupping the delicate, stubborn contour of her jaw.

"I would have felt . . . the pull between us, like a magnet," she breathed.

"Do you feel it now?" he murmured, dipping his head low.

"Oh, aye," she whispered, and she leaned back her head. He touched his mouth to hers.

He felt her lips move sweetly under his, and he pulled her close to kiss her as he wanted to do, swift and hard, until she moaned. Sliding his fingers into her hair, feeling the tresses cascade over his arm, he kissed her until he trembled from the power that rushed through him.

Sweeping her full into his arms, he pressed his hips to hers and felt her lush shape and blessed warmth through flimsy layers of silk and gauzy cotton. He knew she could feel every inch of him hard against her, where he fit intimately between her thighs with only a few thin layers of fabric between them. He continued to kiss her, bending her back so that her breasts, nipples taut, brushed his chest. He felt himself harden further, hot and insistent, his desire impossible to hide.

He had kept himself aloof and alone so long, and now he felt the magnificent potential in this, more than he had ever expected. Yet he would never let himself appear desperate for love — even if, deep inside where he kept his secrets close — he wanted to be loved, and to love, more than anything else in life.

But for a few moments, he could not help but touch her, kiss her, so long as she was accepting of it.

Slipping his tongue between her lips, he felt her sigh and soften. Tracing his mouth down, feeling the warmth of his own breath mingle with her heat, he nuzzled her throat, her ear.

The way in which she arched in his arms was a natural invitation, and when he slid his hand down over her shoulder to find the high slope of her breast, she moaned, writhed a little, so that her breast shifted and he felt the pearled texture of her nipple through the cloth.

Teasing her there with the open palm of his hand, he felt her give way a little in his arms. He felt himself tighten so hard that he gasped against the strength that gathered in him. Once again he captured her lips in a deep kiss, and she wrapped her arms around his neck, moving so that his hand, mounded upon her warm, yielding breast, was snug between the press of his body against hers.

He knew, and his body knew, what luscious secrets she held. Wanting desperately to taste that again with her, he felt his body tighten and swell, and his heart pounded like an engine. Another moment of this, and he would scarcely be able to control himself. Squeezing his eyes shut, he drew a long breath.

Then she pulled away abruptly to stare up at him, her chest heaving, her lips full from kissing, her breasts nudging deliciously through the fabric of her nightgown. "Not now," she said breathlessly. "Not yet. We must — I think we must wait and see where this goes naturally, of its own accord. We are urging it far faster than we should."

He could tell her where this was going of its own accord. But he inclined his head and stepped back, feeling cool air slice between them. His body still burned hot, cloaked in silk folds. Though he longed to touch her, he made himself step back once more.

"As I was saying, madam," he began, trying to master his own breath. "We can start again if you wish, but I will not mince about playing games. You know that I am willing." He reached out to stroke down her arm, his thumb brushing the side of her breast lightly, moving past, though it drove him mad. He wanted all or he wanted nothing from her. "You must choose, Catriona. That kiss and all that comes with it — or none of it."

"N-none?" She blinked at him.

"No games, no insincere vows, no prison in a loveless marriage. Choose to live with that kiss — or without it. Live with the marriage in full, as Countess of Kildonan, or go back to your life as Catriona MacConn. Either way, I will honor my vow to take care of you," he murmured, as he brought her hand upward to kiss it slowly. "But you must decide. . . . Will you trust me, or not?"

Every part of him burned for her. He felt the desire in her, too, like a fine shivering. He let go of her hand. "It's up to you. Now go to sleep, my dear lass. We both need rest. If we are to begin again . . . it should be with a good night's sleep."

Forcing himself, he turned away, though the image of her face was haunting — eyes wide and so blue, cheeks flushed, lips moist and half-open, hair rich as flame. His body pulsed, protested, but he left the room, shutting the door behind him.

Since last night all he had wanted was to feel her heat and fire again. Now, as what he craved most filled him, all he let himself think of was a very cold bath.

Chapter Thirteen

Catriona woke with a start, realizing that she had slept deep into the morning, and heard a knock on the door that preceded Deirdre carrying a tea tray. Within moments, the maid filled a washbowl with steaming water, set out towels, and asked what Lady Kildonan wanted to wear that day, before Catriona had managed to take more than a sip of her tea.

Thanking her, Catriona dismissed the girl quickly, appreciating her efficiency but not comfortable with help for tasks she normally did herself. After a quick wash to rinse the sleep from her eyes, she turned to choose her clothing from among the few outfits she had brought.

Days ago — though it seemed like a lifetime — she had promised to meet Morag MacLeod today by the old bridge. Dressing quickly in warm petticoats under a gray wool walking skirt, she also donned a linen blouse over a chemise and loosely fitted stays. Aware that she would be doing a lot of walking, she chose the sturdy brogans she had brought from Glenachan.

So much had happened since she had last

seen Morag, she thought, buttoning her blouse. So much had changed. *She* felt changed, and she wondered how to explain it to her old friend.

Catriona had always thought of herself as strong but unremarkable, dedicated to serving her family and devoting her modest talents to her heart's work of learning the beautiful old Gaelic songs. She had never thought to marry — certainly not in such a way, to such a man.

A whirlwind had blown through her life with that ice storm, and she was still trying to figure out where it had tossed her.

Catching sight of the same paisley shawl that she had used to cover herself the night before, she folded it carefully and set it in a drawer. Remembering Evan's kisses, she stroked the pretty cloth for a moment, amazed that such passion and promise had entered her quiet life.

She must decide whether to accept the risk Evan offered her and step into the unknown with a man she did not know — or to go back to her familiar life. But that old door might not be open to her any longer. The family that had shaped and defined her now judged her to be of disappointing and unacceptable character. Aunt Judith and her father did not want her back in their house — at least not for a long while.

Sitting, she gazed in the mirror over the

dressing table. Adventure and sexual awareness had not altered her, though her eyes did seem a more vivid blue, her pale skin creamier, her cheeks and lips more flushed. Her bronze-bright hair was still unruly, but she liked its wild gloss as never before. In some ways, she looked almost bonny, she told herself.

Yet she sat too tall in her chair, and her shoulders were square and capable, not delicate. Her bust was rather full, and though her waist and long legs were nicely slim, she was glad that the sensible cut of her clothes hid the flare of her hips. Catriona Mhór, she had always been called, Big Catriona — taller than most men she knew. Such a girl was not lovely, she thought.

Evan's offer last night had surprised and touched her. The Earl of Kildonan could claim any woman he wanted, she was sure — besides a titled fortune, he had keen intelligence, quiet, captivating charm, and good looks. Last night she had expected him to propose a delay of a few weeks or months before they went their own ways, but his suggestion had astonished her.

Fate and a supposed obligation to her had brought the earl a plain, gawky, fire-haired Highland countess, and yet he was willing to honor the marriage. Frankly, she was amazed. While she understood his sense of obligation, she had not expected him to want to remain married regardless of whether or not she carried a child — and she would not have an answer about that particular matter for at least three weeks, she thought, pausing to rest her hand on her abdomen.

Still, Catriona was not sure she could trust him. He had not mentioned selling off parts of the estate, as Grant had indicated, although he had mentioned his intention to leave Kildonan soon. Perhaps she would discover that he was like his father after all, once he had settled the affairs of his Highland estate. She certainly would not go south with him, dooming their marriage to a split sooner or later.

Shaking off her thoughts, she twisted her hair into a simple low knot and secured its weight in a black net with a velvet bow. Deirdre had told her that the others were having breakfast in the small dining room, with food available until ten thirty that morning. It was nearly ten now by her little silver pocket watch, and she was honestly hungry. She hurried out of the room.

The wing that contained her room connected to the central tower by a long whitewashed, windowed corridor. Once she reached the old tower keep, the small drafty corridors and multitude of old oak doors seemed mazelike. Turned around at first, Catriona found her way to the main foyer, where she encountered Mrs. Baird, who led her up some stairs to the small dining room.

Entering, Catriona saw a dark room whose coziness came from sunlight, old red brocade and worn rugs, polished walnut furnishings, dishes gleaming on a huge sideboard. The four people seated at the table turned as she came in. Lady Jean, Sir Harry, Arthur Fitzgibbon, and Evan all looked toward her. While the men stood, Jean hastened forward, smiling.

"Come in! We're on our own for breakfast — it's our custom here." She drew her toward the table. "Evan, your sleepy bride is finally awake!" She beamed at both of them.

"So I see. Good morning, my dear." Evan came around the table toward her to take her hands and give her a light kiss on the cheek. She felt it all the way to her toes.

He smelled so good, soap and starch and a hint of sweet coffee, and something else that was wholly Evan, that reminded her of the clean air in the mountains. Catriona smiled at him shyly, then blushed as she saw the others watching them.

She sat when Evan pulled out the chair beside his own and thanked Jean, who brought her a cup of steaming coffee. Although Catriona liked tea in the morning, a sip of the stronger brew's fortifying effect seemed to be just what she needed. Going to the sideboard, she served herself porridge and bacon from warming dishes, then resumed her seat.

"I trust you slept well, Lady Kildonan," Sir Harry said. Jean must have kicked her husband under the table, for he winced and glanced at his wife.

"Quite well, thank you," she answered.

"You're dressed for walking, Lady Kildonan. What's on the agenda for today?" Arthur asked. She had liked Fitzgibbon the moment she met him — a square-jawed man of average height with a strong, athletic form, his thick brown hair forever falling over his brow, his eyes china blue. He often smiled, and though he sometimes babbled on about subjects not of tremendous interest to others, he was obviously a valued friend here.

"Walking?" Evan said. "Mr. Grant did recommend that Lady Kildonan and I both rest after our ordeal on the mountain and yesterday's stresses. I thought you might appreciate a quiet day exploring the castle, my dear," he said to her, "and I thought to spend time with the account books and the estate records."

"Rest? But you know what today is," Jean said. "It's your Walking Day, Evan." She glanced at Catriona. "You two were married last night. I know it was not the most typical of weddings, but there is a lovely Highland tradition whereby the bride and groom walk out on the day following their wedding and greet the local people. Catriona deserves to have some wedding traditions to remember."

"Aye, she does," Evan agreed.

215

"Then you must honor Walking Day. It's so fitting for your wee Highland wedding." Jean smiled.

Evan looked at Catriona. "What do you think, my dear? Are you aware of the tradition?"

"I am," Catriona said. "On the day after the wedding, the bride and groom go walking through the village to greet everyone. But the nearest village is several miles from here, and since we did not have the usual wedding . . . I do not think Walking Day is really necessary for us." Or appropriate, she thought, glancing down at her half-empty plate.

"Take the ponies and call it Riding Day," Sir Harry suggested, chuckling. "The estate encompasses all of Glen Shee and more — some eighty-two thousand acres," he added for Catriona's benefit. She nodded.

"I'm sure my bride knows the history of Glen Shee better than any of us," Evan remarked, glancing at her.

"Was your family always here, dear?" Jean asked.

"MacConns have been in Glen Shee for hundreds of years," Catriona answered. "Long before the Mackenzies were earls."

Evan cleared his throat and set down his coffee cup. "No doubt, since my grandfather was the first Earl of Kildonan. Before that we were untitled lairds outside this glen, until the Kildonan lands were acquired through marriage in the seventeenth century. So, are you interested in a Walking Day with your groom, madam?" he asked.

She sensed some tension in his voice, but she was sure the others had not noticed. They were a blithe trio, chatting away contentedly — but the newlyweds were not a blithe duo, Catriona thought. Last night's tension still echoed between them.

"I have an obligation every Wednesday," she answered. "I supervise a knitting scheme."

Evan looked blank. "What the devil does that mean?"

"Silly," Jean answered for her. "A knitting scheme is a project done in the community."

"A scheme of knitters — sounds like a female conspiracy," Arthur said, chuckling at his own jest.

"In a way." Catriona smiled. "I am a member of the Ladies' Highland Association, and we have devised a few projects to help the people of the remote regions who have suffered in the changes of the last decades. The knitting scheme is one such project. Yarn is supplied to the croft wives, and then one of the local women and I go around and collect what they have made — socks, mittens, and scarves. Then more yarn is given them, and so on."

"What do you do with these things?" Evan asked.

"We send them to Lady Saltoun, the wife

of the chief of Clan Mackenzie. She collects the knitting and sends the items to the Highland regiments. We have a contract for a thousand pairs each of socks and mittens and five hundred scarves. Most of the items will be shipped to India and some to Canada. Then a little money is paid to the croft wives, who have little other source of income now."

"Very commendable," Evan said, nodding.

"Excellent charitable work," Arthur approved. "Lady Kildonan has the makings of a fine countess." He smiled at both of them.

Catriona reached for her coffee cup when Evan reached for his, so that the clink of china was the only sound for a moment. Again, no one seemed to notice their brittle moods.

"I agree, Fitz," Evan said. "My dear, if you would like to combine your Walking Day with your Knitting Day, I shall go with you to meet your friend. What do you say?"

She gulped, then nodded. "I'll fetch my plaid."

An old woman waited not far from a stone bridge that led toward a high, forested hill. Evan and Catriona walked toward her, their long sticks in hand to aid them in hiking over the hills. The woman watched them, frowning a little.

She looked like a grandmother, Evan

thought, for she was elderly, and though she looked strong and stocky, her skin was weathered and her hair gray beneath a faded plaid shawl that hung to the hem of her dark dress. She wore patched leather shoes and gripped a long gnarled stick. On her head was a mutch, a cap of pleated white linen gathered at the top with long side pieces, rather a pretty thing, which he knew was worn by married Highland croft wives. Her appearance had such a medieval air that Evan was almost surprised when she spoke, as if she were some ghostly visitor.

"Catriona Mhór," she said in Gaelic, "is this your new husband? He's a very fine man to look at."

Understanding most of the words, Evan glanced at Catriona, bemused. "I am?" he murmured.

"He is," Catriona answered, and she blushed. "I mean, he is my new husband," she amended while Evan laughed. "We'll speak English now, Morag, if you please. Lord Kildonan, this is my friend Mrs. MacLeod — Morag MacLeod, wife of John MacLeod, a crofter who lives on the lower slopes of Beinn Alligin."

The old woman studied Evan with a sour, doubting expression. He inclined his head and offered his hand. "It's Evan Mackenzie, Mrs. MacLeod. I'm pleased to meet you."

"Why?" she said suspiciously.

"Morag," Catriona said in a warning tone.

"Pleased to meet you, sir," Morag said, giving him a bold stare. Then she looked at Catriona. "Countess of Kildonan now, eh? Hmmph. I suppose I will congratulate you on your marriage, though it is a surprise to me why you did it. And I will call you Mrs. Mackenzie, for that is what you are now."

"Catriona will do, as always," she said. "Please."

"If you were a crofter's wife, as you might have been one day, I'd be putting the mutch on your head today, with a new plaidie for your shoulders," Morag went on. "But now that you are the lady of Kildonan, you will lose that fine plaid you are wearing and put on stiff little bonnets and lace."

Catriona lifted a hand self-consciously to her bare head, her hair covered only in a fine black net and partly draped by her long, lightweight plaid shawl of cream, blue, and brown. "I suppose I do look like a Highland wife."

"You have married a Highland earl," Evan said reasonably.

"So this is he," Morag said, looking up at Evan. "You're Mr. Mackenzie — pardon me that I do not call you 'lord,' but we are not very fond of such titles here," Morag said bluntly.

"That's fine, Mrs. MacLeod. I prefer Mr. Mackenzie."

"Tall enough for you, girl, and that is good," Morag observed, looking him up and down. "And what a tale! Fell from the mountain right at your feet, I hear, that day you and I were walking out in the mist. And he would have died if you had not taken him to safety in that old shieling and kept him alive through the night!" She peered at him. "He looks bonny enough now. That was fine nursing, eh?" She winked.

"He was not that badly hurt," Catriona said.

"She did indeed save my life, Mrs. MacLeod," Evan said. "And I asked her to be my wife to pay my debt of gratitude."

"Ach, but I heard her wicked auntie will not have the girl in the house now. You must have been very generous indeed, Catriona," Morag said in an exaggerated tone. "And who would not be, with such a beautiful man?"

"Morag!" Catriona said, sounding shocked, while Evan turned away to smother a grin. "Where did you hear all this?"

"From my daughter, this morning. She is Mairi MacAuley, who runs the inn," she told Evan. Her English was surprisingly good, though it was accented lightly. "I heard it from Mr. Finlay, too, when I saw him in the hills early this morning."

"Finlay was out here?" Catriona glanced around.

"He came up to see my old John MacLeod. But he's ridden off to Inverness by now. Said he would be there for a day or two. The news is traveling fast about your wedding," Morag went on. "My two married daughters are buzzing with it, and the word is running from house to house in the glen. What's left of us who still live here, Mr. Mackenzie, if you know what I am saying."

"I know exactly what you are saying, Mrs. MacLeod. And aye, the wedding did come as something of a surprise."

"A surprise," Morag repeated. "I told you not to go out in the bad weather that day, Catriona Mhór," she said. "I had a strange feeling that day, and see what happened."

"I hope it was a good feeling," Evan said.

"I cannot always tell — they are just feelings and could be something foul or something fair. I am not a seer. But I will tell you that the title of Countess of Kildonan will not sit well with many around here for Catriona Mhór. And what are your plans now, sir?" she asked Evan abruptly.

"Plans?" He blinked.

"Will you stay or will you leave this glen?" Morag asked. "Some say you do not want to be here. Which is it?"

"I, ah, have many decisions to make," he said.

"Inherited nearly a year ago, and now he decides to come back and make his plans,"

Morag said in an aside to Catriona.

He was not surprised that the old woman had her doubts about him. He had expected that from the tenants in the glen, thanks to his father's actions and reputation. He turned to Catriona.

"Well, you and Mrs. MacLeod have plans yourselves," he said. "I'll leave you here, then, to go about your business."

"Very well," she answered.

For an awkward moment, Evan and Catriona looked at each other, and he knew she felt unsure, as he did, about how they should say farewell. Then he bent and gave her a chaste kiss on the cheek.

Catriona turned with Morag and walked toward a bridge not far from where they stood. Evan noticed its single stone arch construction, built over a gorge that contained, in its hollow, a wide, fast stream. He glanced past that toward the hills.

High about them soared forested slopes and bleaker, rocky inclines dotted with tenacious grazing sheep and goats. Higher still, the Torridon peaks were ringed with clouds. Everywhere were the sounds and scents of wind, water, turf, and pine. The landscape here had overwhelming power, mysterious strength, and a raw and rugged beauty. Much of this — nearly all his eye could see from this spot — belonged to him.

Glancing toward the bridge again, he noticed that Catriona and Morag had begun to cross its long arch. As he walked along himself, the angle of his view changed, and he saw that the bridge was ruined in the center of the span.

The keystone was missing, and a gash, empty air, separated the two curving sides of the bridge.

Yet the women walked up the slight stone incline, talking, not even looking at the danger. Another step, and another, and they would plummet to their deaths.

Evan started running. "Catriona!" Pounding onto the bridge, he grabbed her, grabbed the older woman, too, and pulled them both away from the brink, dragging them off the bridge onto the safety of solid earth.

"Ach," Morag said to Catriona. "Did you not tell the man about the bridge?"

Chapter Fourteen

"Tell the man what," Evan said, heart still slamming, "about the bridge?" Letting go of Morag, he kept a grip on Catriona's upper arm, as if he had to keep her from falling, although they stood on solid ground.

He knew why he did that. He just did not want to think about it. The shock he had felt when he had seen her at the edge of the gap had left him trembling.

"The bridge is safe for walking, though we do not send carts or horses over it," Catriona said.

"Safe?" Evan blinked at her. "Are you mad?"

"We cross it often, without difficulty."

"As sound as the mountains, that bridge," Morag said.

"Why hasn't it been repaired?" Evan demanded.

"It has, many times," Catriona answered. "But it always collapses again in the center."

He studied the bridge with a narrowed glance. "The arch is too low," he observed immediately. "And the construction may be faulty." Looking down at the water, which ran fast and deep between a high bank on one side and a soaring mountain slope on the other, he lifted his glance again. "That slope has deep runnel tracks from melting snows. . . . Does the stream flood during spring rains?"

"Sometimes," Catriona said. "If the water comes as high as the bridge, more stones break off. Should the arch be higher?"

"No, but that low curvature is unstable across such a wide span. That's one reason it comes down so easily."

"Nah. It is the fairies who take it down," Morag said.

He looked at her. "The what? Fairies?"

"This is Drochaid nan Sìtheach, the Bridge of the Fairies," Morag answered. "It leads to Beinn Sìtheach, the Fairy Mountain, and so the *daoine sìth* do not want many humans to cross over. They take down the bridge when it pleases them to do so, and the humans put it right back up. When I was a wee lass, I remember my father and other men setting the stones into place, and the stones fell even as the men worked. They said then it was the fairies' mischief. That was long before your father evicted my father and others from their own homes, when they were old men and no longer of any use to the lord and the land," she added, with an accusatory glance.

"I'm sorry for that, Mrs. MacLeod," he said. "I am. But please tell me more about what happened to this bridge."

"The fairies wreck it, and we put it back up. But it has not come down for a long time. It is a sturdy enough footbridge."

"There's a hole in the middle!" he said, jabbing his finger in that direction.

"Aye, but it's only a wee bad step. You just have to know the right way to get across."

"A wee bad step." He frowned. "And how, exactly, do you cross it?"

"You must speak a fairy charm."

"A what?" He blinked at her, and at Catriona, who seemed to find nothing odd in the old woman's statement.

Morag nodded. "We say a charm when we go over, and the same when we come back. It keeps the traveler safe."

Evan fisted his hands at his waist. "A fairy charm."

"You'd best tell him, Catriona Mhór, in case he needs to cross the bridge," Morag said.

"By all means, tell me." Evan looked at Catriona.

"Hold your fingers just so," she said, shaping her thumb and forefinger in a closed circle. Reciting some Gaelic phrases, she translated them for him.

Like the birds of the air I fly,
Like the leaves on the wind I fly
Head to foot, crown to sole,
Angels protect me from the fairies of the knoll.

"And that keeps you safe," Evan drawled.

"That and long legs for leaping the gap," Morag said.

Shaking his head, Evan looked toward the bridge, where crumbled keystones hung over a drop of nearly twenty feet. "This is insanity," he said. "I'm closing this bridge."

"But this is a direct route to the lower slopes of Beinn Shee!" Catriona argued. "Morag and I use it every week for our walks about the hills, and there are crofters and herdsmen who live with their families on the mountain slopes. If they have animals or carts with them, they go along the drover's track to the lower bridge, which crosses the same stream several miles farther down in the glen." She pointed southeast, away from Kildonan toward Glenachan.

"Then it will not be inconvenient to close it temporarily."

"It would, for the walk to the lower bridge takes much longer. Some crofter children go to the village school at Kilmallie this way, through Kildonan lands."

"Children! Absolutely, the thing must not be used."

"You do not like bairns walking on your land?" Morag asked.

Evan sent her a sour look. "I like them very well, and I do not want any of them to fall off the bridge. It will be closed until it is fixed or replaced."

"But our charm keeps us safe," Morag pointed out.

"Tragedy happens too easily." He knew that too damn well, he thought, as he walked up the bridge to test the stones. Some bounced disturbingly underfoot. He turned. "As Earl of Kildonan, in the interests of my tenants, I am closing this bridge for repair."

"Since the Earls of Kildonan and Glen Shee never cared much for their tenants before," Catriona said, "why start now?"

He shot her a dark look and walked away to pick up a large rock, big as a hatbox, which he then deposited in front of the bridge as an impediment.

"Stand aside, ladies," he said, and they did, while he lifted and tossed several large rocks of similar size until he had built a crude barrier. Wiping his gloved hands of dust, he looked at Catriona and Morag, who stood staring at him.

"That should do for now. I'll send someone up here with a rope and a sign to keep off the bridge."

"In Gaelic or English?" Catriona snapped. "Not everyone will be able to read it — certainly the oldest and the youngest will not. You would do better to post a guard to keep them away."

"Shall I wait under the bridge myself like a troll?" he snapped back. "This thing is dangerous, and it is disturbing to know that it's been used all these years. Why was my father never informed of its condition?"

"He would not have cared," Catriona said.

"He never came this way that I knew," Morag said. "The hunting was not good enough in this part to please him, I suppose. He never bothered us here, even though it is not far from Kildonan Castle."

Evan let it go, knowing the likely truth in what she said. "Well, if you are determined to go walking today, you'll have to use the lower bridge. I'll drive you there. We can go back to Kildonan and fetch a pony cart or the gig."

"I live three miles from this spot, and I will not walk all the way back up here from the lower bridge," Morag said stubbornly. She looked at Catriona.

As if in silent agreement, the two women lifted their skirt hems and stepped neatly over the rock barrier.

Evan strode after them, but as he reached the apex behind them, he felt a subtle tremor. His additional weight, when the women stood near the weakest point of the arch, was unwise.

"Catriona," he said, "come back. You, too, Mrs. MacLeod. Carefully." He held out his hand.

"Your new husband is a worrier," Morag told Catriona.

Without a backward glance, they said the

charm in singsong voices and then cleared the breach lightly and rapidly, helping each other with outstretched hands. Standing on the other side of the span of ragged rock and empty space, Catriona turned.

"There, you see," she said. "Good day, husband. I will return by suppertime." She turned and took Morag's arm, and the two women walked down the opposite half of the bridge.

Evan stood staring after them as they struck out on a steep upward ascent on a heavily forested hillside. Far above, the fairy mountain and other, more distant, peaks soared into a cloudless blue sky.

He stared downward to where the water rushed fast and deep over boulders far below. In coming to Kildonan, he had never expected that he would have to confront a collapsed bridge. Though the structure was small, its very existence reminded him too sharply of a magnificent thing of iron and steel, its red-painted girders gleaming in the sunlight as it crashed downward into a harbor in Fife.

Difficult as those memories were, he could not turn away from the comparatively minor challenge of a simple stone bridge in need of repair. The sight of Catriona on the ruined structure had made his heart plummet with fear — but he would face this, and make certain that nothing happened to her, or to anyone else.

He walked toward the center and tested his weight here and there, holding on to the parapet. He felt a dangerous shimmy underfoot, where the ragged edge jutted like teeth into open air. The keystone and crowning stones were missing. Glancing down, he saw a pile of rubble, impossibly old and worn by water, lying in the midst of the deep, fast stream.

He moved back, frowning. If anyone stepped fast and hard along that edge, sooner or later the stones would give way.

And when that happened, all the fairy charms in the world would not prevent the old bridge from coming down.

A little stone house with a thick thatched roof sat at the top of a steep slope. Looming over it was a massive wall of dark rock with patches of green moss and rusty-colored bracken. A few wild goats clung to its heights, Catriona saw, as she and Morag walked closer.

Tendrils of smoke rose from a hole in the center of the roof, and two goats nibbled on a block of turf beside the closed door. She saw no other signs of life about the place.

"Is Mother Flora at home?" Catriona asked Morag.

"She's always here, except when she walks the hills for her exercise. She refuses to come away from her home otherwise. But I warn you, she usually sends me away when I come up here — after she takes whatever food or gifts I have brought."

"I hope she will agree to sing her songs for me. I brought paper and pencil in case she does, so that I can take notes."

"I would not be too quick to take out your paper," Morag said. "She knows we're coming — I came up here the other day with my daughter-in-law and got her promise that she would see you. Look, her door is not open. She's going to make us knock and beg to come in, the old witch."

As they walked, Catriona looked around. This remote slope was part of the foothills of Beinn Sìtheach, although the angle prevented her from seeing its uppermost peak. The wind cut brisk and cold, and Catriona drew a deep breath of the air, a nearly intoxicating essence that combined pines, grass, water, and the strength, somehow, of the mountain.

She could feel the magic in these hills — if there really were such creatures as fairies, surely they existed here, on the powerful and mysterious mountain slopes named for their kind.

The climb was a straight path worn in the grass, but so steep that Catriona felt the burn of effort in her legs — and she was used to walking inclines. She reached out to take Morag's arm to assist the older woman, only to be waved away.

When they reached the kailyard of the cottage, both goats blinked at the visitors. A cat slipped around the corner and climbed from the turf block to the thatched roof, tail curling.

Morag knocked on the worn wooden door. No answer came. "I know you're in there, Flora MacLeod!" she called.

Finally the door creaked open, and a tiny old woman peered out at them. She was bent and fragile, her face a delicate mesh of lines, her eyes a bright aqua blue, young eyes in an ancient face. Her hair was snowy and thin under a pleated mutch, and her brown dress was nearly a rag, its hem shredding about her feet, which were covered in patched leather shoes. She clutched a faded plaid around her shoulders.

"Ach, it's you, Morag MacLeod. What do you want?"

"I've brought you fresh vegetables," Morag said, lifting the basket she carried. "And a visitor. Let us in out of the wind, Mother Flora. We've had a hard climb up here to see you."

"It's a fine day and the climb will do you good, Morag MacLeod. You're fat as a pig." Flora looked up at Catriona. "How tall are you, girl?"

Catriona blinked. "A little under six feet."

"Huh. More than that, I'd say." She studied her. "Red hair, too. My husband was a tall red-haired man. Would he be your grandfather?"

"I — I don't think so," Catriona said.

"He was a lusty man with many by-blows before I met him. After that he only wanted to be lusty with me." Flora grinned, showing a scattering of teeth.

"Mother," Morag said, but Catriona saw her smile and knew that Morag and Flora had blunt honesty in common, at least.

"What's your name, tall one?" Flora asked.

"Catriona MacConn. My father is the reverend of Glenachan, and I think you knew my mother, Sarah."

"Ach, so I did! She was not so tall as you, but with the same beautiful red hair." Flora smiled. "Mine was blond, once."

"Are you going to let us in or not?" Morag asked.

"I like turnips," Flora said, peering at the vegetables in the basket Morag gave her. "What else do you have for me?"

"Would you like some socks?" Catriona asked impulsively. Reaching into the large basket she held, which contained the knitted things she and Morag had collected from a few croft wives elsewhere in the area, she drew out a pair of knee stockings in a bright pattern of red, black, and white.

Snatching them with arthritic fingers, Flora looked up. "What are you waiting for? Come in. Watch your head, tall one."

Ducking her head under the lintel to step inside, Catriona expected to find little more than a hovel. Instead, the interior was dimmed by smoke and scant light but cozy, with a few good pieces of furniture and a bed neatly made with a thick blanket and a flat pillow. The floor, though, was littered with peelings of food that crunched underfoot, and the house smelled suspiciously like a byre.

"She lives like a goat," Morag muttered.

"Sit down," Flora instructed, and Catriona and Morag took seats on a bench beside the fire, while Flora sat on a wooden chair with a threadbare cushion behind her back.

"Have you got anything else in that basket?" Flora asked, reaching over curiously to poke her fingers inside. She pulled out a scarf. "I need one of these."

Morag snatched it back. "Teach the girl your fairy songs first, and we will give this to you."

Scowling at Morag, Flora then turned to Catriona. "Why do you want to learn my fairy songs?"

"I've been collecting the old Gaelic songs for years and writing down the verses and melodies." Catriona reached into the basket again and pulled out some folded pages. "I have learned over a hundred and thirty so far. They are listed here —"

Flora waved her hand. "I do not need to see that. Bah. Why do you want to turn the old songs into scratchings on a page?"

"She is saving them so people generations from now can sing them," Morag said. "People who do not know the old Gaelic songs."

"If they do not know the old songs, then why would they want to sing them?" Flora asked. "Are you married, girl?"

Catriona blinked at the sudden question and glanced at Morag, who frowned. "I am," she said carefully.

"And what husband lets his pretty young wife collect songs like butterflies when he should be putting babies in her belly? You'll have many healthy babies, with those fine hips and such a good bosom," Flora observed. Catriona blushed, speechless.

"She was married only yesterday," Morag said. "Give her time to see what will happen."

Flora grinned. "Is your groom a MacLeod? There are not many handsome young men left in Glen Shee. I hope it is not that sour doctor from Kilmallie who Morag brought here once or twice. He does not know as much as I do. So who is it?"

"He's . . . Mackenzie of Kildonan," Catriona said. She felt Morag stiffen beside her.

Flora narrowed her eyes. "You're the Countess of Kildonan?"

Catriona nodded. "I am."

"I will not share my songs with the wife of

Kildonan," Flora announced. She pointed toward the door. "Get out of my house!"

"But, Mother —" Morag began.

"Hush, Morag." Catriona picked up the basket and stood, summoning her dignity, though tears stung her eyes. She had feared this would happen, had known from the moment she became Countess of Kildonan that her new status could drive a wedge between her and the people and culture she loved. "I am sorry —"

"Just go!" Flora stabbed her finger toward the door. "Leave me to my memories and my grieving, and do not take my old songs from me, too. They are the only solace I have now. Go!"

"But Catriona is deserving of your songs," Morag said.

"She is countess of these lands, and her husband took part in the clearances on that day of sadness, years ago. I saw him with his father, watching as the people were sent from the glen!"

"Ach, that's true," Morag murmured. "I remember."

"Will you let the son take my songs away, as his father took my kin?" Flora demanded.

Catriona bowed her head. She, too, had seen Evan that day, riding with the despised earl. Yet she was Evan's wife now, and no matter the state of her marriage, she would keep her thoughts to herself.

"The old earl sent away fourteen of my children and ten of my grandchildren. They were all grown then, with their families," Flora said, ushering them to the door. "They left me alone here, with few of my own left to take care of me. And not the best ones either," she added, darting a glance at Morag.

"Now, you listen to me —" Morag said.

Catriona stepped through the doorway, ducking her head, and turned. "Flora MacLeod, I am sorry for the past," she said. "I, too, grieved that day for kinfolk and friends who left Glen Shee. But neither my husband nor I caused that tragedy. We share your suffering, and we share your hope that one day those who left will return to Glen Shee, where they are loved and remembered. Come, Morag."

She walked away, her skirt and plaid blown by the wind, her senses filled with the mountain air, but tears blurred her vision. Morag, grumbling, followed.

As they crossed the yard, she heard Flora begin a song of mourning in raspy, quavering tones, although the quality of the voice she had once possessed was still evident. Hearing the song, Catriona turned.

Where shall we go to make our plea
When we are hungry in the hills?
Hiri uam, hiri uam

The old woman sang a lament, the same *tuireadh* that Catriona had sung herself, years before, the day the people left Glen Shee. Standing on a hillside overlooking the road, she had honored their leave-taking in the only way she knew.

Now, raising her head and drawing a breath, Catriona added her voice to the melody. Her notes were higher and more pure than the old woman's, but the harmony was strong and haunting.

> *Where shall we go to warm ourselves*
> *When we are chilled with cold?*
> *Where shall we go for shelter*
> *Since my love's hearth is dark?*
> *Hiri uam, hiri uam. . . .*

As the song ended on a soul-wrenching note, the echo of its passing rang out over the mountains.

Flora emerged from her hut and walked toward Catriona, looking up at her with an intense blue gaze. "You," she said. "You were the one who sang a *tuireadh* for the people that day."

Catriona nodded in silence.

Flora looked at Morag. "Did you hear her that long-ago day?"

"I did," Morag said. "And I knew it was her all this time."

"Why did you not tell me?" Flora

grabbed Catriona's arm and dragged her back toward the house while Morag followed. "Come!"

Chapter Fifteen

"Morag sings like a frog, so I could never teach her my special fairy songs," Flora said, once they were all back inside the cozy croft house. While Morag gaped at her in protest, Flora went on. "But I have always wanted a pupil worthy of the music. Your voice is pure, Catriona Mhór, and you understand the old songs — why they are beautiful and valuable."

"Thank you, Mother Flora," Catriona said.

"But you are Countess of Kildonan. This is not good. However, I liked your mother well." The old woman frowned.

"Catriona Mhór is worthy of your songs," Morag insisted. "She wants to protect and save them. Set aside your resentment of Kildonan for now, and give her your teachings."

"But her husband cannot be trusted," Flora said. "How could my songs be safe in his house? The outlanders and holiday climbers would ask his wife to sing her pretty little songs. Bah, that is not the way, with pianos and primness. These are beautiful, powerful songs. Their magic must be appreciated, and the new earl will not understand that — just like his father."

"Evan is not like his father," Catriona said.

"He is a good man, and he will love these songs for what they are. You misjudge him." Suddenly she felt fiercely protective toward Evan.

"And he is a beautiful man, too," Morag said. "If you would ever come down off this mountain, Mother Flora, you would see him for yourself."

"Ach, there was no one finer than my husband," Flora said. "But I might set you a test, tall one. Did your mother teach you any of my songs?"

"She knew many of them, but only one of your fairy songs."

"Sing it for me now."

Catriona closed her eyes to remember. Tilting back her head and sitting tall, she began the beautiful air that her mother had sung years ago to lull her children to sleep.

> *My joy and my heart*
> *My laughter and my tears*
> *My child, my little child*
> *Hill o hu ro*
> *Hill o hu ro, hiri o . . .*

As Catriona trilled the last notes, beautiful mouth music rather than true words, the melody seemed to chime and fade.

"Ah, nicely done," Flora said.

"Is that the test? Then she passed," Morag said.

"Of course it's not her test. That is the fairy song my own great-grandmother heard from the fairies themselves, when they came to peek at her child in the cradle. So you want to know the rest of what I know, eh?"

"I do," Catriona said.

"Well, you do have the fairy's own gift of singing. But first we must know if the fairies approve. Hmm . . ." Flora looked around the room thoughtfully. Then she stood and went to the window to take something from its place on the wooden sill. "I want you to bring me a crystal stone." She held out her palm, in which was a smoky crystal a few inches in length.

"That's a Cairngorm stone," Catriona said. She knew that the quartz rocks, which occurred in translucent shades of brown, could be found on Highland mountain slopes and were named for the mountains to the east. Catriona had sometimes found them while walking the hills. "I would be happy to get one for you."

Flora set the crystal in the windowsill, where it winked, whisky colored, in the light. "Bah, that sort is easy to find. I want one that is far more rare. I want a fairy wand."

"A what? There is no such thing," Morag said.

"They exist, but they are not easy to find," Flora said. "They shine with their own magic light. If you can find one and bring it to me,

I will teach you my songs."

"The stones that are called fairy wands?" Catriona nodded. "I've heard of them in the old tales, but I don't know anyone who has ever seen them. I would not know where to find one or what it might look like."

"They exist only at the top of Beinn Sìtheach." Flora pointed upward at the ceiling to indicate the great mountain that shadowed her house.

Catriona stared at her. "No one has ever gone all the way up there. It is said to be impossible to climb that peak." She knew that well enough — Evan had fallen in his attempt, and her own brother had died halfway up those rocky slopes years ago, when she had been a child.

"No one said it would be easy. But if you want my songs, you must find the will and the heart to do this. They say the mountain peak sparkles in sunlight because the fairy crystals are so thick there. But I want the most special one of all — the sort that shines in moonlight."

"Moonlight? That's crazy!" Morag said. "There's no such stone, and you cannot send the girl up there in the darkness!"

"Hush, you. It is her choice," Flora said. "The most precious fairy wands hold a magic light, and they are best seen in darkness and moonlight. If you want the songs, go up there. If you deserve the songs, the fairies themselves will see that you find a way to go up there and that the stone falls into your hands. And that you get safely down again. So it will not be so hard as you think — if the fairy kind are with you."

"Ach, you've lived with your crazy dreams for too long," Morag said. "She is the Countess of Kildonan and a newlywed bride, not a half-magic creature from one of the old tales!"

"How do you think I got the fairy songs myself? They are not given to just anyone. An old singer set me a task long ago, too."

"What was it?" Morag asked. "Flying over the mountains on your broomstick?"

"If you must know, crabby one, it was to win Rory MacLeod's heart and make him my own," Flora shot back. "It was the power of love. And I did it, and it was harder than climbing that mountain ever could be, I can tell you that. Ah, but the winning of that man — that alone was worth any price." She smiled, then looked intently at Catriona. "Well? What say you?"

Catriona frowned. She had wanted to learn the old, legendary fairy songs all her life, ever since she had discovered the particular magic that Celtic music held for her. It was her dearest dream to learn and preserve the old Gaelic songs, while the culture waned and changed all around her.

The rare and beautiful fairy songs had always lured her more than others, and no one knew as many of them as Flora. Without them, the work of Catriona's heart would never be complete.

She must do this somehow, she told herself. Just last night, Evan had said that he took risks, while she preferred the security of the familiar. He wanted her to take a chance on their marriage — but she felt entangled in doubt and fear.

Now she must find the courage to climb that mountain peak and go higher than anyone else, higher than her brother or Evan had gone. Somehow she must find the fairy crystal that Flora wanted — or her life's work would never be finished.

"I will do it," she said, hardly believing her own words.

"Good. But hurry," Flora said. "I'm a very old woman."

Later, returning to Kildonan Castle alone, Catriona pleaded genuine fatigue and had a late tea in her room. She had come back by way of the old bridge that she had crossed a thousand times before. Evan had not been there to see her leap the gap again, and just as well, she thought. He had been on his way to meet her, and their paths had intersected on the rolling moorland that led to the castle, where the long grasses were dark gold with autumn and the winds cut cold and damp.

He did not mention the bridge, nor did she, and they had walked back to Kildonan in relative silence, chatting only politely about their afternoons. She had walked a long way, and he had spent time going over the books of the estate and talking in the stable with Mr. Gillie about the livestock. Both she and Evan were tired, she knew, and he seemed pensive, while her own thoughts were focused on her meeting and her mission, which she could not discuss with Evan.

When he asked about the music, she sang for him the fairy tune that her mother had taught her. Listening with the quiet, attentive manner that seemed so much a part of him, Evan had asked her to repeat the song. When she was done, he had touched her shoulder, murmuring his thanks and praise.

A simple caress, but the curious thrill she felt at his warm, affectionate tone and his genuine appreciation for her song equaled the power of a kiss.

They had parted in the foyer, Evan going to meet with Arthur in the library, while Catriona went to her room to change.

After her solitary tea and some reading, she had fallen asleep, waking to darkness and Lady Jean knocking on her door. Feeling foggy and craving even more sleep, Catriona was glad to hear Jean report that Evan, too, was resting soundly and that neither of them would be expected for dinner.

"You both survived quite an ordeal a couple of days ago in that awful storm on the mountain," Jean had said with sympathy, "followed by the wedding and the challenges of coming here to your new home." She smiled. "No wonder you both need rest, just as Mr. Grant advised."

At the mention of Kenneth Grant, Catriona had suppressed a shudder and nodded in silence. She let Jean take charge, running her bath, closing the draperies, building up the fire in the hearth. Jean left then, sending Deirdre up with a tray of hot soup, bread, and sweet tea. Once Catriona was settled in the bed with its abundance of pillows and quilts, she had fallen asleep.

Deep in the night, she awoke and got out of bed to use her private water closet. Then, pausing by the door to the little sitting room, she felt so tempted and curious that she had padded through to stand at Evan's door. Though the urge to knock was strong, she only lifted her hand to rest her palm on the wood.

She thought she heard him pacing, for the floor creaked and she heard the soft thud and scrape of slippered steps. Something had awoken him and kept him up.

When his steps paused, she sensed him keenly on the other side of the door. Leaning her brow against the wood, she breathed slowly and imagined she heard him breathing, as well.

But she did not knock. As much as she wanted to breach the threshold between them and explore what he seemed so willing to risk, she could not summon the courage.

For a moment, closing her eyes, she thought of slow, heated kisses, of passion like a river, of needs tapped by desire. All she had to do was knock . . . and soon the marriage would be made.

But she wanted more than affection and desire. She wanted love, deep and real, and all that went with it.

Lowering her hand, she returned to her room, sliding beneath the covers to bury herself in snowy linens and loneliness, all the while aware that she did not have to be alone tonight.

What she wanted was finer, but seemed just out of reach.

Chapter Sixteen

Glad to be outside in sun and wind, Evan was particularly pleased to have a physically demanding chore for the space of the morning. He worked alone on the broken bridge, fetching rocks from among those scattered on the hillside. Wedging them one by one between the broken stones that edged the gash in the bridge, he did his best to shore up the loose stones.

Straddling the breach, he secured several rocks on both sides. Then he walked to a wooded area to gather some stout sticks and broke them to appropriate lengths, fitting them across the gap space. This added some needed countertension to the sagging haunches of the bridge.

After breakfast he had sent word to Finlay MacConn, but Davey MacGillechallum, his gillie at Kildonan, had returned with the answer that Mr. MacConn was still in Inverness. Catriona had not known why her brother had gone there, and she quickly left to meet with Morag MacLeod. They needed to gather some finished knitting from a croft wife who had not been home the day before.

Evan had made sure, before he left for the

bridge, that Davey had taken the two women the long way in the pony cart, instructing the lad to take them as far as the terrain would permit. Since Catriona had insisted on returning by way of the fairy bridge, Evan had promised to meet her in the late afternoon.

By the time he was satisfied that his makeshift repair would hold, he was covered in dust and thirsty. He had a flask of whisky and water in his inside jacket pocket, and he took a sip, his thirst barely satisfied. Wiping his forearm over his brow, he walked down the steep embankment to drink from the cold, clear stream at the bottom of the gorge, then scrambled back up again.

In the distance, he saw two men walking along the road from the direction of the smaller estate of Kilmallie, which bordered his own lands.

"Ho there! Kildonan!" Arthur Fitzgibbon waved, and Evan recognized the gentleman with him as Kenneth Grant. Waving in reply, he waited as they approached. They both carried long-barreled hunting guns and wore tweed suits and caps, Arthur in the knickers and boots that he preferred, Grant in darker coat and trousers.

"Kildonan! While you were gone, Mr. Grant invited me out for a bit of shooting on his lands," Arthur said, brandishing his gun. "He lent me his rifle — not that I've seen many of this sort, a fine weapon with a true aim. We had an excellent morning."

"Did you?" Evan asked, shoving his hands into his pockets, still without his jacket, which lay draped over the parapet of the bridge. "What did you bag?" He saw they carried nothing beyond a gun and a canvas knapsack apiece.

"Three brace of grouse on the moorland between here and Kilmallie, five partridges on the crofter's hill to the south, and a brace of wild ducks along the reeds by the river. We sent them back to Kilmallie and Kildonan with Grant's gillie."

"Excellent. I'm sure Mrs. Baird and Cook will be pleased to have something fresh and interesting to prepare for dinner," Evan said. "Mr. Fitzgibbon enjoys hunting, though I had not planned to do any during our stay here," he told Grant.

"Not a hunter yourself, Kildonan?" Grant asked, leaning his gun against a boulder. "Your father was quite the sportsman and had quite an array of guns and an impressive row of stags' heads mounted on the wall in his billiard room."

"Aye," Evan agreed. Since his father had died after his gun accidentally went off during a morning spent deer stalking with guests on the Kildonan estate, hunting was not one of Evan's preferred subjects or pastimes. "You sound familiar with his collection, sir. Did you hunt with my father?"

"Sometimes. I came to Kildonan Castle fairly often when your father was in residence," Grant said. "That was during the years of your estrangement, of course. Not only did I treat the earl as his physician, but we hunted regularly together. He taught me a good bit about deer hunting. Superb stalker, your father."

"Aye, I was aware of that, though I never had the opportunity to go out with him myself, past the age of about ten, when I was allowed to walk with the beaters," Evan said. He had never learned, as an adult, to enjoy hunting for sport. "He did have a fine collection of guns, but most of them are gone now. I had the lot of them packed up and shipped south, where they fetched a handsome price."

"Sold them?" Grant blinked.

"The price helped pay off some of his debts and some of the duties on the estate," Evan said. "I had no need of them and my sister objected to having them displayed throughout the house, considering how our father died."

"Of course. How stupid of me to overlook that," Grant murmured. "Unfortunate and tragic incident, sir. I wish I had been with him that day. I was away at the time and returned to find him already gone." He frowned, looked about thoughtfully. "If you do not hunt, sir, what sport do you prefer? Surely you find some way to relax and test yourself physically. Do you enjoy golfing, per-haps, in the Lowlands?"

"Kildonan is an excellent golfer, though he prefers climbing for sport," Arthur said.

"Just now you look as if you've been tossing cabers," Grant drawled, "or breaking rocks in a quarry."

Evan glanced down at his stone-dusted clothing, his loosened collar and rolled sleeves, the light sheen of sweat on his shirt. "Actually I've been doing some work on the old bridge."

"Why in blazes would you do that?" Arthur peered at him. "Have you been hauling stones like a laborer?"

Evan turned and pointed. "The center has collapsed, though the Highlanders still use it for a footbridge. Damned dangerous," he growled. "I have been trying to shore it up in case anyone attempts to cross it, but it must be closed off from pedestrians and replaced entirely."

"And it's about time," Mr. Grant said. "I mentioned the state of that bridge to the pre-vious Lord Kildonan more than once, but he was not inclined to have it repaired. Too damned expensive, was his comment."

"Oh?" Evan raised a brow. "Father never mentioned it to me at all, though I would think he would have done so. I am a bridge engineer by profession."

"I understood that you and the previous

Lord Kildonan were estranged, sir," Grant replied.

"Not entirely. I have not lived at Kildonan for years," he said, "but my father and I corresponded on matters to do with the family and the estate. He knew I would inherit someday, and he kept me apprised with occasional reports."

"I see. I was not aware. Forgive me."

"Nothing to forgive," Evan replied. "As to the bridge, I will have my factor post a sign and rope barriers. As soon as it is feasible, the bridge will be replaced. I will take on the expense, of course."

Kenneth Grant nodded. "Magnanimous of you, sir."

"Not at all. It's my responsibility."

Arthur glanced around. "Where is Lady Kildonan today?"

"Off in the hills with her friend Mrs. MacLeod," Evan said.

"Ah, the Highland knitting scheme," Grant said. "I am so impressed with Miss MacConn's — excuse me, Lady Kildonan's — project here in Glen Shee that I have suggested the idea to some of the ladies in the parish of Kilmallie. They began the scheme on my own estate, though without the admirable dedication of Lady Kildonan."

While Grant spoke, he stared at Evan intently, his narrowed brown eyes saying something entirely different than his mild, pleasant

256

tone. For a moment, though it seemed absurd, Evan would have sworn that the man disliked him — even hated him.

He frowned, aware that Kenneth Grant had known Catriona for years and had been with the rescue party that had arrived at the shieling hut to find Catriona and Evan in suspiciously intimate circumstances. Perhaps the man disapproved of their encounter or the necessary wedding that followed. Because Grant had been a friend to the previous earl, Evan felt safe in guessing that Grant, at least, did not resent the new earl.

"I'm pleased that my wife is involved in charitable work," he answered blandly.

"May I look at the bridge?" Grant asked, and the three men walked toward it. "You've done a good job with the shoring up," Grant commented. "Though it's true that the Highlanders in this area have been leaping that gap for a long time and no one has been injured seriously. They're nimble as goats, most of them."

"Nevertheless, I intend to come back here later to see that Catriona gets across safely," Evan said.

"Of course. You're her husband now." Grant smiled, and again Evan saw a flash below the surface of something dark, something at odds with the man's amiable demeanor.

Something about Kenneth Grant bothered

him, Evan thought. Part of it was a nagging feeling that Grant looked familiar, but he could not pinpoint in his memory where he had seen him before.

"Mr. Grant is a climber, as well, Kildonan," Arthur said. "He and I have been discussing the merits of serious mountain-eering. He has told me about some of the singular challenges of the Torridon peaks. He's quite familiar with them."

"Oh? Fascinating, sir." Evan stepped aside to collect his jacket and slipped it on, then picked up his hat before heading down the slope with the two men. "So you've done some climbing around here, Mr. Grant?"

"Aye, though I haven't yet made it to the top of the highest one — Beinn Shee — that somewhat jagged peak at the center there." He pointed to the loftiest height in the range of snow-topped mountains that ringed the glen. "I've made attempts in the past, but they've been spoiled by bad luck and bad weather. Temperamental mountain, that one — no one has climbed all the way to the top, they say. I've had better luck scaling moun-tains elsewhere in the Highlands and on Skye."

"Excellent climbing on Skye," Evan said. "Fitz and I did some climbing there a couple of years ago."

"Yes, we took on Sgurr nan Gillean in a fine mist," Arthur said. "Had a fine guide, too, and with his help, we were lucky enough to make it to the top that day."

"That's an impressive peak, sirs, the highest in the mighty Cuillin chain, and some say well nigh impossible. You are expert climbers, indeed," Grant said.

"Not expert," Evan demurred. "Cautious but persistent might be a better description. Sgurr nan Gillean has a rough surface that provides a good grip all the way up, despite its sharp incline. We simply did not give up."

"We've heard that no one has yet climbed Beinn Shee all the way to the top," Arthur said. "So I thought it a perfect peak for our Alpine group to conquer — those of us who are keener on the hard climb than the scenic scramble. I think the ladies will decide to forego it, as well they should. Kildonan, we should invite Mr. Grant to join our adventure. He knows these mountains well, and his medical expertise will be an added security."

"A fine idea, if Mr. Grant is interested."

"I would be honored to accompany your group." Grant smiled.

"Our friends are due to arrive this afternoon," Evan said. "We will send word to you about our climbing plans."

"It sounds as if you would be an excellent addition to the Scottish Alpine Climbing Club," Arthur said.

"My expertise is nothing to boast about, I'm sure," Grant said with some modesty.

"By the way, you'll want the best Highland guide if you plan to attempt Beinn Shee."

"I agree. Can you recommend one?" Evan asked.

"The most experienced is John MacLeod, a crofter — he's Morag MacLeod's husband, and his rather ancient mother lives on the lower slopes of the Fairy Mountain. Old John has been up and down all the slopes and peaks along the Torridon range for most of his life. He has been my guide more than once in scaling the other Torridons. But he's getting on in years. Actually, I'd recommend your factor, sir. Finlay MacConn knows these mountains as well as anyone. Though I cannot say if he's been all the way up Beinn Shee."

"Finlay? Really?" Evan shoved his hands into his pockets as he walked, looking intently at Grant. "I wasn't aware."

"He and his brothers and father used to climb regularly. But that was before the reverend was injured and before the older son's death on the mountain."

Evan looked quickly at him. "My wife's eldest brother — aye, I heard something of that from her."

"Yes. Donald MacConn went climbing one day and the weather turned bad — just as it did for you, sir. He was not as fortunate as you to be rescued so graciously. He slipped and fell to his death. Finlay and his father went searching, and Reverend MacConn was injured also, when he fell — terrible weather that day, treacherous slopes. The reverend never fully recovered and has been a changed man. Luckily, he had his faith to comfort him in his grief. His wife died shortly afterward, as well — her illness was brought on by grief, in my estimation. After that, many of their kin were sent away by your father's evictions. The MacConns of Glenachan have not had an easy time of it."

"Indeed," Evan said. "I had not realized the extent of it."

"There is a great deal you do not know about your bride," Grant said. "But that is only to be expected in the circumstances." A smoothness to the tone, a sly assurance, made Evan glance sharply at him.

"Ah, but I am a quick study," Evan replied.

"Indeed. Ah, before I go, Lord Kildonan, allow me to make a request of you."

"Certainly, sir." Evan waited, feeling slightly wary, although he could not say why.

"I heard word in Inverness from my solicitor there that you might be entertaining offers for portions of your property. That, in fact, you have interested buyers already."

Evan narrowed his glance. "Aye," he said. "It is something I am exploring at this time. The estate is very large, and there is some benefit in reducing its size." He was not going to admit to Grant that one of the expected guests was coming to look at the estate to perhaps buy a large part of the land and rent the castle on an extended arrangement, as well.

"Then allow me to make an offer, as well, sir. If you are going to reduce the size of Kildonan's estate, I would be very interested in buying the land that borders my own property of Kilmallie, at the farthest eastern end of the glen. I have been wanting to expand my own sheep runs, and this might prove the perfect arrangement for both of us."

"Thank you. It's an interesting offer, and I will seriously consider it," Evan said. "We'll speak on it again."

"Excellent. Good day, then. I must be on my way, for I promised to visit the rectory at Glenachan and take tea with Reverend MacConn and Mrs. Rennie." He gathered both his gun and Arthur's, which had been a loan. "I must get back to Kilmallie to change. I enjoyed shooting with you, Arthur."

"Please give Reverend MacConn and Mrs. Rennie my regards," Evan murmured. "We shall invite them to dinner soon." He knew that sooner or later the time would come to smooth the rift between Catriona and her father and aunt.

"I will pass that word along to them. Until later, sirs." Grant touched his bowler hat and strode away.

Evan turned to walk with Arthur toward Kildonan Castle, which looked golden in the sunlight. Against a backdrop of rugged mountains and blue sky, it formed a striking picture.

"Selling some of the land to Mr. Grant would be a good step toward reducing the size of the estate," Arthur commented.

"Aye, and it would keep the land in the hands of a Highland laird, which is important to me," Evan said. "But there is something about the fellow . . ." He stopped, aware that Arthur might consider the man a friend.

"Oh, I agree," Arthur said. "Good fellow, but there's a look of the wolf to him. I'd be wary of his offer. He'll fleece you if he can. Picked up two grouse I shot today and claimed the brace as his own. Not sporting." Arthur shrugged.

Evan huffed in wordless comment. Then he narrowed his glance as he looked toward Kildonan Castle and noticed several people strolling the castle grounds, including four women in wide skirts and carrying parasols. Stopping, he shaded his brow.

"Who's that?" Arthur asked.

"I believe our guests are here early." Evan quickened his pace as he strode down the hill.

Catriona walked toward the fairy bridge after parting with Morag in the hills, fully aware that Evan did not want her to take this route. However, it was the fastest way back to Kildonan Castle, and she had no qualms about crossing the bridge, which, though broken, had not crumbled any further for decades. Her customary route home after walking the hills with Morag was to take the drover's track back to Glenachan House in Glen Shee — miles away from this spot. But life and fate had abruptly ousted her from the home and the routines she knew.

As she left the forested lower slope and approached the bridge, she could hear the rush of the water in the gorge. Looking up, she saw Kenneth Grant standing on the other side of the bridge. Slowing her step, gripping her walking stick, she stopped to stare at him warily.

"Lady Kildonan, how nice to see you," he said.

She walked closer, knowing this was the only way across, though she felt as if she entered a trap. "What do you want?" she asked.

"Only to make sure you cross safely." He held out a hand.

"I can manage on my own, thank you."

"I saw your husband earlier today. He's quite concerned about the condition of this bridge. He worked like a laborer all morning to make some repairs — just so you would be safe."

She looked down and saw additional stones

wedged in the raw edges of the break and stout sticks braced across the gap. "I see. It looks quite sturdy. I really do not need help, Mr. Grant. You can go home."

"Oh, but I thought we could talk again. Come on," he said, beckoning.

Looking about rather frantically, she saw a man walking the moorland in the distance between the castle and the bridge. Evan was coming to meet her. The sight of him lifted her spirits so much, quickly and unexpectedly, that she no longer feared Kenneth Grant. She felt a new, surprising confidence against his threats.

Reaching the middle of the bridge, she leaped the gap with no difficulty. As she set her feet down, she felt the improved stability in the old stones.

Grant took a long step toward her and grabbed her arm so fast that she gasped. As he yanked her toward him, she stumbled, and her left foot slipped off the ragged edge of the breach, knocking out one of the prop sticks.

Then he tilted her backward, so that she latched on to his arm in desperation. Waving her arm as she held her walking stick, she tried to use that to keep her balance. Grant struck it violently out of her hand, and she heard it clatter all the way down, then splash into the water.

"Be careful, my dear," Grant said, and he

pulled her back up to stand beside him in a stable spot on the bridge. "You nearly fell."

Catriona stared up at him, heart slamming. Had he truly meant for her to stumble, or had he nearly lost his balance, with her beside him? She knew what he would claim. Stepping back, she pulled with her arm, but he would not release her.

"I had no idea you planned to marry Kildonan when we met last," he said. "You should have told me."

"I did not know it either when we spoke. You are hurting me —" She twisted in his grip.

He lessened the pressure, but did not let go. "Be careful not to fall again, my dear," he murmured. "And remember what you and I talked about."

"I don't understand why you are doing this — why are you so angry with me, so set on punishing me and my family? We have always trusted you."

"I trusted *you*, my dear, but you hurt me to the quick with your hasty marriage. I do not intend to hurt you, but I had always hoped that if you decided to marry, you would turn to me for that. What changed when Mackenzie came into your life? Was it the man himself, so charming to a lonely young woman? Or did you set out to trap him for his title and his fortune?"

"How dare you suggest that! You know the

circumstances. We had no choice but to marry." She felt vulnerable standing with him on the narrow bridge, on a part of the arch just below the crack — but Grant did not allow her to move off of it to the safety of the path.

"So that is an admission of your sin. I thought so. When we found you in the shieling hut, I saw the way you both looked at each other . . . and I knew then that he had taken you and that you had welcomed his affections. So the Plain Girl of Glenachan could not resist Kildonan. Devil take the man," he growled.

"No — you do not understand —" But she would not explain the details to him or to anyone.

"I have waited a long while, biding my time, but I never expected that you would give yourself to a stranger. I never thought that particular man would come back here, to be truthful. I had heard that his sister and Sir Harry would run the estate and that Kildonan would soon sell off much of it. I am understandably upset, for his return has ruined my life — as well as yours." He stared at her, looking cold and suddenly dangerous.

She yanked her arm. "What is it you want from me?"

"I want what he has taken from me," he growled, pulling her to him, bending to kiss her mouth while she twisted in protest.

267

Lifting his head, he held her tightly. "And I want you to take heed, Plain Girl," he finished.

She glared up at him. "My husband and my kinsmen will not tolerate this when they find out —"

"They will never find out, because you cannot tell them. You will pay a price for my silence, as I told you before. I can ruin your family. They will leave this glen . . . like the others did."

Breath heaving, she watched him in silence and shock, knowing deep in her gut, like a twist of fear, that he was right. She had no choice and could not speak or her family would suffer. The people of the glen would suffer, too, without Finlay to help them, without her father to shepherd their souls.

"So will you keep silent and be my helpmate and mistress? Or will you tell your precious earl and risk your world collapsing around you?" He cupped her head to kiss her again, but she wrenched away.

"Leave me be," she hissed.

"Is it prison for Finlay, then, and ruin for Thomas? Pity. I like them both. Well, I have written my letter to the sheriff. It only needs posting." He let go of her.

She stepped back, rubbing her forearms. "I never thought you could be so hateful."

"Perhaps it was bred in me. Where shall we meet again to discuss our bargain? We could use the same shieling hut where you dallied with your earl. You could tell your earl that you are going out with Morag MacLeod."

"No," she said, breathing hard.

"Give it some thought, Catriona," he said, voice low. Then he glanced toward Kildonan Castle in the distance. "Ah, look. Your bridegroom is coming to your rescue." He pointed.

Catriona turned and saw Evan walking up the hillside toward them. "Evan!" she called, while Grant squeezed her arm. "Evan!"

Chapter Seventeen

"Kildonan! Here!" Grant waved and called, to Catriona's surprise. Then he tugged her off the bridge and waited with her at the top of the hill as Evan came closer.

Her heart pounded, and she fought tears, yet she stood calmly. She realized that Evan would know nothing of what had just transpired. From the low angle of the hill, he could not have seen them clearly on the bridge.

Grant was right. She could say nothing now, if ever.

"A lucky thing you came, sir," Kenneth Grant said as Evan reached the top of the hill and came toward them. "Your bride had quite a fright. She nearly fell from that infernal bridge. I'm very glad I happened to be passing this way."

Evan's face turned grim as he strode toward them. "Dear God," he growled, and he pulled Catriona into his arms to hold her. She sagged against him, resting her head on his shoulder, and an astonishing flood of relief poured through her.

He drew back, keeping an arm around her. "Are you hurt?"

"I'm fine." She wanted to dive back into the safety of his embrace. Instead, she clutched the back of his frock coat and stood close to him while she faced Grant with loathing.

"Your bride crossed the bridge as usual, but she stumbled," Grant said. "I happened to be close enough to catch hold of her. You are wise to barricade the area and forbid use of the bridge, sir. It should have been done long ago."

"I am in your debt, sir." Evan shook Grant's hand.

"Not at all. A pleasure to help such a bonny lady. You are indeed a lucky man. Good day to you both." He bowed, barely glancing at Catriona. "I will see you soon, when we go climbing."

"We'll look forward to it," Evan answered. Kenneth Grant doffed his bowler hat and walked away.

"Climbing?" Catriona asked. "He's going to climb with you?"

"Arthur and I saw him earlier, so we asked him to join us. How lucky that he saw you on the bridge. I was on my way to meet you myself — but would have come too late. Dear Lord, Catriona, what a fright you gave me," he said, drawing her closer.

When she thought he might take her into his arms — might kiss her — he only draped his arm around her and turned to walk with

271

her down the long hillside. She was surprised to feel a deep disappointment, for she had tried to make up her mind that they must begin again as acquaintances and proceed from there.

She glanced over her shoulder and saw that Grant was no longer in sight. "Evan, I . . . do not mean to be ungrateful, but must Mr. Grant come along on your outing?" she asked bluntly. "I do not care for him lately. You do not know him as well as I do," she added.

Evan tilted his head, looking puzzled. "But he is your savior, my lass." He said it lightly — but he did not know the truth behind the incident, she thought.

"No," she said, snuggling against him, indulging her feelings for that moment, "you are my savior. I did not feel safe until you came up that hill, Evan."

He stopped then and murmured something low and deep that she did not hear, but she wished she had. Sweeping her hard against him with one hand at her back and the other behind her head, crushing her hair in its net, Evan bent his head and kissed her.

Surprised, she caught her breath and felt a strong, wild response rush through her. Closing her eyes, she leaned in to him, savoring the tender, powerful movement of his mouth on hers, feeling his hard, fierce strength as he pulled her against him.

Looping her arms around his neck, she arched into him and kissed him back with equal fervor, surrendering to the utter delight of feeling so loved, so safe — whether or not it was true.

Wrapped in his embrace, she stood with him on the open moorland, knee-deep in grass, the wind billowing her skirt and her plaid. She felt dizzy, felt enchanted, aware of the watchful dominion of the mountains, the clouds sweeping overhead, and she and Evan joining beneath those elements like a crystal point of power. She never wanted the feeling to end.

And then he let her go and held her away from him. She could see his breaths coming hard, could feel the tremor in his hands as he gazed down at her, his hazel eyes gone brilliant green, his expression deeply serious. "Forgive me," he said. "I promised that I would leave the decision to you about such things. But I almost lost you today, Catriona," he went on. "You gave me the devil of a fright. Promise me you will keep off that bridge."

She exhaled, shook her head. "I cannot promise that. Morag and I need to go back and forth to those high hills somehow."

He let go of her and resumed walking beside her, though she wished they could turn back time to a minute ago — or back to the wonderful night she had spent in his arms, before life became so complicated and uncertain.

"There are other ways to go into those hills," he said.

"Do you expect us to climb down into the gorge and leap the stones in the burn? Morag is over seventy years old."

"Then she should not be leaping the gap on the bridge either." He cocked a brow as he glanced at her.

"She's been crossing that wee bad step for longer than I have. And I always make sure she gets over safely."

"You could both fall one day. That fairy charm did not do you much good today. No, Catriona — I want you to take ponies along the drover's track from now on."

"That's impractical here, where the hills are steep and rough, and the tracks are in poor condition now that there are no herds of cattle being driven along them. It would take us hours longer on ponies, and we could not visit the most remote crofts. There are not many people left in this glen," she said, "but there are several in the high hills who look forward to our weekly visits."

"I see. Well, we will think of something. Come, lass, you need to go home — you look shaken. Have you had your tea?"

"I'm fine," she insisted. "And I had tea with Morag and her husband."

"I left the gig under those trees over there. I'll take you home to Kildonan." He tucked her under his arm again, and she came into that circle gratefully. They walked in natural tandem, their bodies fit in a complement of curves and hollows in motion. Leaning her head on his shoulder for a moment, then lifting it, she said nothing more as they walked down the long hill.

She did not know this man, yet he tapped a deep passion in her that she had never realized was there. Falling swiftly and almost literally into her life, he fit into place as if an empty space had waited just for him. She felt safe with him, somehow, and wished they had never left that shieling hut, never learned more about each other than what was most important: that they could care about each other, they could love each other, they could flourish together.

Walking in the circle of Evan's arm, she realized that not only did she feel more secure and more relaxed, but that Grant and his ugly threats had diminished like shadows in sunlight.

But like the fleeting sunshine in this glen of mountains, she knew it could not last.

Riding in the gig, she and Evan had covered the distance of the rough, hummocky grassland and were nearing Kildonan Castle when Catriona looked up. She noticed several people making their way along the incline of one of the steep hills behind the castle, on the side of the glen opposite Beinn Shee and the fairy bridge. She touched Evan's arm and pointed. "Look — who is that?"

"Ah. Our guests. The climbing club arrived while you were out, along with a good friend of mine, who I hoped might come to Kildonan. After luncheon they were eager to get out and about, so Jeanie and I directed them toward that rather respectable hill. The view from there is spectacular."

"It is," she said, having climbed it before. "The whole of the glen and the range of the Torridons can easily be seen from up there. We call it Sgairneach Mhór in the Gaelic."

"What does that mean?"

"Big stony hill," she said, and his laugh, deep and relaxed, soothed through her.

Some of the climbers perched on the hillside while others scrambled up the rocky slope. They wore suits and gowns, hats and bonnets, carried walking sticks and parasols. She saw several men and women divided in two groups, one near the top of the hill, the other lower down. Between them was the rough height of the hill, covered with bracken and rock, creased with narrow runnels filled with water and scattered with sheep.

She stared in disbelief. "They look like they're dressed for church, yet some of them are four hundred feet up."

"A plucky but proper bunch," Evan drawled. He turned the gig and drove toward the foot of the slope. Halting the vehicle, waving up to those who halloed down to them, he got down from the gig and went around to the other side to assist Catriona.

She liked the hard strength of his big hands on her waist, and she loved the way he slid her effortlessly, slowly along the front of his body, making her blush, making her re-member secret moments that she should not properly think about — but wanted to think about, and feel, again.

He set her down and took her elbow, and she winced suddenly. Kenneth Grant's treat-ment of her had left bruises on her arms. When Evan glanced at her, she only smiled.

"Have you got the stamina for introduc-tions?" he asked.

"Of course," she said, but her voice was brittle and she tightened her hands nervously.

Together they climbed the lower part of Sgairneach Mhór, and Evan lent her his walking stick to help her balance as they went up the rocky, inclined field. The gushing water in the runnels added another layer of sound to the whip of cold breezes, the echo of human voices, and the baaing of the sheep.

The incline was so steep that Catriona had to crane her head far back to look up. She moved in silence behind Evan, although she was so used to climbing that she could have overtaken him easily. But she wanted to hang back, not eager to meet his friends so soon.

Lady Jean and Sir Harry were there, she saw, and Arthur Fitzgibbon, as well, but the others were unknown to her. They were of an age with Evan, she noticed, except for an elderly gentleman and lady in the lower group, who seemed fit and energetic. All of them laughed and chatted, calling up and down the hillside as if engaged in lawn tennis or golf rather than a steep climb.

Lady Jean and the other ladies all wore charming little bonnets, dark day dresses, and short jackets, and carried parasols. Looking up, Catriona even noticed crinolines and pretty side-buttoned boots.

Next to them she felt like a fishwife in her tartan shawl and plain skirt and blouse. She had no bonnet and gloves, her bronze-colored hair was slipping loose from its low knot, and her cheeks were no doubt flushed with wind and exertion. Tucking strands of hair back, she gave it up as futile.

The older lady waved. "Lord Kildonan, we have perfect weather for an excursion in the Scottish hills — a cloudless sky, pleasant breezes, and a nice hill — though not as exciting as the Alps, where Lord Wetherstone and I took our summer holiday." She looked stout but strong, and her black gown, veiled bonnet, gloves, boots, and fringed black parasol were all of the finest quality, Catriona noted.

"Kildonan, there you are, back again." The older gentleman extended his hand cordially. Wearing a brown suit and long coat, he was not tall, but he was broadly built, with white side-whiskers framing his jowled face.

Evan took Catriona's arm. "My dear," he said, "let me introduce Lord and Lady Wetherstone, who came up from London." He indicated the older couple, who nodded to her. "And Mrs. Anna Wilkie and her husband, Reverend John Wilkie, from Stirling." They were a young couple standing with Jean and Harry. "May I present Catriona née MacConn, now my wife — Lady Kildonan."

"Lady Kildonan, what a pleasure," Lady Wetherstone said, taking Catriona's hand, smiling. "Congratulations."

Mrs. Wilkie also offered her hand and her congratulations on the marriage. She was a beauty, Catriona saw, a blonde of the fine china variety, small boned with translucent skin and blue eyes. Her hair was perfectly arranged beneath a little gray bonnet, and her jacket and skirt of pale gray wool complemented her delicate coloring. She held a pretty blue parasol over one shoulder.

Catriona felt big and gawky by comparison, certain that her vivid coloring and size made her look like a shaggy red cow beside this exquisite creature. The young woman smiled at her with genuine kindness, and Catriona liked her so well in that moment that all thoughts of self-conscious comparison fled.

John Wilkie, her husband, was tall, blond, and handsome in a mild but charming way. Talking with him for a few moments, Catriona discovered that he was a reverend of the Established Church. She told him that her father had the living of the Free Church at Glenachan — and then she wondered, when Lady Wetherstone lifted both eyebrows high, if she should have kept that to herself a little longer. After all, earls did not generally marry the daughters of ministers.

"Thank you — I am so happy to meet you," she repeated to each newcomer. "How kind of you to come to Kildonan Castle."

Standing there with her plaid slipping down from her bare, tousled head, wearing such unsophisticated garments, she was sure her manners must seem quite ordinary. She had not been raised in the privileged classes, as these people no doubt had.

But her mother and her tutors had taught her and her siblings good manners from an early age. She would have to rely on that training to see her through this experience. Welcoming the guests, she expressed gratitude and otherwise said little, only smiling and nodding.

She stayed by Evan's side, glad for the firm touch of his hand now and then on her elbow or the small of her back as he conversed with his friends.

"Hulloo! Come on up. What's keeping you?"

At the shout, Catriona looked up to see a woman waving to them, standing nearly at the top of the steepest part of the hill. She clung there with the ease of a mountain goat, her feet planted aslant, her hands on her hips. "Come up!"

"I think we're being challenged," Evan said, and he waved back. "Hulloo, Jemima! We'll be up!" He looked around. "Who's for it?"

"Not me," Lady Jean said, and she looked at Sir Harry, who shook his head when Lord and Lady Wetherstone also refused.

"I'll go up with you," John Wilkie said. "My dear?"

"I'll stay with Lady Jean," his wife replied. "Lady Kildonan, will you climb, or stay with us?" she asked, while Lady Wetherstone fixed Catriona with a direct and curious stare.

"Oh, my wife is a natural at this sort of thing," Evan said, extending his hand out to her and leaving her no choice. As his fingers closed firmly over hers, he pulled, and she stepped up beside him on the slope. Reverend Wilkie followed them, but kept several yards below, taking his time.

"Thank you," Catriona murmured to Evan as they mounted the slope beside each other. "For another rescue."

He grinned at her. "I thought you looked pale at the idea of entertaining the guests on the hill while I went up. And I thought you might like to meet the others on your own ground — these spectacular hills," he said, glancing around.

The climb was easy, an incline littered with rocks and tough old heather plants all the way to the conical top. Catriona clambered upward with Evan behind her and Wilkie below them.

She used the walking stick a little and neared the top where the others waited, enjoying the view. The wind buffeted her cheeks and whipped at her skirt, and she paused before reaching the very top.

The view was magnificent. Kildonan Castle perched between a slope and a shining lochan that reflected the castle, the sky, the mountain peaks. Glen Shee spread out for miles, colored wine, gold, and green, its hills dotted with croft houses and sheep. Narrow burns and small lochs glimmered like bits of mirror dropped in the grass.

Massive mountains surrounded the glen like proud, fierce guardians, the highest peaks coated with snow. Catriona raised a hand to her brow and turned, looking. The wind tore at her hair, loosening strands and spilling them across her cheek.

"Beautiful." Evan came up beside her. "Have you collected your courage yet?"

"My courage?"

"It's not easy to face these people when

you've just come to the castle yourself. You're still settling into your role."

"What role?" she asked crisply. "We have not yet agreed on what that should be."

He reached out to sweep back the loose tendrils of her hair, tucking them behind her ear. Shivers spilled down her back, quite unlike the chill of the wind or the dread of meeting more guests. "I have been thinking about that," he murmured.

"So have I." She stared up at him, yearning suddenly, but not sure enough to show it.

"Oh, here's Wilkie." He turned as the reverend joined them.

"What a glorious view," John Wilkie said. "Let's see it from the top," he suggested, and he turned to go higher.

Evan took Catriona's elbow to guide her off the rock. They made their way up the last part of the hillside. At the top, a narrow ridge of hills dipped and undulated like a dragon's spine as they flowed along the line of the glen.

"Welcome to the top!" Arthur said, coming toward them with the others.

"My dear, let me present my cousins — Miss Jemima Murray and her sister, Miss Emily Murray. And this is Sir Aedan MacBride," he said of the tall, dark-haired gentleman who stood behind the Murray sisters. "Meet Catriona, now Countess of Kildonan."

"And mistress of all you see around you," Arthur added, while Evan laughed.

Catriona smiled. "I'm so pleased to meet you."

"As are we. What excellent news — a countess for our earl at last!" Pretty, brown-haired Miss Jemima Murray had a fearless quality about her, a wide smile, a rich laugh, and a firm handshake. Catriona quickly learned that Jemima was not only Evan and Jean's second cousin, but the tour leader and vice president of the climbing club. Arthur Fitzgibbon, Catriona then discovered, was its newly appointed president.

Privately she thought Jemima capable of leading an army, let alone a few travelers, for her energy and enthusiasm seemed infectious and boundless.

Miss Emily Murray was her sister's pale opposite, a quiet-spoken young woman who seemed as naturally athletic as Jemima, though shy as she took Catriona's hand and smiled quickly.

Catriona would have noticed the last gentleman in the group anywhere. He seemed singular not only because of his good looks, but also because of his air of simmering intensity. Black haired and blue eyed, a true Celt in appearance and a gentleman in demeanor, Sir Aedan MacBride of Dundrennan was the only man in the group wearing a kilt and jacket. He moved with athletic, unconscious grace in the garment, even while hillwalking, and reminded Catriona somehow of a Highland warrior prince.

"Lady Kildonan!" He took her hand in his gloved one briefly. "Kildonan and I have been friends a long time. He's a fortunate lad to have such a Highland beauty for his countess."

She laughed, thinking of her unkempt appearance. "Thank you, sir. My husband has mentioned you fondly and told me that he spent holidays with your family. I've always admired your father's poetry, by the way."

"Madam, he would have been most pleased to hear it," he said graciously.

"The views are so stunning," Jemima said. "We could take a picnic out to these hills and attempt to climb several peaks before sunset — I'm sure it could be done, and it would be quite an exhilarating day. What do you think, Lady Kildonan? You know these hills better than we do."

"It can be done," Catriona said. "Climbing some of the higher peaks takes several hours, but once you are up in the heights it is often possible to walk from peak to peak along the ridges — providing the weather is good." She glanced at Evan, who held her gaze for a moment.

"Perhaps Lady Kildonan can direct us to the most interesting hills to climb," Emily

Murray said. "We'd like a bit of a challenge, of course."

"You'll find plenty of challenge here in Glen Shee," Evan answered.

"Some of the highest peaks have never been climbed, I hear, such as Beinn Alligin and Beinn Shee," Jemima said.

"Then you and I will conquer their heights, Miss Jemima," Arthur said gallantly.

Jemima laughed, the sound echoing. "Certainly! Evan will go also, and my sister, Emily, and Reverend Wilkie. Sir Aedan plans to stay only until tomorrow, but I believe the Wetherstones will climb with us, and Mrs. Wilkie, as well. Evan — you will go, even though you are now . . . a newlywed?" Jemima looked doubtfully at Catriona.

"I wouldn't want to miss it. Perhaps my bride would like to join our effort, as well." He looked questioningly at Catriona.

While listening, she looked out over the beautiful expanse of the mountains, glen, and lochs. The wind pushed hard and chilly at her, sweeping her skirts against her legs, and she spun to look again at the mountain where her older brother had died years before and where her father had been injured, body and soul.

Of all mountains, Beinn Shee was not one that she ever wanted to climb. But Flora had given her a quest, and her life's work would be incomplete unless she braved those slopes to find the crystal the old woman wanted.

Having reached the top of many other slopes and peaks over the years, Catriona understood why Evan and his friends wanted to climb these mountains. Up on those heights, she had experienced a wild, incredible sense of freedom that drew her back again and again.

The thought of reaching those heights with Evan was irresistible and powerful. No matter what happened in their marriage — whether she stayed with him or left — she knew that she must climb that mountain beside him.

Turning, she mustered a smile. "I would love it."

All was quiet late that evening as Evan made his way through darkened hallways that were lit by lamps the butler would extinguish on a final check of the house. His solitary footsteps echoed on stone in the corridors of the central keep, despite the carpets strewn there. As he entered the wing that housed his private rooms with Catriona, his footsteps were muffled in the modest, more modern dimensions of the long hallway.

Pausing at Catriona's door, he was tempted to knock. Instead he stood listening to the peacefulness, imagining her quiet, even breaths as she lay sleeping.

After a simple Highland supper shared with their guests in the small dining room — a meal of mutton stew, brown bread, and a sugar-crusted lemon cake — Catriona, as hostess, had proposed that the ladies retire early. Evan had not been surprised by her considerate regard for their guests, most of whom were tired after a day of traveling and hillwalking.

Her suggestion was welcomed. Lady Jean, being with child and readily fatigued, was the first to depart, followed by the other ladies and some of the men. Making quick apologies, they went to their various bedrooms in the castle's main tower and two wings.

Evan shared port and cigars with Sir Aedan MacBride and Reverend Wilkie, the only two who lingered after dinner. Wilkie, the author of several books about his travels and climbing adventures in Europe and Britain, revealed such a fine knack for storytelling that he kept Evan and MacBride entertained until past midnight with his tales.

Two glasses of port warmed Evan's blood, and good company and healthy fatigue had relaxed him. He stood in the silent corridor outside Catriona's room and fought the urge to touch her door handle.

All he wanted, just then, was to go to her, take her into his arms, sink down with her in that big, comfortable bed. He wanted to recapture the night when they had held each other, caring so deeply about the other's welfare that their own needs seemed unimportant.

Compassion and desire, in a crucible of danger, had created love — real love — that night. He grew more sure of it each day. Although the concept staggered him, the power of the feeling had awed him, even changed him somehow. Standing at her door now, he knew he was not the man he had been only days ago, when he had first climbed up the mountainside in the mist.

Could love happen immediately, like flint and spark, creating flames so hot that they flared into passion within hours? Could that heartfelt fire create embers that would last forever, an eternal flame?

He would not have believed it possible, but he felt a pure, subtle magic flowing through him, stirring him, as if his soul was rousing from a long sleep. Filled with new hope and certainty, with caring and desire, he knew this could not be less than love — real love — the sort that existed in fairy tales and legends.

Yet all hung in the balance. He and Catriona could destroy what they had discovered — or they could build on it gloriously.

Drawing a deep breath, he counseled himself to wait, to let her decide, to refrain from forcing a choice. Otherwise he would never know what she truly wanted.

She had saved his life, and in turn he had attempted to save her. Now he realized how much she had saved him, how lighter his burdens seemed. And hope, once extinguished, was flickering to life like a candle-wick sizzling with a new spark.

Standing in the darkness, he leaned a shoulder on her door and felt a sudden, strange sense of falling again — but this time he was falling in love, and he could not stop the plummet.

Chapter Eighteen

"Oh! What a grim occasion," the half-whispering voice said, "matched only by the dreadful weather." A loud sniff followed. "I cannot imagine such a hasty little wedding! And only days ago!"

Catriona slowed as she came down the hall toward the small dining room, ready to meet the others for breakfast the morning after their arrival. The remark, not meant for her ears, was obvious enough, and it stung like a bee.

She hesitated before a turn in the hallway, unsure if she should march boldly on, or turn and flee.

"It was a quiet little wedding and very romantical," she heard Jean say. "They knew each other as children, you know. Love blossomed very quickly for them, and they could not bear to be apart." She sighed, an audible yearning.

Bless Jean, Catriona thought. She was stretching a distant childhood association to the point of a rather large white lie — after all, Catriona and Evan had been children in the same glen, although they had barely met each other. Yet Jean attempted to embellish an awkward situation and a hasty wedding, indeed.

Catriona would love her for life, she decided. She glanced down the hallway to make her escape, but saw Mrs. Baird at the other end of the hallway. The housekeeper paused to talk to an unseen maid in one of the rooms farther down the corridor.

"Really," Lady Wetherstone, the first voice, said. "I pressed the little downstairs maid for an explanation of the earl's sudden marriage, and she told me they were alone together for an entire night on the mountain! No wonder they married!"

"Lady Jean said she saved his life that night," another voice murmured. Catriona recognized Anna Wilkie's soft tones. "And he married her immediately out of gratitude and to preserve her honor. His childhood sweetheart — there can be nothing more wonderful, in my opinion." She, too, sighed.

Lady Wetherstone huffed. "Well, I can understand a man being tempted under such circumstances — she is a fetching creature, though that red hair is a little wild and she's so tall that she quite startled me, especially in her Highland tartan. She looked like a peasant wife rather than a bride and a countess."

Catriona sank against the wall and folded her arms, deciding that she did not care for Lady Wetherstone very much — although she would never be so rude as to describe her flaws to others.

"I think she's very lovely. And I thought her Highland outfit was charming," Anna replied. "I'd love to have a tartan shawl like that — it was beautifully made."

"She's a very unlikely countess, all the same, even if they did elope, or whatever it was," Lady Wetherstone said.

"Lady Kildonan will be a credit to this house," Jean said in a low, insistent tone, "and a credit to my brother. Just look at them — how they gaze at each other, how they murmur so softly that no one else can hear them. Remember that they cared for each other at the risk of their own lives. They were made for each other, and that sort of love is rare and precious. We should be in awe of it, in my opinion."

"I agree," Anna Wilkie said.

"That is because you are both young and silly," Lady Wetherstone said, "and full of romantic notions. And, Lady Jean, your heart is softened by your expected blessed event, I have no doubt. Now, which door did you say leads to the gardens? I would so enjoy seeing them this morning."

"It's misty outside, but not so thick that we can't enjoy the view," Jean said. "We can take a short hallway to a stair and down past the kitchen, if you do not mind going that way."

Their footsteps sounded and soon faded,

and Catriona breathed a sigh of relief. Straightening her posture and smoothing her brown silk skirt, then taking a moment to pat her red hair — wild as a beacon fire, apparently — in its prim little net, she walked resolutely down the hallway to open the closed door of the small dining room where the others remained at breakfast.

"Wilkie tells me he's written yet another book," Arthur told those gathered at the breakfast table. His glance skimmed past Evan, Wilkie, Sir Harry, and Catriona.

She glanced up attentively, teacup lifted. "How interesting! What is this one about?" She had no idea that Reverend Wilkie wrote books of any sort, but she was not going to reveal her ignorance.

"Mountaineering — they're all about mountaineering and hillwalking," Arthur said. "I read the first one and enjoyed it immensely. Quite a good account of a trek through the Swiss Alps. What was its title again, sir?" He looked at John Wilkie.

"*Scrambling in the Alps*," the young reverend answered. "I've also written *Scrambling in Skye*. And my most recent is called *Scrambling in the Grampians*."

Beside her, Catriona heard Sir Harry snort softly as he reached for the toast rack. On her other side, Evan caught her glance and winked briefly. She wanted to smile, but refrained.

"Awful title, pardon me, sir," Arthur commented, "but any book that honors one of Scotland's noble, ancient mountain ranges is worthwhile. And you pen excellent travelogues. If you're interested, Lady Kildonan, I have with me a copy of Reverend Wilkie's book about the Alps." He looked at Catriona, who nodded in silent thanks.

"I understand you have written another book, as well, Mr. Fitzgibbon," Wilkie said.

"Yes, my third. *The Geological Structure of the Alps* was my first, followed by *Glacial Theories in the North Highlands of Scotland*. My most recent was *Hebridean Ice Age Formations*. But no one has read any of them, I'm afraid." He smiled.

"Your students have read them, and a new crop reads them again every year," Evan said. "And I've read the blasted things myself."

"Well, yes, *you* would," Arthur said, as if it were expected. "Not that you agree with them."

"I'm not convinced that a glacier can be described as a body of viscous fluids," Evan answered.

"Could be if the body was frozen saltwater, Kildonan."

"In some cases, perhaps, but most glacial formations in Scotland will prove to be freshwater, I think. Though I admit I'm quite keen on your practicums concerning the thermal conductivity of various stones."

"Oh," Catriona said, blinking. "It all sounds . . . so interesting." She knew she sounded unconvinced.

Evan chuckled, as did Sir Harry, and Arthur as well, though reluctantly. "Fitz is Professor of Natural Philosophies at Edinburgh University," Evan explained. "He was a very young professor there when Sir Aedan and I attended his classes. He's collected all sorts of accolades by now, and he's a respected fellow of the Royal Society of London."

Catriona murmured her admiration, having never heard of the society.

"While Lord Kildonan," Arthur countered, "was the youngest member ever admitted to the Royal Society of Edinburgh — at eighteen he wrote a brilliant essay on the extinct volcanoes of Scotland. He's quite a geologist, and he has put it to good use."

"Are you also a scientist?" Catriona asked Evan, and realized that it must seem odd that she knew so little about him.

"No. I specialized in engineering studies," Evan answered. "Though I need a good understanding of rocks and geological formations in my work."

"He's a most talented bridge designer," Sir Harry said. "I've worked with him myself in that regard — my family owns a steelworks, Lady Kildonan," he explained to Catriona.

"Ah," she said. "Then the bridges my husband builds are more than the stone variety."

She thought of his efforts and concerns regarding the fairy bridge.

"Aye," Evan said curtly.

Catriona remembered that he had once mentioned a bridge collapse resulting in the deaths of some of his friends. She glanced at him in quick concern, regretting the subject.

"Mr. Fitzgibbon, I understand you came north to study the geological composition of the Torridon mountains," Wilkie said.

"Yes!" Arthur said avidly. "The local mountains here are primarily formed of Torridonian sandstone — the chocolate and red varieties — and Lewisian gneiss, which is a hard black stone identical to that found on the Isle of Lewis and the Isle of Skye. Natural crystal formations occur in these slopes, as well."

"Crystal? How fascinating," Catriona said, leaning forward.

"Are you an admirer of geology and rock formations, Lady Kildonan?" Arthur asked.

"I admire the mountains that contain Glen Shee," she answered, "Beinn Alligin to the west, Liathach the Giant to the south, Beinn Dearg north, and Beinn Eighe east of the glen. I much admire their peaks, corries, ridges, and stacks. But I know little about their composition or their thermal properties." She glanced out the window toward the blue, misted shape of Beinn Alligin. "At times the sun seems to shine through the upper peaks, as if they were made of thick glass. It's quite an enchanting effect."

"No magic whatsoever," Arthur said pragmatically. "Those are crystal beds, I would guess. That can happen at the very tops of the mountains, if the embedment is large enough."

"Oh, do not deflate the lady's dream," Evan said. "I rather like the thought of enchanted crystal mountains." He smiled at her over his coffee cup.

"Did you know that Beinn Alligin means 'Jeweled Mountain'?" Catriona asked. The men shook their heads, looking interested. "The point of the tallest peak, Beinn Sitheach in the Gaelic, is said to be made of pure crystal."

"Ah, Beinn Shee — the Fairy Mountain," Evan said. "I have very fond memories of it." He grinned at her, teasing, and Catriona smiled, too, for a moment loving the exchange. He looked so happy — so content. She wished it could always be that way between them.

"No one knows for sure about the crystal," she went on, "because no one has ever gone that far up. Professor Fitzgibbon, do you think there could be crystal beds up there?"

"It's very possible that they exist in good measure on the peaks," he said. "There are huge beds of white quartz among many of the northernmost Scottish mountain ranges, mixed in with black gneiss, above beds of sandstone and massive bases of metamorphic rock. As for the crystal, the most common forms in the mountains would be white quartz and perhaps some sizable deposits of smoky quartz — what we in Scotland call 'Cairngorm stones.' "

"Aye, it's quite common to find those sorts around the hillsides," she said. "Tell me, have you ever heard of a particular sort of crystal . . . that glows in moonlight?"

"Moonlight?" Arthur blinked. "Perhaps they are phosphorescent."

"Of course," Evan said. "Certain types of minerals have phosphorescent properties," he explained to Catriona. "That is, they glow with their own inner light and can be seen in dark crevices — eerie to see them winking like little balls of light in a cave or a deep cleft in a rock. A very curious phenomenon and not well understood."

Catriona felt a sense of excitement. "Are they crystals?"

"Crystalline formations?" Arthur frowned. "Well . . . not exactly, but sometimes phosphorescent minerals can be trapped inside crystals. Phantoms, we call them. Lovely things — quite rare. Definitely to be treasured when they are found."

Nodding, barely able to keep control of her excitement, Catriona smiled. "Have you ever heard of something called . . . a fairy wand, or a fairy crystal?"

Evan frowned, tapping his fingers on the tablecloth. "Aye. Certain types of clear or pale-colored crystals are called that, if they have several terminations clustered together, so that they resemble miniature fairy castles. Pretty little things. I had one once, as a boy. . . . Don't know what happened to it," he mused. "I used to collect rocks and crystals — had a box full of them." He smiled at Catriona. "Why all the interest, my dear?"

"I was hoping that a fairy crystal — particularly one that glows in the dark or in moonlight — could be found on Beinn Shee."

"Why?" Evan almost laughed, she thought, as if in surprise.

"I . . . promised a friend that she could have one of those, if it could be found."

"On top of Beinn Shee? That would be nearly an impossible task," Reverend Wilkie said. "I believe Beinn Shee has another name in the Gaelic, and though I cannot remember the Gaelic words, I remember the translation — the Inaccessible Pinnacle. They say it cannot be climbed, at least in the last part of the peak."

"So I have heard," Evan said. He glanced at Catriona. "Fitz and I made an attempt on the more challenging part of the north rock face when we first arrived, but the weather turned foul quickly. And, well, other distractions came up. Worthy ones, however," he added.

"Kildonan had a bit of an adventure on that mountain he will not soon forget," Arthur said. "But we must make another attempt. What do you say, Kildonan?"

"The idea still intrigues me," Evan said. "A mountaineering challenge, after all, is one of the reasons I came back to Kildonan."

"Then I shall suggest it to Miss Jemima and the rest of the group when they come back from their walk around the gardens. Shall we go later today?" Arthur asked.

"This afternoon Miss Murray and the ladies are organizing a picnic on one of the most scenic peaks, where the climbing is not too difficult," Reverend Wilkie said. "If the weather holds out, perhaps we could attempt Beinn Shee tomorrow or the next day. Lady Kildonan — you will join us, I hope?" He smiled.

"The day after tomorrow is Sunday," Catriona said. "Will you and your group have an outing on the Sabbath?"

"Oh, I had quite forgotten," Wilkie said with a laugh. "Well, being an Established Church minister of the moderate sort, I am not a strict Sabbatarian, nor are any of our group, to my knowledge. Does the thought of going out on a Sunday outing make you uncomfortable, madam?"

She avoided a direct answer. "You may find that the local people will not approve if they see you out and about on Sunday," she answered. "They may not speak very freely to you or serve you food if you stop for hospitality. And you may have trouble finding a guide or gillie to go with you, depending on whom you ask. As for me . . . I follow Kildonan practices now," Catriona said, and she forced a smile.

"My wife's father is the minister of Glenachan, at the other end of the Glen Shee," Evan said. "Free Kirk," he added.

"Oh," Wilkie said. "Then you were raised —"

"Strict Sabbatarian," Catriona acknowledged. "We were allowed to do nothing on Sundays but attend church, pray, and read the Good Book. We did not even cook or clean — all Sunday meals were prepared on Saturday evening. As for hillwalking, or riding in carriages for pleasure — my father forbade it, other than the brief walk needed to get to his church."

"Perhaps you would care to attend church on Sunday and then remain here, though I believe Miss Murray is planning a group outing," Reverend Wilkie said. "But I quite understand. I hope to attend the local church myself in the morning before climbing — that would be your father's, then?"

"Aye. Reverend MacConn of Glenachan. He would be very pleased to see you there," she said. "As for me . . ." She paused and looked at Evan.

"Whatever you would like to do, my dear,"

he said quietly. "You could go to church with your family, or perhaps observe prayers on your own and then join Miss Murray's outing. It's entirely up to you now."

She watched him for a moment, realizing that he was right. Much of her life had been spent in the shadow of strict authority, either that of her father and aunt, or the practices of the Free Church. She had always longed for freedom, finding it in small ways but never claiming it outright for herself — perhaps that was why she loved to walk endlessly in the hills on the excuse of the knitting scheme, and why she found such fulfillment in learning and cataloguing the old songs, when so many times during the year she was not permitted to sing at all.

And besides, she suddenly thought, Kenneth Grant would attend services in her father's church, as he always did. She had seen Grant there every Sunday for years, and had greeted him pleasantly, never suspecting that he might harbor ill will toward her or her family. Yet now, as she recalled the way he sometimes stared at her during the church sermon — flat and serious, with hidden thoughts — she knew far too well how dark his thoughts were. She had no desire to encounter the silent threat of his presence.

Evan smiled, faint and patient, and she knew that he waited for her answer. He would not dictate to her what she must do, or not do, on Sundays. And she realized, too, that he was offering her a chance for more freedom.

But she would have to take one of those risks he had talked about — the challenges that were easier for him to face than for her. She would have to step outside the perimeters of the life she had always known. Evan asked that of her in other ways, too, but he had left the decision to her, showing her patience and acceptance rather than force. He had no intention of infusing her decisions with his own will and opinions.

This was what it was like to be loved, she thought then, loved and supported for who she was, and given what she needed. The thought was a revelation.

She smiled slowly. "Go out on a Sunday? I just may do that," she told Evan. "I will think about it."

Chapter Nineteen

"To a grand picnic on the heights, ladies and gentlemen," Lord Wetherstone said, and he held his wineglass high.

Seated on a sun-warmed boulder beside Evan, Catriona raised her glass with the others, who sat on blankets or on various boulders. After sharing the toast, they resumed their luncheon, chatting in small groups while they ate an assortment of cold sandwiches, fruits, cheeses, and cakes, along with lemonade and wine, served on china with linens and glassware. Davey and Allan, the two gillies from Kildonan, had carried the baskets up the wooded slopes to the four-hundred-foot-high level where the group now gathered.

Catriona sipped, then set her glass down on a flat space on the rock she shared with Evan. Their picnic site was located in a corrie halfway along one of the slopes of Beinn Eighe. The slightly tipped natural bowl was shadowed by the mountain on one side, while the other half was filled with warm sunlight, the whole open to brisk winds.

The corrie commanded a wide, glorious view of Glen Shee and the mountains, and the fine morning mist had lifted to a cloudy but silvery day that gave pristine detail to the vast panorama. Jemima Murray had suggested stopping in the corrie for their picnic to admire the view and enjoy the fresh mountain breeze.

Catriona had been glad of that, for she was ready to rest and had a good appetite after more than two hours of walking and climbing. After leaving pony-drawn carts at the end of the road that ribboned through Glen Shee, the group had walked two miles along a wooded trail, then climbed steadily upward on a rough path that followed a long slope that was covered with tall pines and knee-high thickets of rust-colored bracken.

Stopping to gaze at a high, spectacular waterfall that spilled in frothy streams down raw rock, Catriona and the others had found it impossible to talk and be heard above the water's roar. Revived by the damp mist thrown off by the falls, they had quenched their thirst with the cold, clear water that swirled in the pool beneath the waterfall, and then they continued upward.

Higher still, the climb was easy but steep. Each traveler wielded a stout walking stick, and the two tireless gillies were available to help Lady Wetherstone and Anna Wilkie, whose stamina faded. Here the view overlooked the pine forests on the lower slopes, and the bleak turf, grass and tough old heather, were studded with stones of all sizes and varieties.

Sitting now and enjoying the chance to rest, having finished half of a ham sandwich and then some fruit compote, Catriona looked around, inhaling the fresh, clean, pine-scented air.

Laughing at something Evan said as he chatted beside her with Aedan MacBride, she felt a peacefulness, a lightness of spirit that she had not felt since childhood. Looking down on the glen, she thought about what she might have been doing today if she had not met and married Evan Mackenzie so quickly.

Perhaps she would have been slicing vegetables for that night's stew in the kitchen with Aunt Judith, or supervising the washing of bed linens, or dusting the parlor. She might have escaped for the afternoon to walk with Morag MacLeod, collect knitting, and learn a new song. Late at night, she would have sat in her bedroom with a single candle, bent over the painstaking work of transcribing music and copying lyrics in Gaelic and English, then adding annotations, to add to her growing collection of Gaelic songs. Then she would have climbed into the lonely bed that she would never have shared with a husband — for just days ago, she had been the Plain Girl of Glenachan.

Now she sat in clear sunshine halfway

above a beautiful world, enjoying fine company and excellent food, sipping wine, a lady of quality attended by the best servants.

And her husband, the earl of these lands, sat beside her, his shoulder pressed to hers now and then, blocking the wind and providing unspoken comfort and security. His mellow voice and quiet laughter thrilled through her, and the sight of his handsome profile, as cleanly drawn as a masterpiece, made her melt inside.

She felt happy, she realized — free and content, filled with hopes and excitement. Though it seemed more like a precious dream than reality, she wished she could hold on to it.

Evan leaned over to refill Catriona's wineglass, still involved in conversation with Sir Aedan MacBride. Reverend and Mrs. Wilkie sat with Emily Murray and Lord and Lady Wetherstone, while Arthur Fitzgibbon strolled over some large, smooth boulders with Jemima Murray, reaching out now and then to assist her. Davey and Allan began to clean up the luncheon, putting away the food, wrapping up the dishes and placing them in the baskets.

"Fitz has cornered Cousin Jemima," Evan remarked, watching as Fitzgibbon stood with Jemima on a boulder, his wide gestures becoming professorial. "He's explaining his glacial theories on the shaping of Scotland's mountain profiles by the pressure of masses of ice over eons of time. You see, my lass," Evan said, leaning slightly toward Catriona, "he believes that Skye and Lewis tore away from the northwest mainland eons ago."

"Which does make sense when one looks at the particular kinds of rock found only in those regions," Aedan commented.

"Aye," Catriona said. "Lewisian gneiss, for example, appears on Lewis and Skye as well as in the Torridons. Its distinctive striations of black gneiss and white quartz can be quite attractive." She grinned mischievously.

"Ah, you've been cornered by Professor Fitzgibbon, as well," Evan said, lifting a brow.

She laughed. "He did sit beside me at supper last night."

"I wonder if Miss Murray's interest in mountains runs to lectures in natural philosophy," Aedan mused.

"Could be. She seems spellbound," Evan said, and Aedan chuckled. Catriona saw Miss Murray lean toward Arthur in rapt fascination while he chatted enthusiastically, waving his hand toward another angle of the mountain view.

"Sir Aedan," she asked, "do you also have an interest in climbing and geology?"

"I do some climbing, though not for sport as Kildonan does," he answered. "There are respectable hills in the area of Strathclyde, where I live, though I climb more out of necessity than for enjoyment. As for rocks, I am familiar with geology due to my work — I'm a civil engineer. I build highways, mostly."

"Ah, an engineer like my husband?" she asked.

"We took engineering classes together at Edinburgh University. I was interested in building routes and pathways, and Evan was fascinated by the physical principles and the beauty of bridges. We have another friend who designs lighthouses — but he has always been very keen on putting himself at risk."

"So the risks of climbing do not appeal to you?" she asked.

"By nature, I'm not one for risks, madam," he said, his blue eyes sparkling. "I like life to be quite steady. My wife says I am dull in that way — though I prefer to think of myself as reliable and determined."

"Though he'll blast his way through a mountain if it gets in the way of his determination," Evan drawled.

Catriona laughed. She liked Aedan MacBride, and she liked that Evan seemed so relaxed and laughed so easily in his company.

"And besides, I did not come to Glen Shee to climb, Lady Kildonan, but to visit your husband," Aedan said. "He can be a daredevil like our friend Dougal Stewart, who builds the lighthouses. I came to see what new mischief Evan has wrought for himself."

"Quite a bit," Evan replied wryly, and then sipped his wine.

"So I see," Aedan said, and grinned. "I arrived at Kildonan just in time to learn your good news, apparently. That was a surprise."

"Aye, it was," Evan said succinctly. Catriona avoided answering altogether by glancing around. "A pity you did not bring Lady MacBride with you. Talk of surprises — news of your own wedding astounded me last year. You swore never to embroil yourself in matrimony," Evan said.

"Change can be healthy, even for those of us who resist it." Aedan lifted a brow as he looked at Evan.

"Well, I'm glad you found time to come up here, if only for a day or so," Evan said. "You said that you're bound for Skye?"

Aedan nodded. "The Parliamentary Commission asked me to evaluate the landscape for a new road there. And Dougal is starting a new lighthouse on the northwest coast of Skye, so we will both be there for a while, and we could both use your expertise, Evan. That's partly why I came here."

"Dougal wrote to tell me about his new project. He asked if I would come out to do some diving with him and examine the underwater foundations of the new structure."

"Diving!" Catriona said. "I thought your expertise was in bridges and geological formations."

Evan nodded. "Bridges and dockworks, both of which can rest on bedrock in rivers, lochs, or harbors. Diving skills can be quite useful, so I became a master diver several years ago. Dougal Stewart sometimes asks me to go down the deep to look at the integrity of the geological foundations."

"Oh, yes," Catriona said. "That sounds quite dangerous."

"It can be," Evan admitted. He glanced at Aedan. "Have you seen Dougal recently?"

"He and Meg — Dougal's wife, Lady Strathlin," Aedan added to Catriona, "visited Dundrennan a few weeks ago."

"Lady Strathlin?" she repeated. "I've heard the name. She was very generous to the Highland people in their . . . time of trouble during the evictions." She glanced at Evan, wondering if he noted her reference to the clearances in which his father had taken such a heavy hand.

"Lovely quiet lass, Meg," Evan said. "One would never know that her fortune exceeds that of the very queen. She and Dougal are well suited. That lad never has to work another day in his life, yet he carries on with his lighthouses. I think he enjoys his rather mythic struggles to put the things up."

"Just as I find a strange, unholy pleasure in blasting through hillsides to build roads," Aedan said. Evan chuckled.

"And you?" Catriona asked Evan. She relished not only the conversation, but the attention of two attractive, intelligent men, one of whom truly seemed like her husband, at least for this wonderful afternoon. "Do you find putting up your bridges to be mythic and exhilarating?"

Evan's smile disappeared. "No," he said abruptly, and he frowned at her so deeply that she almost gasped.

"You certainly enjoyed making repairs on our little bridge the other day." Her response was sharp.

"Bridge?" Aedan asked. "You were repairing a bridge?"

"There's a small masonry arched bridge on the estate that is in poor repair," Evan explained. "The damned thing is a hazard, yet the local Highlanders use it anyway. My wife nearly fell off it."

"I did not," she burst out.

"Fell? Good God," Aedan muttered. "Of all things —"

"Never mind," Evan barked, sending Aedan a quick glare. "The bridge will soon be replaced." He sipped his wine again while Catriona stared at him, dumbfounded by his sudden show of temper. Then he calmed. "Tell me, Aedan — how are Christina and your little one?"

"Both in excellent health, and Christina is even finding time again for her academic work." Aedan smiled at Catriona. "Our son was born in September. Kept us up half the night for the first month, but now the sprite seems to be settling in." He beamed proudly, and she thought again what a handsome, interesting man he was and how lucky his Christina must be.

She glanced at Evan, so tall and stunning and strong beside her, with his dark, wavy locks and mysterious hazel-green gaze, his deep voice that spun chills along her spine, his touch that could conjure such willing fire in her.

And she realized, sitting beside him, how fortunate she was herself, for this space of time in her life. Evan Mackenzie intrigued her and deeply attracted her. Marriage to him was the fulfillment of a blissful dream — why would she want that to end?

Suddenly, watching him, she wanted more with him, wanted his passion and his attention, desired his love and craved to feel his children inside of her. The depth and power of the urge almost sent her reeling where she sat.

She wanted to love him, wanted to give herself to him wholly, without question or reservation.

"I do hope you will both come have a peek at the bairn," Aedan was saying. "Christina would love to see you again, Evan, and I know she would be delighted to meet your bride." Aedan smiled at Catriona. "It's early

November now — why not spend Christmas with us at Dundrennan House? Dougal and Meg will be there with their two little ones, as well."

"Oh, that sounds lovely — oh," Catriona said, stopping herself, glancing down, unable to look at Evan then. They could be in the midst of dissolving their marriage by Christmas.

Evan took her arm as he sat beside her, his touch on her elbow warm and protective. Something inside of her melted to feel that, but she gave no hint of it. "We will certainly discuss it," he answered Aedan. "Won't we, my dear?"

She nodded, wishing that she truly had the freedom, and the privilege, to agree and accept the invitation on behalf of herself and her husband — her beloved husband.

"The descent is much easier than the upward climb, even if we are all so fatigued we could lie down for a nap anywhere along this path," Jemima said.

Evan laughed in agreement and glanced at Catriona, who walked beside him. Just for the excuse of touching her and being near her, he would have taken her arm or hand to assist her, but his bride was probably the most seasoned hillwalker in the group. She moved downhill with a natural grace, her dark gray skirt swinging about her ankles. It was short enough for comfortable walking, and now and then he had a glimpse of layers of ruffled petticoats and the slender contour of her ankles above sturdy leather brogans.

His Highland bride, he thought, smiling faintly to himself. The other ladies were experienced climbers and hillwalkers, but their outfits did not differ significantly from what they would wear to a tea party or a social call — wide skirts, parasols, gloves, shawls, and pretty little bonnets. Catriona's clothing looked practical and comfortable, and her Highland plaid shawl in brown, blue, and cream was not only flattering but its colors and pattern somehow harmonized with the earthy, simple beauty that surrounded them.

As they walked down a long wedge of the hill that was scattered with stones and rocks, Jemima and the others stopped repeatedly to admire the scenery or to examine pretty examples of rocks, and with Arthur more than happy to lecture about the geological varieties, their progress was slow. But the day was pleasant, the air not too cold, and there seemed no threat of rain despite gray clouds and veils of mist on the mountaintops.

"Oh, look, what's that?" Mrs. Wilkie asked, pointing to an adjacent slope, where a cluster of rocks had a deliberate beehive shape. "It looks like a cairn of some kind."

Catriona put a hand to her brow as she looked in that direction. "Aye, that is a very old cairn. No one quite knows what it commemorates, though."

"Is it a grave?" Lady Wetherstone asked, pausing. She seemed glad of any excuse to stop and catch her breath.

"I doubt it, unless it's a very ancient one," Catriona said. "Most cairns are piles of stone put up to mark an event or to honor someone who has died or has passed literally by the spot on their way to somewhere else. This has been here a long while. Over there, beyond it," she added, pointing, "is a remarkable thing, even more ancient — a stone with a natural hole in it."

"I have heard of those! I must see it — do you mind if we take a scenic detour?" Reverend Wilkie and his wife began to walk in the direction of the cairn, and the others followed.

Mildly interested, Evan strolled beside Catriona, who soon led the way. But the stone, when they reached it, frankly amazed him. Standing nearly five feet high, it was an upright monolith with a sizable hole in its upper end, like a crude stone sewing needle stuck in the ground.

"What a perfectly odd thing," Jemima said, sticking her hand into the hole. Emily, her sister, did the same, and then peeked through.

"It's quite pretty," Emily said, running her hand along it. "There are carved markings here — swirls and crosses and things."

Sir Aedan stepped forward. "Pictish carvings, perhaps." He bent to trace his finger over the designs. "My wife is an antiquarian expert in this sort of thing. She would be absolutely fascinated by these marks and very envious that I saw them without her."

"I'll make a rubbing impression on paper and send it along for Lady MacBride," Catriona offered, and Aedan smiled.

"Fascinating thing," Reverend Wilkie said, walking around the standing stone. "Actually, I've heard that stones with holes in them are the gifts of the fairies."

"I know a local Highland wife who would agree with that," Evan said, as he thought of Morag, who had spoken to him with such refreshing bluntness. He smiled privately at Catriona.

She nodded. "Many of the hills here are inhabited by fairies, so it has long been said," she murmured. "It is Gleann nan Sitheach, the Glen of the Fairies, after all."

"Fairies? I'm not so sure," Arthur said, coming close to examine the stone. "Holes are rare, but can occur naturally in stones, most often from the wearing action of water over eons. More than likely, this stone was transported here by some ancient tribe to be used for some superstitious purpose."

"This particular stone is thought to have magical properties," Catriona said, nodding.

"I've always heard that."

"How marvelous!" Anna Wilkie set her face in the hole next. "What sort of magic?"

"They say if you look through the hole, you will see the future," she answered.

Wilkie stepped forward. "What do you see, my dear?"

"The whole of this wonderful glen — it's like paradise," Anna replied. She stood and smiled at her husband. "That must mean our future will be lovely." He took her hand.

One by one, they each peeked through the stone. Evan took a turn, too, looking through it toward the downhill angle, as the rest had done, to see the vast, beautiful spread of the glen and the mountains marching into a misty infinity. "Our futures all look good, apparently," he said, and he turned toward Catriona, who had hung back, the only one who had not had a turn at the stone.

"Do you want to see your future?" he asked quietly.

She shook her head and gazed at him. "I intend to decide that for myself."

Her words had an almost physical impact, like an excitement deep within. He knew what she meant. "Good," he murmured.

They stood with the upright stone between them, she above and he below on the incline of the hill, each with a hand on the cool, gritty stone. He rested his fingers on the inner curve of the hole as he spoke.

"There's another use for this stone," Catriona said, as the others turned to listen. "This is called the Marriage Stone. In ancient times when a couple wanted to wed, they would come up here and say their vows, holding hands through the hole in the stone. That way they had no need of a priest," she added.

"How convenient," Lord Wetherstone said, as some laughed.

"How fitting that our newlyweds should stand there now," Anna Wilkie said, looking up at Evan and Catriona. "Though it's too early for you to renew your vows quite yet!"

"We must come back up here another time, then," Evan said. He looked up at Catriona just above him on the slope, and she returned his gaze somberly, the only person not smiling.

"Look how far ahead the gillies are!" Lord Wetherstone called. "We shall have to hurry to catch them."

As the others made their way down the hill, Evan stood waiting for Catriona. She did not move to follow, but stayed there with the stone between them. Her gaze swept the landscape and found and met his glance.

She moved her hand so that her fingers brushed his where they rested inside the hole. A casual, accidental contact, yet it seemed almost deliberate. A fluttering sense spiraled through him. He took her fingers in his before she could pull away and drew her closer in silence.

She did not protest, only watched him, her gaze direct and serious, filled with meaning and with a single question.

He knew the answer, somehow had always known it, and he wondered if she knew it as clearly as he did. Stepping up on the hill to come around to where she stood, he kept his fingers closed on hers inside the eye of the hole.

"Catriona —" Then he bent his head, unable to help himself, and she tipped her face upward and met him kiss for kiss, tender and slow, so slow, while he tightened his hand over hers inside the magical stone.

Pulling in his breath, he drew her to him with one hand while he kissed her again and then renewed it even more deeply when she leaned toward him. Entwining his fingers with hers, their hands woven together inside the stone, he felt her hunger begin to match his, felt her lips open beneath his, sensed the small, moist tip of her tongue. A feeling spun down to his feet like lightning.

The wind whispered cold over the slope, and he knew this could not continue, not here, standing exposed and windblown on a rock-strewn hill. Through the fog in his head, he heard someone call, heard another laugh. He pulled away reluctantly, but kept her hand with his, inside the stone.

"Tonight," he said. "Come to me tonight." He knew he should not push her to agree, but he could wait no longer — his body could not wait, nor could his soul. He felt compelled to have her, to merge as part of her again. And he still did not understand what drove him like this — the feeling was new, but more powerful than any other he had known, and its strength felt eternal.

Drawing back to look at her, seeing how the wind had tousled her hair and kissed her cheeks, he knew that he loved her. For him, their joined hands in the ancient stone seemed like a silent promise. He needed no other vows with this woman. He knew what he felt, what he wanted, had known some of it from the first night.

And he was fast losing reason to question the urge and the certainty. This union was sudden but right, and it would last. He trusted whatever voice in him insisted so calmly and clearly. But she was not sure — she took few risks — and he could not rush her.

He leaned forward and kissed her cheek. "We must go," he murmured. "They're enjoying this almost as much as I am."

"Evan," she whispered beside his ear. "Oh, Evan . . ." His name on her lips sounded like the wind that fluttered her plaid, and he heard desire and anguish in it.

"Catriona, my own," he murmured, and

somehow the sound of her name was like the voice of the mountain, that strong, that splendid. He felt strangely as if she worked some magic over him, and he its willing subject.

He leaned to kiss her again. "Tonight," he urged.

Then he let go of her hand. She stepped back, went around the stone, and headed down the slope toward the group who waited, smiling up at them.

Following, he realized that she had not answered him.

Chapter Twenty

"What a jolly fellow this is — a grand Highlander in full flourish!" Lord Wetherstone paused before a portrait of a Highland chieftain. "Another of Kildonan's ancestors, I suppose?"

Strolling between Lord and Lady Wetherstone, Catriona stopped with them to gaze up at the portrait in question. After returning from the hillwalk late that afternoon, most of the guests had rested after an enjoyable tea. Evan had gone to his study to look at estate records, while Catriona sat down to transcribe some Gaelic songs, all the while feeling a fluttery excitement as she tried to decide if she would go to Evan that night, alone in their rooms.

Later, after another simple supper, Evan had offered to conduct a tour of the castle for those guests who had not yet retired for the night. The circuit took them up the main stairway to the long portrait gallery.

"Oh, this is one of the best portraits we've seen so far," Catriona said, looking up. "What a handsome Highlander he is."

"Yes, but he looks like a savage with that wolf fur and all those weapons, and he's wearing such an awful lot of tartan," Lady Wetherstone observed. "Why is there so much cloth bunched around him? Lord Kildonan and Sir Aedan are wearing kilts tonight," she said, glancing at Evan and his friend behind them, "but their plaids are not like this one in the portrait at all."

"All Highland men wore such folded kilts, long ago," Anna Wilkie said, catching up to them. "It seems improper to us to show one's limbs, of course, but when the garments are worn by Highland men, there is a certain wonderful aesthetic, don't you agree, Lady Kildonan?" Anna looked at her. "Such marvelous masculine strength on display." Her pretty smile was surprisingly mischievous, and Catriona almost laughed to see it.

"Oh, aye, Mrs. Wilkie, I do agree," Catriona said.

She thought Evan looked rather marvelous himself, dressed in a pleated kilt of dark green and blue tartan with red and white accent stripes, along with a black jacket and waistcoat and tasseled knee stockings. Glancing at him now, she admired the powerful cut of his well-developed calves and strong, flat knees and felt a curious little thrill at the hint of his long, taut thighs beneath the woolen pleats and sporran. That led to images of the rest of his tightly muscled body, and though she blushed to herself, she could not help smiling.

Aye, she thought, perhaps she was ready to go to him tonight — she did not think she could resist it much longer.

She had been particularly fascinated by the portraits in the gallery, for many of the faces depicted there reminded her of Evan. Her husband's dark good looks and greenish eyes seemed to be an inherited trait among generations of Kildonan Mackenzies.

"That's the authentic Scottish kilt," Catriona said, looking up at the painting they stood beneath, a portrait of a fierce Highland warrior swathed in red plaid, brandishing a claymore and a brass-studded targe. "Plaids were originally one length of material, worn wrapped and belted about the waist. The free end was tossed over the shoulder and tucked to form a large pocket for carrying things," she explained. "At night, the Highlander could wrap himself in the long yardage of his plaid and sleep comfortably outdoors."

"Taking off one's clothing to make a bed out of it? What a dreadful thought," Lady Wetherstone replied.

"I rather like the idea," her husband said. "We could have used them on our outing today — what a brisk wind that was! And one would not have to bother with a change of clothes, a knapsack, or a blanket with such a practical garment, eh, Kildonan?" He grinned at Evan.

"Aye, that was the idea," Evan said, joining

them. "Highlanders are a creative and re-sourceful lot. This grand Highlander is Sir Niall Mackenzie, by the way, second laird of Kildonan. He was called Clever Niall. He had this tower keep built, which forms the center of the castle."

"However did a poor Highland warrior acquire the fortune to build such a fine castle?" Lady Wetherstone asked.

"Cattle thief," Evan said succinctly.

"Ah, Clever Niall," Aedan MacBride murmured, coming up to join Evan and the others.

While Catriona and the rest chuckled, Evan led them toward another portrait. "This is my grandfather, the first Earl of Kildonan," he said, indicating a rather stiff gentleman in a black evening suit with white waistcoat and white neckcloth. The chair behind him was draped with a length of plaid to indicate his Highland origins, but Catriona noticed that no plaid touched his staid person. A military medal adorned his coat lapel.

Evan's grandfather had a grim, humorless expression, and his back and long legs were ramrod stiff. He was among the handful of Kildonan Mackenzies who did not resemble Evan and Jean but had the brown eyes and brown hair of the other side of the family.

She began to wonder what Evan's child and her own might look like — would it inherit the red hair and blue eyes prevalent in her line, or the greenish eyes and dark, glossy hair that occurred so frequently in his? Pausing beside the others, she put a hand subtly to her abdomen and wondered if a miracle was already occurring inside of her — or if it could soon be started there. All she had to do was decide, and accept, and the rest could follow.

But their passionate union the first night they met might have already produced a child. She ducked her head and allowed herself to wish it were so for a moment, and she felt grateful knowing that sometimes it was possible for love's many miracles to be that simple.

"He was already a viscount — Lord Glendevon — inherited from his father," Evan went on. "The earldom was granted only thirty years ago by Queen Victoria after his brave showing in India. He single-handedly rescued an entire besieged regiment and managed to bring back a fortune in gold and jewels, most of which he donated to the crown. That was enough to earn him the queen's gratitude, I suppose, since she honored him by creating him earl of his own estates — the whole of Kildonan and Glen Shee."

"Yes, I remember hearing that story," Wetherstone said. "A small earl by some standards, but nonetheless a peer appointed by the queen. So you are the third earl, sir. Interesting."

"A few generations back, we were really no different from most of the people in this glen — small lairds with herds of cattle and some sheep, involved in clan wars and loyal to our kin above all else." Evan looked pointedly at Catriona for a moment. "To be honest, I have never been comfortable with my titles, and I would not mind being simply a Scottish laird. That would be more than enough for me." He smiled faintly.

Lady Wetherstone and the Wilkies, along with MacBride, strolled ahead to study the portraits at the far end of the hallway. Catriona looked back toward Evan, hesitating between her duty as hostess and her desire to be near her husband. Lord Wetherstone and Evan lingered with the grandfather's portrait in quiet conversation.

"A pity to reduce the estate, really, with its proud history," Wetherstone said, rocking back on his heels as he contemplated the starched figure of the first earl.

"Reduce?" Catriona glanced quickly at Evan, who did not seem to hear her.

"Aye, a shame," Evan answered Wetherstone, "but the place cannot be managed properly from a distance of three hundred miles. I have a town home in Edinburgh — and I am often far away from there, working on engineering projects. Sir Aedan, for example, would like me to go to Skye to consult on a road project there. Being laird of such a large estate needs my full attention. Otherwise the needs of the glen will simply not be met — and I would be a very inadequate laird, indeed."

"I understand your position, absolutely. Dividing it into smaller estates and renting out the castle seems a better solution," Wetherstone commented.

"Aye. At least that is what I had decided to do," Evan said, looking toward Catriona, "when I first came back here to Kildonan." He held her gaze, and she saw something in his eyes, in that moment, that she could only describe as pain.

She caught her breath and glided closer, not caring a whit if it seemed rude to leave those who had wandered ahead. This conversation had her whole, and intense, attention.

Her heart beat fast, for she realized he was discussing the possible sale of Kildonan to Wetherstone and his lady wife.

"Yes, I see your position," Wetherstone said. "If one comes all the way up here, one would want to stay for a while. Perhaps spend at least the hunting season or the summers here. Certainly not winter — wouldn't want to be stranded here, eh?"

"Certainly not," Evan murmured. His glance flickered again toward Catriona. She felt as if they were having a silent conversation of their own — he somber and almost apologetic, she increasingly indignant — and she further imagined that it would become very fiery, very shortly, as soon as they were alone.

After those luscious, fervent kisses at the standing stone that afternoon, she had craved to be with him that night. But now, realizing the awful implications of this conversation, she felt the flames of anger and fear rather than desire. She could not bear to see him give up Glen Shee and Kildonan to another man — an Englishman, no less — who would dictate changes as he saw fit.

Nor could she bear to lose her new home with her husband just when she felt that the dream might come true. Kenneth Grant had claimed that Evan would definitely sell — and she hated the fact that Grant could be right about anything to do with Evan.

"Well, now that I'm seeing this wonderful place for myself," Wetherstone said, "I'm seriously considering the purchase. How is the hunting? Good, you say?" He looked at Evan.

"Evan?" Catriona asked quietly, glancing at her husband. She did not care about the question of hunting. She wanted to know the full truth behind this dialogue.

His gaze skirted hers, piercing and quick, before he looked at Wetherstone. "Excellent hunting, sir. My father was quite the sportsman, and his hunting trophies are throughout the place. There's a sixteen-point stag head mounted in the smoking room if you're interested. I've never been keen on hunting myself. Arthur can tell you something about Kildonan's appeal to sportsmen. He was out with Mr. Grant, a local laird and physician, just today."

"Ah, so there is a physician nearby? Very good. My dear, there is a physician in the glen," Wetherstone called out.

Lady Wetherstone turned and came back toward them. "Is there? Excellent. That was one of my questions."

"He's not a qualified physician," Catriona said abruptly.

Evan and the Wetherstones looked at her as if she had sprouted another head.

Lady Wetherstone blinked. "Oh dear! An impostor?"

"Not an impostor, but he never finished his education and does not know as much as he claims. Not that Highlanders care about medical degrees, but a Southerner might take issue with it. For medical knowledge in this glen, madam, we often consult croft wives skilled with herbs and potions. Although they may give you a strand of knotted red thread to carry with you, or rub snails upon your person, or recite a fairy charm" — here she looked hard at Evan — "they will invariably help whatever ails you."

"Oh!" Lady Wetherstone looked at somewhat of a loss. "But one would be so healthy living here in the Highlands, with such invigorating air. One might never need a doctor." She smiled.

"Such a healthy environment," Lord Wetherstone agreed.

"Oh, aye, except for the lung fever," Catriona said. "We are particularly prone to it here in the winter months — and both young and old are so susceptible." She shook her head. "But a good remedy for the cough is to swallow some roasted mice several times a day and rub a stone covered with one's own saliva on the chest. Works quite well, I hear," she said. "So you need not worry about ailments here."

"Oh, oh!" Lady Wetherstone raised her lace-mittened hand to her mouth and looked slightly green.

Evan narrowed his eyes to glare at Catriona over Lady Wetherstone's head. "Certainly if you and your lady wife were to purchase part of the Kildonan estate," he said, turning to Wetherstone again, "you would never regret it. The scenery here, as you learned today, is utterly spectacular."

"It is quite beautiful, and it seems so good for the soul," Lady Wetherstone said, recovering a little.

"Aye, we often go to the hilltops to watch the most terrible storms sweep toward us from the islands to the west," Catriona said. "They are magnificent to watch. Until lightning strikes or the wind tears the roof off the house. Then you'll be glad to be snug in your castle."

"My dear," Evan said in a warning tone. "And the hillwalking, of course, is immensely enjoyable. The landscape is so wild and romantic, really."

"So vast," Catriona agreed, "that one could get lost in it. And the weather is so unpredictable that one never knows what will happen next." She smiled at Evan. "Isn't that true, dear?"

"Sometimes," he said between his teeth. "I did want to point out that we have at present about fifty thousand sheep on the estate, sir. The income from that can be very respectable."

"Aye. Imagine catching all those sheep to clip them and gather the wool for market," Catriona said, leaning forward a little. "And Highlanders are said to be so lazy — though I don't find it to be true, but I have never had to catch and clip sheep myself. Perhaps I would be a laggard, too, if I had to do that instead of sitting in my cozy wee house." She laughed lightly. "And it is so inconvenient to hire Lowlanders to come up here to do the work seasonally."

"My dear," Evan said, taking her elbow and squeezing, "I think Sir Aedan would like to discuss some of the other portraits with you." He tried to steer her away, but Catriona stood her ground. She was enjoying herself suddenly, after her initial bout of fury with Evan. She felt certain and righteous, like a warrior queen defending her homeland from invaders.

"Lady Kildonan," Lord Wetherstone said, "how would you describe life in the Highlands, then? Would you recommend this as a place to live?"

"I love it here, and personally I would never leave it. *Ever,*" she answered, pulling her elbow out of Evan's grip. "But I am a strong and healthy woman and raised to this place. I walk everywhere, usually several miles a day, sometimes uphill all the way. And, of course, life is a bit more rustic here, but we are used to it."

"R-rustic?" Lady Wetherstone inquired, likely still thinking about roasted mice.

"I have never known many of the benefits and conveniences that Southerners enjoy on a daily basis, but then I do not miss them. We bring up most of our supplies and foodstuffs regularly from the markets at Inverness or Fort William, as our kitchen gardens can be meager. If you enjoy oranges or lemons or bananas, you will have to pay dearly for them. And if you like good roads to handle a sociable or even a gig — well, you could speak with Sir Aedan and see what he advises," she added, smiling. "Oh, and regular postal service, recent newspapers, and even English-speaking staff and merchants are hard to come by here. I suppose the Gaelic culture of the remote Highlands can seem like a foreign country to outsiders. Is that a consideration for you?"

"Oh, my," Lady Wetherstone said, glancing at her husband.

"May I ask why you're interested?" Catriona inquired sweetly. "Are you thinking of taking a longer holiday in the area?" She slid an intent glance toward Evan.

"My dear," he said in a near hiss, "thank you. I think you've been quite enough help." He turned her firmly with a hand at her waist. "Mrs. Wilkie looks to be in need of rescue. Sir Aedan and Reverend Wilkie are discussing salmon fishing."

"Very well. So nice to speak with you, Lady Wetherstone, Lord Wetherstone. I hope to continue our wee chat tomorrow." She inclined her head and turned, skirt swirling.

Evan still had a hand at her waist, and he bent low. "I do hope we can continue our wee chat tonight," he murmured, and his tone had a distinct, new edge.

"Oh aye, now I am really looking forward to it," she said between her teeth, and she glided out of his grip.

"O! Si rùn mo chéill'a bh'ann," Catriona sang, pacing back and forth on the worn carpet in the little sitting room. *"Hu ill o-ho-ro, hu ill o!"* She repeated the phrases again,

singing them softly and intently to herself. *"O! Si rùn mo chéill'a bh'ann!* Oh, my secret love was she!"

After dashing over to a little table placed between two armchairs, she picked up a pencil and scribbled down the musical notation on the scale she had drawn on the page. She sang the phrases again, near to a whisper, her fingers going madly, softly, in the air as if on the keys of a pianoforte. "Oh, my secret love was she, *Hu ill o-ho-ro!"* Biting her lip, she nodded to herself in time with the music in her head.

The hour was late, but she was not tired — certainly not — after that tense exchange with Evan earlier, under the guise of politeness. After the guests had retired for the night, she had paced her room, waiting for Evan's knock. When it did not come, she had gone to his door.

Hesitating, she then let anger fuel her and knocked boldly. He had not answered, and after a few minutes she had opened the door to find that he was not there. All her courage in finally knocking on his door had been for naught.

Unable to rest or sleep, she had turned to her work. Days ago, she and Evan had burned several pages of her songs to keep the fire going in the little shieling hut. She had not found much time since to write down the tunes again. Taking up the work now gave her an outlet for her agitation and a focus for her energies. Four of the lost songs were completed, and she had nearly paced a path in the old worn Turkish carpet on the floor.

And still he had not come back.

"My secret love was she," she sang again in translation, and left the refrain for the next verse. Fingers flying in the air, for that helped her to transcribe the music, she scribbled down more of the tune, then wrote the next few Gaelic lines, singing them, then translating them and singing them again. "Lips like raspberries, mouth like wine . . ."

"Oh, my secret love was she," Evan sang.

Catriona jumped. She dropped her pencil and let it roll away. He stood in the open doorway of his room, filling the frame, his shoulder leaned on the jamb, his opposite hand propped against the lintel. He wore the black jacket, waistcoat, and kilt he had worn at supper, but his neckcloth was gone, his collar open. His hair was mussed, and his eyes gleamed.

"What a bonny wee song," he said. "My secret love was she. *Hu ill o-ho-ro, hu ill o* . . ."

He sang it in perfect pitch, his voice deep and true, with such a mellow quality that she felt shivers listening to the beautiful sound. She had not known that he could sing like that.

But there was much she did not know about her husband. She had never seen him drunk, either. She stood.

He leaned his weight heavily on his hand, lowered his head, and fastened her with an intense stare from under dark brows.

"Aye, an excellent Highland tune," he said. "Sing it after dinner next, will you? Our guests will be so entertained. *Hu ill o, my secret love was she*. A wee touch of the Highland flavor here at Kildonan, provided by our own Lady Kildonan."

She walked toward him.

"Lips like raspberries," he sang low. "Mouth like wine . . . What was the rest?" he asked. "Hair like fire? Temper like . . . ah, the terrible storms that sweep in from the islands? The ones that blow the roofs off the houses? The ones you climb up into the hills to see — when you are not lost," he ground out, "or fevered or busy consuming mice."

"You've been drinking," she said, folding her hands tightly.

"Aye, thank you," he said, and he pushed away from the door. "Does the minister's daughter disapprove? The same minister's daughter that fed it to me by the spoonful not so long ago and enjoyed a wee dram herself, before she got out of her clothes?"

She lifted her head indignantly and tightened her clasped hands in silence.

"Madam, pardon me, that was poorly done," he murmured.

"It was," she agreed. "My disapproval depends on what was consumed, how much — and whether it is a habit."

"Whisky, enough to keep up with Wetherstone — who is a sponge for the stuff, apparently — and no, it isn't a habit," he said. "I've only been very drunk one other time in my life, and I did not much like it. I prefer a clear head," he said, stepping toward her, "when I must deliver bad news."

"And what might that be?" She straightened her shoulders as he came closer, but she stood her ground, staring at him resolutely, though her heart pounded.

Chapter Twenty-one

"I've just had a long chat with Wetherstone," Evan said, "and the grand fellow has decided not to buy a single bit of Kildonan sod after all, nor rent the castle at the handsome price he had earlier proposed to me. Not that he dislikes the Highlands, mind you," he went on, stepping toward her again. "He is very keen on hunting holidays and climbing tours. But his wife is not keen to live part of the year in the remote northwest Highlands among savages. I wonder why." He folded his arms. "They'll purchase an estate near Inverness, or one closer to Stirling . . . and civilization."

"That is good news," she said. "At least for them."

"And for you, too, no doubt. The bad news, my dear countess, is for me and for my solicitors, those money-hungry devils that await me in Edinburgh."

"Solicitors?" she asked.

"I need funds, madam, and this estate must provide them. And I very much needed Wetherstone to follow through on his promise to purchase a good deal of this property — more than half. Now I have lost his offer.

But you knew that would happen," he said. "You deliberately undermined my plan, and it didn't take long. Lady Wetherstone is so upset that she's taken to her room with a sick headache. Not only is Lord Wetherstone upset about learning the supposed truth of life as a Highland laird — he's not happy about being shut out of his wife's room!"

He thundered the last, pointing at her own door. Catriona said nothing, though she raised her eyebrows high at the unwanted image of Lord and Lady Wetherstone amorously together.

"Of course I can sympathize with the man on the latter problem," Evan went on, "since I share the same dilemma."

"You could have come to my room whenever you wanted," she said. "I've waited to hear your knock on my door since our first night here, yet nothing. You've left me alone."

"As I promised," he pointed out, fisting his hands at his waist. "And did you knock on my door? It would have been open to you if you had. But my knock would be pointless, wouldn't it, for both of us? Apparently you have no intention of staying on as my wife. That became clear to me tonight."

"How so?" she demanded. "Because I do not want you to sell this place to someone else, especially to an Englishman? Because I think you should have discussed it with your wife first?"

"How could I," he growled, "when the agreement was made weeks before I had a wife? Lord Wetherstone and I discussed this in detail in Edinburgh two months ago. You had nothing to do with it then." He strode a few steps, shoving fingers through his hair, turned and strode back.

"I have something to do with it now," she said.

"Oh, aye, you've had quite a hand in it," he muttered, turning to cross the same carpet she had paced earlier.

"You could have told me," she said. "Just as you could have told me that you were the Earl of Kildonan!"

"And what was I supposed to say? 'Oh, greetings. I'm the new earl about to sell the place out from under you. Pass that blasted blanket so we can keep warm in here'?" He flashed out a hand in an angry gesture.

"You could have come to me and explained," she said. "I have lain alone in that bed, awake well into the night, thinking about the future — our future, as you asked me to do — and while I was beginning to believe perhaps we could have a wonderful life here after all, as earl and countess, as man and wife, as — mother and father someday" — she gasped a breath, hurting to know that her deepest needs and desires

343

might be snatched away — "you were plotting to sell the land, rent the castle, and go south as fast as you could!" She was shouting now. Tendrils of hair came loose, slipped down, and she ignored them, breathing heavily as she watched him.

"I did not know," he said quietly, "that you were thinking that way — I rather thought it was the other way — that you meant to dissolve this marriage. How was I to know?"

"You could have asked me!"

"I was waiting! I gave you a chance to think, as you wanted! Starting over, do you recall that? Though I'll be damned if I'll come courting with flowers and pretty speeches. I'll play no games. Be my wife, or not, as you will. But let me know which way your head is turning with the changing winds, madam!"

"Yours is clearly turned south," she snapped, "toward Edinburgh and your life away from here."

"Not from desire, but from need," he returned, his voice quiet but firm now. "I must have funds, as I said. Some of this estate must be sold. There is no choice."

"Why?" She folded her arms. "Another matter you could have discussed. How can I agree to be your wife in full, if I do not know much about you? Drinking, debt, secret identity — these are not good signs! And how can you be in debt, when your father milked this land for profit over years!" This, she realized, deeply bothered her. She simply could not understand how he could need even more funds from the estate, when the fortune his father had created for him was said to be vast.

"What do you know of me, or my affairs?" It was a challenge, his voice rough-edged. "Tell me — what do you really know of me?"

"I know you have kept secrets from me," she snapped.

He nodded. "Then you know that I often keep things to myself. It is my nature, though it is not always wise of me to do so. I admit my flaws, madam, and that is one. Go on. What else do you know of me?"

"I know you are — the son of the man who sent most of my friends and family out of this glen." She drew in a breath that caught and almost became a sob. "I know that."

"Since he did not raise me past the age of wearing knickers, then I am free of his influence for the most part," he said. "My mother and her family have had the stronger influence, and they are Highlanders in their roots and their souls, fine people who now live and do good work in the Lowlands. I love the Highlands, Catriona. For years I denied that in myself. But since I have been here — and have been with you — I see that it is in my soul, and there is nothing I can do about that."

"Then why sell this place?" she demanded. "Why leave Kildonan and leave me? Why give these lands over to others who will misunderstand our needs here, our lives, and cause more problems like we had under your father's influence?"

"Leave you?" he asked softly, as if she had said only that.

She nodded, gasping suddenly to fight tears. "If you sell your right to Kildonan and Glen Shee . . . I will not go with you. I will not leave my glen."

He pulled in a breath, glanced away. "Your father and aunt were about to send you down to Glasgow."

"I would have gone to live with friends in the high hills here. Even if we would be evicted later," she added bitterly.

"I would not send you away."

"Wetherstone might. Grant might," she blurted. "I know he wants to buy some of these lands, too — he told me. You must not sell to him."

"Grant? Why not? His lands border Kildonan. He is at least a Highland laird in residence here. He will not care if he cannot get his oranges and newspapers on time," he snapped, waving an arm. "Perhaps I shall sell him as much of this land as I can, now that Wetherstone has lost interest."

"Why sell? Why not stay here — stay with me" — she was near to crying now, but would not let the tears fall — "and be a Highland laird yourself?"

He frowned at her for a long moment. She thought perhaps the drink was spinning in his head, wondered if he would answer. "The Highlanders of Glen Shee are not fond of the new earl."

"They could be," she said. "Prove yourself to them."

"How?" He huffed a laugh.

"You wanted to fix the bridge," she suggested. Her heart began to pound with new hope. "You could give them back their homes."

He crinkled his brow as if puzzled. "Impossible."

"Not at all." She knew that for a fact. "They could be found. Brought back."

He dismissed it with an impatient shake of his head. "I have to sell Kildonan. And I have to fix that blasted bridge," he growled. "That must happen."

"Do you think no one will buy land with a broken bridge on it? Don't be ridiculous."

"I cannot tolerate having it on my land," he said. "You do not understand."

"Then tell me," she said. "And tell me why you have to sell. If I am your wife, I should know these things."

He took a long step toward her, took her by the waist, drew her toward him so that her body met his, with layers of clothing between them. Yet she could feel him hard and strong against her. "Are you going to remain my wife? Which way does that wind blow, Catriona Bhàn?"

He remembered, she realized. He remembered that he had called her fair, when others had labeled her only big or tall. That thought, and the warm press of his hands at her waist, made her feel as if she were beginning to melt from within.

"Catriona," he murmured when she did not answer. He lowered his head, nuzzled her nose with his, soothed his lips over her cheek. "Catriona . . ."

Indeed, she was melting, would turn to a willing puddle of desire in his arms if he did not stop touching her, sliding his lips on her cheek so softly —

Or kissing her mouth. When he did, she sighed out, near a gasp, and opened to his kiss, could not help herself. He pulled her to him, where he was so hard and insistent for her, and his mouth took hers almost roughly, the taste of whisky clean and pungent on his breath, on his lips and tongue. She circled her arms around his neck and kissed him in turn, for she could not stop, feeling her heart slam in tune with his.

Then she pulled back, shoved to get free, for she could feel how intensely he wanted her then, and she wanted him, too, with an almost desperate need. Yet she fought it, pushed away, and he let her go. And that stepping away broke her heart a little.

"And so the Highland winds change again, do they?" He lifted his hands as he stepped back, and she felt the almost physical tug in the empty space between them.

"How can I be the wife of a Highland man," she said, "if he is not in the Highlands? Why must you sell?"

"Are you my wife? That is a knotty question, isn't it?"

She lifted her head. "We have not had much time to decide that."

"I do not need much time," he growled. "I know what I want — you, my dear lass. I do not need proof, as you seem to want. I just know. And God save me, I cannot say why I feel this way," he muttered. "Particularly at this moment."

She folded her arms, felt her chin wobble. His revelations astonished her, gave her hope. But she kept to the safe path, as she always must, while he was willing to swing out into the riskier areas. "I am not asking for proof," she said. "I only want to know why you want to sell my home out from under me — not this castle. That is yours. Glen Shee — that is my home."

He nodded once. "My father left considerable debt — he put a good deal of money into Kildonan and its thousands of sheep, but he did not clear all the debts before he died. I had some immediate funds and made up most of the deficit. But I have . . . another debt, and sales from the estate must go toward satisfying that."

"What debt is that?" she asked.

He blew out a breath, looked away. "What does it matter? It will be paid, no matter what I have to do."

She realized that he would not tell her, and that she would be a harridan to press him for it. That must come in its own time. Some secret troubled him deeply, and she must wait and have faith that whatever it was, he would handle it with the same integrity that she saw in him in all matters.

Standing there in silence in the small, quiet space that wedged between his room and hers, she knew how much she wanted to be his wife. But she could not leave Glen Shee. It would tear her apart, and she would not be the same woman, wife, lover.

"So you still intend to sell to make up this debt, whatever it is?" she asked softly.

"Aye," he said, half turned away from her, head down, hands bracing his waist.

"Then . . . even if we start again, as we agreed, we will have to end it," she said. "I will not leave Glen Shee. I will not."

"Stubborn lass," he murmured, and he glanced at her over his shoulder, still half turned from her. "What makes you think we can only make a marriage here in Glen Shee?

What has that to do with it?"

"It has all to do with it," she said. She stood quietly, strongly, shoulders squared. "It is part of me. I cannot undo that. If it is not part of you, I understand — but I cannot leave here."

"And if you had been evicted with the rest, those years ago? Would you not have coped, madam?"

She shook her head. "I would have withered," she said softly. "The mountains — the earth — I am part of that, somehow. I would have faded. As many of the people who left have done."

"How do you know?" His glance was sharp.

"I know." She lifted her head, reminding herself that some secrets must be kept. He had them, and she had them, too.

He looked up, toward the window that he now faced. Though it was dark outside, the moon, near full, hung over the mountains far beyond the curtained glass. "The marriage is in place," he said. "We cannot go back to its start, and we cannot leap forward to its end. We have tasted each other, and we both want more. You cannot deny it."

She kept her head high. "I do not deny that."

"Then make your decision, Catriona. Is the marriage worth it to you? Are you willing to make the effort, even if you do not know where we will be or in quite what direction you are headed? It is something like climbing, madam," he said, indicating with a nod the mountains in the distance. "One sets out to climb because the peak is enticing, alluring. So beautiful that it must be conquered and made your own. It holds some sort of bright promise, far off there, so unknown, so far above what you have known, so much finer, better, greater. Do you know what I mean?"

"I know," she said. "It is hope and dreams."

"Aye. And you know it's there. You have gone up those heights a little, and you are compelled to go farther. You make the commitment, the promise. And then find that it is not so easy as you thought. There is effort involved, as well as joy. You must work for the joy. Are you willing to put heart and soul into the venture no matter where it takes you?"

"I might be," she said.

"I am," he said. "Though I do not know where it will go. But I know the mountain is beautiful. Strong. And will make me stronger and better for knowing it. The mountain gets hold of you," he said, turning to look at her. "It gets into your blood, your dreams, becomes part of your soul. It is beyond beautiful, and you will never be the same if you make the commitment and stay with it. You will be a thousand times better for it. It will test you and then transform you — when all you thought to do was conquer it and call it your own."

Listening — for his voice was of that caliber that vibrated in her very soul, melted her resistance and her heart, could dissolve her anger and fear if she let it, that beautiful, deep, resonant velvet voice — she walked toward him, compelled, standing close, enthralled.

"Go on," she whispered. "The mountain."

"If you pledge to stay with the climb —" He turned, moving so that he stood very close to her, looming over her like a mountain, the only man she had ever known who was so much taller than she was, so much more willful, and so very beautiful in body and soul. "Be prepared, Catriona."

"For what?" she whispered.

He leaned toward her, reached out, swept his fingers along her cheek. "For the passion you will experience when you attain that height. You will never know anything like it in your life. When you commit to the risk and find the courage to follow this through," he said, leaning close, "your soul will open up. I swear it. I know it."

She stared at him, and he leaned close. His knuckles brushed along her jaw. Shivers poured through her as she watched him, searched his eyes.

"And you want me to take a risk," she said.

"I am saying there is great reward in the risk." His fingers slipped deep into her hair, tugged at the knot wound in the net. "The mountain is the other, the beloved, the unattainable and the attainable, all at once." He whispered as he spoke, and she felt him slipping the pins loose, one by one. She closed her eyes for a moment.

If she wanted, she could stop him now, she could ask for more time, for more explanations. Or she could simply follow the quickening of her heart and see where it led, as she had done before with him.

"It's true," she murmured. "I do not generally take much risk. I had a demanding father, and I was raised in a strict religious household. . . . I was never allowed much freedom, though I admit . . . that I always wanted it, and took it where I could, on my own."

"In your songs," he said. "In your wanderings in the hills."

She nodded, grateful that he understood. "One time only," she said, "I found my courage and followed my heart. That was when I met you . . . and . . ."

"And loved me, as I loved you, that night." He still whispered, and his fingers felt divine, warm and sure as he pulled the pins out of her hair.

Catriona nodded wordlessly, watching him. The net binding her hair came loose, and the copper tresses spilled over her shoulders. Evan drew the net off and pushed it and the hairpins carelessly into his pocket. Then he gently combed his fingers through the mass of her hair.

He stood so close that she could feel the heat emanating from his body, could smell faint traces of cigar smoke and mountain air. His hands felt like magic, yet all he did was slowly stroke his fingers through her hair, from crown to shoulders.

She closed her eyes slowly, tilted back her head. Feeling as if she might dissolve, she knew she was being seduced by her own husband — and she did not want to stop him this time. Her body tingled subtly, began to throb needfully in places, and she felt a growing hope that he would touch her elsewhere, that he would kiss her and pull her into his arms and finally love her.

He bent closer, so that she sensed his breath, clean with whisky, gently passing over her cheek.

"When we met," he said, "you faced a great risk. And considering the trouble it brought you — your supposed state of sin and this marriage — it is understandable if you regret taking the risk." Still his fingers stroked, caressed the heavy silk of her hair, until she thought she would go mad with wanting more.

"I took a risk then, and I knew it. And I do not regret it. Any of it," she whispered, looking up at him. Head to foot, she stirred and burned for him, the awareness in her body overtaking her senses.

But she closed her eyes briefly and knew that she must confess what she had done that first night. "I wanted that to happen between us, Evan. It was my fault."

He paused his hand, cupping her head. "Your . . . fault?"

She nodded. "I wanted to know what it was like to be loved . . . like that, with you. Just once, for I thought the chance would never come again in my life. When we kissed and then tried to keep each other warm, I felt it so strongly — I wanted to be with you desperately. You never owed me an apology for what happened — and you certainly did not owe me marriage." She looked away. "You did not ruin me. I offered myself."

"Ah. So I was used, is that what you are saying?"

"You . . . were trapped into needing to marry me. Though I did not mean for that part to happen. I swear it." She looked down in misery, yet felt relieved to confess. She wondered if he would be so angry that this would be the end, rather than a new beginning.

"You just meant for the other to happen, because you wanted to know what it was like," he murmured.

She nodded. "With you." When she heard his soft huff of laughter, she looked up in surprise. He took her by the shoulders, his hands large and easy upon her.

"Catriona, we both needed warmth and the solace of each other. What happened was utterly natural for our bodies. You did not act wantonly — you only responded to the very strong urges of a healthy body, though it was new to you. But it was not my first experience. I should have stopped, but somehow I could not. And I suspect you could not, either."

She watched him. "I thought . . . I made you do that —"

"Shocking lass," he said tenderly, lifting a brow. He slid his hands to her waist, snugged her against him. "It's a very good thing you married me."

"But I never meant to hold you to any obligation. You have no use for a poor Highland wife. I have no title, no fortune, nor even an inheritance, no social importance, no influence. If you have debts, you should have been free to marry an heiress."

"Oh? And what makes you think I want a wife with those qualifications?"

"You are an earl — you need a true countess, raised to that life. I fear that later you will regret this marriage, when you realize how unsuited we are and how little you have benefited. And then you will resent me and cast me aside, and we will live apart, or separate altogether. I do not want a marriage like that."

"Neither do I." His tone took on a sharp edge. "My parents had a marriage like that. I never want that for myself; nor do I want a society success for a wife, regardless of money or influence or whether or not she enhances my status."

"But you are a peer of the realm —"

"As I tried to tell you before, I think of myself as Evan Mackenzie, not the Earl of Kildonan. And Evan Mackenzie is content with a wife who will match him wit for wit and strength for strength, a wife who will see his flaws and still care about him. A wife whose generous, loving nature will make him a better man. A better man, not a better earl," he stressed.

"But —"

"Catriona Bhàn," he murmured softly. "Hush."

He tipped her chin with a knuckle and lowered his head, and the touch of his lips upon hers was slow and deep, and within that kiss was the promise of all she had ever wanted and more.

She sank forward into his arms.

He filled with fire the moment his mouth took hers. The kiss began with hard insistence and grew tender and exploring, lips fitting, melding, caressing. She opened to him, sighed, the taste of her sweet, the sensation one of forgiveness. Somehow he knew he had waited for her most of his life, and he felt as if he had kissed her a thousand times, as if somehow he knew her wholly, totally, and felt that she knew him that well, too.

Above all, he was aware that he loved her, without doubt, no matter how brief their acquaintance. That no longer astonished him and rather took on the sheen of a miracle in his heart — that he could love, that it could enter his life so easily, when he had known suffering in the past and had not forgiven himself. Now the love that brimmed up inside of him felt like a blessing, like a gentle flood of warm rain, a soothing reassurance from some other, powerful source. That revelation blended now with urgent, deep-seated desire.

Aye, he was a little drunk, he knew. An evening's worth of whisky heated his blood and whirled in his head. It warmed his affection for her, loosened his will, weakened his resistance. He wanted her, and she was willing, and this time he need not stop as he had done on their wedding night. She was his wife, and whatever must be confessed and negotiated between them would find its time. Passion ruled this moment, and it was all he wanted, all he needed now. He knew she needed this, too — he sensed it in the hungry tenderness of her kisses. He heard it in her soft, breathy sighs.

Holding her, feeling her arch toward him, her body taut and beautifully curved against his own, he felt stirred to a depth of madness. He moved his mouth on hers, with hers, nipping and caressing. He skimmed his hands over her torso, wrapped his fingers around her slender waist. Sliding upward, hands easing over her silk bodice, he traced the shape of a breast beneath her layered clothing.

She gave a little gasp as he did so, and he let his hand round over and massage that fullness through an inhibition of cloth — he could feel the bud but could not touch her as he wanted, not yet. Grazing his fingers upward, he began to undo the small buttons that closed the bodice of her gown, exposing the pale, flawless skin. His hand, splayed on her rib cage over the layers of clothing, sensed the thunder of her heart under his hand and her deepening breaths.

He kissed her again, with such an urgent hunger that she moaned beneath his lips and moved her body against his as she pleaded for more. He caught her to him with one arm, her body curving gracefully in the support of his grasp, her arms circling his neck. Heart and blood pounding, he restrained his urges, kissing her slowly, so that her lips gradually opened like a flower and her tongue emerged to touch his.

Soon his fingers slipped free the last button and her bodice fell open to reveal her lush breasts, quickened with her breaths, pushing out of the confinement of stays and chemise. His body surged, hardened like steel in fire, to see that. Dipping his head to kiss her there, he could sense the whiskied warmth of his breath sliding between her breasts. He pushed the dark silk away from her shoulders, and she slipped her arms free, then looped her bare, pale arms around his neck again.

He straightened with her then, facing her, his own body intensely stimulated by the scent, the feel, the sight of her. She stood before him in chemise and stays and skirts, and he remembered another time when she had stood before him, half-nude and shivering, on the day he had begun to love her.

Tracing his palms down her bare arms, he turned her in silence. Fingers, his and hers, worked at tapes and ribbons until her other garments slipped off, one by one. He hardly marked what they were, where they tumbled. Overwhelmed by the urge and the freedom to touch her luscious skin, to kiss her shoulders and the long arch of her throat, he turned her again and bent his head to taste the sweet skin of her breasts, filling his hands with the cool, silky weight of her hair as it spilled down her back.

She reached up and tugged off his jacket, and he let it go. As her fingers worked the buttons of his waistcoat, he let that go, too, and the shirt after it, so that he stood in kilt and stockings, and she in chemise and knickers. She stepped into the deep circle of his arms, and he kissed her, touched her everywhere, where she was cool and where she was warm, all of it driving him mad, driving him onward.

When she arched again in deeper invitation, he slipped her chemise over her head and tossed it away, so that she stood nearly naked before him. The deep, ripe swells and curves of her long, beautiful body, her sweet willingness, her breathy excitement pushed him beyond thought. Sweeping his hands over her breasts, tipped firm, he found the tapes at the waist of her knickers and drew the knot out, so that they slid from her hips, pooled.

Now she stepped into his arms, slid her fingers through his hair, and traced her sweet breath along his cheek, his ear, so that he pulled her hard against him, and her body moved within his embrace like a siren. He did not know now if he was seducer or seduced — at first he had urged her toward this, wanting her so much he could no longer bear it. Now he felt, for a moment, that she was like the strong and beautiful spirit of the mountain, and he was powerless under her spell.

His will was weakened by the whisky, and he could not hold himself back much longer. He was aroused to an irresistible level, his hardness demanding, his heart slamming within him.

Sweeping her suddenly into his arms, hearing her little surprised laugh, he carried her through the connecting door and into his bedroom, dark as a cave, the forest-green walls and mahogany furnishings almost black in the moonlight, the golden flame of a candle burning in a hurricane glass on the bureau revealing the white pool of turned-down bed linens.

Setting her on his big four-poster bed with its deep mattress, he sank down with her into plush softness. He had not enjoyed that cushioned, sinking comfort until now, when suddenly the bed seemed a heavenly place for hot passions on cool linens, with the woman he loved wrapped in his arms.

She looped her arms around his neck, pulled him down to her, and he kissed her and slid his body along the length of hers. When she propped her knee up and he lay a little on top of her, he felt as if they fit together as well as if they had been made for each other, long legged, matching shoulder to shoulder, hip to hip.

Cool fingers, their touch hot as fire, traced over his bare chest, over his flat waist and the pleats of his kilt. He could feel the warmth of her touch through the wool as she pushed aside the cloth and slipped her hand up and under to caress his thigh, making him gasp inwardly. Eager and inquisitive, her fingers slipped up his leg while her other hand tugged at the buckle of his belt until she freed the kilt, and he pushed it away, wanting to be unencumbered with her.

She found him, shaped and grasped him, drawing out her touch, but he could not bear it, not now, not yet, and moved away, intent on sensing her pleasure and knowing he had given that to her. She arched against him, her body exquisite under his touch as he stroked her torso, her breasts. His fingers skimmed her abdomen, a taut span between her hips, while she whimpered and moved toward his touch, and her lips opened under his, tongue seeking, sweeping moist and so ecstatically hot over his.

Dipping his head to kiss her bared breasts, he tasted her, lingered, while her fingers tightened on his back and combed through his hair. He felt the fine quivering throughout her body, sensed the deepening swell of her breath, and he thought he might burst himself.

He cupped her face in his hand and kissed her deeply, felt the heat rising between them like flame. Remembering the essential warmth they had sought from each other on the night they had first met, he felt it again and knew he would never stop loving her, knew that each time he touched her, kissed her, he would remember that her warmth and generosity had once saved his life. And each time he loved her and felt that heat build between them, he would feel a little part of his soul coming back to him, through her and the loving they created.

She had told him once that a little part of the soul could be lost in times of tragedy, and suddenly he knew that was the key to why he loved her, why she held such magic for him. She brought him to life, somehow, restored him when he was weak. Not fully, but enough — like a breath, or a sip, enough to wake him and startle him into living, into feeling more awake in heart and soul and mind than he had ever been before.

He did not know why or how, just that it happened only with her, when he saw her, touched her, loved her. When the magic had him in its thrall, as it did now, he could not stop touching her, could not hold himself back from loving her.

She writhed in his arms, showing the subtle pleasure she felt, and he slipped his hand downward to find the enticing warmth between her legs, the sweet, deep heat of her most hidden part. As he touched her there, teased her to the brink, she moved and whimpered and pleaded, opening for him, surging against him. He covered her, and she took his solid weight with the support of the soft bed beneath them, and he thrust, slowly at first and then deep, feeling himself begin to tremble, feeling the power pour through him in waves, cleansing and remaking him.

For he was not the man he had been only weeks ago. He was finer, stronger, better, and she was part of that. She was the catalyst, the element that drove him to reach heights he had never dreamed possible before. He had never thought to love like this, never, and yet when it came upon him, it was so easy, a natural flow of heart and soul, and all it asked of him was to admit the possibility and then to surrender.

Chapter Twenty-two

Turning another page in the accounting book on the desk, Evan glanced up at Finlay MacConn. His young factor and brother-in-law stood on the carpet of the sunlit study, his brown woolen jacket hanging loosely from his wide shoulders. Frowning, Finlay bunched his hat brim in his hand and looked at his sister.

Catriona stood beside the empty leather chair before Evan's desk, which both siblings had refused. Calm and still, her hands joined, she looked both demure and seductive, her beautiful curves clad simply in one of the dark walking skirts she preferred and a high-necked white blouse that complemented her translucent skin and the warm sheen of her hair. Her usually pale cheeks were blushed pink, her blue-gray eyes steady, and her chin raised proudly, almost defensively.

Evan resisted the urge to smile at her, remembering their shared delights of the previous night. Neither Catriona nor Finlay seemed in a mood for smiling or even relaxing, which puzzled Evan. Surely meeting with the earl over the estate records held no threat to any of them. Finlay was a very capable factor, from what he could tell. He wondered, though, if Catriona was still tense about Evan's decision to sell parts of Kildonan. Perhaps she had spoken to her brother about that.

But when he saw yet another glance pass between his wife and her brother, he wondered at the message there — and suddenly felt that they knew something that he did not.

Evan skimmed his fingertips down another page of columns filled with numbers and lists of tenants' names. He sat back and tapped a knuckle thoughtfully against his lips. "We have eighty-two thousand acres," he finally murmured. "What was the number of sheep in the last count?"

Finlay cleared his throat. "Fifty-one thousand, four hundred and twenty-seven, as you'll see I wrote there in the book, last spring," he said. "Although that may not be exact, but close enough. It's devilish hard chasing the sheep down from the hills. That's how many were caught and clipped last April, sir."

"An enormous task," Evan commented. He turned the page to look at other notations. "And this? Twenty-six men hired up from the South for the gathering, clipping, packing, and transport of the wool?"

"Aye," Finlay answered. Again he looked at Catriona.

"And tenants?"

"Excuse me, sir?"

"How many tenants do we have on Kildonan lands now?"

"Well, since Kildonan includes the whole of Glen Shee," Finlay said, looking up at the ceiling as if thinking, "and not all of those are involved in tending the sheep . . . there are about eighty households, with perhaps four hundred ninety residents of all ages."

"Does that include the men hired in the last ten years to live in the glen and look after the sheep?" When Finlay hesitated, Evan repeated the question. "How many are those?"

"That includes the eighteen men with their families, sir. They're all Lowlanders and Englishmen."

"I see." Evan paged back in the large book, looking at the careful rows of figures entered by Finlay and the last factor, Kenneth Grant's father, with some entries by Evan's own father, though he did not see his father's handwriting very often. "How many residents did Glen Shee hold before?"

"When, sir?" Finlay asked.

"Before," Evan said, looking pointedly at Catriona.

"Thousands," she answered. "Perhaps two thousand, five hundred in your great-grandfather's day — before this was an earldom and before the clearings began so that the land could be turned to sheep runs. Now we are less than five hundred here."

Evan nodded pensively. "It seems odd to me."

"What does?" Catriona asked almost sharply.

"With all the sheep on these acres and all the work each spring needed to get the wool to market . . . for the last two years, according to these figures, less than thirty men did all of it."

"That was what your father wanted," she said. "The fewer men and their families, the better. More room for the sheep."

Evan flipped another few pages, found pages dated to earlier seasons, and ran his finger down the columns. "For the two years before that, we employed several more men for the clipping and wool packing . . . and yet the estate had less sheep. Thirty-five thousand in the flocks but five years ago." He looked up.

"Perhaps Mr. Grant's father, the previous factor, was not very good at record keeping," Catriona suggested.

"Aye, he was better at other things," Finlay muttered.

"Such as?" Evan looked up.

"Evicting," Catriona said. "He was good at evicting."

"And so was my father. Is that what you mean to imply?"

"Aye." She stared at him boldly. "You know that's true."

Of course he knew that, but he gave no sign of it. He turned pages until he came to a clean one. "I'd like a census."

"A what?" Finlay asked. "A counting of sheep or tenants?"

"I want a list of the tenants," Evan said. "I want to know who lives here, where they live, and how many are in each household. I want to know what work they do for the estate, if any, and how much they are paid for the work."

Finlay gulped, Evan saw, and slid another glance toward his sister. Whatever the fellow was hiding, he was not good at it, because there were high spots of color on his cheekbones.

"And we could do with another exact count of the sheep," Evan said. "We should keep the count going every month, adding and subtracting as needed. That way we will know, next spring, just how many men we will need to do the work."

"Aye, sir," Finlay said. "There are some tenants who can act as my assistants in the counting and the census of residents. I'll ask them to get started. Is there anything else, sir?"

"Aye. Another matter has come to my attention. The old bridge at the foot of the Fairy Mountain, as you call it here, is in poor condition. I have barricaded it myself," he said, glancing at Catriona, "but apparently that does not deter some people from using it, despite the obvious danger."

"The old bridge has been broken a long while, but it seems sound enough," Finlay said. "I've used it often myself. I would not bring a cart across it, but otherwise I think it can be trusted."

"I disagree," Evan answered abruptly. "I intend to design another bridge myself and hire a crew to build it. But that will take time. For now, we'll have to find a few able men to do some tough labor. I'll show you how I want it repaired and shored up. Can you gather enough workers for that?"

"Aye, sir," Finlay said, with another quick glance toward his sister. "We'll meet you there whenever you like."

"Good. Next week will do." Evan frowned, glancing from his wife to her brother. The tension between them was taut as a wire — he could sense it from his seat behind the huge walnut desk his father had used.

He of all people should understand, he told himself. All along, he himself had kept a few secrets from Catriona, things he did not think would affect her.

But he had not imagined until now that she might keep secrets from him, too. If he had the right, she did as well. Still, the thought that she might need to keep something from him was troubling. Was she hiding a truth from her husband — or from the earl?

★ ★ ★

Arm in arm with Finlay, Catriona walked toward the entrance, glancing back over her shoulder. Evan remained in his study reviewing estate documents. Something told her that he stayed there to give her a chance to be with her brother.

Finlay bent down. "Does he know anything about the new tenants?" he asked. "Did you tell him?"

"No," she said. "I have not said a word, as I promised. Thank you, Baird," she told the butler, who stepped toward them. "I will see Mr. MacConn out." When the butler nodded and retreated into the dining room, she turned to Finlay in earnest, keeping her voice down. "Did you record the names of our new tenants in the estate books or write down the work they did and were paid for last spring?"

Finlay shook his head. "I have those records elsewhere. I was hoping he would not notice so soon. I swear, Catriona, I thought the man might never come up to Kildonan at all and leave the running of the estate to me and to his sister — who paid little attention to the details of who lived here and how many." He whispered urgently as they stood isolated by the front entrance. "But now your husband has seen the discrepancies between the amount of wool processed from Kildonan lands — and the number of men who did the work. He suspects something, indeed. Now the question is, what will he conclude, and what will he do about it?"

She glanced away, feeling her heart turn anxiously as she thought of Kenneth Grant, who also knew that Finlay had been quietly bringing evicted tenants back into the glen to act as sheep herders — and who could turn her brother into the authorities for it. "Evan is a good man, Finlay," she whispered. "He is not like his father and . . . and some other men. I think we can explain to him what we've been doing."

"I have one more family to move into the glen. When I went to Inverness, I found some of the MacLeod family — they were working on the shores bringing in the nets, and it is not the sort of work they are accustomed to. They lived in a hovel on the beach, nearly starving. I will bring them through the glen tomorrow."

"On Sunday?" She stared at him.

"It is the only day we could manage it — I brought them back here with me and left them temporarily at Mrs. MacAuley's inn. She can only keep them a day or two, as she expects travelers to arrive soon. After the MacLeods are settled, that will be the last of the new tenants for a while."

She nodded. "It will have to be. Where will they live?"

"In the old shieling on Beinn Sìtheach."

"What! The place where Evan and I — but it is a ruin," she whispered. "We nearly froze to death on a bitterly cold night. A family with children could not survive the winter there."

"A few of the other crofters have gone up there in the last few days to repair the roof and patch the walls and bring in furniture and stock it with food and dry peats," he said. "Now it is good enough to house a family. And it is the only place that was available — They will build another croft higher in the hills next spring, I think. For now, this will do."

She nodded. "Evan and some of the other guests plan to go to services at Papa's church tomorrow. Be careful, Finlay."

He nodded. "I will." He bent to kiss her cheek quickly.

"Finlay," Evan said.

Catriona turned, jumping a little in surprise, not realizing that Evan had come up so quietly behind them.

"Sir," Finlay answered calmly.

"Our friends are considering a climb up the slopes of Beinn Shee a few days from now," he said. "You were recommended as a guide. Would you be willing to take a group of us up the mountain in a few days?"

"Of course, sir," Finlay said. "Depending on the weather and what route is taken, it can be an easy climb or a very difficult one.

Are they experienced hillwalkers and climbers, sir?"

"Some are," Evan said. "I confess that I did not make it to the top of that mountain myself, along the toughest route. But if I had, perhaps I would never have met your sister." He smiled.

"I'm sure you would have met her one way or another," Finlay answered. "But you would not have had your adventure together, and so you would not now be married." He grinned.

"True, and so I must be grateful to the mountain for defeating me that day," Evan said, and Catriona saw a quick dazzle in his hazel-green eyes as he glanced at her. "By the way, we've asked your sister to join us on our climb."

"Up there? I doubt she'll go to the top of that particular mountain." He looked at his sister.

"I will go," Catriona said, lifting her chin when Finlay looked surprised. She knew he thought of their brother Donald, who had died on Beinn Shee — but Finlay was unaware of Flora's request that Catriona bring back the fairy crystal from that daunting height.

"If you would come Monday morning for breakfast, that would be excellent," Evan said. "We'll discuss plans and perhaps go the next day or the day following."

"Tell your friends to get good rest tomorrow night and be ready for a climb on Monday," Finlay said. "If the weather is good, we should go up that morning. The weather is too unpredictable here. Why make plans for another day, if the one you have is good enough?"

"Aye," Evan said, glancing at Catriona. "Good advice for all of us to remember."

"I'll be here early," Finlay said, "though your census and sheep count will not be done by then." He smiled a little, though Catriona saw that it was forced.

"Take the time you need for that. Good day, then. Perhaps we'll see you at kirk services tomorrow." Evan turned and walked back down the hall toward his study.

Finlay turned. "So you're going up Beinn Shee, as well?"

She nodded. "I must. . . . I'll explain later."

"Well, if you go, I would rather it was with me than anyone else. It can be a beast of a mountain to climb. It would be better if these holiday climbers would go up one of the other peaks." He watched her for a moment. "Are you happy, Catriona?" he asked suddenly, softly.

She hesitated, then nodded. "I am. Happier than I ever thought I could be. This has all happened so fast — but I am hoping it was all for the best."

Frowning, he nodded. "May it last, then. If Kildonan does not make you happy all of your days, I will see to it myself that he pays for it. Will you be at services tomorrow?"

"I — I should, but Papa and Aunt Judith were so angry about — what happened with me and Kildonan. Neither of them have even sent word to me since I left."

"Father has fretted the whole while you've been gone, yet he has not felt at ease coming here himself to see how you have been getting along. He would like it if you came to services and brought your husband, though he would not admit it. Remember to come in time for the reading of The Book. You know how Aunt Judith would disapprove if you came late on a Sunday."

She nodded. "I'll be — *we* will be there."

Chapter Twenty-three

Steady rain pattered the window glass in the library, providing a layer of soothing sound while Catriona transcribed some songs. Seated in a leather wing chair, she gazed now and then through a set of tall windows. Beyond the fine sheets of rain and sweeping lawns and forestland, she saw the mountains swathed in mist and a vast sky filled with clouds.

The library, located in the same wing as her room and not far from the passage to the dining room, was not large, though it was cozy. The walls were lined with bookshelves and divided by tall windows at one end and pocket doors at the other. Walls and shelves were painted a quiet green, the chairs were covered in worn sherry-colored leather, the floors were scattered with beautiful old rugs, and the windows that framed the landscape were draped in dark green velvet. Of all the rooms at Kildonan, including her own serene but formal bedroom, Catriona liked the comfortable, shabby atmosphere of the library best.

Glancing out the window, Catriona noticed Kildonan's gig speeding away from the castle.

She knew it carried Sir Aedan MacBride, along with Lady Jean and Sir Harry, to Kyle of Lochalsh and the small harbor there. Lady Jean and her husband had decided to accompany Sir Aedan, who had business to attend on Skye, and they intended to spend time in a resort hotel in Broadford before returning to Edinburgh.

When she had wished them all farewell that morning, Jean had embraced her and thanked her — to Catriona's amazement — for coming into their family. Still stunned, Catriona had turned to Aedan, who had kissed her hand and repeated his invitation for her and Evan to come to Dundrennan House for Christmas. Wanting very much to accept, she had only smiled in silence, while Evan promised that they would certainly consider it.

Out in the corridor, she heard footsteps and voices raised in chatter. Jemima's husky laughter floated down the hallway. Catriona knew they would not come to the library for her, for she had pleaded fatigue and said she had a good deal of work to do in order to excuse herself from the day's outing. Due to the cold rain and mists, Jemima and the others planned to go out in two covered carriages, which would take them along the scenic shores of Loch Torridon.

Mr. Grant had offered to act as their guide, and that was the chief reason Catriona had decided to avoid the outing.

Shortly after Finlay had left, Mr. Grant had arrived to see Lady Wetherstone, who had complained so of a nervous headache that her husband had summoned the local doctor. A dose of laudanum reassured the Wetherstones about Highland medicine but had confined the lady to her bed for the day. Afterward, Mr. Grant had joined the others in the drawing room, and he and Arthur Fitzgibbon had discussed sightseeing opportunities on a such a rainy day.

Greeting Kenneth Grant coolly, Catriona had taken her music pages into the library and had asked Mrs. Baird to ensure her privacy. Although she could not avoid Grant indefinitely, she did not want to see him so soon after spending the night in Evan's arms. Nothing could be allowed to spoil that.

A knock sounded on the door, and Evan stepped inside. As she looked up, her heart gave a quick, girlish flutter.

"Catriona, pardon me," he said quietly. "I know you wanted some time to yourself in here. I need but a moment."

"Come in." She sat forward, some of the papers spilling unnoticed to the floor. "What is it?" She wondered, with a quick and guilty nervousness, if he wanted to talk to her about Finlay.

He strode toward her and half knelt to retrieve the pages, handing them back to her.

"Reverend Wilkie came to me not long ago to say that they are all looking forward to attending services at Glenachan in the morning. So we'll all be going, I suppose."

"Oh! And you will, too?" She realized with a quick tug in her heart, how much she had missed her father, despite the bad episode surrounding her hasty marriage. When he nodded, she continued. "My father conducts prayers and the reading of The Book early in the morning before service," she said. "I will be expected."

"Then we'll both be there. I'll tell the others we'll meet them at the kirk."

"Thank you." She smiled, grateful for his willingness to respect her family and relieved that he had not brought up the subject of Finlay or the tenants.

"Are you rewriting some of the songs we had to burn," he said, glancing at her pages, "to keep each other warm?" She saw a gleam in his eyes and felt an answering swirl within herself.

She nodded. "I'm nearly done with those, and I'm also writing down a few that Morag MacLeod taught me this week."

"How many do you have in total?"

"With these, a hundred and thirty-four songs, all done in Gaelic and English, with musical scale and whatever interesting annotations I've learned about the songs."

He stood, and she did, too. "That's quite

an admirable task you've taken on. I'm proud of you. Is it nearly done?"

"A collection of the old Gaelic songs could never be complete. I suspect there are literally thousands of songs all over the Highlands and Islands — no one knows for sure. It would take a lifetime to discover them all. I've set out to learn the songs of the north-west Highlands. In the last few years, I've visited every croft house in this glen and many in the neighboring glens," she said. "And I've traveled as far beyond that as my father would allow me, to meet with the singers who were said to know the music."

He slid an arm around her waist. "No wonder you are adamant about staying in the Highlands."

"I must, Evan," she said. "For the songs and for other reasons — I simply cannot leave here."

"But once you've gathered the songs, you can refine the collection anywhere. And in Edinburgh, there are publishers who would no doubt be very interested in your work."

She pulled away a little. "Still thinking about selling?"

He pressed her to him. "Last night," he murmured, "we agreed on peace for a while on this subject — at least until our guests are gone and we can discuss this more freely."

"Aye," she said, frowning. "We did. But I

will not leave here, and I'm not interested in publishing the songs."

"No? Scottish ballads are very popular now."

"And prettified for the public," she pointed out. "I could not do that to these songs. The true Gaelic songs are part of the ancient, magical soul of the Celtic Highlands. My mother taught me the first songs I ever sang, and I began to collect them in earnest when I realized, after so many people left this glen and took the old songs with them, that I could do something to save the music I loved, with the Gaelic culture fast disappearing from the Highlands."

"More evidence of your heartfelt love for this place, and its heritage." He paused, and in his serious expression she saw understanding and respect. With his arm still around her, he turned with her and strolled to the other side of the room, where a fireplace and mantel, beneath a large portrait, divided the crowded bookshelves along that wall.

"This was painted a few years before his death," Evan said.

The oil painting was a half-length portrait of the previous earl, Evan's father. She had never met him in person — had never wanted to do so — yet now she felt curious about George Evan Mackenzie.

Tilting her head, she studied the picture.

Despite the gray hair, bullish build, and broad waistline, he resembled his son in the handsome, chiseled planes of his face and the brilliant hazel-green eyes, but in the puckered brow and downturned mouth she saw discontent and the unforgiving expression of a lonely, angry man. She knew that his countess had left him many years before the date of the portrait, taking their two children, Evan and Jean, with her to the Lowlands.

"What made your mother leave him, Evan?" she asked softly. Of all the questions she could have asked, for some reason that one troubled her most and came into her mind immediately.

He sighed. "My mother is a strong-willed person, as he was," he said. "She loves the Highlands as deeply as you, I think — and is still active in ladies' charities to benefit the Highlanders. She will approve of you quite heartily, I think." He squeezed her shoulder a little. "But back then, when I was a lad, she disagreed with my father's decision to expand the estate and fill it with sheep runs and hunting reserves to expand his fortune. And she hated his cold treatment of his tenants but could do nothing to stop him. He was a harsh laird and a harsh father at times," he went on, "but he was not a harsh husband. He loved her in his arrogant way. I think he grew worse when she left, out of spite, perhaps. The worst clearings on these lands were long after we were gone from here, in the years when I was at university. He might have changed for the better if he could have gotten past that unbreakable pride of his. He could never admit that he was wrong about anything."

She leaned her head on his shoulder. "Those qualities have not been passed on or taught to his son, so far as I can see."

"Thank you," he murmured. "I hope not. Though I hope I have his keen intellect and his superior determination. But my mother and her family influenced the rest of my character, I think."

She sighed and wrapped her arms around his waist. Remembering last night's passion and gentleness in his arms, a delicate thrill of pleasure went through her as she felt his arms come solidly around her. She felt safe and wanted in his arms. She felt — loved, she thought, though he had never said so. And she could never imagine packing up to leave him with two children in tow, as his mother had done to his father.

Yet she knew that Evan still had his secrets, and she wondered if she would ever learn the truth of why he felt he must sell parts of the estate. Looking up at the portrait of his harsh father, she feared that one day a conflict would tear the current earl's marriage apart, as well — for she would not be able to bear it if he sold Kildonan and asked her to leave with him.

Evan tipped his head. "Catriona, I have been meaning to ask you something."

"Aye?" She waited, heart pounding with near dread, considering the track of her thoughts.

"Years ago, on the last day my father evicted people," he said, so low it was nearly a growl, "I was there."

"I know," she said softly. "I saw you with him."

"Which did not help my reputation in your regard or the regard of others in Glen Shee, I'm sure. But when I left the glen that day," he went on, "I was angry. You should know that my father and I fought bitterly about it. I thought I would never be able to return here again — certainly not with my head held high."

She looked up, feeling a sudden wash of sympathy for him and for what he must have endured as the son and heir of an arrogant, selfish man. She waited, listening.

"I was sure that what he was doing was wrong and that he had ruined this glen and hundreds of lives. But this is what I wanted you to know," he said, resting his hands on her shoulders. "As I rode off that day, I heard a young woman singing. She stood on a hill, her hair bright as copper" — he brushed his hand over her red-gold hair under its net — "and the song she sang went deep into my heart. I shared her grief, though she could not have known that."

"She knows it now," Catriona said softly.

"So I thought," he said. "It was you that day. And I heard the same voice singing the day I fell down the mountainside. I came to my feet and was lost in the fog and disoriented by the blow to my head. But I went toward your voice through the mist and found the drover's path. If I had not, I might have slipped and fallen farther down the mountain."

"You heard me singing? I was coming back from walking out with Morag," she said, her voice hushed with awe. "I was practicing the song she had just taught me. I never knew that you heard and that it helped you find me."

"Your song saved me, love." He wrapped her close in his embrace, and she rested her head on his wide, strong shoulder, breathing in his scent, his presence.

"Oh, Evan," she whispered. "I did not know." There was still so much she did not know about him — so much to learn.

He drew back, looked at her. "So you see, you saved my life more than once," he said. "Let me help you now. Is there something I can do?"

She looked up at him in surprise. "Help me?"

"My father's actions caused much grief in this glen, Catriona. I know that, and I realize that the culture suffered as well as the people. Now you are doing your best to try to save that heritage. Is there some way I can help you?"

For a long moment, she stared at him, a little amazed at first. His sincerity was genuine, and she felt a surge of trust and gratitude.

But she could not tell him about Finlay and the tenants — not yet, though she was beginning to feel that she could confide in him one day soon and that he would understand. Remembering Kenneth Grant's threats, she knew she must wait a little longer, until she had spoken with Grant again — as much as she dreaded that — and persuaded him to leave the matter be.

Then she nodded, knowing what she could ask of him. She had not intended to tell him about Flora and her fairy songs, but now she explained about her desire to learn the old tunes, while Evan listened, his gaze keen.

"The fairy music is said to be unique to Glen Shee," she went on, while he nodded his understanding. "I have heard only a few of the songs, but I know they have a special magic of their own. If I leave Kildonan and Glen Shee, Evan, I can never learn those songs. And then who will? Flora will not share them with just anyone, and I fear they will disappear altogether one day. She is very old and very stubborn."

"And she is willing to teach you?"

"She will, if I pass a test she has set for me." She told him about the fairy stone that Flora wanted from her, though she expected Evan to tell her that it was nonsense.

He tilted his head, listening. "And you are willing to look for this stone for her?"

She nodded. "I will, if it is the price of those very precious songs. If it is even possible — I do not know."

He gave a dry laugh and shook his head. "And I thought you were unwilling to take risks!"

"I am learning to face them," she said, "from you."

"And I'm learning from you, love," he murmured, and he took her by the shoulders. Leaning forward, he kissed her for a moment, long enough for her knees to quiver.

"I would go up to the mountain and get the stone for you," he said, "but you need to do that yourself. Only you know what to bring back to her. But I can help you get there safely, and I can help you find the stone. We won't be alone, though — judging by the enthusiastic planning I have heard around here in the last couple of days, the top of that mountain will be very crowded. What do you say, Catriona Bhàn?"

Smiling, half laughing, Catriona flowed back into his arms. He kissed her, then kissed her again, each one tasting sweeter and newer than the last, while the rain drummed against the windows.

Then he drew back, catching her hips firmly against his, rocking with her a little. Not only did she know what he wanted, she wanted it, too, here and now, her heart pounding fast with the very thought.

"So, my love, you requested privacy in here," he murmured, leaning forward to nuzzle his nose to hers.

"I did," she whispered, and her body began to pulse and ache for him, knowing his secrets as he knew hers.

"Good," he said, and he drew her away from the fireplace and the overbearing portrait gallery. Tugging on her hand, he pulled her into a small book-lined alcove that held a single leather armchair. He drew her into that confined space and bent to touch his lips to hers in a swift, hard kiss that plunged through her like tender lightning.

Catching her breath, she leaned back in his embrace and wrapped her arms around him. As his hands loosened the buttons of her blouse and as she tugged at his jacket, she began to laugh softly, for a feeling bubbled up through her, a mix of joy and freedom, of passion and delight. Fumbling with his clothing as he fingered the buttons of hers, she kissed him and pressed against him, while he chuckled with her.

"I think we'd better hurry," she whispered,

catching him in another fast, fresh, hungry kiss.

"This time," he said, lowering his head to nestle his lips upon her breast, nudging down her stays to free her nipple to the hot, moist sweep of his tongue, so that she gasped aloud and arched back, "this time, Catriona Bhàn, I think haste would be lovely," he whispered, his breath soft on her skin.

He took her mouth swiftly, so that she arched again and would have cried out, but he stifled that with his lips and tongue and a few deep, deep kisses. When his hand drifted under her skirts, shoving aside petticoats, finding the convenient slitted cloth of her knickers, she gasped again, for the sensation of his hand, deft and hard, slipping between her legs was divine excitement. Her heart pounded in a frenzy, and soon she was undulating in his arms, kissing and being kissed, wishing she could loosen all of her clothing, all of his, to savor his body against hers, let his lips wander wherever he cared to taste her.

He sank into the chair and pulled her down to straddle him, her skirts rucked in a billowing cushion all around her, spilling over the arms of the chair. With quick fingers she freed his trousers just enough, and when she grasped him, warm and hard, in her caressing hand, he groaned low and shifted. Moments later he helped her guide him deep inside of her, so deep, his thrusts nurtured in the hidden space of her body, the two of them hidden in the alcove, their silent, bursting passion further concealed by the demure drape of her skirts.

What rushed through her felt so dynamic, so hot and new that she could not think, only moved and rocked and followed its course. Breathing with him in endless rhythm, she let the keen internal lightning possess her.

This felt so right, she told herself, so wonderful, and the thoughts repeated in her mind, settling deep in her heart — *this feels so right.*

Chapter Twenty-four

On Sunday mornings, it seemed to Evan — ever since he had been a small boy gripping his mother's hand in church — the light had a gentle quality, the air seemed calm, the weather always of a peaceful variety, and birdsong sounded more melodic.

Not so at Glenachan House, where the atmosphere seemed close and almost thunderous, the light dim and shadowed, and no birdsong was in evidence — none would have been allowed.

Evan sat beside Catriona at midday dinner in her father's house. He glanced around at the tense faces of her family — her father at the head of the table, his head leonine and shoulders large, his expression somewhere between a glower and puzzlement, her sour-faced and silent aunt, her brother uncharacteristically subdued and frowning. Catriona was quiet and lovely — she could seem nothing else to him now, Evan thought.

They ate quietly, with little conversation, sharing the good but plain fare of cold roast beef, vegetables, and thick buttered bread, all prepared the night before in keeping with the strict Sunday regimen of the household. He was surprised when Judith Rennie and Catriona got up from the table and returned from the kitchen with an excellent dessert of apple tarts and damson plum pudding, followed by strong, good coffee. He would have thought that sweets, and anything that could be excessively enjoyed, would not have been permitted at the reverend's table.

The meal followed a morning spent in prayer and the reading of the Bible, referred to simply as The Book. Upon arriving early, Evan and Catriona sat at the dining room table with the others while her father intoned verses from the Bible for an hour. Then they had gone to the nearby kirk to join a small gathering of Highlanders in the parish and guests from Kildonan Castle. Thomas MacConn delivered a sermon in Gaelic on the Good Samaritan, which was then repeated in English for the English-speaking guests from Kildonan Castle.

An interesting choice of sermon topics, Evan thought, considering MacConn's own daughter had been chastised by her family for saving a man's life.

Perhaps the sermon had been intended as MacConn's gesture of apology, Evan realized, for he had been relieved to see that Catriona was warmly received — with as much affection as gruff MacConn and his tight-lipped sister could summon, Evan suspected. He himself was treated with respect and a cool friendliness. Reverend Wilkie and Reverend MacConn had conversed about writing sermons, and Evan's guests were treated to cakes and lemonade after a very long kirk service, although his friends left before the midday dinner was served to the family.

Finally, as the meal ended, Evan hoped that he and Catriona would be free to leave, but her father began another round of readings from The Book. Listening politely, unable to leave without appalling rudeness, Evan was unable to join his guests as host, which was also his duty that day.

Finally, when he realized how long Mr. Gillie had been sitting outside in the gig waiting for them, Evan made his apologies, expecting Catriona to fetch her shawl and bonnet, relieved to escape with him. But she hung back, hands folded primly, face bearing a tense little smile. She looked as if she had no intention of leaving Glenachan again.

His heart did a sudden flip, for he wondered if she indeed had decided she would stay, now that she was back in the strict family fold. Had their influence descended on her so quickly, like a shadow? Had she concluded that the marriage was indeed pointless after all? Her expression was neutral, her eyes shuttered. He could not read her mood or state of mind.

"You may fetch me back to Kildonan later this afternoon, if you will," she told him. "After tea."

"Certainly," he murmured, unaccountably relieved. For a moment, the very thought of living without her had struck him like a physical punch. All day he had been keenly aware of his burning passion for her and of the strength and newness of the love he felt. Now he realized how much he wanted her, hour by hour, to be in his life in even the smallest, most mundane ways.

"I'm sure you would like to go with your guests today," she continued. "It's such lovely weather, and I think Miss Jemima had planned another scenic outing by coach."

"A scenic outing," Judith Rennie said haughtily, "on a Sunday?"

"Aye," Catriona had answered, turning to stare at her aunt. "On a Sunday." She lifted her chin with the gentle stubbornness that Evan had come to know. Yet he saw, too, that she did not intend to defy or disrespect her father to go with him.

Hiding his disappointment, Evan kissed her hand, reluctant to kiss his bride's cheek with her father frowning and her aunt glaring at them. Then he bid them farewell and left.

The gig from Kildonan had barely left Glenachan grounds to head out on the moorland road when Catriona turned away from the window in the drawing room to look at Finlay.

"When?" she asked.

"Soon," he said. "We'll need to give Lord Kildonan enough time to get to the far end of the glen, of course. And after we've wrapped up some food to feed the MacLeods, we'll take the pony cart and fetch them from Mrs. MacAuley's inn. She'll have fed them well — they are her cousins after all — but they'll want plenty of foodstuffs for their wee cupboard. Then we'll take them up to the shieling and get them settled in. I'm just waiting now for another who's promised to help us."

She nodded, expecting that he meant one of the MacLeod clan, perhaps Morag and her husband or Mrs. MacAuley's son. Glancing out the window again, she saw that the gig had disappeared from sight. For a moment she felt a deep tug of conflict, knowing she could have gone with Evan and no one would have questioned it. She could have spent a Sunday of freedom and pleasure in his company, although her father and aunt would not have been pleased had they known that she wanted to ride where he rode, walk where he walked, just for the pleasure of his company and the pleasure in a beautiful day. That did not seem like a sin to her.

But there would be other Sundays with Evan — she fervently hoped so, hoped that they would somehow find another solution to his problems than selling Kildonan and splitting their marriage.

For today, she had a more important mission. While she knew that her brother was capable of moving the MacLeod family into the shieling hut without her help, she wanted to be there for him and give him support in what he did.

Besides, she was the Countess of Kildonan now and could make the new inhabitants of Glen Shee feel like welcome friends rather than fugitives.

The door of the drawing room opened, and her father entered, leaning on his walking stick as he often did. She glanced quickly at Finlay, wondering what their father would say if he knew their plans for a Sunday afternoon. She stood, turned.

"Are you ready, then?" Thomas MacConn asked Finlay.

"Ready?" Catriona glanced from one to the other.

"To help the new residents move into the shieling," her father answered. "I promised Finlay that I would help him."

"But — Papa, it's Sunday!" she blurted, more out of surprise than that it bothered her.

He turned and gave her a rare smile. She remembered that he used to smile often when she had been a young girl, and she had not realized until that moment how much she had missed his smile. "I know it's Sunday, lass — and this is God's work we're doing."

He held the door open and beckoned for the two of them to follow him.

"Lady Kildonan found you here, along this very track? How fascinating," Jemima said. She walked beside Evan on the drover's track that led over the mountain peaks and down toward the glen. "A pity Jeanie and Harry left Kildonan already — she would have loved to see where you were stranded. She said it was all so romantical."

"Oh, quite," Evan answered wryly. "Me with a bloodied head and unconscious, no doubt a lead weight to manage, and the poor lass dragging me over treacherously icy slopes. Romantic, indeed. I'm surprised she did not deliver me a blistering lecture on climbing in fog and sleet, to be honest." He grinned.

"She was very brave, your countess," Emily Murray said. "I do not think I would be half so brave in the same circumstance. Where was it you fell?" she asked, looking around.

Evan stopped, turned. "There," he said after a minute, pointing upward and to the left. "That rocky slope."

Reverend Wilkie, walking with his wife just behind Evan and his cousins, turned to look, shading his forehead with his hand. "That black and wicked slope all the way up there? That's a long, hard fall, and it's a wonder you survived it. If you climbed that part of the mountain and got up that high, you're either a very good climber . . . or a very stupid fellow." Wilkie grinned, his teasing good-natured.

Evan chuckled, shrugged. "I started out that day thinking myself the former and ended up believing myself the latter."

"Until you met your angel savior," Jemima said. "And then you thought yourself a very lucky lad."

"Indeed," he murmured, smiling to himself.

"Surely there are easier ways to get up to the top of Beinn Shee," Jemima said, studying the steep slope.

"Aye, there are, but after a certain point all the routes are difficult, from what I know of it," Evan said.

"Since our Scottish Alpine Club has unanimously agreed to climb Beinn Alligin and Beinn Shee while we're exploring the Torridons," Jemima said, "we'll have to find a route to please all of us. None of us want to scramble up vertical black rock."

"Only Kildonan and Mr. Fitzgibbon," Emily said. "And perhaps Mr. Grant — he seems keen on the rougher climbs."

Wilkie, in quiet discussion with his wife, turned. "Kildonan — Mrs. Wilkie and I were wondering where your wee shieling hut might be."

"Just over that ridge," Evan said, pointing. "Off the track a bit and down a hill beside a burn."

"I think we'll have a look. I'm interested in any chance to explore for the book I'm writing on the Torridons." Wilkie smiled and took his wife's arm as they walked toward the ridge.

"Oh, finally, here come Wetherstone, Mr. Grant, and Mr. Fitzgibbon," Jemima said, turning as the men came over another hill. "They've lagged behind all afternoon. They cannot do that when we go on the more challenging climbs — we must all keep together. Look what happened when Mr. Fitzgibbon and Cousin Evan were separated!"

"I would not mind getting lost if it meant I might meet some wonderful stranger," Emily said, and she gave Evan such a charming and mischievous smile that he had to laugh.

"Ho, there, Kildonan!" Arthur called as he walked closer with Grant and Wetherstone. "Plotting our route for tomorrow?"

"Aye, Fitz. I think we'll send you up that black wall so you can examine Lewisian gneiss," Evan drawled. "The rest of us will take ponies along the drover's track, with gillies and picnic baskets, and meet you at the top."

"So long as it's not sleeting, I'd do it." Arthur grinned.

"True, that verglas coating was miserable to deal with," Evan said.

"I'll help you plan the route, Arthur, if you care to go up," Kenneth Grant said, his manner grim and serious. "I've gone as high as anyone on those dangerous slopes. The rocks are unstable in places, and the ridge is so sharp that walking is nearly impossible for any man — let alone ladies wearing skirts." He slid a glance toward the women.

"Mr. MacConn has agreed to guide us when we go," Evan said. "You're welcome to come along. We'll appreciate the expertise."

"Of course," Grant said.

Arthur reached into his pocket. "Look at this. I found some particularly nice Cairngorm stones while we were walking back there." He drew out a glittering cluster of smoky quartz crystals, while Jemima and Emily exclaimed over their beauty.

"Kildonan!" The Wilkies appeared at the top of the slope, waving, and came nearer. "I thought you said that was a deserted hut," the reverend said. "Are you sure?"

"Aye, missing half its roof," Evan said. "Just over that hill."

"There's a charming little cottage there," Anna Wilkie said. "Someone is at home. We saw smoke curling from the thatched roof and a cart and horse outside. Very picturesque. I shall make a sketch of it for your book about scrambling in the Torridons, my dear," she told her husband.

"Charming cottage?" Evan gave her a puzzled look. He began striding in the direction of the shieling, while the others followed.

403

Reaching the rise of the hill, he stopped in astonishment.

The same dilapidated shieling hut where he and Catriona had endured a night of bitter cold in a sudden passing ice storm, the same hut that had been missing half its roof, with open chinks in the walls that let in the freezing north winds, was now a neat, cozy Highland cottage.

The roof had been repaired with fresh sections of thatch. The yard was swept, and a stack of peats sat beside the door, which was painted with a new coat of red paint. The stone walls were patched, the new mortar still white. Smoke curled lazily from a hole in the center of the roof, and a cart and horse stood beside the house.

Remembering that Finlay had mentioned his desire to fix the old shieling hut, Evan wondered if he had seen to it that quickly — and further wondered who could be living there now.

The door opened, and someone emerged. He saw coppery hair and the lovely, familiar form of his wife. She turned to speak to the person behind her, and Finlay came out, followed by Thomas MacConn.

Wondering why they were all out on a Sunday, Evan folded his arms and stood on the ridge of the hill, watching. A crisp breeze blew his coat about his torso, filtered through his hair, chilled him. A good day to keep moving, he thought, not a day to stand exposed on a hill in the cold, blowing wind.

A third man came out with them, then a woman who carried a baby in her arms. Two children stayed shyly behind her. All the strangers wore shabby clothing, Evan saw, and the children had no shoes, though they seemed to be healthy little sprites. Catriona took the woman's hand, then leaned down to touch the children's heads. She spoke to them, then stepped away.

The MacConns headed toward the pony cart, while the family went inside the repaired, cozy shieling and closed the door.

"What the devil is going on here?" Evan muttered to himself.

"Oh, Kildonan." Grant stepped up beside him and looked at the scene below for a few moments. "I intended to tell you about this once I was sure — but look, here's proof."

"Proof of what?" Evan snapped.

"For a while I have suspected that your factor was moving in tenants without your knowledge or permission. Former evicted tenants, in fact. Apparently that is his latest group of refugees."

Evan narrowed his eyes and saw Catriona and her kinsmen preparing to climb into the cart. As he and Grant stood there, Arthur, the Wilkies, and the Murray sisters joined him.

Pausing suddenly, Catriona looked toward

the hill where all of them stood watching. She said something to the MacConns and then began to walk toward Evan, the skirt of her dark gown whipping in the wind. Her brother and father followed more slowly.

Evan strode down the hill to meet her, his long legs taking him far ahead of the others, so that he met her at the bottom of the long, grassy slope that led toward the drover's track.

He stopped and waited as she came the last few feet. "What is the meaning of this," he said in a low tone. "I know what Grant told me. Now I want to hear what you have to say about it."

She looked at him for a moment, then past him toward Grant and the others, who approached. Then she lifted her chin. "We found homes and gave work to some of the Highlanders who left Glen Shee several years ago," she said.

"Not we," Finlay said as he approached them. "I have done this."

"And I," Thomas MacConn said. All three MacConns faced him with strong, straight postures and defiant expressions.

"How many families? How long has this been going on?" Evan asked quietly.

"I've moved eighteen families back into the glen in the last two years," Finlay answered. "They were all evicted by your father. To do this was entirely my decision as factor."

"I helped him," Catriona said.

"Hush," Finlay said. "I found them where I could — living in the gutters of Glasgow without employment, gathering kelp and driftwood on the seashores, collecting rags for pittance. I brought them here and gave them materials to fix their old houses, which were abandoned and burned. And I gave them work."

"Shepherding," Evan said. "Clipping. Gathering."

Finlay nodded. "And repairing homes for others," he added, tipping his head to indicate the shieling hut.

"Many of them have been weaving cloth, as well, from wool produced by their own few sheep, which can bring in a small profit for a family," Catriona said.

"And I suppose they've been knitting," he said, dry and grim. Catriona nodded. He saw the new family come out of the shieling and move toward them uncertainly.

Evan felt at a loss for what to say, what to do. He knew that the estate's profit depended on a handful of men handling several thousand sheep, except for the extra workers needed in the springtime. He knew that his father agreed with the economic philosophy behind the clearances — that huge numbers of sheep should replace people, and the fewer Highland families in a region the better. For centuries, Highlanders had held huge tracts of land, using it only to support families by means of small vegetable gardens, a few sheep and cattle, the working of crafts. Besides sheep runs, thousands of acres could be lucratively rented for hunting reserves and holiday resorts.

Evan narrowed his eyes and watched the MacConns in silence. The new family walked closer, and behind him, he sensed his own guests nearing him. All of them waited for him to say something, to demand recompense and justice, to threaten to have Finlay arrested for undermining his employer's orders and requirements.

Catriona watched him more intently than anyone. She stood very still, her hair bright as fire in the cool gray air, her skirts fluttering in the wind. Though her face was pale, she stood with strength and determination. Evan was reminded of some ancient Celtic warrior queen prepared to defend her people.

He respected her love for the residents of this glen and for its musical heritage. She preserved and defended both with all the devotion of a mother or an earth goddess. He loved that compassion in her, the strength of mountains.

And he could appreciate the courage and resourcefulness that Finlay — and Catriona, too — had needed to do this.

"See, it's just as I suspected," Grant said in a smug tone, coming up behind him. "This is shocking insubordination in your own factor and will undercut the profits from these lands. The man should be arrested for criminal acts. And the reverend is with him — and on a Sunday! The man could lose his living for something like this, if it should be reported. Distressing," Grant said. "And Lady Kildonan," he added, "are you also involved in this unsavory situation?"

"Grant, be quiet," Evan said. He did not turn, though he was tempted to silence the man with a ready fist.

"What the devil! It's a good thing I decided against buying part of this land, Kildonan," Wetherstone said. "I would not want such rebellion on my estate. Mr. Grant, I'd advise you to reconsider your offer, as well."

"It wouldn't be a problem," Grant said smoothly. "I would have them evicted again — with another factor, of course. And the current factor would be excused. Probably imprisoned."

Evan had heard enough. He jabbed the point of his walking stick suddenly into the ground and looked at Finlay.

"Did you enlist the new tenants to work on the old bridge?" he asked sternly. "I gave you those orders the other day."

"What? Fix the bridge?" Finlay asked.

"Exactly," Evan said. "I need a work crew, and I expect you to gather the workers from among the new tenants you were authorized to move into these lands."

"Authorized!" Grant sputtered.

"Well, of course," Evan said, turning with a tight smile. "Did you think Mr. MacConn did this all on his own?"

"Actually, I did think that," Grant snapped. "I still do."

Evan rounded on him. "My father, the previous earl," he said angrily, "sent hundreds, perhaps thousands of people away from this glen over ten or twelve years. He replaced them with sheep. The sheep are flourishing, taking over these hills" — he waved an arm — "but many of the people are not flourishing where they were sent. It is time for them to come home. We have enough damn sheep that we could use the help. Do you not agree, Lady Kildonan?" he asked brusquely, swerving to look at her.

"I do," she said firmly. She looked at Grant, flared her nostrils proudly. "I absolutely agree with my husband."

"What the devil is this about, Kildonan?" Wetherstone asked.

"He's lying to protect his wife and her family," Grant said. "The Highlanders were sent away from here because they were useless."

"An oversight on my father's part," Evan said. "Highlanders are determined as the dickens," he told Wetherstone. "Hardworking and intelligent, too. When they have a mind to, they can do damn near anything better, faster, more cleverly than men hired up from the South. By the way, I'll need a second crew for another job as well, Finlay." Evan turned back. "The exterior walls of Kildonan Castle must be harled with plaster again. The present coat is in poor condition. The work will take months, and perhaps should be started after the sheep clipping is done in the spring."

"Aye," Finlay said. "Anything else, Lord Kildonan?"

"One thing more," Evan said.

"What is that, sir?" Finlay asked.

"Damn fine job of running the estate in my absence, Finlay," Evan said. He looked at the newcomers. "Greetings," he said, inclining his head. "Welcome to Kildonan and Glen Shee."

"This — this is Mr. William MacLeod, his wife, Helen, and their children," Catriona said, bestirring herself from what seemed plain astonishment. "They've just come up from Inverness . . . to work on the estate. Mr. and Mrs. MacLeod, this is Lord Kildonan."

The MacLeods nodded, and William doffed his hat. "Thank you, sir, for . . . all the help."

"You can thank Mr. MacConn and Reverend MacConn for that," Evan said. "And

411

Lady Kildonan, of course." He yanked his stick out of the ground, then stopped. "Mr. MacLeod — are you a relative of Morag MacLeod, or Flora MacLeod, who lives up in the hills?"

"We are, sir," William said. "Mother Flora is my great-grandmother."

Evan smiled. "She'll be glad to see you, I'm sure," he said. He glanced at Catriona for a moment. "My dear, I had planned to meet you at Glenachan House later, but since you are here, would you care to come back with us by way of the drover's track? We've been out for a bit of a hillwalk."

"Aye," she said. She turned to hug her brother and then gave her father a kiss on his cheek, murmuring something that made the tall, burly man blink as if he fought tears. Gathering her skirts, she ran toward Evan.

He turned abruptly and hardly waited for her, his feelings still in turmoil. Immediately recognizing Finlay's altruistic motives, he had tried to circumvent trouble with Mr. Grant in particular. But he realized with dismay that Catriona's secret — helping those people — ultimately meant that she would never leave Glen Shee.

She could never bring herself to leave, he amended as he walked ahead of her without speaking. It was not in her to be apart from this place. He had learned beyond a doubt that she loved the glen and its people more than anything — or anyone — else. The knowledge hurt deeper than he could express.

"Evan!" She caught up to him, her stride soon matching his. The others had walked far ahead of them, including Mr. Grant, all of them clearly anxious to keep their distance from Evan, who was still seething. "Evan, wait."

He turned in silence.

"Thank you," she breathed. "I will explain, I promise. But what made you do that?" Her eyes looked bright.

"Loyalty," he growled. "I'm a Highlander, though I may not seem like one to you." He turned away and lengthened his stride, leaving her standing on the path.

Chapter Twenty-five

The day was soft, silvery, and cool. Catriona shivered in a chilly breeze as she walked between Evan and Finlay, just ahead of the others — Arthur Fitzgibbon, the Wilkies, the Murray sisters, Lord and Lady Wetherstone, and Kenneth Grant. They had ridden in pony carts to the far end of Beinn Alligin, which curved around the head of the glen, its hills and peaks draped in mist. Now Catriona and the rest of the group made their way over the upper moorlands toward the mountain.

She drew her plaid shawl closer, glad that she had worn warm, if plain, clothing — a skirt and jacket of thick brown wool, flannel petticoats, sturdy ankle boots, and the Highland shawl. Her humble outfit did not befit a countess, she knew; nor was it as fine as the other ladies wore — once again they had dressed for mountaineering as if they were attending church services — but her clothing was practical for strenuous hiking and climbing.

The men wore comfortable tweed suits, bowler hats, and tough-soled boots. Two or three, including Evan, carried canvas knapsacks. All of them, ladies and men, had sturdy walking sticks. In addition, Catriona knew that Evan, Finlay, and Arthur had stout Manila ropes in their knapsacks, along with hooks and axes, in case equipment was needed on steep slopes or they encountered ice, snow, or slippery inclines.

"This time of year does not offer the best days for climbing," Finlay said, glancing up at the cloudy skies as he walked along with them. "May and June are best. In spring the floods are too risky, in high summer the midges will make you miserable, and in fall and winter the weather becomes unpredictable. Though if you are all determined to go up, it cannot not be put off until another day. We could have poor weather again, perhaps even snow."

"Winter weather affords some excellent scenic views," Arthur said as he walked behind them. "The Alps are perpetually covered in snow, and that does not deter climbers — rather attracts them."

"Snow and ice on these mountains," Finlay said, "can be treacherous, as Kildonan discovered. Look around you — some parts of the Torridons have a good head of snow and will keep it all year. Though where we are going today, we will not see so much of it, I think."

Ahead, the mountain rose into the pale gray sky, dark and massive, its upper contour variegated with high broad shoulders and ridges, knobby points and pinnacles. The highest point at the center of the curving mass of the mountain was Beinn Shee, its steep conical peak split down the center eons ago by a landslide. The deep cleft formed two sheer rock cliffs that faced each other above an inclined wedge of rubble and turf.

Frosted white with snow and embeddings of white quartz, the line of peaks undulated along the ridge with a strangely fluid grace despite its massiveness. As the group began the long walk up rock-studded meadow, Catriona slowed to look ahead at the gigantic cleft that dominated the mountain profile.

Her eldest brother had died there when she had been a girl, and Evan had fallen there, too, in his attempt to scale the vertical rock, sliding down snowy tracks to the hills that led to the drover's path where she had found him. And now Catriona herself had promised to climb that wicked black sheer to find a fairy crystal that old Flora insisted could only be found on Beinn Shee.

Had she been mad to agree to it? She felt like a peasant girl in a fairy tale, she thought, sent on a quest for a magical talisman, accompanied by a handsome and beloved prince. But the prince was angry and disappointed in her, and for all she knew, would not stay with her in the end. He had no need to do so, after all, for she had betrayed him in order to help others.

But now she realized that the quest she once thought so important was not what she truly desired — to love that prince and to be loved by him. Without that essential magic, the gift of the fairies had lost some of its luster.

All morning, Evan's manner had been cool and distant, his words low and neutral, his hands brief whenever he had touched her waist or elbow to help her over the rougher areas. She did not need the help, but so welcomed his nearness that she had accepted readily. All the while she wondered what he thought, what he had decided to do. Last night he had not come to her room, although she had waited for him, hoping to explain privately why she and Finlay had brought evicted tenants back to the glen without the earl's knowledge or sanction.

Finlay turned now to face the others who followed behind them. The Wilkies and Wetherstones, the Murray sisters, and Arthur Fitzgibbon and Kenneth Grant came closer.

Catriona turned, too, avoiding Grant's skimming glance. She had nothing to say to him and hoped he would have nothing to say to her ever again. But she did not let on, for she did not want to spoil the climb for the others, who were unaware of the tensions that tugged between a few members of their group.

"We'll go this way toward the upper slopes of Beinn Alligin. That high notched peak in the center is Beinn Shee," Finlay explained, pointing. "These lower hills lead to the mountain and the drover's track and cut over to the main ridge."

Reverend Wilkie took a leather memorandum book from his coat pocket and made some notes and sketches. "Can we follow that course along the length of the mountain to the other end?"

"That can be done," Finlay answered. "Beinn Alligin is in the shape of a crescent several miles long. But we'll only go to the center of it — past the first cluster of peaks, called the Horns of Alligin, and to Beinn Shee and Sgurr Mhór, the Great Peak. Then we'll turn and come back this way."

"Mr. MacConn and I decided the best route would be to turn at Sgurr Mhór and follow the ridge back again," Evan said. "At the other end, the descent ends in a ruined bridge that is unsafe. So we've arranged to have the pony carts waiting for us where they left us earlier."

"I did hope we might attempt to climb Beinn Shee, for some true mountaineering," Jemima said, and her sister, Emily, nodded.

"We can go up to the peak," Finlay said, "and it is possible to go around it, but not advisable to scramble inside the cleft, which we call Eag Dubh — the Black Notch. At least not for you ladies," he added with a smile, though Catriona sent him a scowl.

"Beinn Shee itself cannot be climbed safely, Miss Murray," Grant said, stepping forward. "Though some foolhardy folk have tried." He glanced at Evan.

"Kildonan and I made a good attempt," Fitzgibbon said defensively. "Would have made it, too, but for the weather."

"Mr. Fitzgibbon and I started our climb from the base of Beinn Shee and worked our way upward," Evan said. "It was a very difficult ascent, and the descent — well, was not something to recommend."

Catriona glanced up at him quickly in silence. He did not look at her.

"Our route today will be challenging enough," Finlay said. "This is no afternoon hillwalk, up in time for luncheon and down in time for tea. And the weather is a bit unpredictable," he added, glancing up. "It may rain, and if it threatens in earnest, I'd advise that we head down, no matter how far we get."

They began to walk again, making their way up rock-strewn hillsides tough with heather and gorse, and came to a fast-running burn where the water churned white over rocks. Finlay arranged a strong rope, held secure on either bank by Arthur and Grant. Catriona and Evan crossed first to help the others in leaping from stone to stone using the guide rope.

After most everyone had crossed the stream, Lady Wetherstone stopped like a horse refusing a fence. Her husband and Evan coaxed her, but when the hem of her gown got wet, she insisted on turning back. Lord Wetherstone agreed to take her back, though he seemed clearly disappointed to miss the day's outing.

"What a savage place, with no proper bridges, nor even roads or paths — and climbing a mountain means walking all the way," Lady Wetherstone complained loudly to her husband after they had said their farewells for the day. "Why, we climbed Alpine mountains twice as high as these Scotch hills, and had an easier time of it! Do you recall, sir? They put us on donkeys at Chamonix, with halters led by adorable little children, and we rode nearly to the top, thousands of feet up! And never a stream to cross without a bridge!"

Catriona caught Evan's frowning glance and guessed that he shared her thought — perhaps it was best, after all, that the Wetherstones declined to purchase Kildonan property. The lady especially lacked appreciation for the Scottish Highlands.

Farther up, tall pines soared from rocky inclines, and water slid downhill in surging courses. The slopes became sharply angled stone fields, and tufts of moss, grass, and heather clung to the mountainside. Sheep and occasional wild goats grazed, clinging somehow to impossible inclines, skirting away placidly as the humans came near. Eagles skimmed past, and Catriona glanced down to look upon their shining wings and tails, their feathers outspread like fingers.

She walked just behind Evan and Finlay, followed by the Murray sisters and the Wilkies. Arthur and Grant brought up the rear of the group, moving more leisurely because Arthur stopped frequently to examine varieties of rock, gathering specimens and taking notes in a small journal.

Glancing back, she saw Grant look up at her, his gaze keen and disturbing. He had said little to her or to Evan that morning when he had arrived at Kildonan, having been invited days earlier to join the climb. So far she had managed to avoid him and planned to continue. No one else knew of his threats to her, which had been neatly ended by Evan's actions yesterday. She realized with a sense of relief that she need never tell Evan — or deal with Mr. Grant again.

But she had caught Grant's cold glance directed at her once or twice, and the chill she felt had been deep and real. Now, as she walked up the hill, she sensed his silent presence behind her like a dark shadow.

She could say nothing to Evan, who still did not know of Grant's threats regarding Finlay or his physical advances toward her.

The memory of those ugly incidents gave her an urge to shift closer to Evan, and their arms bumped. He took her elbow in silence. Despite the unresolved rift between them, she felt protected and comforted, and she gave him a faint smile.

Catriona climbed slowly and steadily, pausing often with the others to admire the wide and magnificent views of the mountains to the east, Loch Torridon to the west, and a tantalizing glimpse through veils of fog of the sea and the blue isles of the Hebrides. Fragile mists drifted past, but the rain held off.

Finally they reached the knobby ridge that flowed from peak to peak like the curved spine of some great mythic beast, the steep hillsides its sloping back and body. Three thousand feet up — for they had climbed that far in three hours — the height was dizzying, the world below misted and lovely beneath the wide sky.

Arthur picked up a few stones and watched them bounce and skid thousands of feet. Laughing, Jemima picked up a rock to do the same.

"Try not to look down," Grant cautioned her. "It could give you vertigo. Pity if a bonny lass should follow those stones."

He turned to look at Catriona and smiled, flat and humorless. Her heart slammed, and for a terrifying moment she wondered if he was capable of real harm. She could not forget his threats, and she remembered the awful instant where he had tipped her off the old broken bridge. But she still could not understand why he would be angry or frustrated or why he would have reason to harm anyone.

Ignoring him, she turned away and was deeply grateful for Evan's ready hand at her back as they moved along the ridge in single file. Finlay took a rope from his knapsack and tied it around his waist, then tied it around the waists of Jemima and Emily to reassure them. At first the sisters had been giddy with the exhilaration of the climb, but they grew quiet and serious as the effort became more demanding. Reverend Wilkie took another length of rope and tied it around his waist and his wife's.

When Evan offered to do the same, Catriona shook her head and moved onward. But she was glad for his strong, familiar grip on her hand or elbow now and then. A lifetime spent in the high hills gave her no fear of heights and sharp inclines, but despite her experience she found the strong, cold winds on the exposed ridge disconcerting.

Thin clouds moved in to ring the mountaintop below them, and Finlay urged the others to rest for a while on a fairly level spot between two knobby peaks, where they shared lemonade in flasks and a simple meal of oatcakes and cheese, carried inside knapsacks. Anna Wilkie and the Murray sisters made sketches that they tucked away in deep skirt pockets, while Reverend Wilkie made notes in his memorandum book, and Kenneth Grant and Arthur paused to speak to Evan, then wandered along the ridge to sit and look at the magnificent view.

Here the air felt clear, thin, and cold. Smiling to herself, Catriona sat on a sloping wedge of rock and earth, tucking her booted feet under her skirts while she looked with awe at the stunning vista that spread out for miles.

She glanced up as Evan sat down beside her, resting his arms on upraised knees, joining her in companionable silence for a few moments.

She began to speak, and he did, too, both tripping awkwardly over the other's words. Their helping hands and the bond of the climb had begun to heal some of the rift between them. She wanted to explain, to apologize, but soon the Wilkies came to join them, as did Finlay and the Murray sisters. Then Kenneth Grant came toward them, too, dangling a silver flask in his hand. He held it out and turned to offer it to Catriona. She refused with a shake of her head.

"It's not lemonade, but something more invigorating," he said. "I think we could all use a little of it up here. That wind cuts like a knife."

She realized suddenly, from the strange edge in his tone, that Grant might have been drinking a little already. "We certainly don't need any invigorating drink when we're walking along the Beinn Alligin ridge," she said.

"Of course not," Grant agreed. She could see he was sober for the most part, though a little more effusive, smiling more than normal. "But you know it's customary among mountaineers to sip a fortifying liquid when one reaches a peak. Usually it's brandy, but since this is Scotland, I brought a flask of whisky for the occasion." He lifted it and took a sip.

"We haven't reached the peak yet, so I would advise putting that away if you want to keep your head about you," Evan said, glaring at him. "And a sip is customary — not the whole flask."

"Not yet on the top, but nearly there," Grant said, and with the flask, he saluted the split peak beyond them. "We'll soon scramble over these small rocky pinnacles here and then be at the great Black Notch, the fairy's own hollow into the earth. And a few sips should definitely mark that occasion." He indicated with a sweeping hand the area where they sat — a conglomeration of black ledges and steps that formed three rough pinnacles that could be scrambled over or walked around.

"Up there," Grant said, "climbing to the summit of the Eag Dubh, the Black Notch, is no real challenge. We can just take the high ridge behind it and keep going if we want. But to really climb Beinn Shee, one must scale the Black Notch, and no one has ever done it. Not you, Lord Kildonan, nor the brother of your lovely countess and Mr. MacConn." He nodded. "Lady Kildonan," he said. "Why don't you tell us the story of the Eag Dubh?"

She stared up at him and saw Finlay's face harden into anger. Stunned, she could not imagine that Grant meant for her to tell the story of her brother's tragic fall or her father's injury. But there was another story, and she nodded, glad to deflect her brother Finlay's attention from Grant.

"Its full name is the Eag Dubh na h-Eigheachd," she said, "which means the Gash of the Wailing. This part of the mountain has been avoided for generations by shepherds and others. Legend says that sometimes crying or wailing can be heard from the great split in the mountain and that it may be the call of fairies caught within the rock. But these are not fairies who might be disposed to help humans — these are darker creatures who lie in wait or are trapped in the center of the earth. Evil creatures," she went on. "Some say the wailing sound is the voice of the mountain crying for a sacrifice.

426

They say that when the voice is heard, it does not stop until . . . someone dies there."

The others stared at her for a moment. Reverend Wilkie began scribbling in his notebook, and his wife looked pale.

"Oh," Jemima said. "I wish we had heard that story before now. I might not have come up here." Beside her, Emily nodded vigorously.

"It's just the wailing of the wind through that stony cleft, and nothing more," Evan said.

Grant nodded. "Of course. It's silly to think it anything more — but it's a good story, nonetheless."

"Lady Kildonan," Arthur said, coming near them. He had been walking around one of the rocky pinnacles. "You asked me earlier about crystals on this mountain."

"Aye!" She turned, glad for the distraction.

He held his hand out, opened his fingers. "Look what I've found. Something very precious — a whole cluster of crystals and quite lovely ones." In his palm, several clear crystals, faceted and multipointed, glittered in the light.

"Oh," she said, getting to her feet. She took them from him, smiling with delight. "Where did you find these? I must see!" He turned, beckoning, and she followed.

The others got up as well, and Arthur led them behind a high rise in the rock, almost like a protective parapet. At the base of the curving section, Arthur pointed to a bed of small, perfect crystals that sparkled and spilled out of the many crevices in the black rock.

Gasping, dropping to her knees, Catriona looked at the crystals and traced her fingers over them in wonder. While the other women exclaimed and knelt to examine them, Catriona scanned the bed for the fairy crystal that Flora had mentioned.

Though the rocky parapet shadowed the area and lent some darkness to it, she saw nothing that glowed with its own light. She glanced up at Evan, who knelt beside her.

"Beautiful things," he murmured.

"Aye," she agreed. "But not what I'm looking for."

"Still," he said, reaching out and snapping off a small, jewel-like cluster to hand to her, "they are lovely, and you may want to bring one to your friend Mrs. MacLeod."

She nodded and snapped off another, finding that it broke away easily. The crystal was perfectly shaped, glossy as thick glass, and though she was thrilled with the discovery, she felt that it was not quite what Flora had sent her to find.

Chattering and enjoying themselves, the others harvested a few crystals for themselves — there were so many, Catriona saw, once she stood again and looked around, that the great black rock seemed to sprout them like flowers and mosses.

Mrs. Wilkie stepped back and turned to take some of the crystals she had found to her husband, when she suddenly cried out, falling to her knees on an incline covered with scree — broken and unstable stones. "Oh!" she gasped, beginning to slide downward. Anna's feet and skirts seemed to dangle in midair as she scrabbled for a hold on the rock.

Catriona whirled to see Evan, Wilkie, and Finlay run toward her. Evan reached her first, dropping to his knees and stretching out his hand to grab her and pull her to him. Pulled up to her knees, Anna cried out and threw herself at him. Wrapping his arms around her, Evan murmured to calm her until her husband reached them. Helping Anna to her feet, Evan stood back as John Wilkie turned his wife into the safety of his arms.

Heart thumping, breathing hard, Catriona hurried over to them as Wilkie led Anna up to the safer area around the natural parapet. Weeping, shaking, Anna walked with a limp, and her husband carefully sat her down on a rocky ledge.

"Her ankle —" Wilkie said, turning toward Grant. "You're a physician, sir."

"Aye. Let me look." Grant knelt beside Anna and took her booted foot gently in his hand, probing and testing, while she winced. He sat back. "I do not think it's broken, but it is badly wrenched. We will have to get the boot off and wrap it tightly to add support. You will have to make your way down the mountainside somehow. Can you do that, Mrs. Wilkie?"

She nodded bravely, her lovely face pale.

Catriona came forward to kneel beside Anna, taking her hand. "Have you got a bandage?" she asked Grant.

He nodded. "I brought some things in my knapsack in case there was any injury." Turning away, he fetched some strips of linen while Catriona unfastened Anna's boot and eased her foot free. Even through the woman's light woolen stocking, she could tell that Anna's fine-boned ankle was swelling. Grant came back and began to wrap the cloth around the stockinged foot and ankle, making a snug bandage. Anna did her best not to wince, but Catriona could see that she was in real pain.

"You'll need some of this, madam," Grant said, handing her his flask. "Drink, and no pretty protests." Accepting the flask, Anna swallowed, grimacing, and swallowed again.

"I'll take her down to the glen," Wilkie said.

"You'll need help — she may not be able to walk the whole way," Evan said. "I'll go with you."

"You will all need an experienced guide," Finlay said. "The safest way down is not quite the same route that we took for the ascent. I'll go, too."

"I'll leave with you. Anna will need another woman with her, just in case," Jemima said, as she stood watching beside her sister. "Emily, will you come down, too? We can always come up here again before we leave Kildonan."

Emily nodded, her brown eyes wide. "The climb and the view are wonderful, but to be honest, I have no desire to climb closer to . . . that Black Notch." She looked nervously toward the massive split mountain peak. "I think I've seen enough of Beinn Alligin and Beinn Shee. I'll come with you. Anna needs us."

Evan looked at Catriona. "We'll call it enough for now and make plans to climb this mountain another time."

Catriona hesitated, glancing toward the massive divided profile of Beinn Shee. Having come so far in search of the precious crystal that Flora had asked her to find, she did not want to leave yet — but she could not explain that to most of the others. Only Evan knew about her search for the fairy crystal, and only Evan and Finlay would understand her need to fulfill that quest in order to learn Flora's fairy music.

"Of course," she said. "Anna needs us.

We'll all go down now." She fingered the clear crystals in her pocket and hoped they would be enough to please Flora MacLeod.

Evan stepped toward her and took her arm. "Would the rest of you mind if Lady Kildonan and I lingered here for a little while? She is entranced with this place, I think, and I'd like to learn a little more about it myself. It is my mountain, I suppose, and I should explore it while I have the chance," he added with a laugh. "You go ahead, and we'll join you directly."

"Ah, it is a romantic spot," Arthur said, grinning quickly. "By all means, stay here, you two. But don't be long."

"We won't," Evan said. He still held Catriona's arm and stood with her while the rest of them gathered their things and began to make their way down carefully. Grant and Wilkie helped Anna, one to each side of her wherever that was possible, and she limped with determination and grit. Catriona ached just to watch her, knowing the young woman was in genuine pain and had a long way to go before her companions could safely carry her.

Then she turned to Evan. "Thank you," she said.

He nodded, smiling. "Now," he said, turning to glance around. "Where do you suppose those fairy crystals could be hiding? And what the devil do the wee rascals look like?"

Catriona laughed. "You are the geologist, sir, not I."

Chuckling, Evan took her hand and drew her along. "Come carefully, madam, and we'll make our way over to Beinn Shee — and we'll hope the mountain is not in the mood for sacrifices today."

Chapter Twenty-six

Easing around the last of the rocky pinnacles that thrust up from the mountain, Evan scrambled upward along a rough ledge of rocky slabs that formed a natural stair around the chimney-shaped pinnacle. From that point, the ridge resumed, leveling out to swerve up and dip sharply, like the undulation of a dragon's back. The dip formed a beallach, a gap or hollow in the ridge. From there, the shape of the mountain soared again to form the high cone of Beinn Shee.

Evan studied the approach for a moment, then turned to look at Catriona. "This might well be slippery," he said. "Place your feet where I place mine — I'll find the stable footholds for you."

She nodded and came up behind him, her skirts and plaid snapping and billowing in the wind. A gust snatched her bonnet from her head so that it dangled by its black ribbons. When she tried to tie it more tightly, it flew free, sailing out and down.

Evan led her along the spiny ridge and down into the beallach, where they paused to gather their breath. Overhead, he noticed that the clouds had grown darker and heavier recently.

"Rain," he said, looking up. The winds blew cold and fast, and he felt the slight push of every gust. "We'd best hurry."

Moving ahead of her, he picked his way cautiously, placing his feet carefully, balancing a foot on either side of the ridge, nearly razor-backed in places. Each time he glanced over his shoulder, Catriona was walking resolutely behind him.

He felt a swell of pride, and love, too, warm and filling, to see her graceful, lithe progress and the courage she so calmly displayed. He stopped to smile back at her.

"You might not like to take risks, my lass," he said, "but you manage them beautifully when you have to. I think I'd better call you Catriona Dàna," he went on. "Brave Catriona."

She laughed. "Your Gaelic is better than I thought."

"I have a little," he called back. "Just enough."

He moved onward with Catriona in his wake, the wind streaming over both of them. Now that he was traversing the incredibly steep angle that led across the ridge from the pinnacles to the higher peak, he was sure that some of their friends would have refused this part of the climb. Just as well that they had turned back earlier, he thought.

Scrambling up the sharply inclined slope of Beinn Shee, its rounded side composed of variegated rock coated with moss and with thin patches of snow caught in crevices, Evan slowed to catch his breath. The mountain beneath him had an immense primeval power, dark and heavy, an upheaval of the ancient earth. Clinging to one of its points, he felt minuscule, incredibly exposed and vulnerable, with the world far below.

But Catriona was right behind him, and he felt the energy of his deep need to protect her and to help her with what she had come here to do. He scrambled onward, relieved to reach the top. He had been on higher, taller, grander mountains — but he had never been on a mountain that projected this much force, this sort of fierceness.

Feeling slightly dizzy, he paused at the top to catch his breath and resisted the urge to look down. Instead, he looked out, along the mirrored sweep of the long loch and beyond, toward the sea and the isles, floating beneath a film of drifting clouds.

A drop of rain spattered his hand, and another one. The clouds were so close that the air he sucked into his lungs felt damp and soft, as if he breathed the vapor of the rain clouds.

He glanced down and extended his hand to help Catriona the rest of the way up, and she sat beside him, breathing heavily.

The great peak was a simple cone, steep but not impossible to climb. The split down the center, however, created two dangerous cliffs that faced each other, one a bit higher than the other. The two sides were connected at the bottom by a pitch of rubble and turf that careened downward, jagged rock and patches of snow. A bank behind the split, forming the back of the hill, provided an alternative route that joined the rest of the ridge.

Seated on the highest point of the cone, Evan stretched forward to look down inside the towering cleft. Beside him, Catriona did the same, and gasped softly.

"Ach Dhia," she said. "I've never seen the inside of this so close. Eag Dubh, the Black Notch, is aptly named."

"And a wicked-looking thing it is," he murmured.

The rock inside the cleft was composed of raw, rough black gneiss, craggy and even bristly in places, the black rock slick with dampness and coated with moss and dabs of snow. Hundreds of feet deep, the two cliffsides plunged straight down like a massive, primordial chimney. Gusts whistled through the separation of the cliff faces, a span of fifty feet or so. Its floor of snow-coated rubble hurtled downward at a precipitous angle that joined the mountain face to drop thousands of feet to the glen floor.

"My God," Catriona said. "You tried to climb this?"

"Fool that I am, I did," Evan said. "I managed to come partly up the lower vertical face on this side before I fell. I hit the bottom slope and kept on going, making tracks in the snow all the way. I landed on a ledge far below and somehow made my way across the hillside and found the drover's track."

She sighed heavily. "My brother died here," she murmured.

"Yes," he said. "It was exactly here?"

"Aye. He was found farther down the slope. He fell as you did, while attempting to scale the notch of Beinn Shee. Finlay and my father and a few others found him days later. He could have been saved if he had been discovered earlier. He was not as lucky as you," she whispered.

He took her gloved hand and brought it to his lips. "I am a very lucky man," he said quietly, and he kissed her fingers. Then he shifted to face her. Wind whipped past them, blowing her skirts about her legs, the gust strong enough to push them where they sat at the edge of the cleft.

He had so much to say, and there was no time for it here, now. He ached to tell her that he loved her, that in falling from these very cliffs not so long ago, he had fallen into the rest of his life. No matter how fast any of this had happened, he felt soul certain of his love for her and his commitment to their marriage. He burned to love her, to share all of himself with her, to tell her about his hurts and his joys, his uncertainties and his achievements, confess his fears and his hopes.

There would be time for all that later, he knew. For now, he would share her quest, and they would go home in peace and start again. But having no time for explanations, he could only express his heart to her the best way he knew how.

He leaned close and kissed her, pulling her to him, seated with her at the top of the world — the top of their world — which he meant to share with her forever. Now he knew that he could not sell Kildonan. His own heart would not allow it. Somehow he would find a way to pay off the debts of the estate and the debts he himself had accrued. For two years, he had been helping to pay the expenses of the three families affected when his bridge had collapsed so long ago.

No one knew about that — he had kept it from everyone but one of his solicitors. He sent cheques to them regularly, three widows and their children, and he had been hoping to set up bank trusts for them once he sold some of the land he had inherited.

That tragedy suddenly seemed so very long ago, such a distant time, something that had happened to a different man.

Now, perched on the crest of this strangely magical hill, looking down into what seemed the center of the earth, Evan felt as if the ravaged gash in his own heart, his own soul, had at last begun to heal.

Loving Catriona, surrendering himself and his stubborn, protected heart to the over-whelming power of love, he had felt a sort of miracle begin to work on him, like light shining upon shadow to reveal the life and the beauty there.

Smiling, he kissed her again, felt her arms wrap around him, felt her forgiveness and her wonder rinse over him. He drew back.

"Let's find that fairy bauble, madam," he said, "and get down from this wicked height. I've got to get you home, where we can do this properly."

She laughed a little, seemed almost weepy and relieved as she kissed him again, then glanced around. "Flora said the fairy crystals can be found only on Beinn Shee and no-where else. But I saw no crystal clusters as we came up the hill."

"Nor did I. But I wonder —" He leaned forward, chest down and hands gripping, to peer over the edge into the abyss, down the expanse to sloped snow and jagged rock. "Those walls are the perfect bed for crystals. They're filled with crevices and creases, split open eons ago. Crystals seed themselves somehow and grow there — or so it seems. It's not well understood."

Catriona flattened out on her stomach be-side him and extended her arm down along the rock face, groping within reach of her fingers. "Evan! There are crystals here — I can feel them but I cannot see them, or get hold of any. See if you can."

He stretched his arm down as far as he could, and he, too, could feel the encrustation of crystal growths inside the cracks and creases in the rock. His fingers touched the smooth and delicate planes of crystal wands sprouting here and there. "There are quite a few of them — they must be everywhere along the sides of these cliffs. The rock is Lewisian gneiss —"

"Black sedimentary rock embedded with white quartz," Catriona said, and Evan chuckled.

"Wait," he said. "I may be able to get down there fairly easily." He sat up and removed his knapsack, rummaging inside to pull out a length of Manila rope and an iron claw.

While Catriona watched in astonishment — and protested insistently — he tied the rope securely around his waist and double knotted the end to the serrated iron claw, which he then pounded tightly into an upper crevice in the rock, near the edge. Then he took his small ice ax and slipped it behind him, into his belt under his coat.

Turning on his knees, he slipped his feet over the side of the cliff. The wind blew hard at him, lashing at his hair and his jacket.

Catriona grabbed his shoulders.

"No," she said. "It's just a crystal. No, Evan! What if you fall? I cannot bear it — don't do this just for me!"

What if he fell? For two years, he had almost wanted to fall, he realized now. As if he moved in slow motion, he glanced down into the black chimney that had almost claimed his life once before. And he thought about plummeting down and down to his death.

Falling into death, falling into love, either way slipping loose the knots that the world imposed to find a sort of blessed freedom. Others had fallen from the bridge that he had designed — the materials had been faulty, the engineering committee had told him later. He could not blame himself for flawed rivets and girders.

But he did blame himself — because he had been there and had not managed to get down into the water to reach them fast enough. He had hesitated in his first dive, pausing to quail for a moment at the immense height, for heights had always bothered him just a little, just enough to cause him to pull up, to think, then to move ahead. He had wondered, that day, if he would die, too, upon hitting the water so far below. And he had always thought that hesitation could have cost someone's life.

Glancing at Catriona, he smiled, shook his head. Someday he would tell her about the bridge and about his thoughts on falling. He would tell her about all those who had gone over the edge, re-create for her his three friends who had died. He might even tell her why he drove himself to climb the heights and dive the depths. Looking, always looking for forgiveness.

But in searching high and deep for that, in pushing himself out of heavy guilt and desperate need, driven by his nightmares as well as aimless courage, he had found what surprised him most. He had found love.

He had to do this one thing for her, small as it might seem in the scheme of life. Leaning forward, he kissed her as she knelt in front of him. Then he slid his legs over the side and pushed away.

He felt the drop in his stomach, felt the lurch as the rope and iron claw caught and held him. He swung on the rope for a few moments until its arc calmed, and then he pushed toward the wall and braced himself against it with hobnailed boots, suspended securely by the rope.

Glancing up, he saw Catriona leaning over the edge, her face so beautiful, so pale and frightened for him. He waved and then set about combing the rock for the crystal she wanted.

Tipping back his head, he saw crystals everywhere — glittering and winking in the gloom between the two rock faces, sparkling like diamonds against black stone. Reaching out, he could pluck any number of them.

Pulling the pickax out of his belt, he hacked at more of them, finding them here and there, to the side and just above his head. They came loose, twinkling into his hand, lovely, drusy things, coruscated and lustrous, others silky bits of clear stone. A few of them showed traces of color — the faint purple of amethyst, the topaz brown of smoky quartz.

He dropped those into his pocket and harvested a few more. But still he had not found what she wanted most — a crystal that glowed with its own inner phosphorescence. He pushed away from the wall with his feet to get a broader picture of the black cliff. Slowing swinging a little back and forth, he glanced to the right — and saw something he had missed before.

Winking in the darkness like a star, a crop of crystals shone inside a crevice just past his right hand. He glanced up at Catriona, saw her watching him. He waved again, saw her arm extend.

Then he swung off to the right and stretched, catching himself on a protrusion in the jagged cliff face. Finding a hold for his feet, balanced there, he reached out.

It glistened just past his fingertips, so that he had to stretch and shift along the wall, the umbilical rope tying him securely to the cliff and to safety. Extending as far as he could, he closed his fingers around it and snapped, and it came off into his hand like a flower. He opened his palm.

Lustrous and lovely, it glowed in his hand, the most perfect natural jewel he had ever seen. Polished by nature, clear as glass, the crystal held another crystal inside itself. A pink glow, like a perfect heart, a droplet of color in the clear stone, gave off a rosy light. Phantoms, these were called, and he knew that one like this was as rare as anything found on the earth. Yet it had been sitting there on its tiny ledge on the fairy mountain, waiting to be discovered.

Beinn Alligin, he remembered, translated to the Jeweled Mountain. Now he knew why. The fairies had been busy, indeed.

He laughed softly to himself and held it up toward the misty light that flowed through the cleft, seeing the pink mineral caught inside the crystal. An exquisite thing. Smiling, nearly whooping in exultation, he slipped it into his pocket and looked up.

Catriona still hung head and hands over the edge, looking down. But she was not alone.

A man stood beside her, with his foot on her back.

"Kildonan," Kenneth Grant said. "It's over."

Chapter Twenty-seven

Catriona felt the pressure of his foot in the center of her back, shoving the breath from her. She tried to roll, but he pressed his weight into her almost casually and leaned over to call again.

"Kildonan, come up!" he said, the threat in his voice deep and ominous.

She peered over the edge to see Evan looking up, dangling at the end of the knotted rope. Her heart clenched with terror, knowing that all Grant had to do was kick free the iron claw, and Evan would plummet hundreds of feet to his death.

But why? she wondered. Why would Grant care to harm either of them?

She rolled again, insistently, and got his booted foot in her side. She struggled against him and managed to rise to her knees with one foot on the sloped ground, caught in the folds of her skirts. Grant reached down and snatched her by the upper arm.

"What do you want?" she asked desperately, twisting.

"I want what is mine by right," he said. "And now is the time to make that claim."

"What is yours?" She could hardly breathe,

with Grant yanking her so hard, with the wind shoving at her, with her heart and breath beating in her chest.

She took an instant to look down and saw Evan clambering up. He had not said a word, had wasted no energy in shouting or arguing. He was just coming relentlessly upward.

"Damn," Grant muttered. "I should just cut the rope and he would be gone. And then off with you, over the side. Two lovers lost in the great Black Notch, two poor souls come too close to the edge."

"But why?" she gasped again. "You have wanted something ever since I returned to Glenachan with Evan — something has angered you ferociously, but I could never understand what it was. And then it seemed to grow worse after Evan and I were married. It could not be that you wanted me or hated my brother enough to betray what he was doing — you could never convince me of that. What is it?"

"Do you not know? Can you not guess?" he bellowed, snatching at her when she tried to twist away. "Are you blind? Look at me!"

She turned and stared at him then, breath heaving. And suddenly what she had not seen before became frighteningly clear.

He had the brown eyes, the brown hair, the classic features of the Kildonan Mackenzies. He was tall and lean, and his voice was deep and mellow. He was the image, suddenly, of Evan's father and even more of Evan's fierce grandfather, in their portraits. And his voice was suddenly very like Evan's own, deep and resonant. The man in the painting had seemed familiar to her, and Kenneth Grant had always looked strangely familiar, too, though she could not place the resemblance.

"You — Are you —" she gasped.

"Aye, Kildonan's son," he snarled. "I'm your precious husband's half brother. Older half brother." He was breathing hard now, jerking her arm with each sentence as if to punctuate his astonishing revelation.

"You? But — Evan does not know," she panted. Looking down, she saw that her husband was much closer than before. Seeing the cold anger and comprehension in his features, she realized that he had heard what Grant had said — at least well enough to learn the truth.

Grant dropped to his knees with Catriona, his grip brutal on her arm as he leaned forward over the cliff edge and reached down toward the iron claw that held Evan's rope safely.

"No!" Realizing what he meant to do, Catriona lashed out with fierce desperation, grabbing at Grant's arm in an effort to prevent him from dislodging the iron piece.

He shoved her away momentarily and leaned forward just enough to look down at

Evan. "One good pull, and the iron hook comes loose," he called.

"Let my wife go," Evan growled, ignoring Grant's threat. He pulled himself higher, hand over hand with mighty effort, his toes finding sure holds, his fingers hard grips.

Catriona threw herself backward, hoping to pull Grant with her away from the edge, and away from the rope that was Evan's only life-line. But the man's greater size and weight held them both in place, too near the edge. Once again he reached his long arm downward to scrabble for a hold on the hook.

As his fingers nearly closed on iron, Catriona tugged at his arm, pushed at him, beat her closed fist upon his forearm to force him to give up. He tried to shrug her off, but she felt ferocious, relentless. She would not stop pummelling, struggling.

No matter what it took, she would not let him kill Evan. She would take Grant over the cliff edge herself, if it was the only way to save Evan's life. "Stop," she said breathlessly. "Stop! Why are you doing this?"

"I thought Evan Mackenzie would never come to Kildonan Castle," Grant grunted, resisting Catriona's assault. "I thought I could buy some of the land, and sue for the rest. I meant to take it to the courts, hire solicitors to prove my claim. But then *he* came up here, and he met you — took you for his wife. And I realized he might stay here and claim the lot of it. The woman, the land, the legacy that should be *mine*."

"Yours! Why!" Catriona cried, and fought him even while she spoke. His strength was greater than hers, his determination dark and fierce — but her own will to save Evan felt bright and powerful. She would never give up this fight.

Grasping, tugging at his arm, she reached over the cliff edge herself and tried to pry loose the man's fingers. A cold wind blew upward from the gap, blowing at her face and hair. She felt dizzy, but did not pull away, her body locked beside Grant's, her arm extending along his own.

"Why? Because I was here — he was not," Grant answered, his voice breathless now. His grip felt like iron beneath her hand. "I spent time with the old earl, hunted with him, fished with him. Talked politics and sheep farming with him. Did you, Kildonan?" he called down.

"Damn you," Evan said, scrambling upward. "Leave her be!"

"I drank whisky with him, held his head when he was sick, listened to his stories late into the night. Played cards with him when he was lonely. Did you, Kildonan?"

Evan did not answer, but Catriona heard him coming closer, heard the scuff of his boots on the rock, the huffing of his breaths. She tugged desperately at Grant's hand and arm.

Despite her struggle, Catriona had not deterred Grant. He seemed unbothered, willing to wait. Fearing that as soon as Evan came toward them, Grant would shove him backward or manage to pull loose the claw, Catriona slid back, pulling at Grant's shoulders and then his waist, trying to drag him away from the edge so that he could not touch the claw. She hoped to give Evan time to reach the rim of the cliff.

"I reassured old Kildonan that he had not done wrong by his wife and his children when he dallied with my mother years ago," Grant went on, turning as Catriona tugged at him. Now he tried to shove her away from him, growling something under his breath.

"Your mother — Who is she —" Catriona gasped, wondering suddenly if she knew the woman.

"She's gone now. A simple Highland girl — died when I was born," he said gruffly. He snatched at her then and renewed his painful grip on her arm, momentarily distracted from Evan and the cliff's edge. "The factor and his wife adopted me, knowing I was Kildonan's brat. They raised me at Kilmallie, taking funds from the earl to keep silent about me."

"But you inherited land and wealth —" Catriona gasped. "You are respected in the glen as the doctor! Surely that is enough."

"Aye, the estate was fattened by the earl's

money. But it's not enough — why should I be only the doctor, and a small laird, when I could be the earl. Come here," he growled, yanking her toward him, wrapping an arm over her to prevent her from fighting him. He looked over the cliff edge. "I was the only son the old earl ever knew — the one he leaned upon!" he called down to Evan.

"You — cannot prove your claim," Evan grunted as he pulled closer now. "Madmen imagine all sorts of fantasies."

"I have proof," Grant said. "Letters he wrote telling me of his love for my mother. Do you know why your mother left him, and took you away? Because he loved my mother. Because he already had an heir in me."

"No," Evan said. "I would have been told."

"Ask your mother why she left him," Grant said. "Oh — you will never have the chance, will you. Soon you'll shuffle off this mortal coil." He came to his knees, dragging Catriona up to kneel beside him. "I'm sorry to make you pay with your life, but I should be Earl of Kildonan. You do not care for this place, I hear. You'd rather be in the Lowlands. But now you have a bonny wife — the girl I would have taken for myself. The Plain Girl of Glenachan," he said, pulling her close to him. "Plain Girl no more. A beautiful woman, and I have loved her longer than anyone," he murmured, looking down at her. "But now I'll have to kill you, too, Catriona, with your earl — for you know the truth. And that hurts me worse than you can imagine."

He looked troubled, Catriona realized, truly distressed. "Kenneth," she said. "Please, listen to me —"

"Ah, good. He's about to join us," Grant said with a sense of satisfaction, looking down.

"Let her go," Evan growled. Catriona saw the top of his head for a moment, and heard the scrape of his heels on stone. She wondered why Grant allowed him to come up now — and felt her blood chill to know that one brother planned cold murder for the other.

"*Ach Dhia*," she moaned. "Evan, keep away —" She pushed at Grant, trying to throw him off balance so that he could not attack Evan as soon as her husband came over the edge.

But Grant pulled her close, holding her so tightly that she could not struggle effectively against him. "Kildonan — I would have married this girl," Grant called out. "She would have been my countess. But if I claim brotherhood with you to gain the land after your death, I cannot marry your widow. Pity," he said, pulling her close. "What a pity. You'll both have to die."

He grabbed her tightly to him then, kissing her, driving his mouth hard over hers. The wind shoved and smacked into them. Poised at the very edge, she felt wildly unstable, as if she were about to plummet. Instinctively she pushed at Grant, and saw with satisfaction that he fell backward. But he lunged for her, grabbed her around the waist and slammed down with her, both of them crouched on their knees, dangerously near the cliff rim.

Suddenly Catriona heaved herself closer to the edge, gripping it with one hand, the weight of her skirts giving her better stability than Grant had. The force of her movement tilted him toward the gap, and he grunted with alarm, but rolled down beside her, snatching at her again.

Stretching her arm downward, she reached toward Evan. If they were both to die, she had to touch him once more. "Evan," she gasped. "Oh, God —"

"Love," he said, and suddenly his head rose near hers, and his hand smacked rock and earth beside hers.

Grant let go of Catriona, hurling her aside so that she slid back down the incline a little. As she scrambled upward again, she saw Grant shove at Evan as he came up over the edge.

With a burst of strength, Evan heaved himself toward Grant, rolling with him, both of them grappling viciously at the edge of the cliff.

Without thought, still determined to help Evan, Catriona lunged toward them, but took Grant's knee in her shoulder and was thrown back. Grabbing at Evan's coat and missing, she felt him push her backward, shoving her out of the way. She slid downward, got to her knees, and scrambled toward them again. But they were flailing, punching, wrestling so violently that she could not come nearer. They struggled only a few feet from her, and only a foot from the cliff edge.

She screamed and tried to grab at Grant's foot, but took a smacking, painful kick to her arm. Snatching at his coat, she tried to yank him away from Evan. The wind grew fierce suddenly, whipping at all of them, adding its strength to the fight.

Grunting, huffing, locked in a wicked embrace, they rolled again and again, hands taut at necks, faces grimacing. Grant shifted beneath Evan and tried to heave the other man away.

A sudden, powerful gust of wind shoved at them. Just as Evan rolled again, Grant kicked his leg over the side into air. The momentum drove him halfway off the edge.

Evan grabbed for him, and within an instant, both men careened over the edge into the dark, gaping cleft, tumbling with weird grace out of sight.

Catriona screamed, her throat dry and tight, her heart falling with them. She scrabbled to the edge, afraid to look over, sobbing. She heard a shout, and peered over.

The rope and claw had held. Evan dangled where he had swung earlier, held fast by the rope around his waist. Kenneth Grant clung to his coat, his legs whipping in midair. Grasping the taut, straining rope, Evan snatched at Grant desperately, holding on to the man who had tried to kill him, the man who still struggled to kill them both, now.

"There's another rope and claw! Get them!" Evan shouted.

Sliding backward, Catriona snatched Evan's knapsack, which he had left on the slope. She grabbed frantically at the rope and claw, which were already tied together, her hands shaking fiercely, and crawled back to the edge.

Evan hung there, his coat half pulled off of him by Grant's struggling, thrashing weight, for Grant had no good hold on Evan and had a grip instead on cloth.

Gasping, sobbing, Catriona hoisted as far over the edge as she dared and pounded and forced the claw into another crevice beside the hook presently embedded there. She tested the claw, which seemed to grip almost instantly, finding hidden holds in the rock face.

"Throw the rope down!" Evan called. She spooled the rope downward and watched as Evan heaved and swung toward the wall on the rope that held two men. He pulled on Kenneth's arm, trying to help him snatch the other dangling rope.

Kenneth lunged outward to snatch at the free rope, letting go of Evan. Almost at the same moment, he kicked out at Evan, and the force of his kick jerked his own hands, loosened his own grip, and he fell, sailing downward, spread-eagled in eerie silence.

Catriona looked away, hiding her face in her hands.

"I think I understand," Evan said much later. They stood side by side near the old fairy bridge, at the top of the hill that overlooked the glen.

The castle sat like a jewel at the foot of the dark hills, and the mists floated over the land, over all of Kildonan and Glen Shee. The whole of it looked dreamlike and beautiful.

Catriona sighed, still stunned and in shock, with a deep, hurtful sadness in the core of her heart for the death of a man she had once called friend. They had left him at the foot of the Black Notch, covered with his coat. Evan had said he would go back up with Finlay and others to fetch him down properly.

She and Evan had come down from the mountain in silence, having circled behind Beinn Shee to follow the ridge to its other

457

end, where it met the slope that led to the fairy bridge.

Nearly home now, she thought, and only the little bridge left to cross. She looked up at Evan in concern and reached out to take his hand. His fingers squeezed hers.

"What is it you understand?" she asked softly.

"What you and Finlay did. Why you did it." He looked at her, his expression somber. The wind lifted his thick dark hair. He had bruises on his cheek. His eyes were beautiful, deep and brilliant, and so sad.

She loved him so. It brimmed and spilled and expanded in her, so much she could not express it. Flowed through her with such force it nearly hurt, as if she would have to grow inside to contain it. Reaching up, she brushed her fingers over a new bruise and touched the old one under his hair, where he had hit his head the first time she had met him.

"What are you saying?" she asked.

"I'm apologizing," he said quietly.

She felt a quick lift in her heart, as if it had wings. Smiling, she shook her head. "I should be the one to apologize about the tenants, Evan. I should have told you. I should have known you would be angry —"

"Angry? No." He gave her a bemused look, and his eyes sparkled just before he smiled. Reaching out, he slipped his arm around her, and the cup of his hand felt warm and good. "I was not angry about the tenants, my lass. That is easy to understand. I know how much you love Glen Shee — you and Finlay both." He looked out toward the long glen below, green, silver, and gold softened by mist and drizzling rain. "I understand that, because I care about the glen, too."

"I know you do," she murmured softly. "I see that now. What then? Why were you upset, if you understood why we did it?"

"Because you did not trust me. Because you thought that I was . . . like my father and would send those people away."

"But you are not," she said quietly. "I did not know it before . . . but I know that now."

Evan watched her, his hazel eyes beautiful, his gaze filled with clarity and quiet power. Feeling overwhelmed by relief and something more, by her own unquestioning forgiveness and the deep love she felt for him, Catriona smiled in silence and tipped her head so that her cheek rested on his shoulder.

He leaned down. "Catriona Bhàn," he whispered. "Catriona Dàna. I love you."

She caught her breath. Raising her head, she looked at him, wondering, stunned a little to hear words from him that matched so perfectly, so exquisitely, the feeling that poured through her like gentle, warm sunlight despite the cool air and rain clouds.

Her heart blew open like a rose with the unexpected joy of it, and tears stung her eyes. Smiling a little, she leaned forward.

Evan leaned forward, too, and kissed her mouth gently. The wind swept over them, fluttering her hair, her plaid, fluttering his hair. She felt still and strong and peaceful, and more sure of love than she had felt of anything else in her life.

"I love you, too," she whispered, and she accepted his kiss again, its tenderness melting her deep inside.

"Oh," he said, pulling at the pocket of his torn, bedraggled coat. "I nearly forgot." Drawing his hand out, he opened his fingers. "Is this what you were looking for?"

Winking, beautiful, the natural crystal sat in his palm, its pink heart captured pristine inside the gleaming, perfect wand.

"Oh," she breathed, taking it from him, turning it in the pale light. "Oh, it's beautiful! Oh, Evan — thank you —" She threw her arms around him, pressed her face into his coat.

He held her, dipped his head down. "Now you can take it to Mother Flora, and she will teach you all she knows."

She nodded. "But — if you want to leave here —" She paused, glanced up. "If you want to leave, I will go with you."

He leaned back a little, looked at her. "You will?"

She nodded, tears pooling in her eyes. "I will. I love this place, and it is part of me, but . . . but you are in my heart now. Like this beautiful crystal — one is within the other, and they cannot be apart. I cannot be without you." She held up the crystal wand, with its miraculous pink heart. "If you must be in Edinburgh —"

"Oh," he said. "I have to be in Edinburgh sometimes, but not every day. I think I can stay here in Kildonan and Glen Shee much of the time."

"Aye?" She looked up at him.

"Aye, my countess," he said, leaning to kiss her head. "With you and our little ones — as many as you like and heaven sees fit to give us. And all our tenants, too, as many of those as you like, as well," he said, pulling her close.

She half laughed, half sobbed, and turned into the circle of his deep embrace.

"Let's go home." He took her hand.

"We'll have to cross the old bridge," she said, as they walked toward it.

"Aye, well," he said, stepping on to its stones and pulling her with him as they walked up the incline of the arch. "What was that fairy charm again?"

She laughed, and he laughed, too, and led her toward the gap in the bridge. Whispering the charm, she heard him repeat it and watched as he stepped across with one long stride.

He turned and half lifted her over, setting her down lightly, and took her into his arms. "Now," he said, leaning down to kiss her, "I believe in magic."

Epilogue

"So this is your groom," Flora said. Hand at her hips, she peered up at Evan, tipping her head back so that she could see him more easily. She stood in the doorway of her little house, while Evan and Catriona stood outside in a cold wind and drizzling rain.

"English, if you please," Catriona said.

Flora nodded, still gazing at Evan. "He's a tall one. Tall enough for you, girl."

Evan suppressed a chuckle. The old woman was an elfin creature, wizened yet childlike. He liked her bluntness, and he liked her keen, direct gaze. He inclined his head toward her and smiled a little, waiting in silence.

Catriona smiled and tucked her hand into Evan's arm. "He suits me well, I think," she said, laughing up at him. "My dear, this is Flora MacLeod."

"I'm pleased to meet you, Mrs. MacLeod," Evan said, extending his hand. "I am Mr. Mackenzie."

"Huh," Flora said. Reluctantly, she extended her small, gnarly hand and allowed him to take it. He bowed slightly. "We all know you are more than Mr. Mackenzie, but we will not speak of it here," she grumbled.

"We need never speak of it, if you like," Evan said. "Think of me as your landlord — or as the husband of this fine lass." He covered Catriona's fingers, still tucked over his arm, with his own. "But I would be most pleased if you would think of me as another Highlander, happy to be here in Glen Shee again."

Flora tilted her head. "And who brought my great-grandson William and his wife Helen and their little ones back to me? Was it you, Mr. Mackenzie?"

"Not I, madam," Evan said. "That credit goes to Finlay MacConn and his father and sister."

"But they are here because you did not send them away."

"I did not," Evan agreed. "I will not. And I think we can manage to bring a few more MacLeods back to Glen Shee, once we find them."

Flora nodded once, curtly, though Evan saw her lower lip quiver for a moment. "Well," she said. "Well, then."

"May we come in, Mother Flora?" Catriona asked softly.

"Huh. I suppose." She stepped back to allow them to step over the threshold. "Watch your heads, both of you. Tall people," she muttered. "My husband knocked his head on that lintel more times than I could count, but he built the inside of the house tall enough to make him happy. Well, sit down."

As they entered the dim little house, Evan found the place roomy and neat, though it smelled suspiciously of goat. Escorting Flora and then Catriona to small wooden chairs, he took a seat on a bench beside the fire.

"What have you brought for me?" Flora asked, leaning forward to poke at the basket that Catriona had insisted they carry with them. "Not more stockings, I hope. I have enough of those. I still need a scarf, though."

"And I have one here," Catriona said, reaching into the basket to draw out the soft, knitted folds of a dark blue scarf.

Flora took it with a low cry of delight and wrapped it around her neck so that the ends dangled down into her lap. She perched her hands on her knees. "What else?"

"Some fruit," Catriona said, showing her a sack of apples.

"Bah," Flora said. "I have some just as nice as those. Morag and Helen brought them the other day." She leaned forward curiously.

Catriona glanced at Evan and smiled, her secret dancing in her blue eyes. More than one secret glowed there, he was sure, but she had not spoken of it to him yet. He wondered if she knew herself. The blush upon her cheek and the vivid sparkle in her eyes of late had given it away to him. He smiled in silence.

"Well, there is one small thing I brought

for you," Catriona said, still smiling as she drew out a piece of folded linen.

Looking at Catriona in silence, Flora took the cloth and unfolded it gently. There, gleaming on the pale fabric, the little fairy crystal sat in her palm, its rosy heart glowing. Delicate rainbows of light and color dazzled along the smooth facets of the outer crystal wand.

"*Ach,*" Flora breathed. "You found it!"

"I found it," Catriona said. She folded her hands in her lap and smiled, watching as the old woman turned the stone so that it winked and sparkled in the light of the hearth fire.

After a moment, Flora lowered her hand, the stone still clasped in it. "You climbed Beinn Sìtheach for me, and for the sake of the fairy songs?"

"I did," Catriona said. "But it was Evan who found the stone. He risked his life to fetch it from the rock."

Flora looked at him. "I heard the story of what happened up there," she said. "Morag told me how the doctor died. Well, it is sad and tragic. He did not know as much doctoring as I know, but he had his place here in the glen. I thought he was a bit crazy, that man. You should have asked me."

"I wish I had, Mother Flora," Evan murmured. "You seem like a very wise woman."

"I am," she agreed. She peered at him for

466

a moment, nodded to herself, and then looked at Catriona. "Well, then, I suppose you want me to teach you my fairy songs now."

"I would like it very much if you would," Catriona said.

"I could do that, I suppose," Flora said. "But we will have to work quickly. In a few months, you will not want to come up here to see me."

Catriona looked surprised. "Of course I will want to come up here to see you. Why would I not?"

"Ask him," Flora said, glancing at Evan. "He knows why."

Catriona turned to him. "You do?"

"Well," he said. "I think so. You have a secret, my dear."

She laughed softly, and the sparkle danced again in her eyes. "And what is that, sir?"

He took her hand, lifting it to kiss her knuckles softly. "Mother Flora," he said, still watching Catriona. "I would ask you one favor, if I could."

"Ask me, Mr. Mackenzie," Flora said. She sounded pleased, and she grinned, watching him. "Ask."

"I want you to teach me one of your fairy songs," he said. "I want you to teach me a lullaby." Catriona gasped, and he saw tears glisten in her eyes as she smiled up at him.

"Ah," Flora said, nodding. "And why should I do that?"

Evan leaned forward and kissed Catriona gently and slowly. Then he drew back. "Because I would like to sing to my son."

Catriona caught back a sob, smiling up at him through her tears. "And what if the babe proves to be a daughter?"

"I'll sing to her, too," Evan whispered, leaning forward again to rest his brow against hers. He rested his hand on her back, and felt the slight, beautiful thump of her heartbeat. A sense of deep gratitude filled him, for her, for the love she brought to him, for the child she protected inside of her. "And when our daughter is older, she can sing the songs to her brothers and sisters, and to her own little ones someday."

Catriona came into his arms then, and he wrapped her in his embrace, smiling to himself. Glancing at Mother Flora, he saw the old woman wipe away a tear.

"Now," Flora said. "Enough of that, you two. We have some work to do. Now listen." She began to sing, her voice earthy and low, filled with quiet power.

Evan held Catriona in his arms, and closed his eyes as he listened. He felt the peacefulness of the old music pour through him, and he felt the healing depth of his love — and hers. A moment later, as Catriona began to sing very softly, Evan began to hum the lyrical, lovely melody with her.

velvet cushion on my desk, winking in the light.

I hope you have enjoyed my Scottish Victorian trilogy, which includes *Taming the Heiress*, *Waking the Princess*, and *Kissing the Countess*. Please look for my next Scottish historical — it's too soon yet to reveal the details, but I know you will love it!

And please visit my Web site at www.susanking.net to learn more information about all of my books. Be sure to drop me a note through the Web site. I love to hear from my readers.

All the best — and happy reading!

About the Author

Susan King, a Ph.D. candidate in medieval art history at the University of Maryland, took time off from her dissertation to write her first historical romance, *The Black Thorne's Rose*. A native of New York, she currently lives in Maryland with her husband and their three sons. Susan loves to hear from her readers; she can be reached at www.susanking.net.